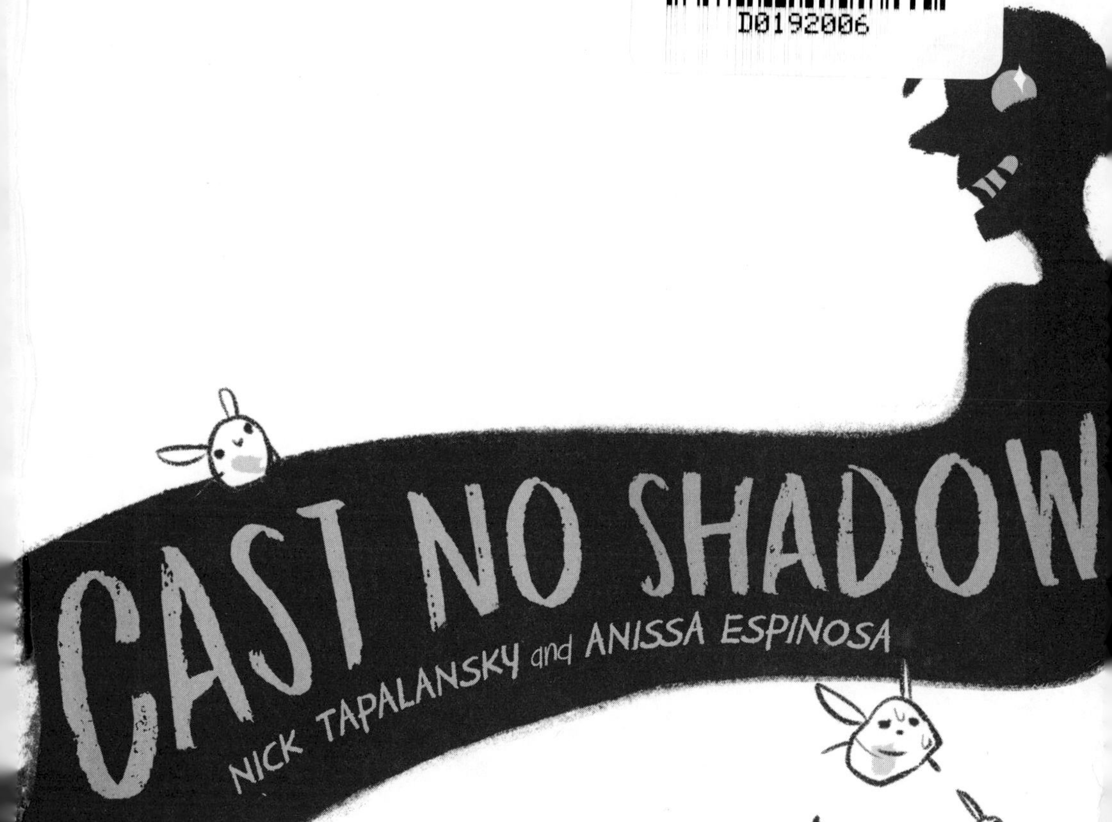
CAST NO SHADOW
NICK TAPALANSKY and ANISSA ESPINOSA

Tone by Alex Eckman-Lawn
Lettering by Thomas Mauer

:01
First Second
NEW YORK

For Nick Harris,
who saw the glimmer of something more in a very humble
beginning, and whose own smiling shadow will always be
a comfort to those who knew him.
—N.T.

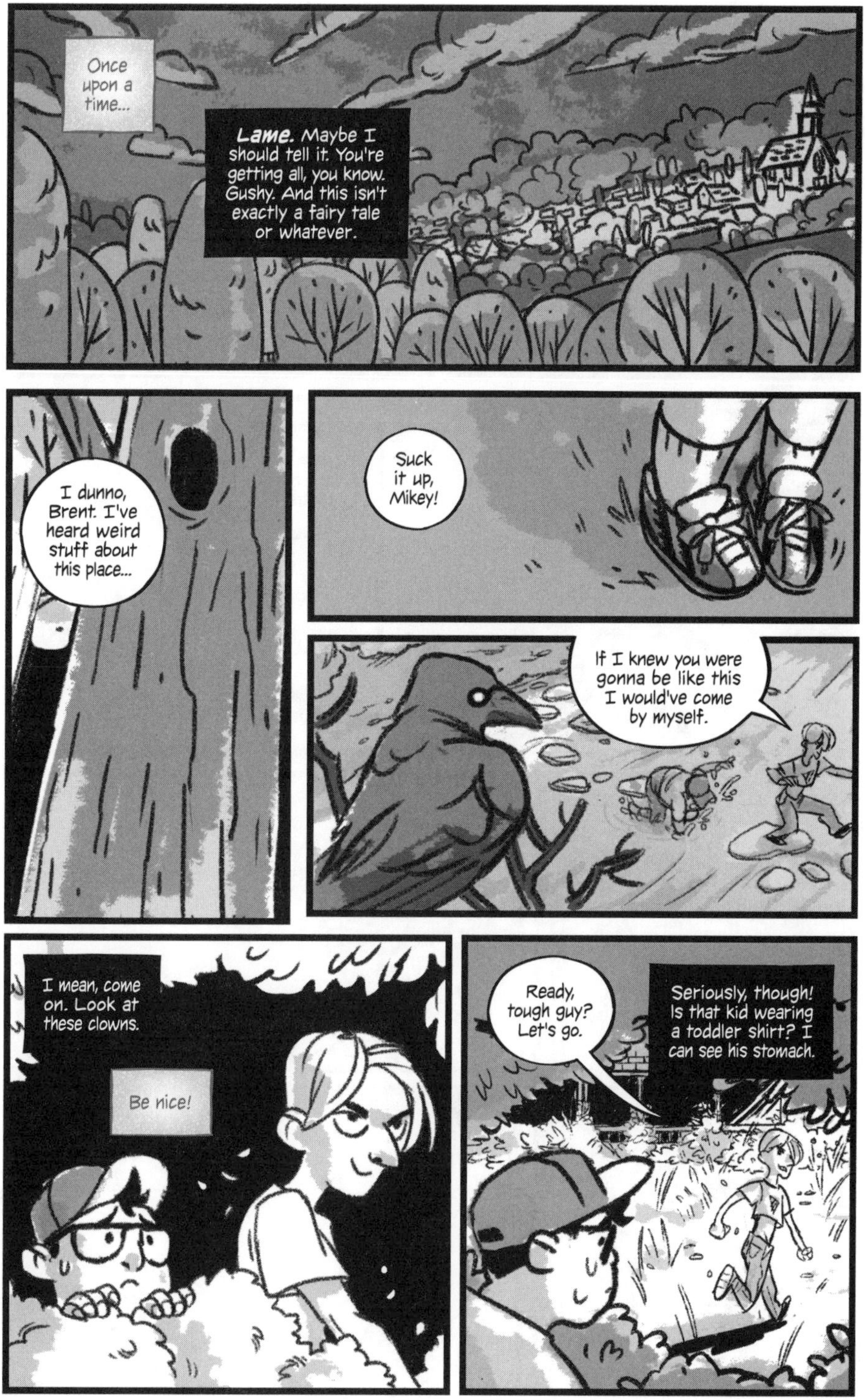

Once upon a time...
Lame. Maybe I should tell it. You're getting all, you know. Gushy. And this isn't exactly a fairy tale or whatever.
I dunno, Brent. I've heard weird stuff about this place...
Suck it up, Mikey!
If I knew you were gonna be like this I would've come by myself.
I mean, come on. Look at these clowns.
Be nice!
Ready, tough guy? Let's go.
Seriously, though! Is that kid wearing a toddler shirt? I can see his stomach.

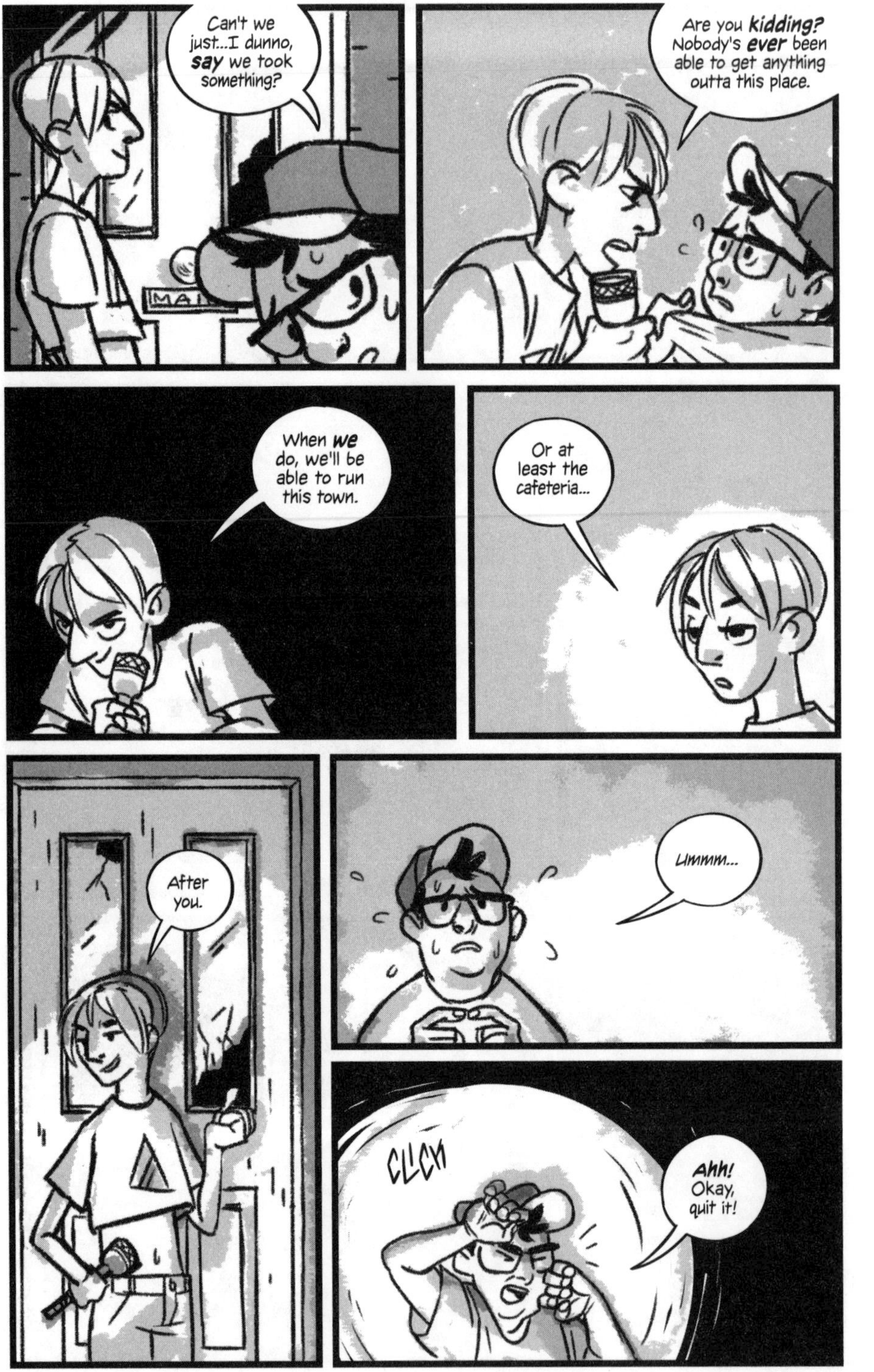
Can't we just...I dunno, **say** we took something?
MAI
Are you **kidding?** Nobody's **ever** been able to get anything outta this place.
When **we** do, we'll be able to run this town.
Or at least the cafeteria...
After you.
Ummm...
CLICK
Ahh! Okay, quit it!

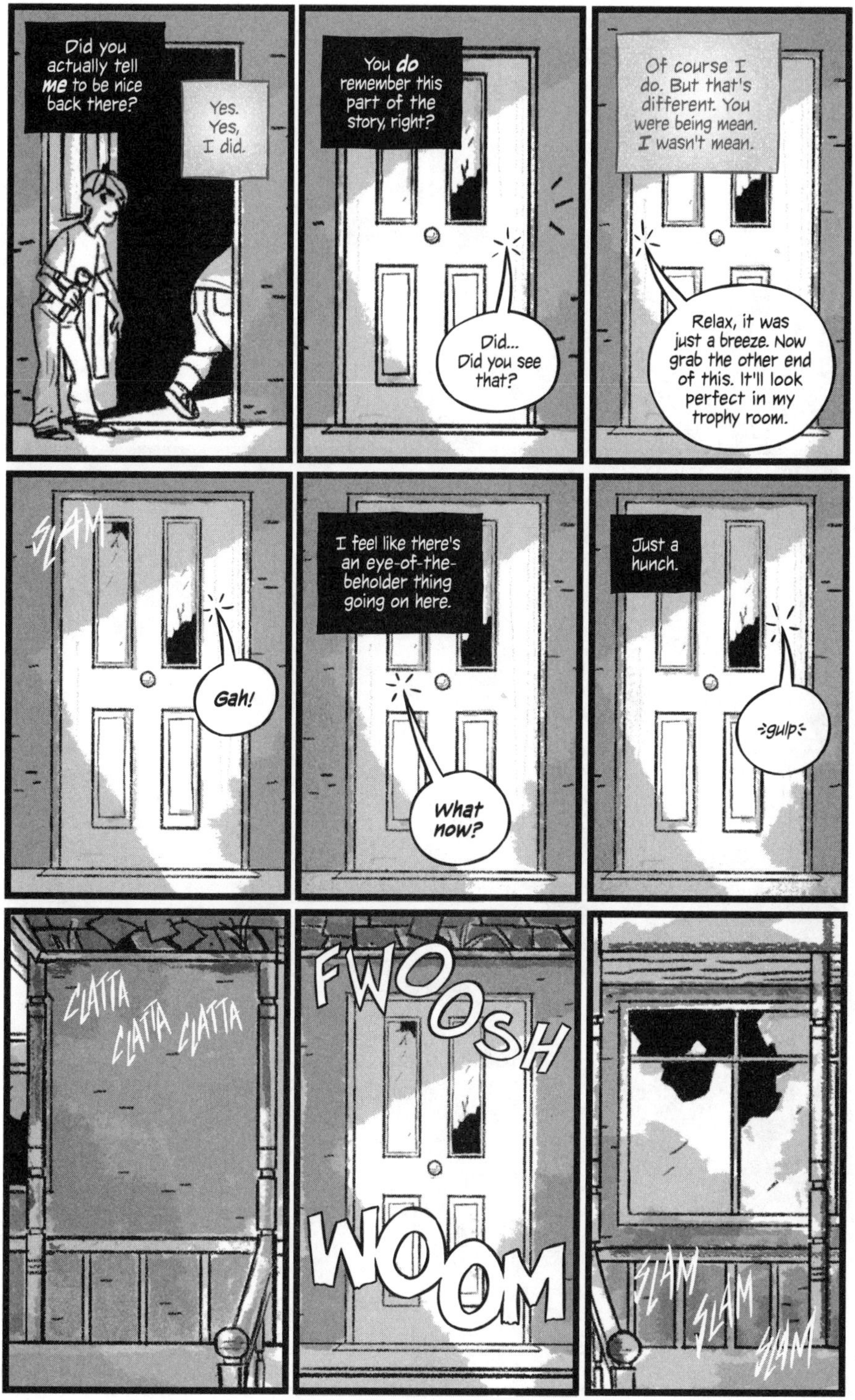

Did you actually tell *me* to be nice back there?
Yes. Yes, I did.
You *do* remember this part of the story, right?
Did... Did you see that?
Of course I do. But that's different. You were being mean. *I* wasn't mean.
Relax, it was just a breeze. Now grab the other end of this. It'll look perfect in my trophy room.
SLAM
Gah!
I feel like there's an eye-of-the-beholder thing going on here.
What now?
Just a hunch.
gulp
CLATTA CLATTA CLATTA
FWOOSH
WOOM
SLAM SLAM SLAM

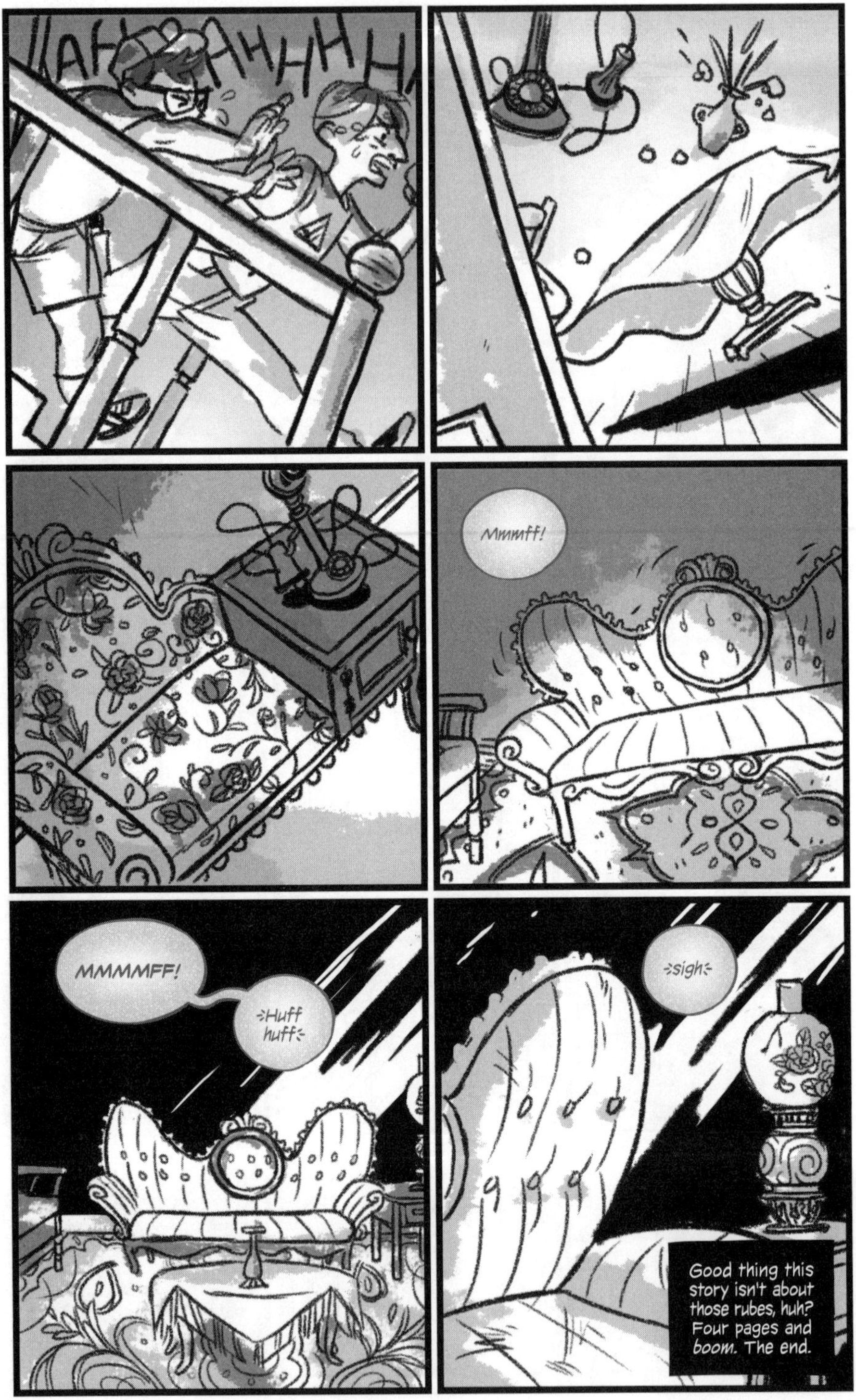
AHHHHHHHHH
Mmmff!
MMMMFF!
Huff huff
sigh
Good thing this story isn't about those rubes, huh? Four pages and *boom*. The end.

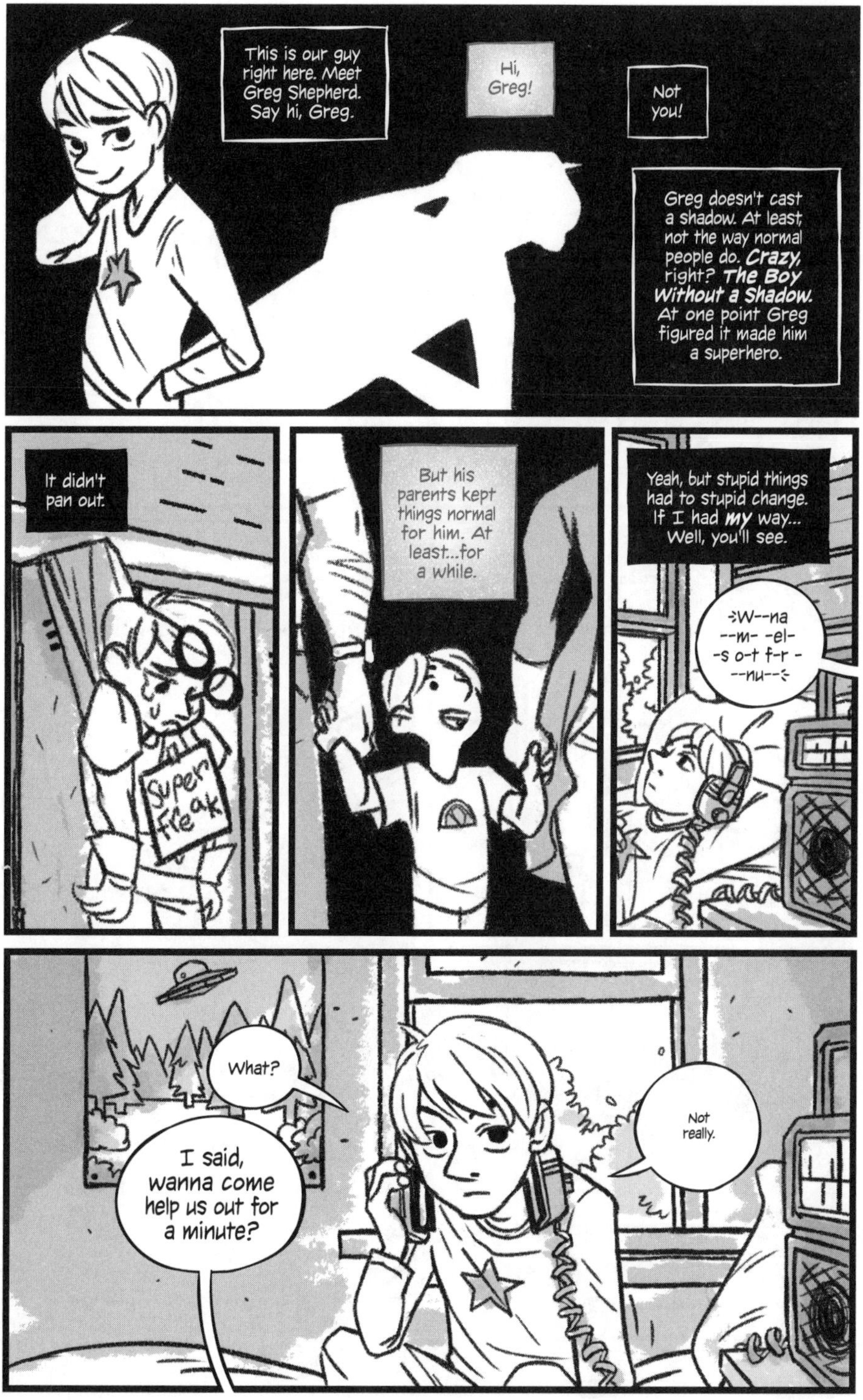
This is our guy right here. Meet Greg Shepherd. Say hi, Greg.
Hi, Greg!
Not you!
Greg doesn't cast a shadow. At least, not the way normal people do. ***Crazy,*** right? ***The Boy Without a Shadow.*** At one point Greg figured it made him a superhero.
It didn't pan out.
Super freak
But his parents kept things normal for him. At least...for a while.
Yeah, but stupid things had to stupid change. If I had ***my*** way... Well, you'll see.
W--na --m- -el- -s o-t f-r - --nu--
What?
I said, wanna come help us out for a minute?
Not really.

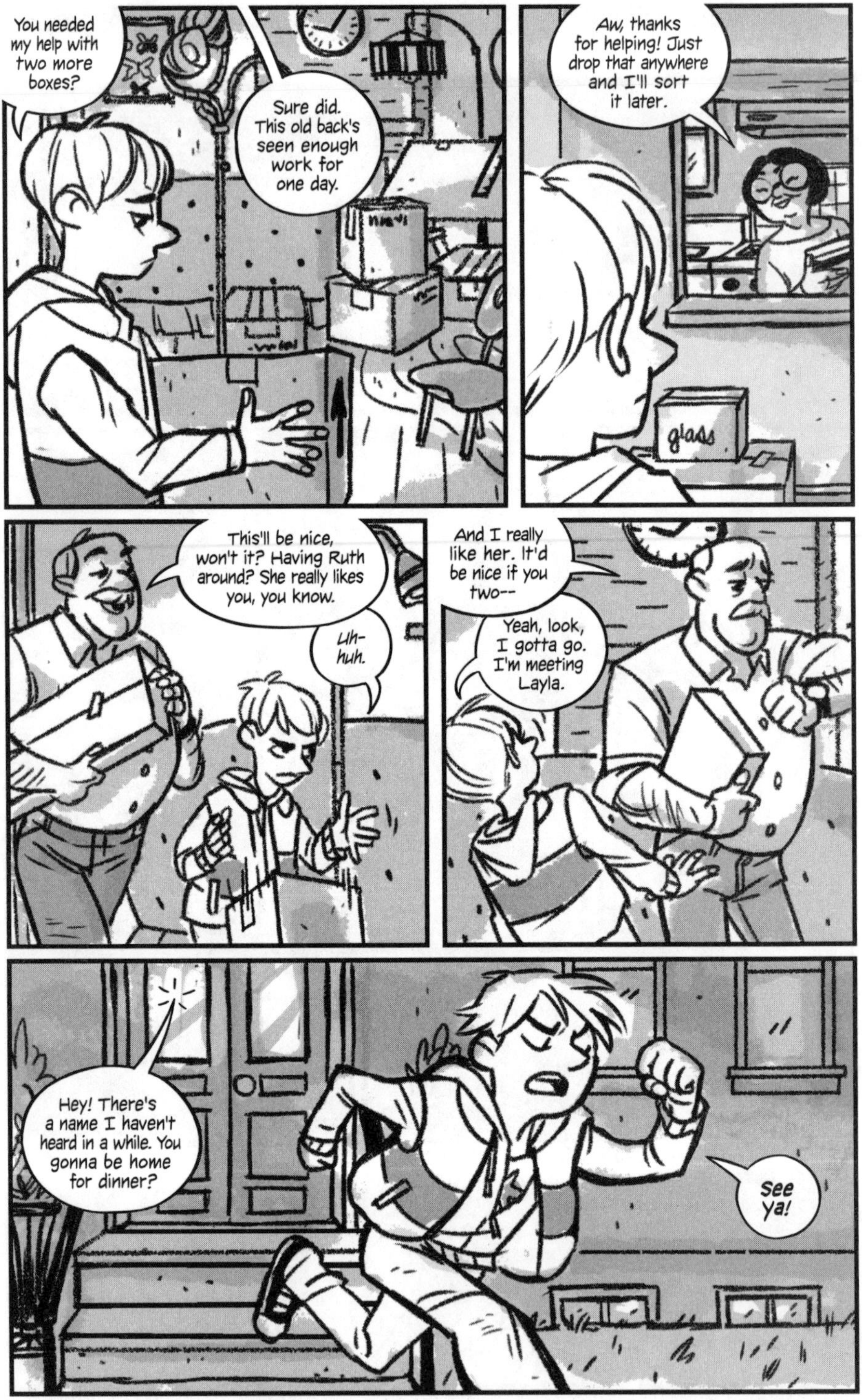
You needed my help with two more boxes?
Sure did. This old back's seen enough work for one day.
Aw, thanks for helping! Just drop that anywhere and I'll sort it later.
glass
This'll be nice, won't it? Having Ruth around? She really likes you, you know.
Uh-huh.
And I really like her. It'd be nice if you two--
Yeah, look, I gotta go. I'm meeting Layla.
Hey! There's a name I haven't heard in a while. You gonna be home for dinner?
See ya!

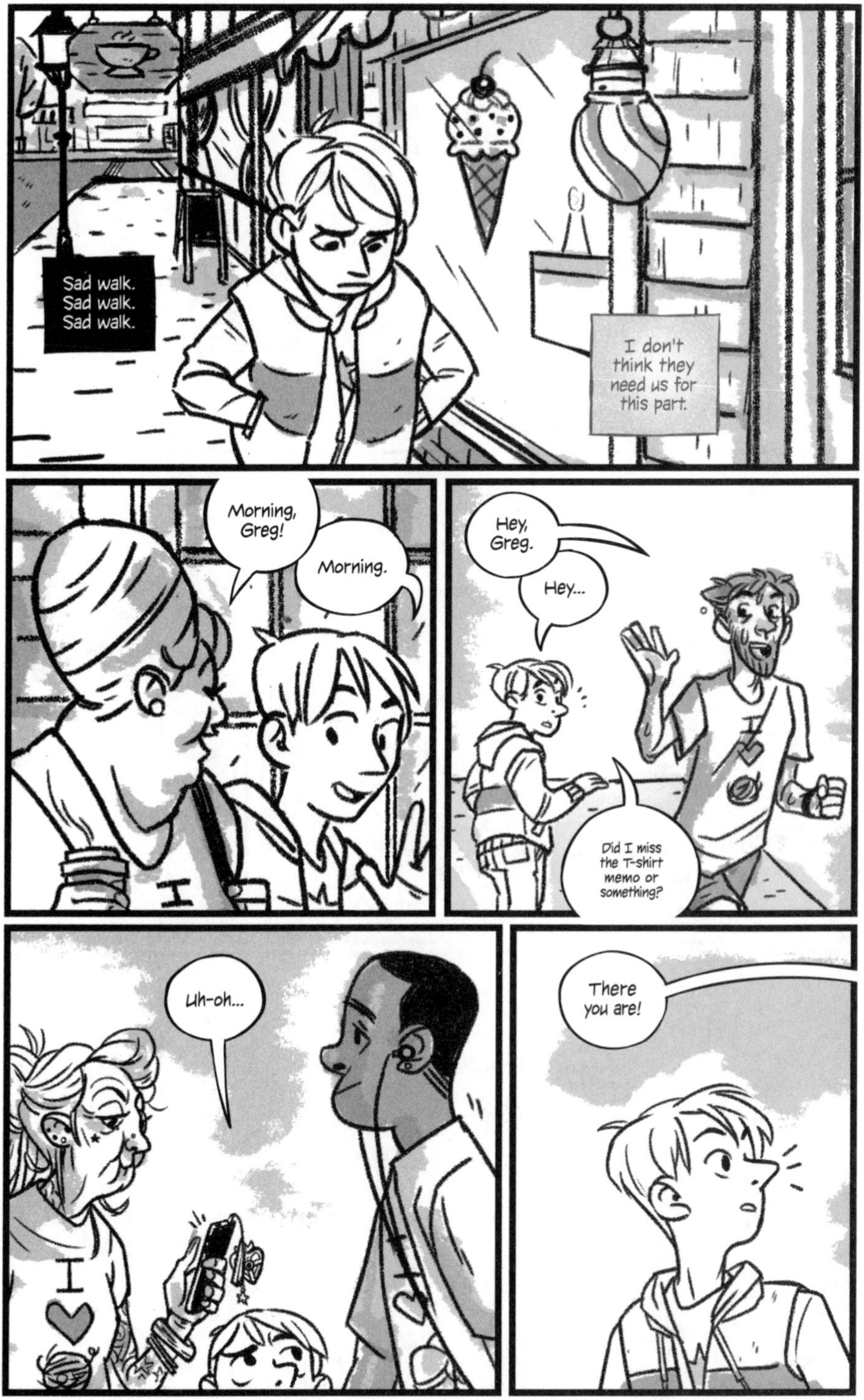
Sad walk.
Sad walk.
Sad walk.
I don't think they need us for this part.
Morning, Greg!
Morning.
Hey, Greg.
Hey...
Did I miss the T-shirt memo or something?
Uh-oh...
There you are!

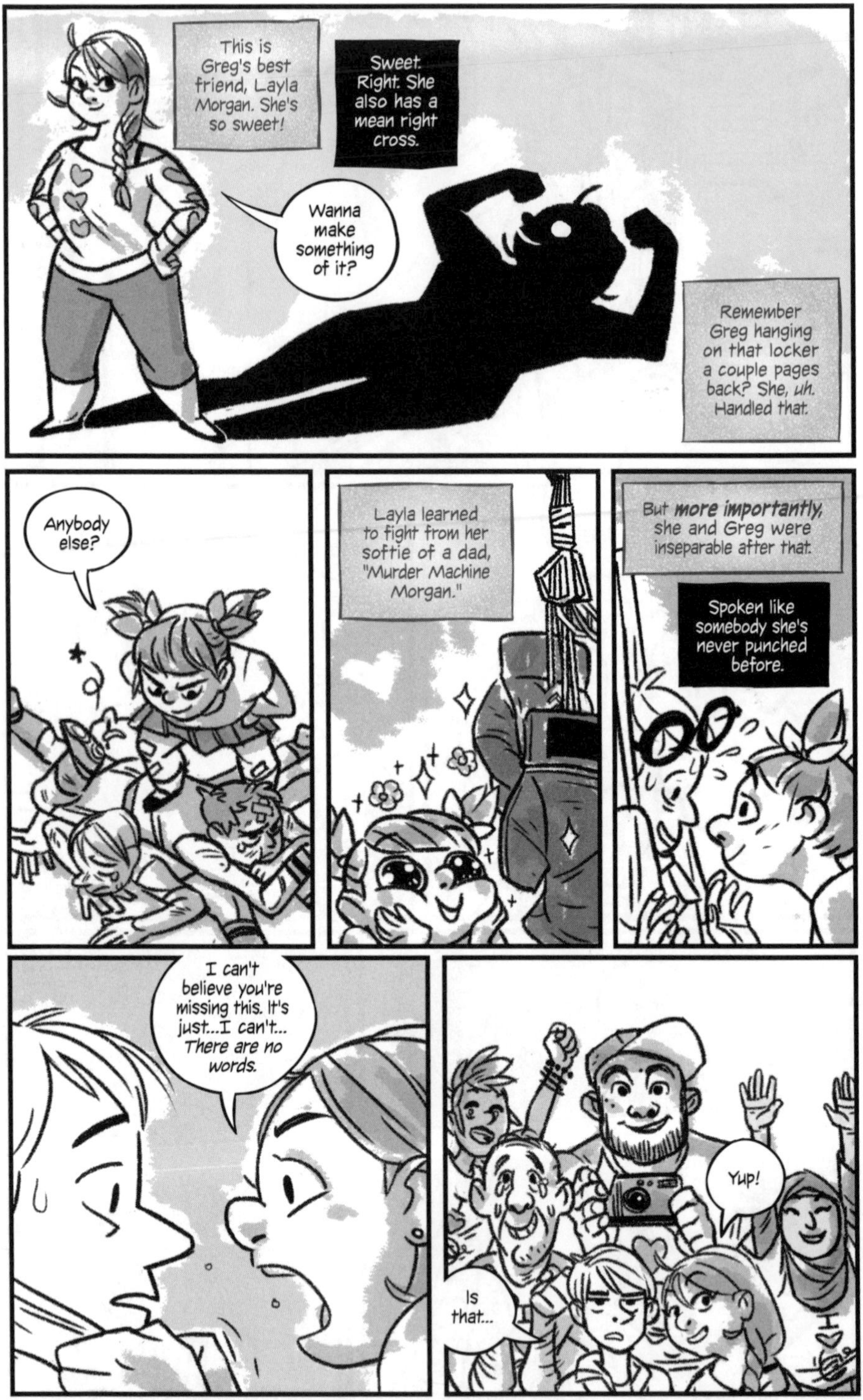
This is Greg's best friend, Layla Morgan. She's so sweet!
Sweet. Right. She also has a mean right cross.
Wanna make something of it?
Remember Greg hanging on that locker a couple pages back? She, *uh.* Handled that.
Anybody else?
Layla learned to fight from her softie of a dad, "Murder Machine Morgan."
But **more importantly,** she and Greg were inseparable after that.
Spoken like somebody she's never punched before.
I can't believe you're missing this. It's just...I can't... *There are no words.*
Yup!
Is that...

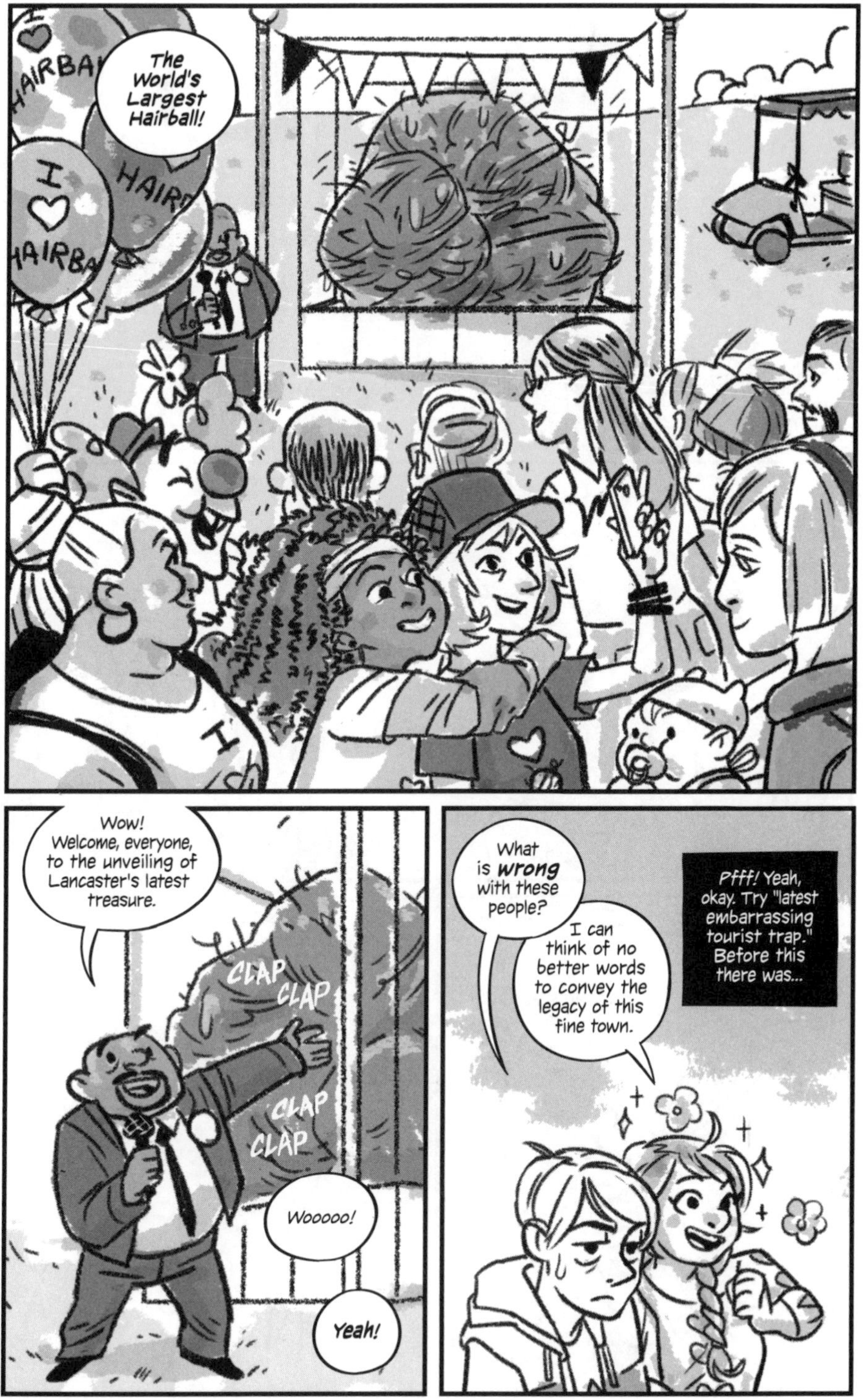
The World's Largest Hairball!
Wow! Welcome, everyone, to the unveiling of Lancaster's latest treasure.
CLAP CLAP
CLAP CLAP
Wooooo!
Yeah!
What is ***wrong*** with these people?
I can think of no better words to convey the legacy of this fine town.
Pfff! Yeah, okay. Try "latest embarrassing tourist trap." Before this there was...

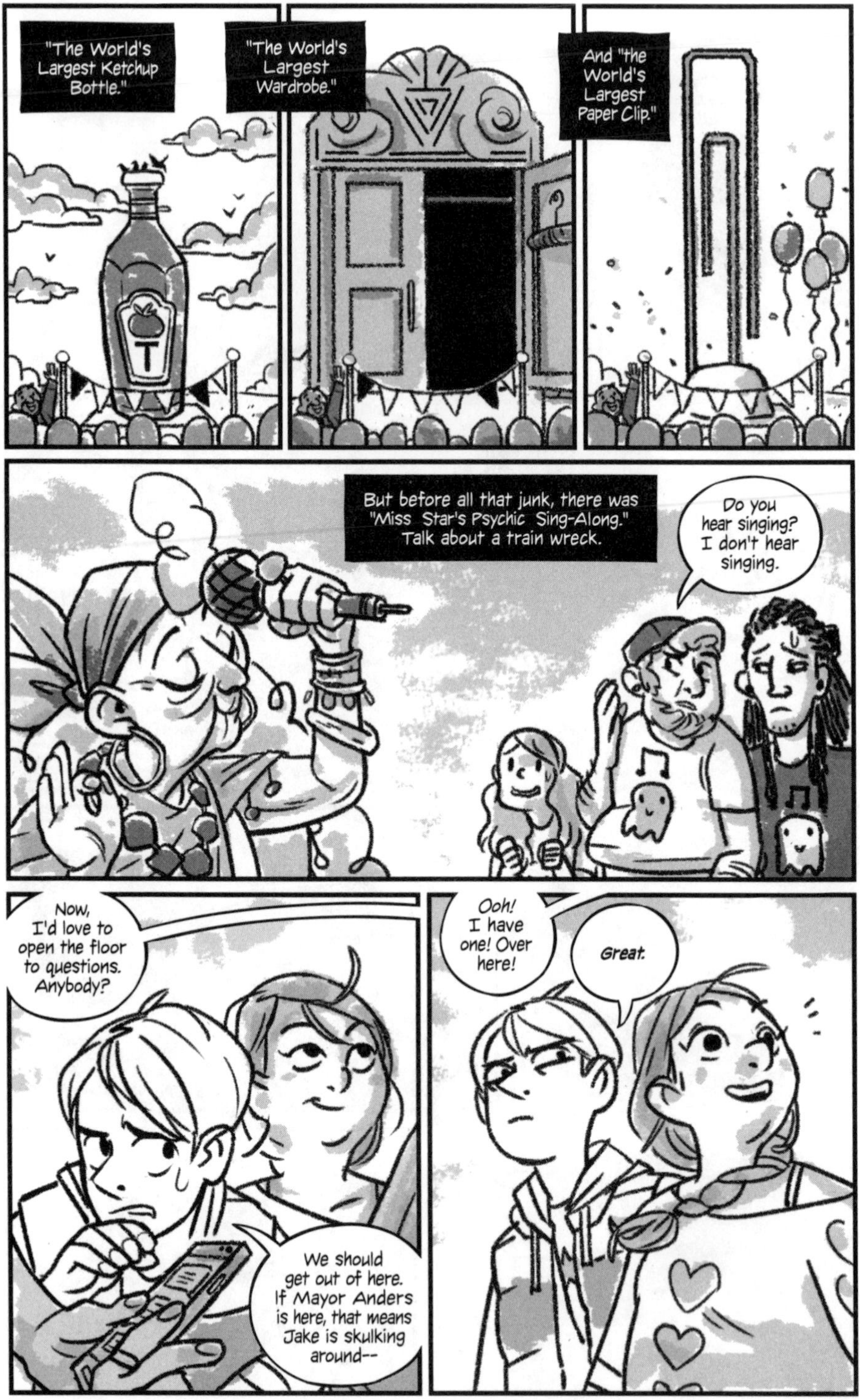
"The World's Largest Ketchup Bottle."
"The World's Largest Wardrobe."
And "the World's Largest Paper Clip."
But before all that junk, there was "Miss Star's Psychic Sing-Along." Talk about a train wreck.
Do you hear singing? I don't hear singing.
Now, I'd love to open the floor to questions. Anybody?
We should get out of here. If Mayor Anders is here, that means Jake is skulking around--
Ooh! I have one! Over here!
Great.

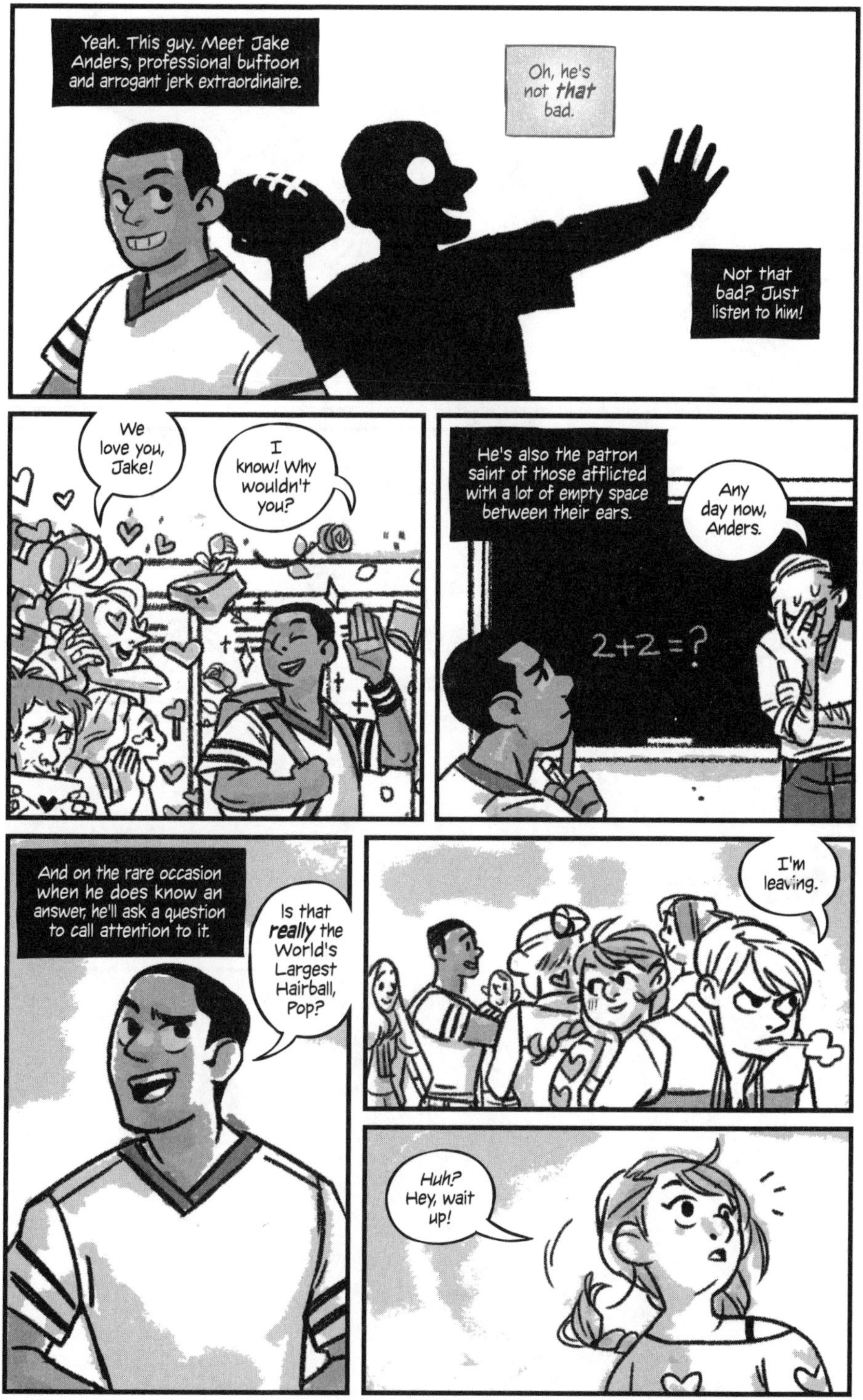

Yeah. This guy. Meet Jake Anders, professional buffoon and arrogant jerk extraordinaire.
Oh, he's not *that* bad.
Not that bad? Just listen to him!
We love you, Jake!
I know! Why wouldn't you?
He's also the patron saint of those afflicted with a lot of empty space between their ears.
Any day now, Anders.
2+2 = ?
And on the rare occasion when he does know an answer, he'll ask a question to call attention to it.
Is that *really* the World's Largest Hairball, Pop?
I'm leaving.
Huh? Hey, wait up!

I know this place wasn't always this weird. Right?

I mean, I seem to recall a time before giant condiments, office supplies, and regurgitated cud.

Normal is totally overrated.

Speaking of, what's it like having Ruth all up in your place? Probably weird, huh?

It's...

Whoops. Now he's done it.

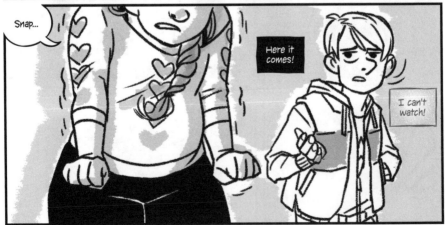

Snap...

Here it comes!

I can't watch!

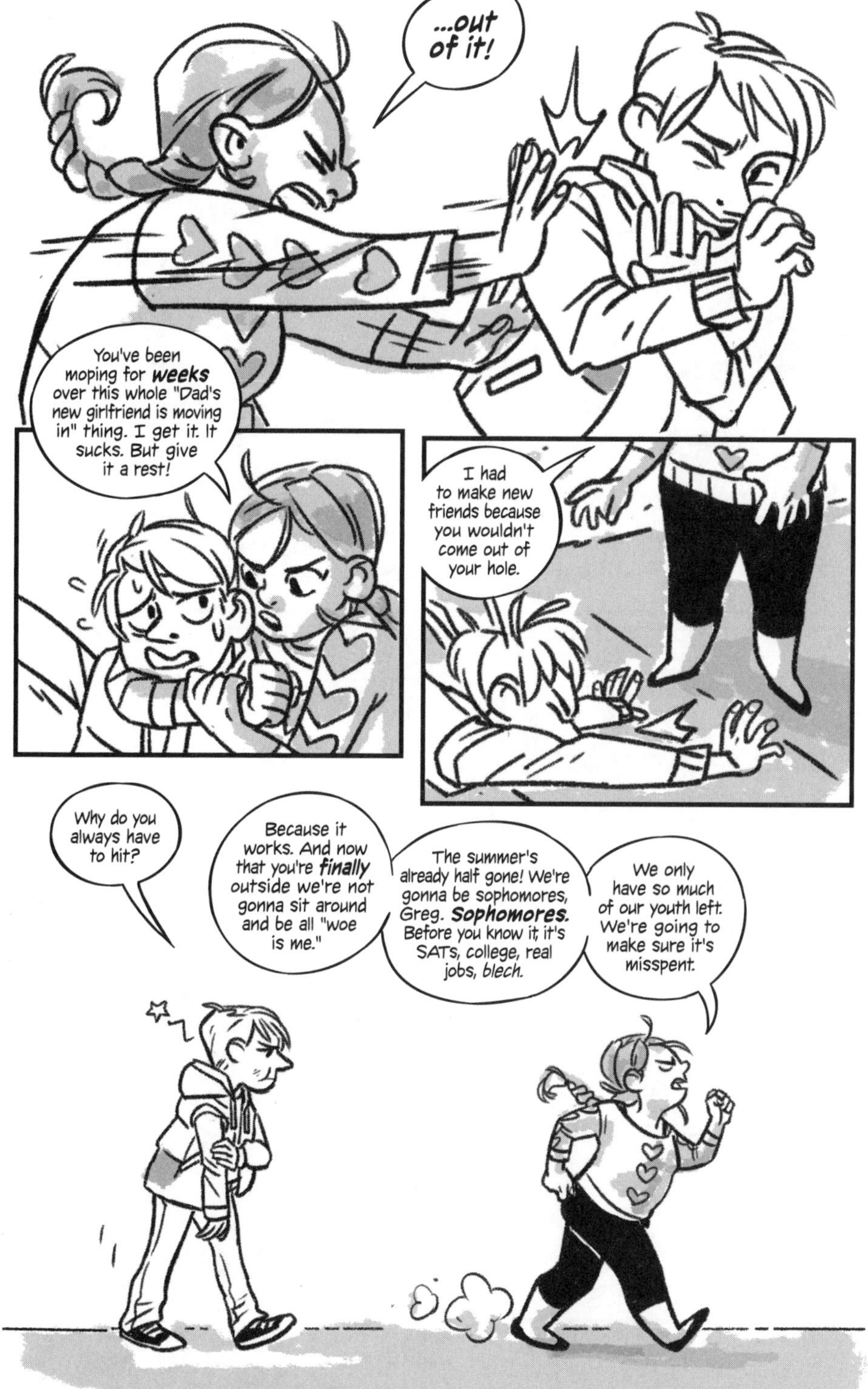
...out of it!
You've been moping for **weeks** over this whole "Dad's new girlfriend is moving in" thing. I get it. It sucks. But give it a rest!
I had to make new friends because you wouldn't come out of your hole.
Why do you always have to hit?
Because it works. And now that you're ***finally*** outside we're not gonna sit around and be all "woe is me."
The summer's already half gone! We're gonna be sophomores, Greg. ***Sophomores.*** Before you know it, it's SATs, college, real jobs, *blech.*
We only have so much of our youth left. We're going to make sure it's misspent.

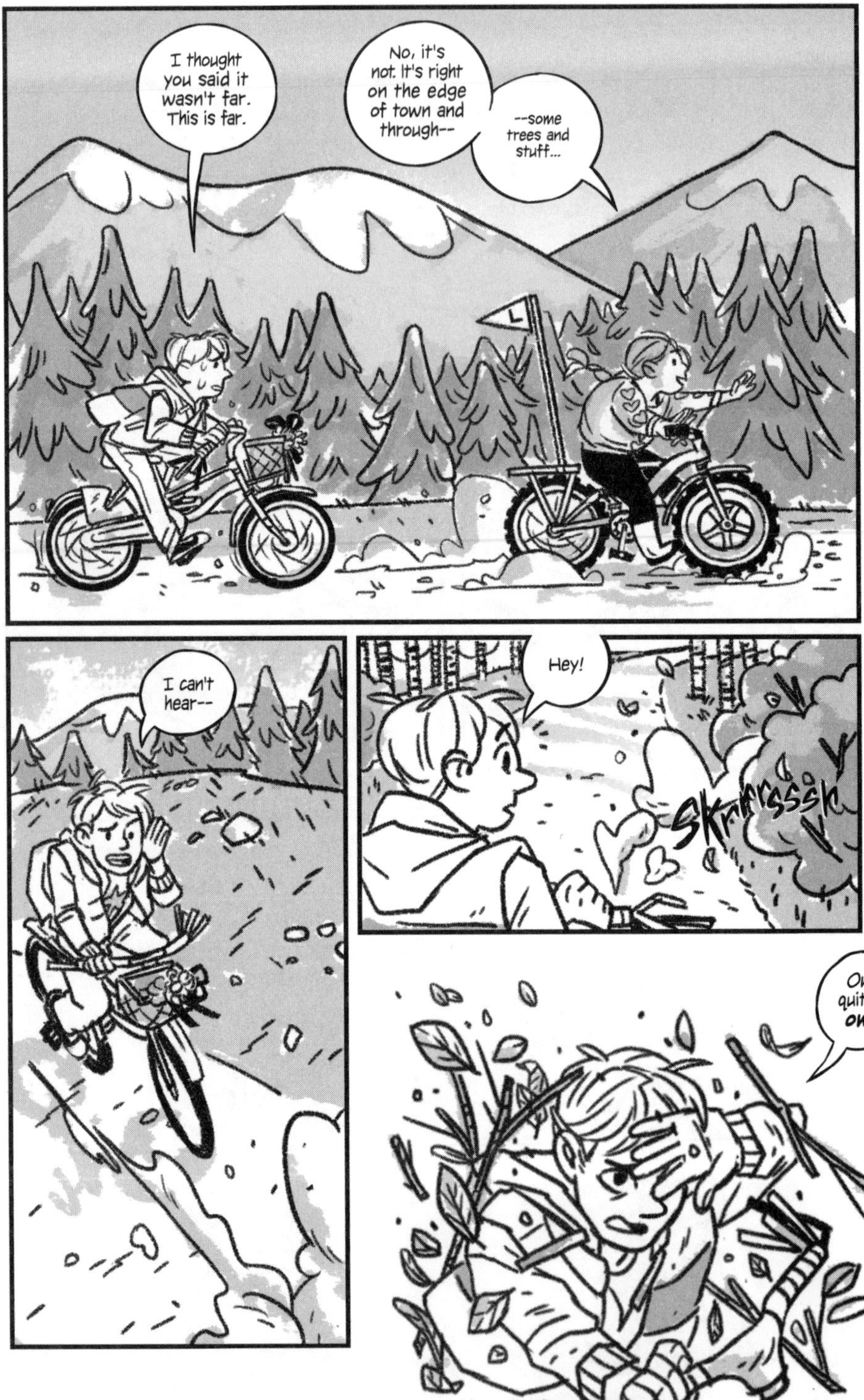
I thought you said it wasn't far. This is far.
No, it's not. It's right on the edge of town and through--
--some trees and stuff...
I can't hear--
Hey!
SKRRRSSSK
Ow, quit it, OW!

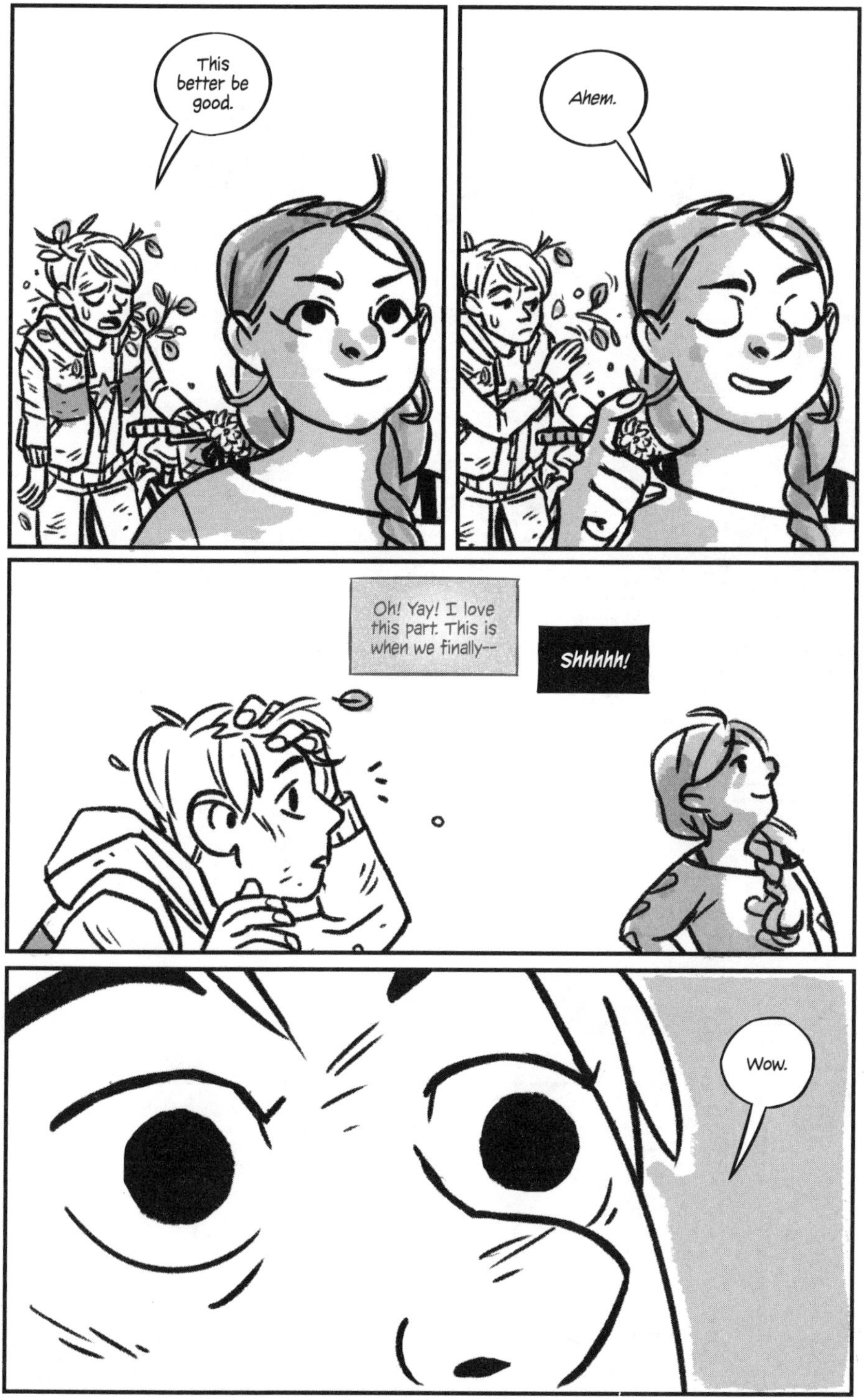
This better be good.
Ahem.
Oh! Yay! I love this part. This is when we finally--
Shhhhh!
Wow.

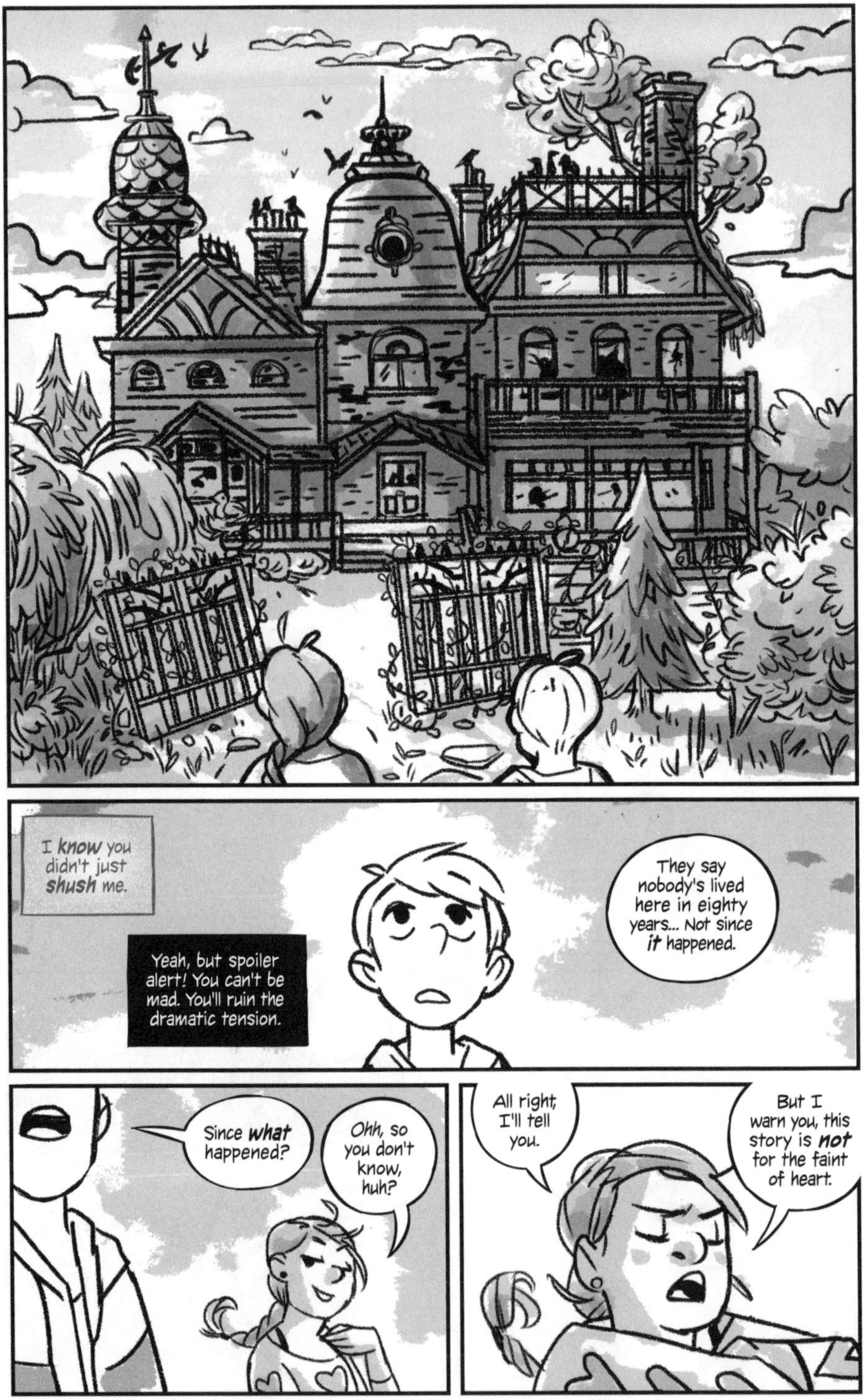
I know you didn't just shush me.
Yeah, but spoiler alert! You can't be mad. You'll ruin the dramatic tension.
They say nobody's lived here in eighty years... Not since it happened.
Since what happened?
Ohh, so you don't know, huh?
All right, I'll tell you.
But I warn you, this story is not for the faint of heart.

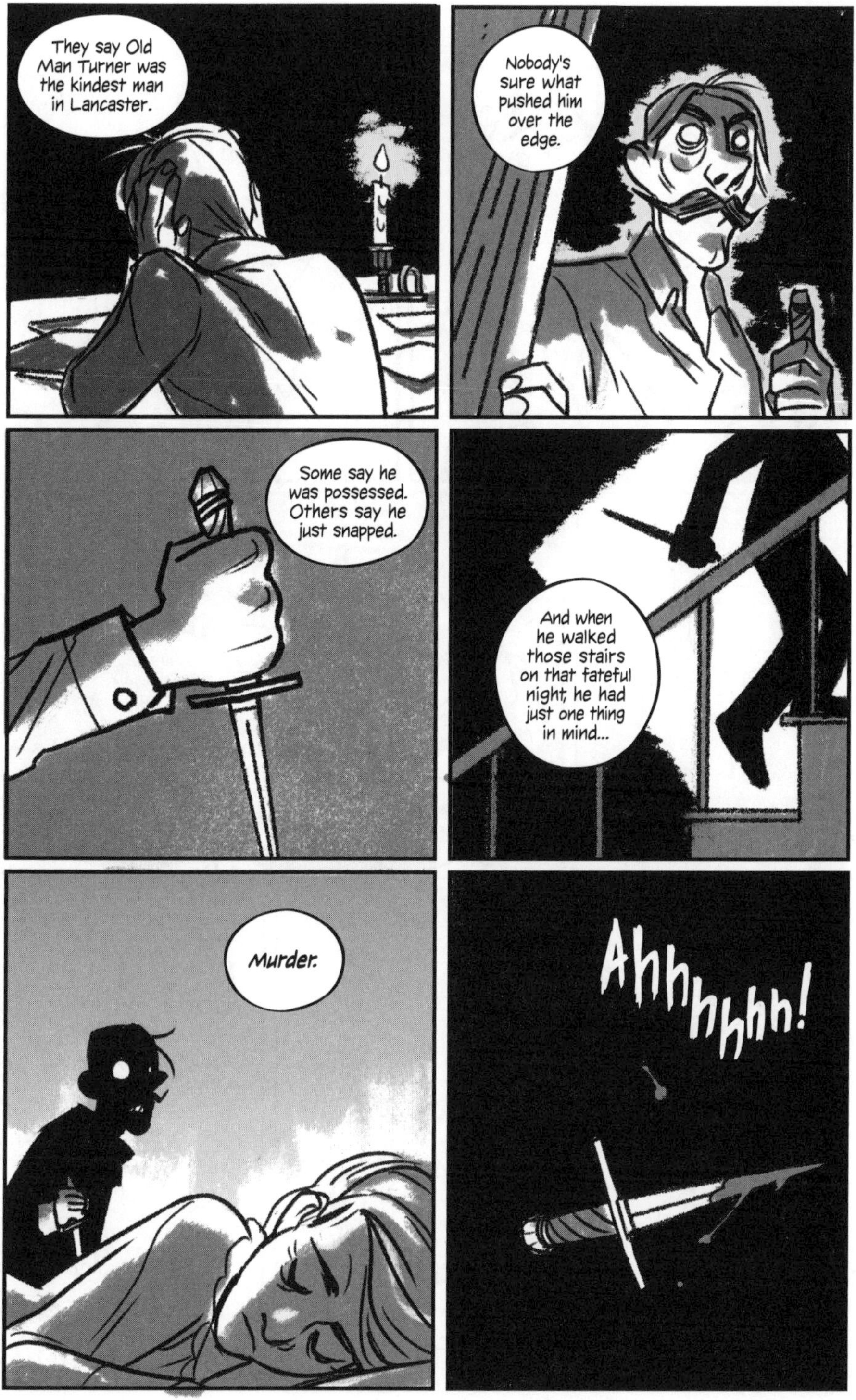
They say Old Man Turner was the kindest man in Lancaster.
Nobody's sure what pushed him over the edge.
Some say he was possessed. Others say he just snapped.
And when he walked those stairs on that fateful night, he had just one thing in mind...
Murder.
Ahhhhhh!

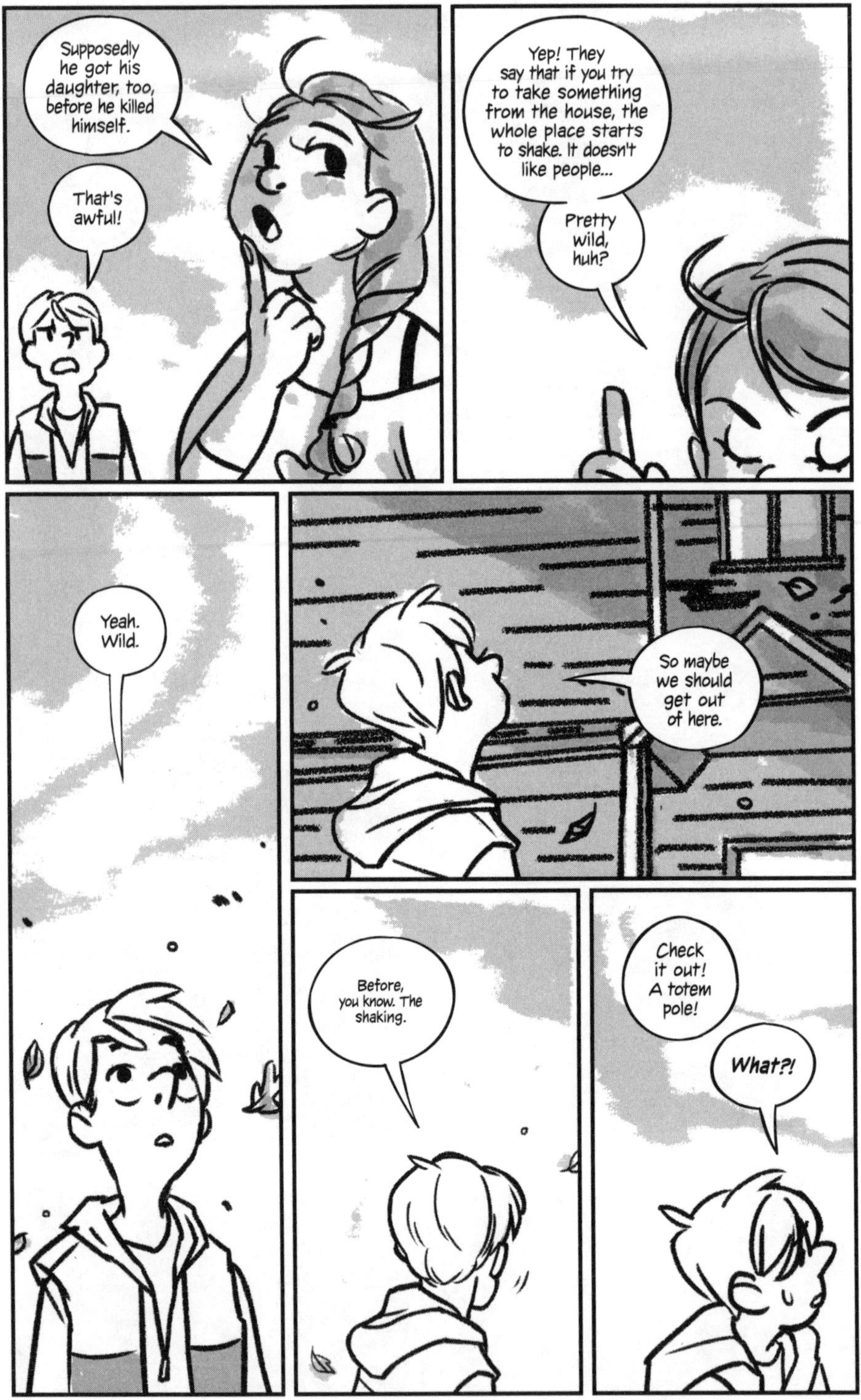
Supposedly he got his daughter, too, before he killed himself.
That's awful!
Yep! They say that if you try to take something from the house, the whole place starts to shake. It doesn't like people...
Pretty wild, huh?
Yeah. Wild.
So maybe we should get out of here.
Before, you know. The shaking.
Check it out! A totem pole!
What?!

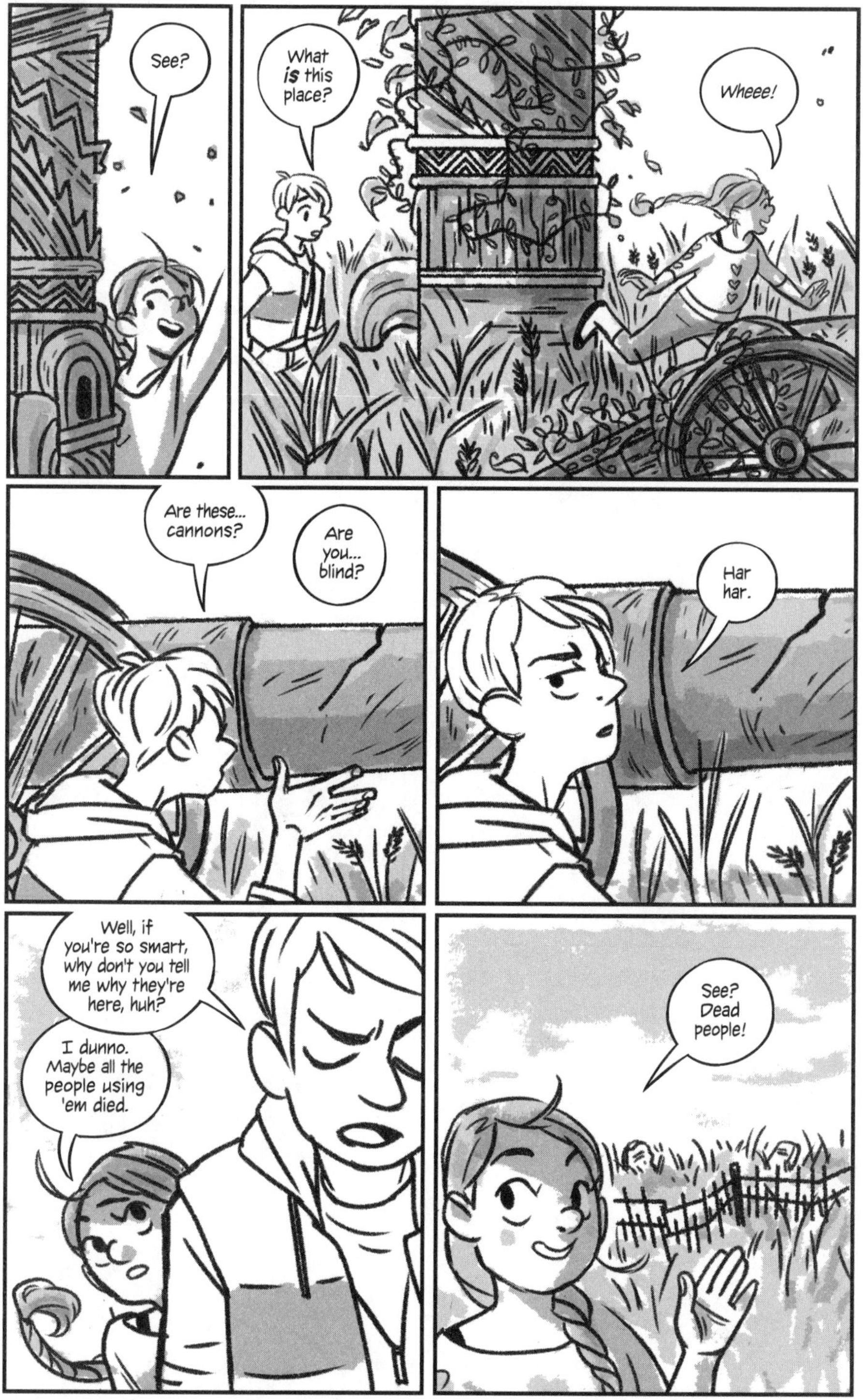
See?
What *is* this place?
Wheee!
Are these... cannons?
Are you... blind?
Har har.
Well, if you're so smart, why don't you tell me why they're here, huh?
I dunno. Maybe all the people using 'em died.
See? Dead people!

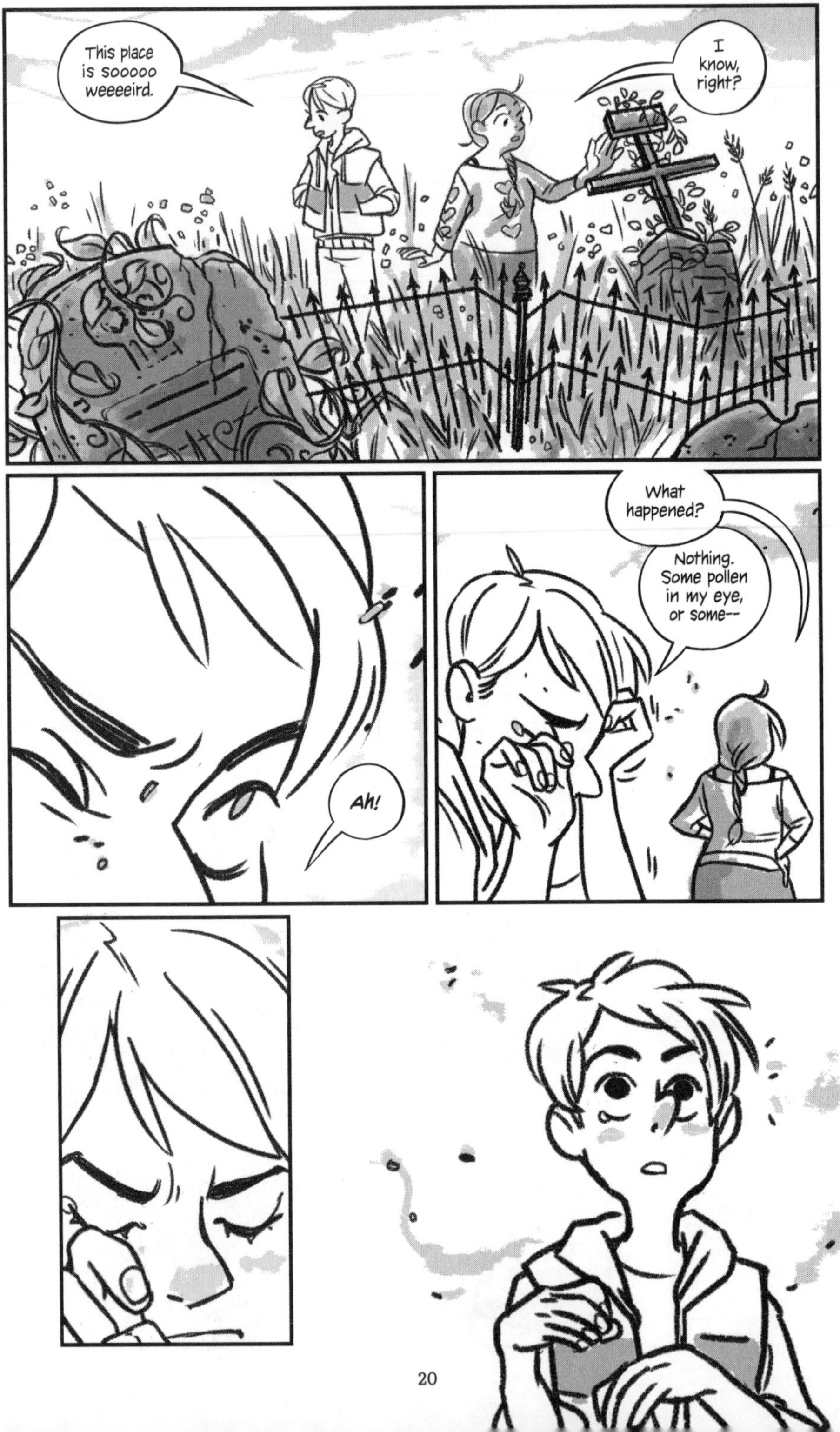
This place is sooooo weeeeird.
I know, right?
Ah!
What happened?
Nothing. Some pollen in my eye, or some--

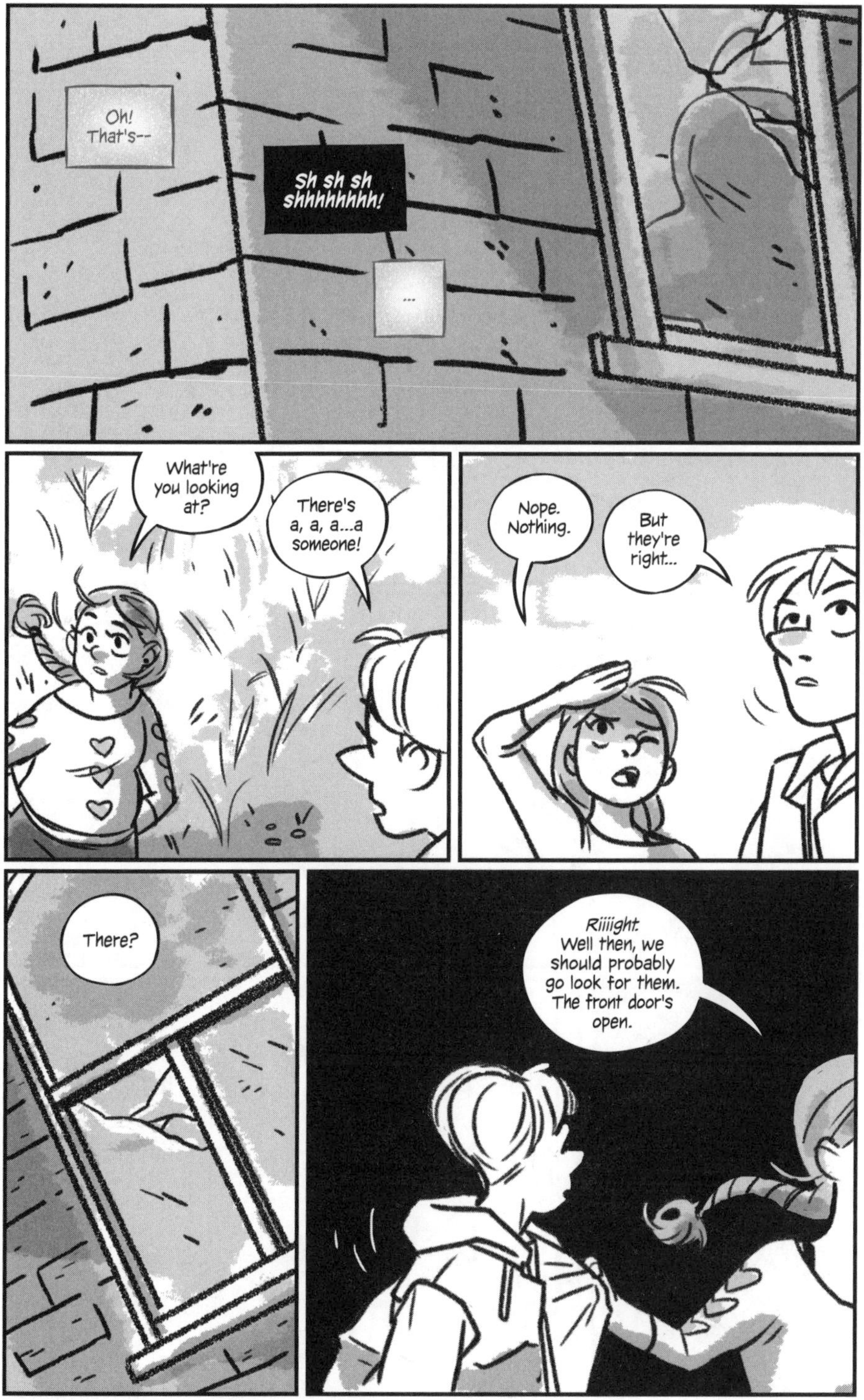

Oh! That's--
Sh sh sh shhhhhhhh!
...
What're you looking at?
There's a, a, a...a someone!
Nope. Nothing.
But they're right...
There?
Riiight. Well then, we should probably go look for them. The front door's open.

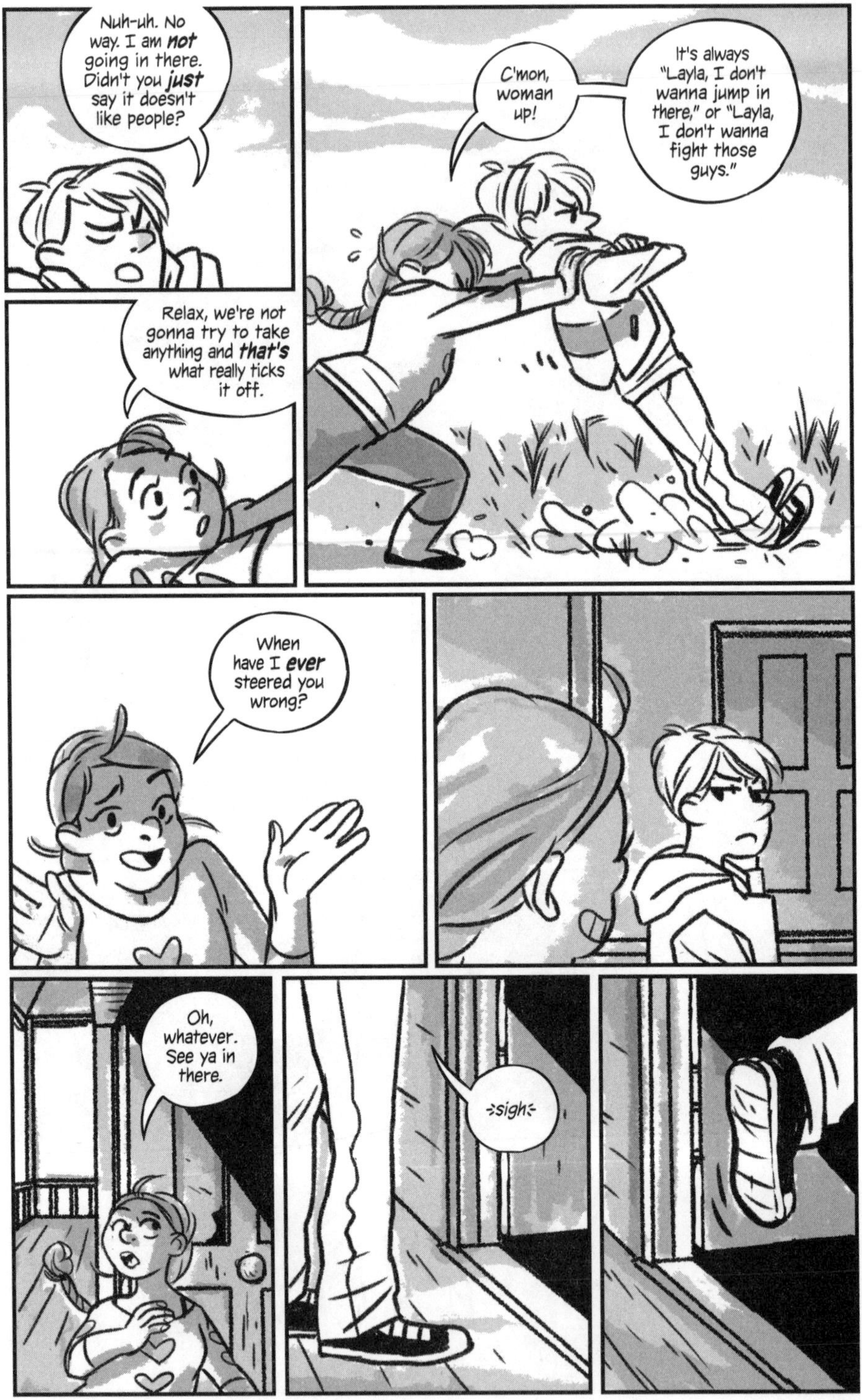

Nuh-uh. No way. I am not going in there. Didn't you just say it doesn't like people?
C'mon, woman up!
It's always "Layla, I don't wanna jump in there," or "Layla, I don't wanna fight those guys."
Relax, we're not gonna try to take anything and that's what really ticks it off.
When have I ever steered you wrong?
Oh, whatever. See ya in there.
sigh

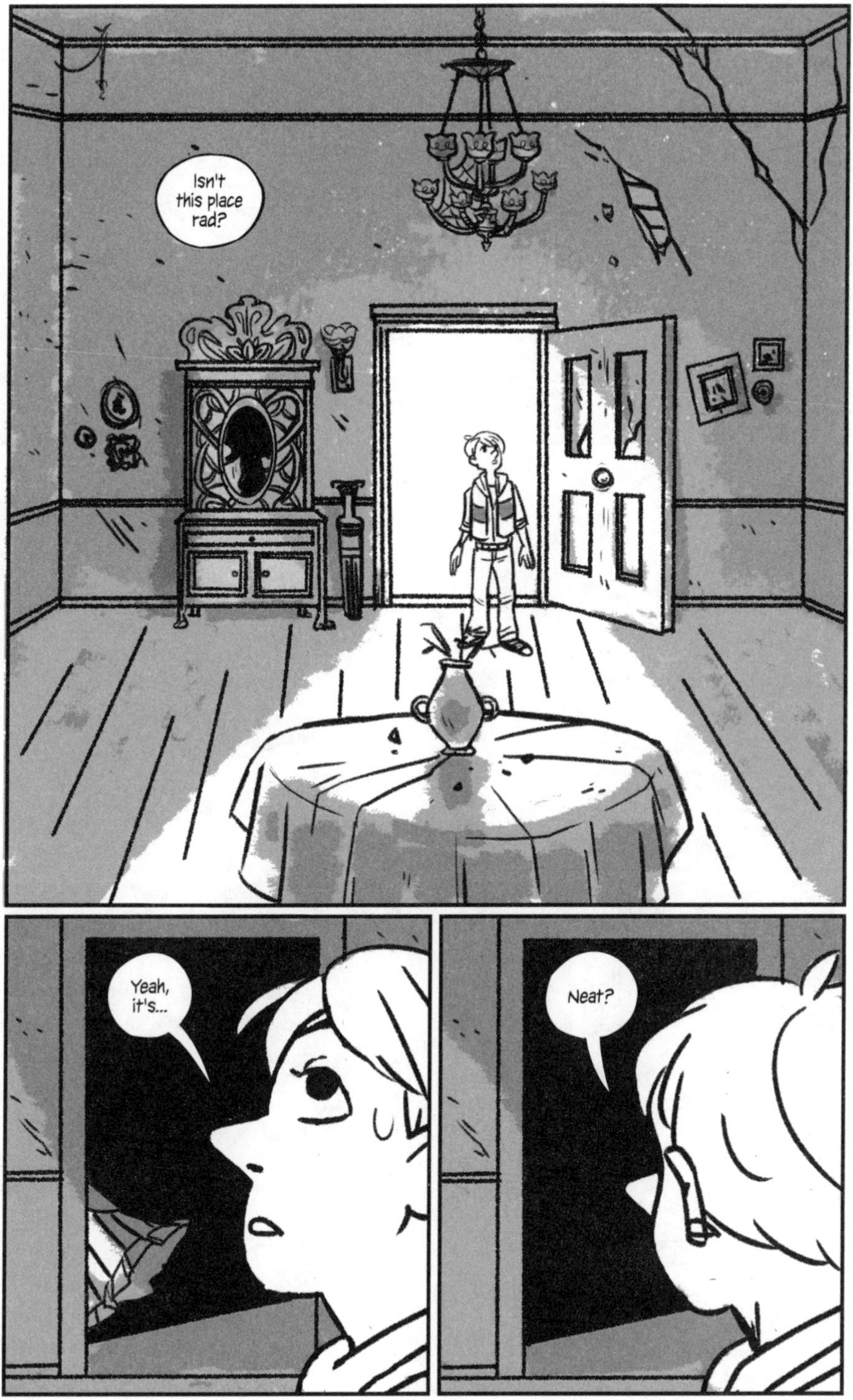
Isn't this place rad?
Yeah, it's...
Neat?

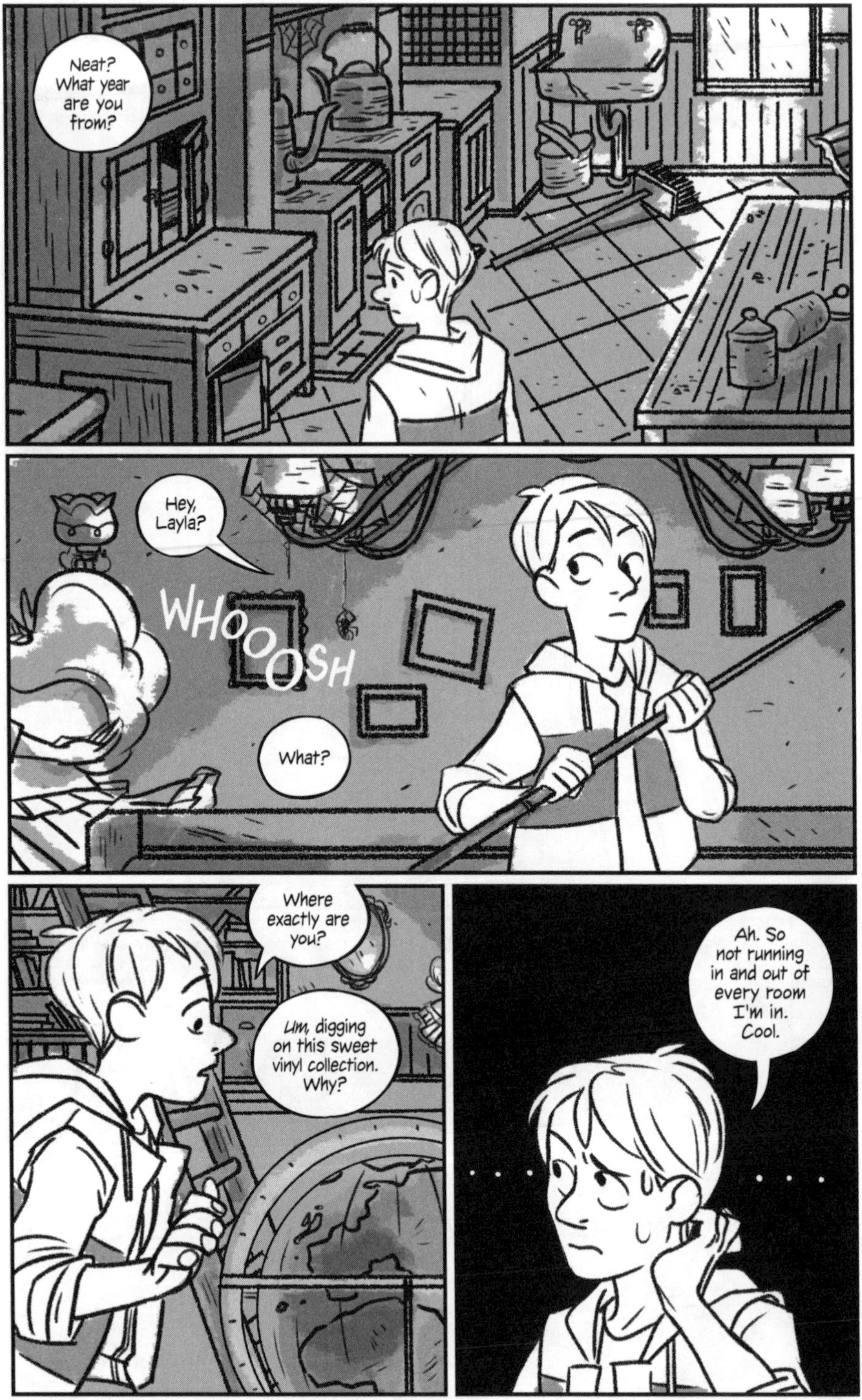
Neat? What year are you from?
Hey, Layla?
WHOOOOSH
What?
Where exactly are you?
Um, digging on this sweet vinyl collection. Why?
Ah. So not running in and out of every room I'm in. Cool.
. . .
. . .

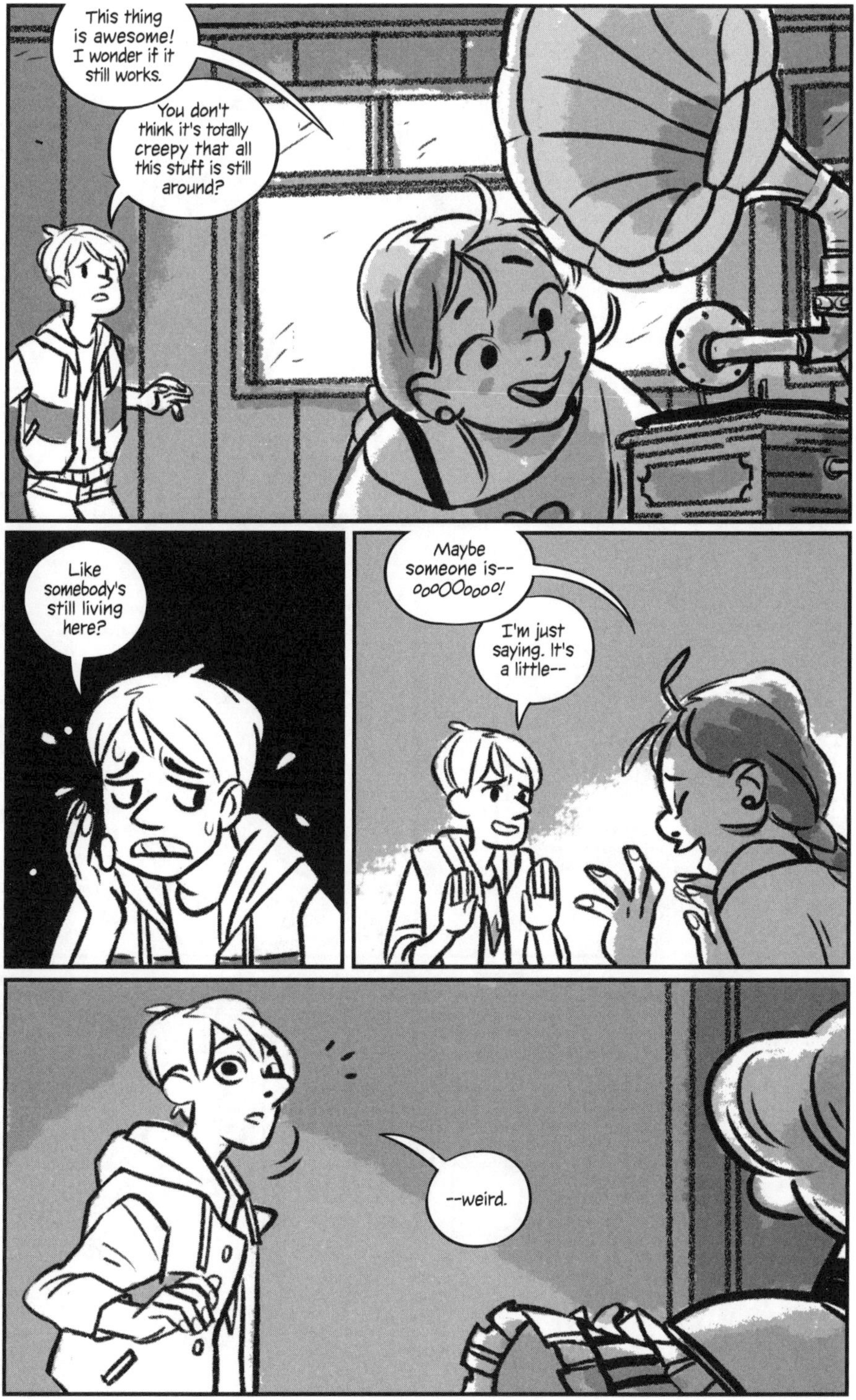
This thing is awesome! I wonder if it still works.
You don't think it's totally creepy that all this stuff is still around?
Like somebody's still living here?
Maybe someone is-- oooOOoooo!
I'm just saying. It's a little--
--weird.

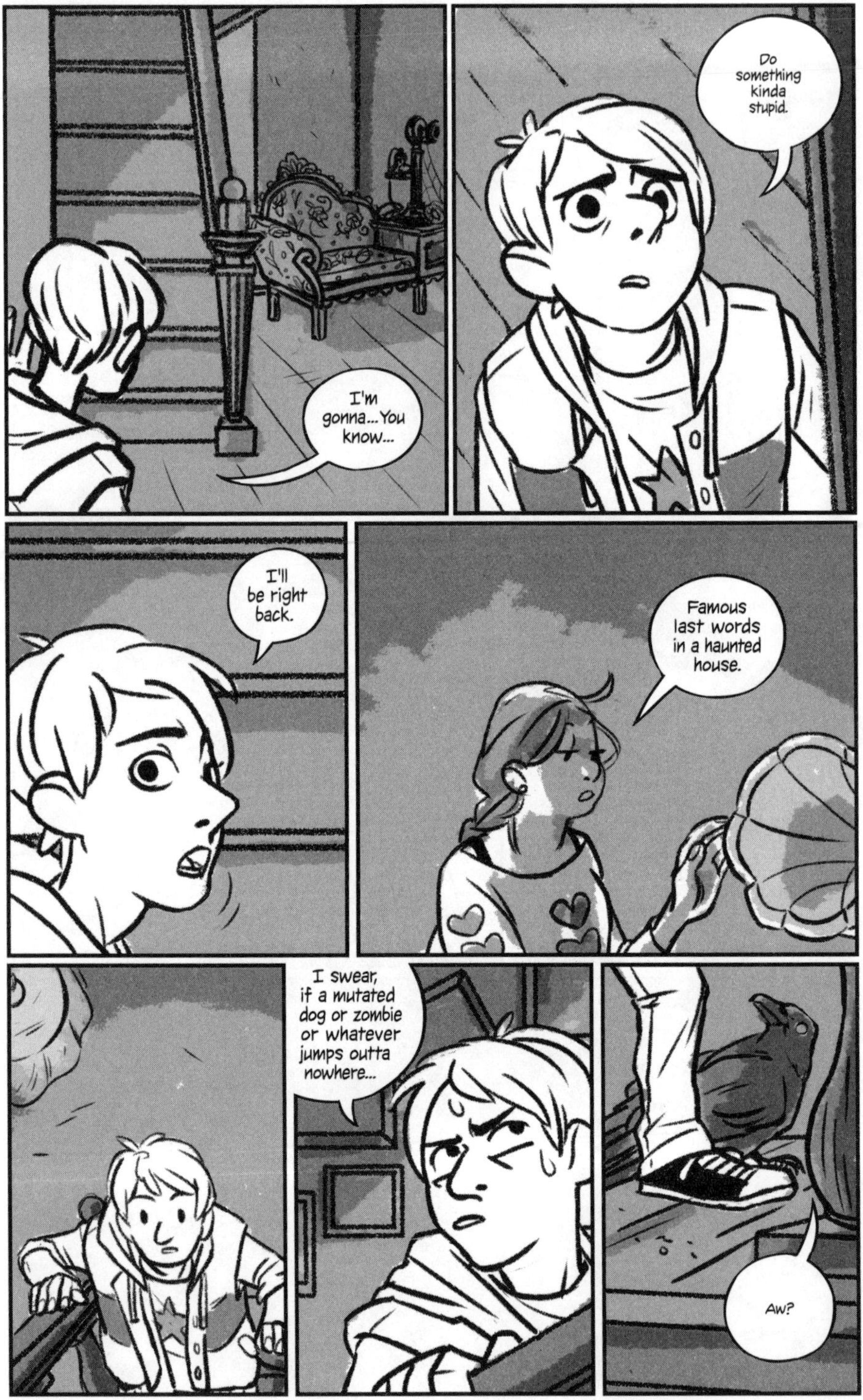
I'm gonna...You know...
Do something kinda stupid.
I'll be right back.
Famous last words in a haunted house.
I swear, if a mutated dog or zombie or whatever jumps outta nowhere...
Aw?

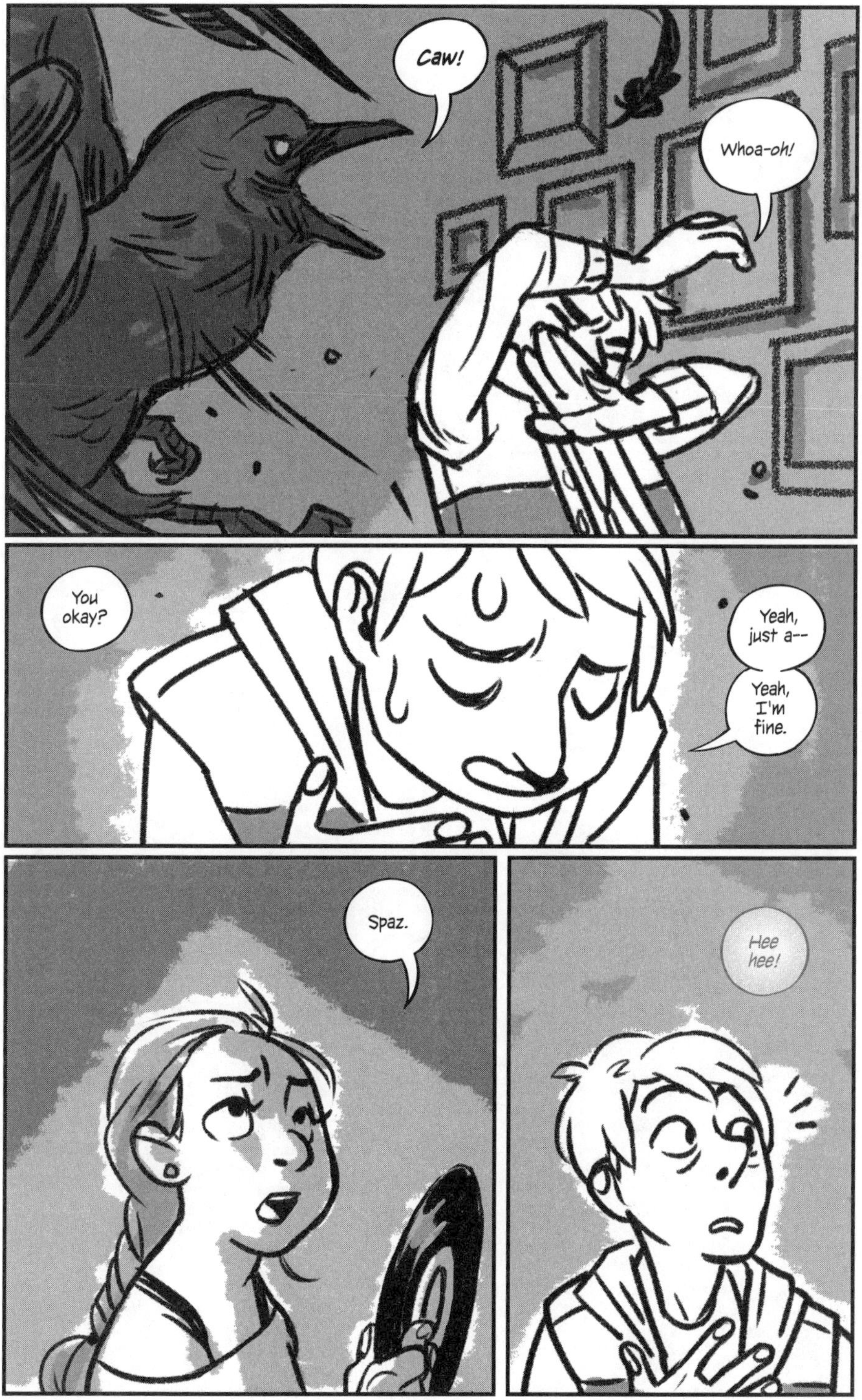
Caw!
Whoa-oh!
You okay?
Yeah, just a--
Yeah, I'm fine.
Spaz.
Hee hee!

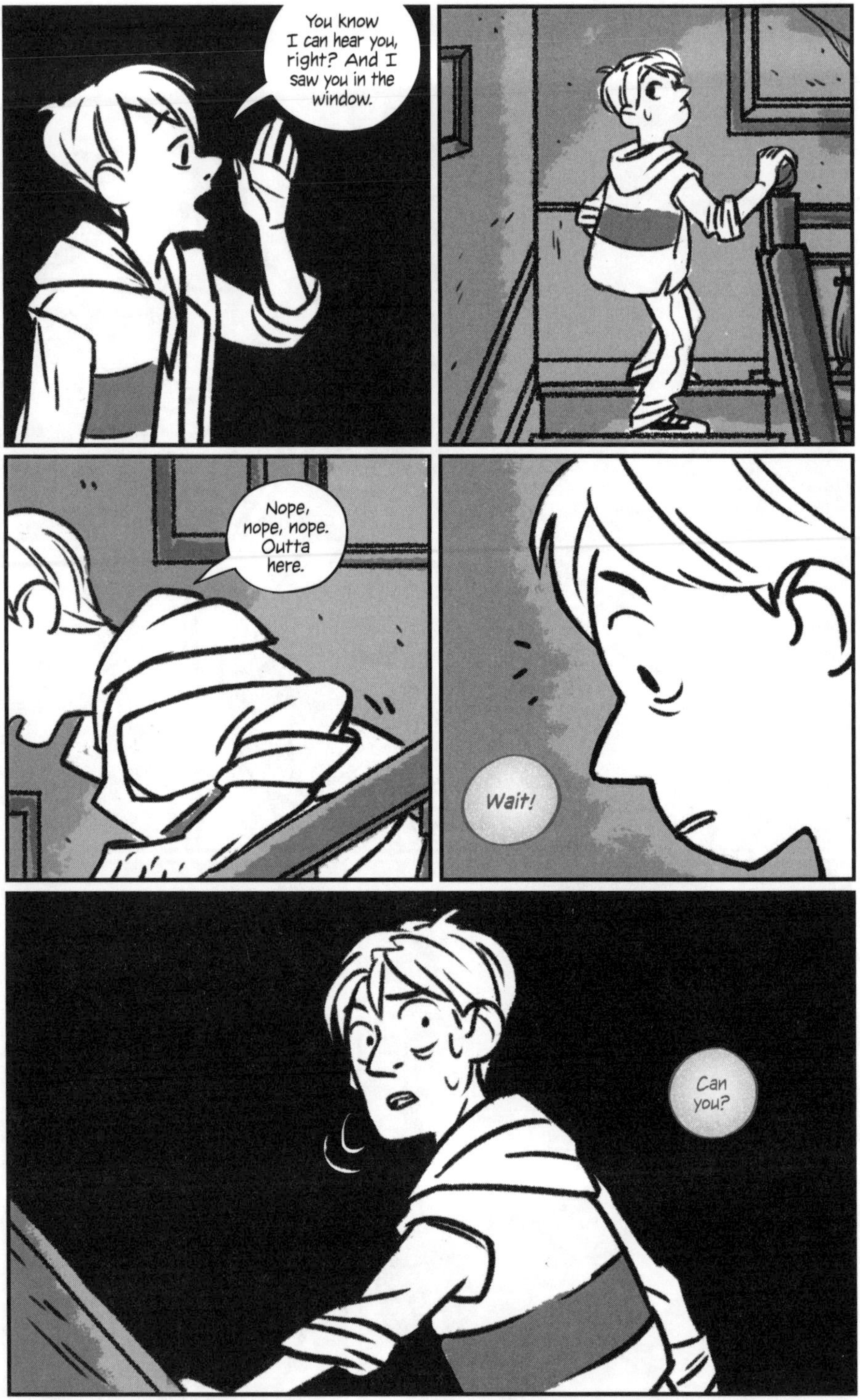
You know I can hear you, right? And I saw you in the window.
Nope, nope, nope. Outta here.
Wait!
Can you?

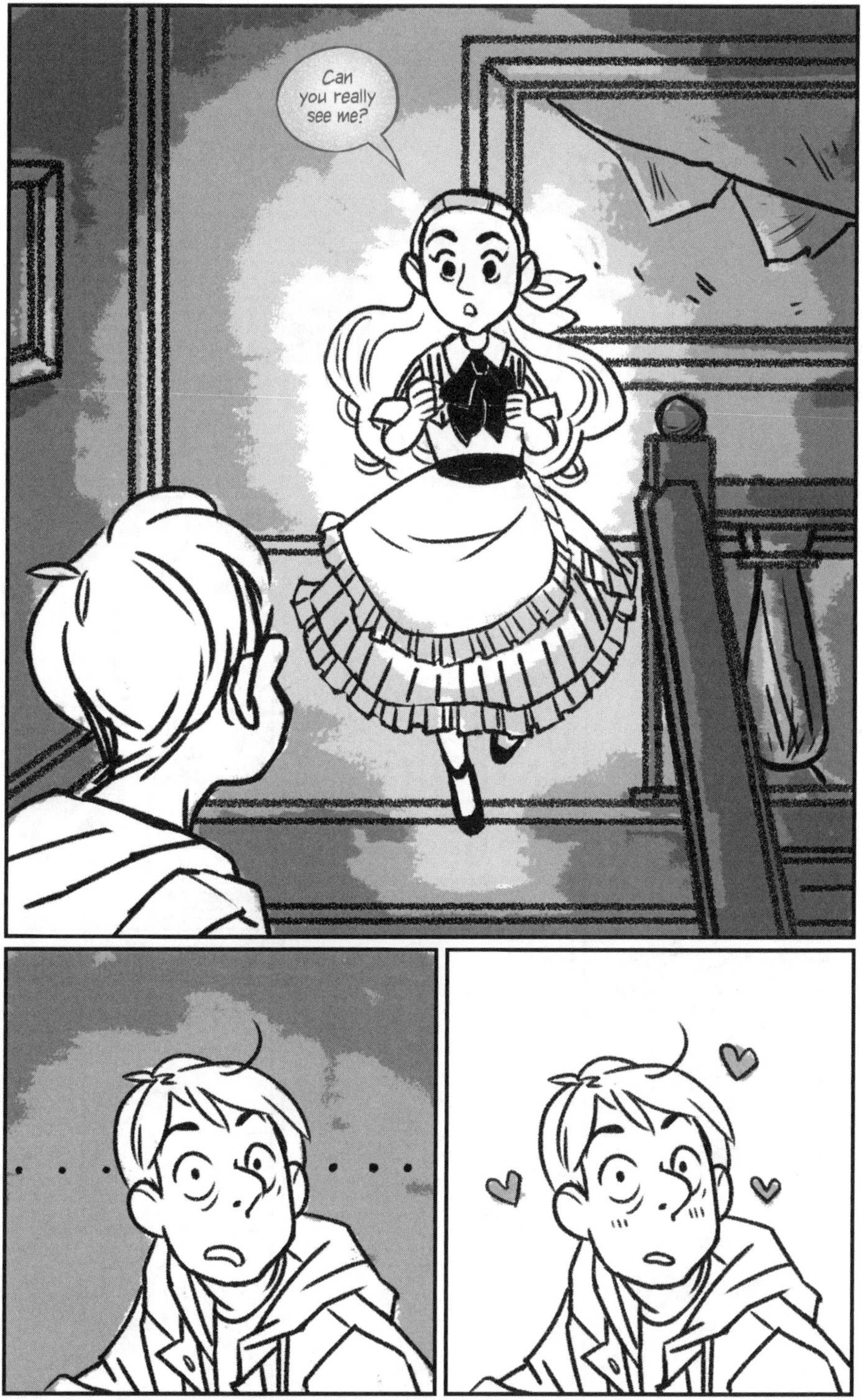
Can you really see me?

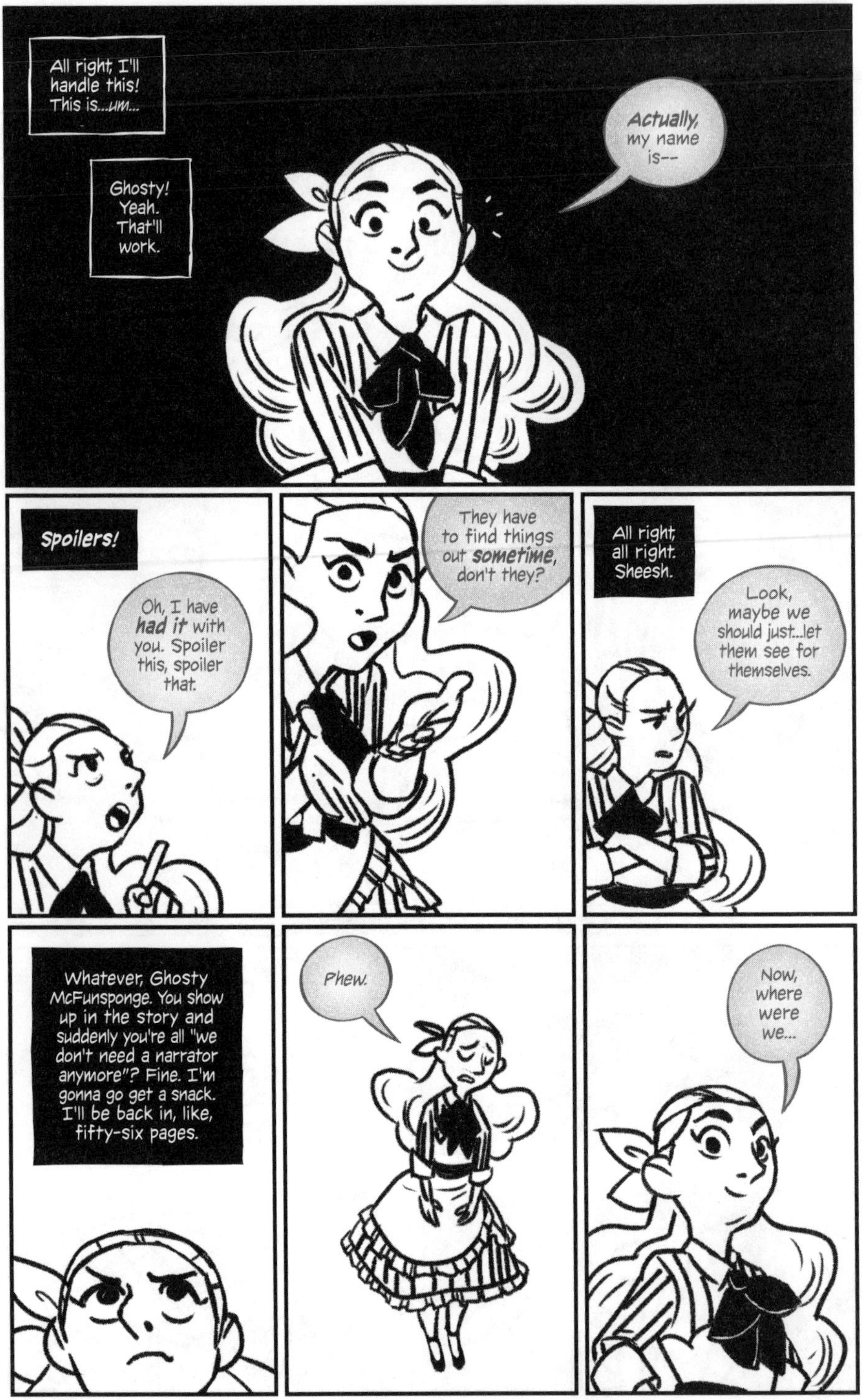
All right, I'll handle this! This is...um...
Actually, my name is--
Ghosty! Yeah. That'll work.
Spoilers!
Oh, I have had it with you. Spoiler this, spoiler that.
They have to find things out sometime, don't they?
All right, all right. Sheesh.
Look, maybe we should just...let them see for themselves.
Whatever, Ghosty McFunsponge. You show up in the story and suddenly you're all "we don't need a narrator anymore"? Fine. I'm gonna go get a snack. I'll be back in, like, fifty-six pages.
Phew.
Now, where were we...

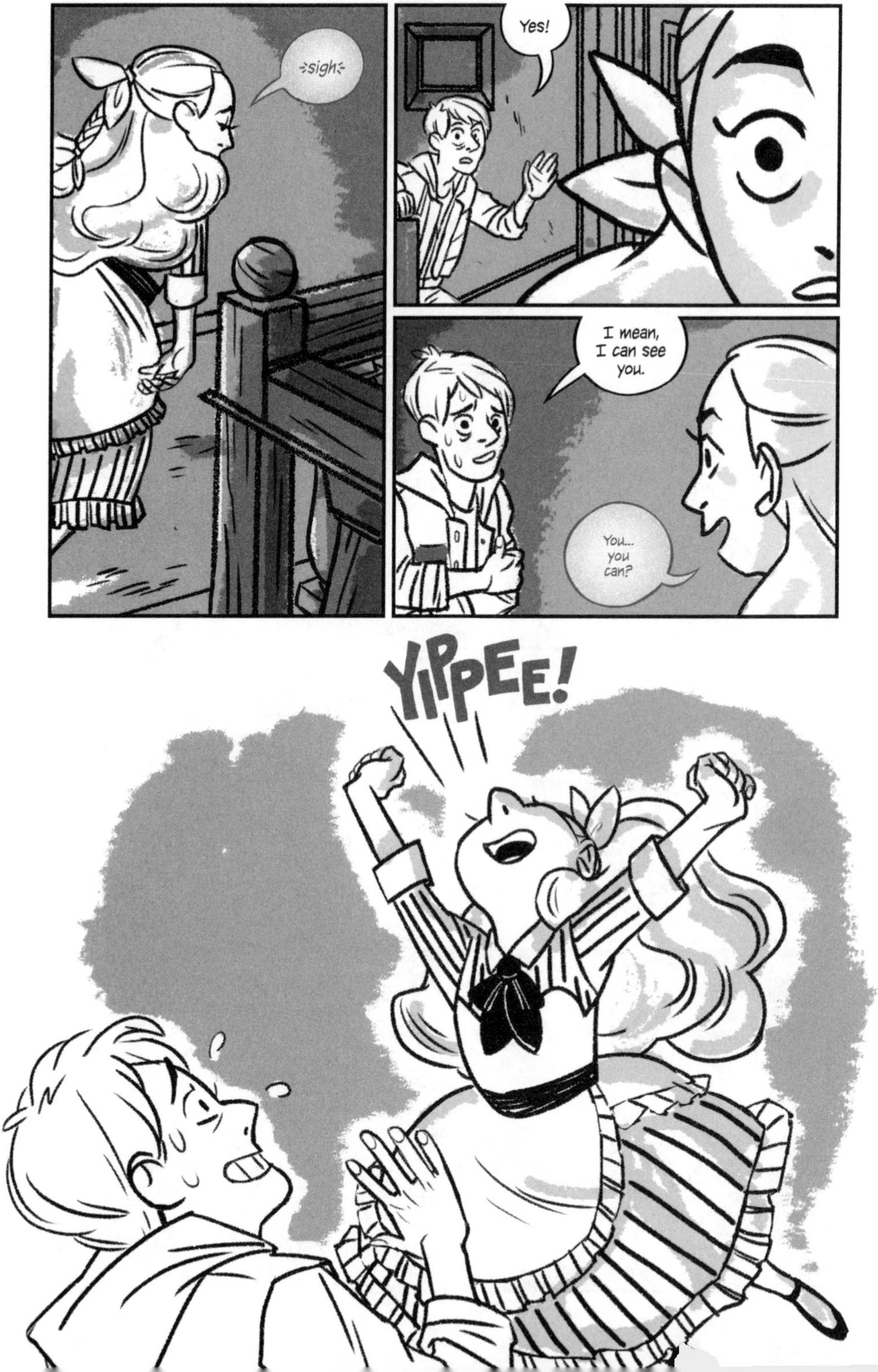
sigh
Yes!
I mean, I can see you.
You... you can?
YIPPEE!

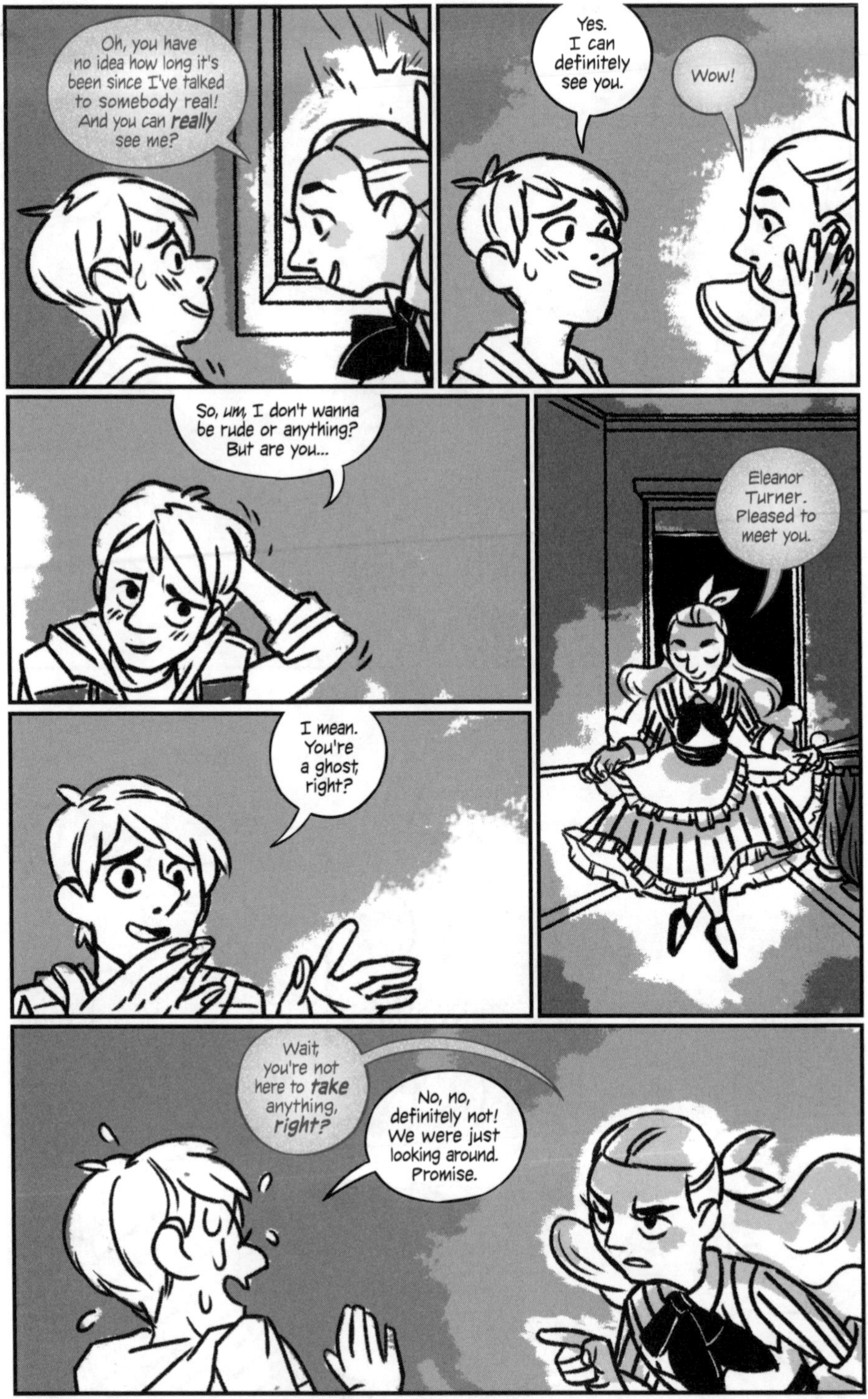
Oh, you have no idea how long it's been since I've talked to somebody real! And you can *really* see me?
Yes. I can definitely see you.
Wow!
So, *um*, I don't wanna be rude or anything? But are you...
I mean. You're a ghost, right?
Eleanor Turner. Pleased to meet you.
Wait, you're not here to *take* anything, *right?*
No, no, definitely not! We were just looking around. Promise.

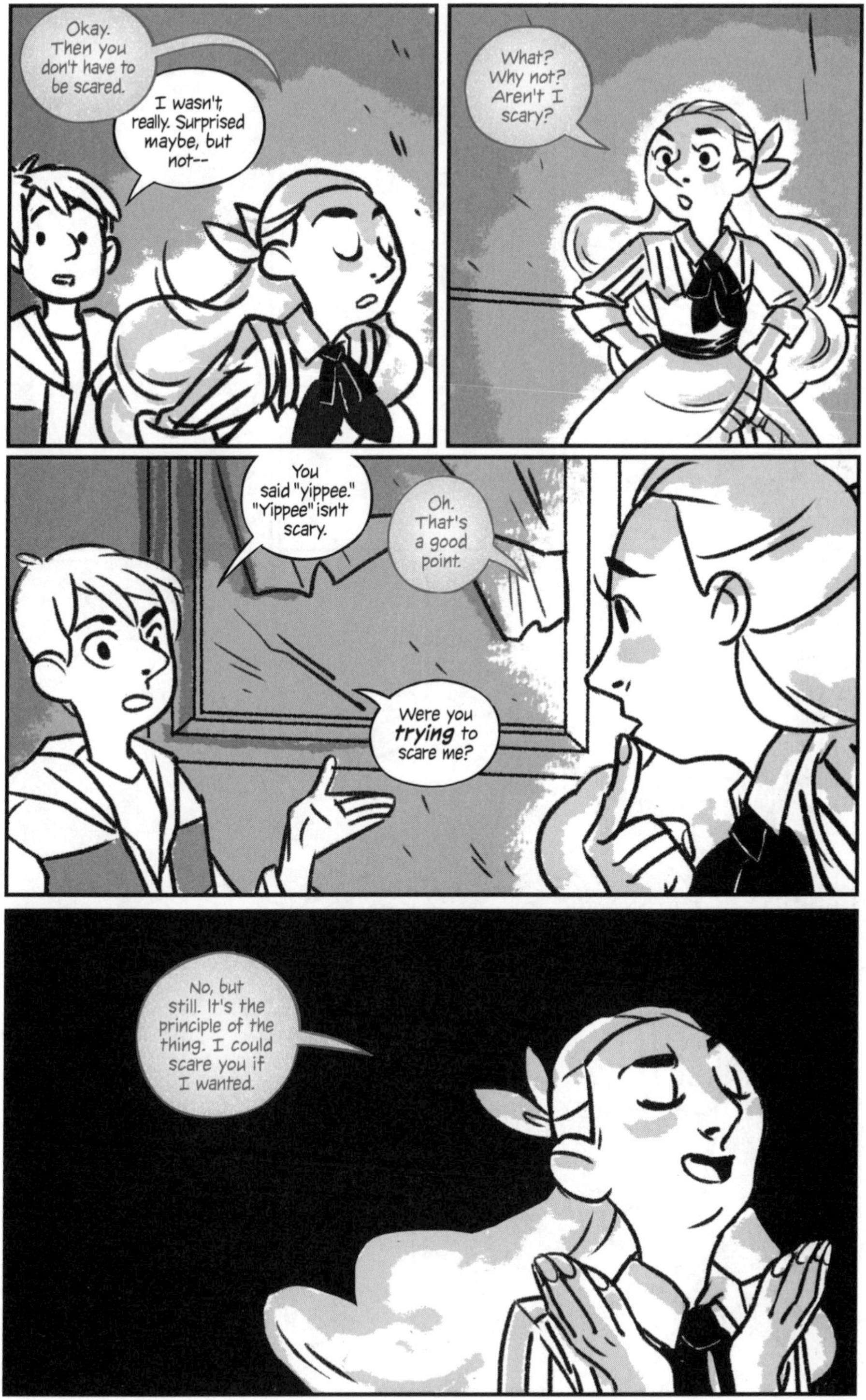
Okay. Then you don't have to be scared.
I wasn't, really. Surprised maybe, but not--
What? Why not? Aren't I scary?
You said "yippee." "Yippee" isn't scary.
Oh. That's a good point.
Were you *trying* to scare me?
No, but still. It's the principle of the thing. I could scare you if I wanted.

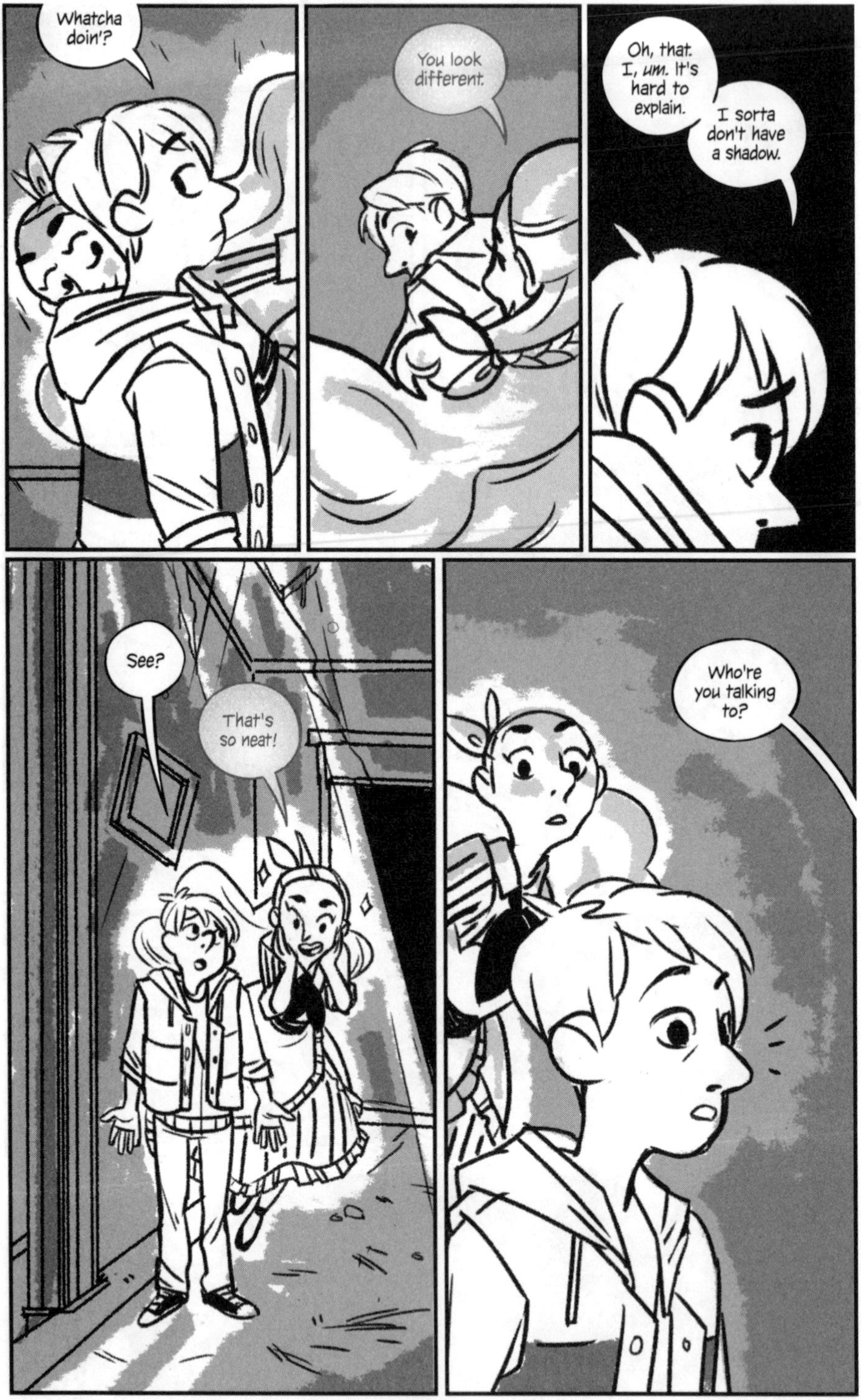
Whatcha doin'?
You look different.
Oh, that. I, *um*. It's hard to explain.
I sorta don't have a shadow.
See?
That's so neat!
Who're you talking to?

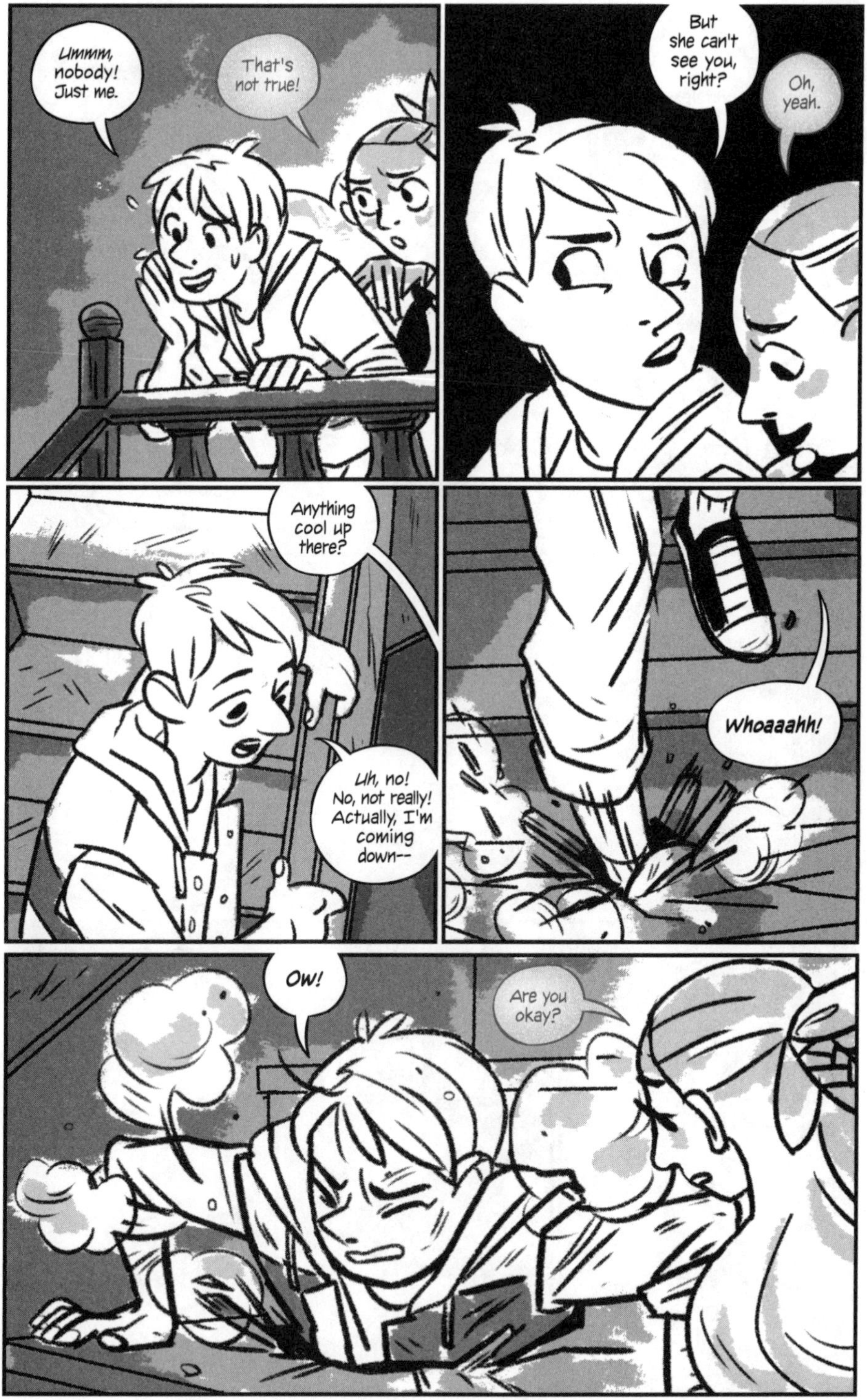
Ummm, nobody! Just me.
That's not true!
But she can't see you, right?
Oh, yeah.
Anything cool up there?
Uh, no! No, not really! Actually, I'm coming down--
Whoaaahh!
Ow!
Are you okay?

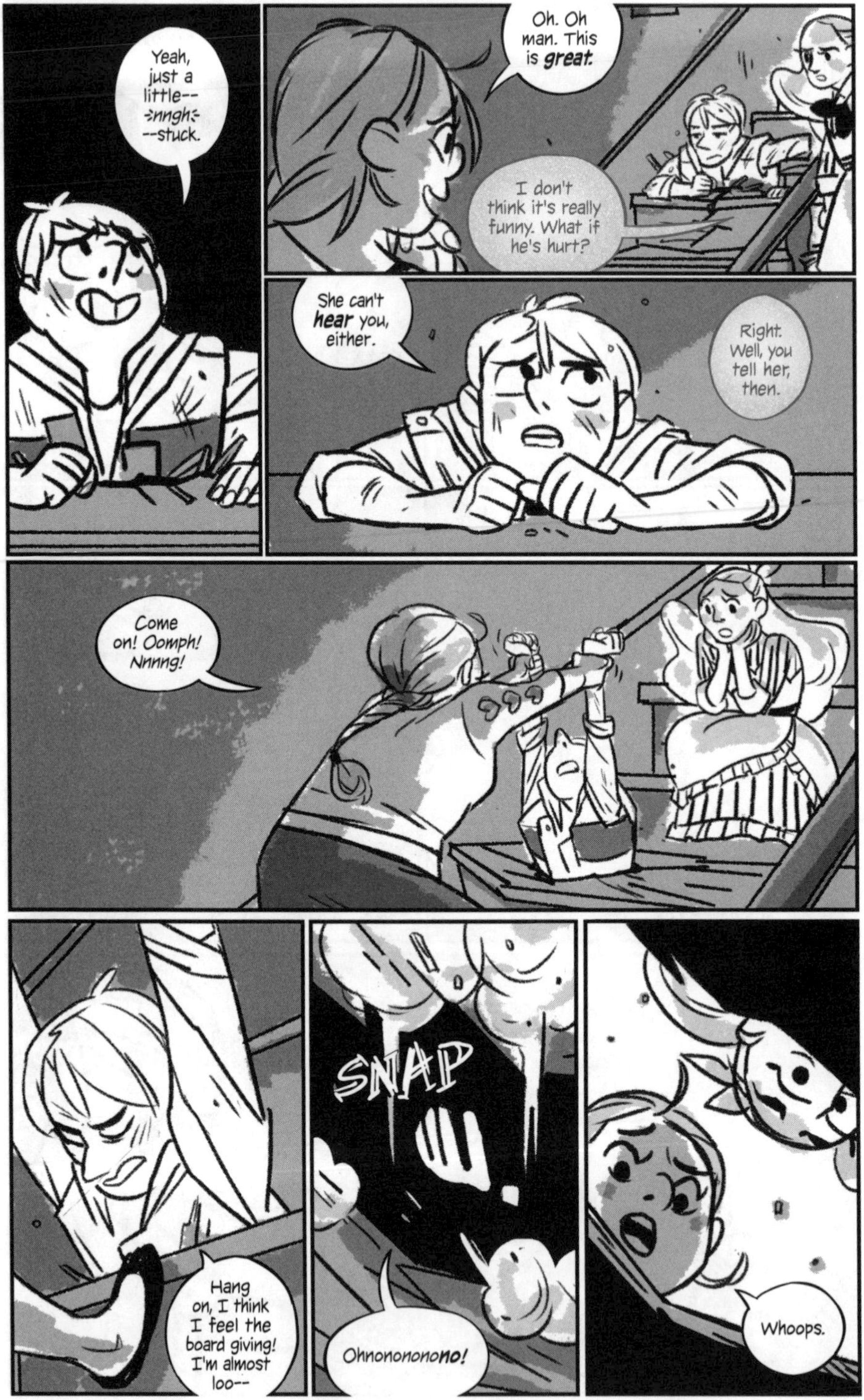
Yeah, just a little-- -nngh- --stuck.
Oh. Oh man. This is **great.**
I don't think it's really funny. What if he's hurt?
She can't **hear** you, either.
Right. Well, you tell her, then.
Come on! Oomph! Nnnng!
Hang on, I think I feel the board giving! I'm almost loo--
SNAP
Ohnonononono**no!**
Whoops.

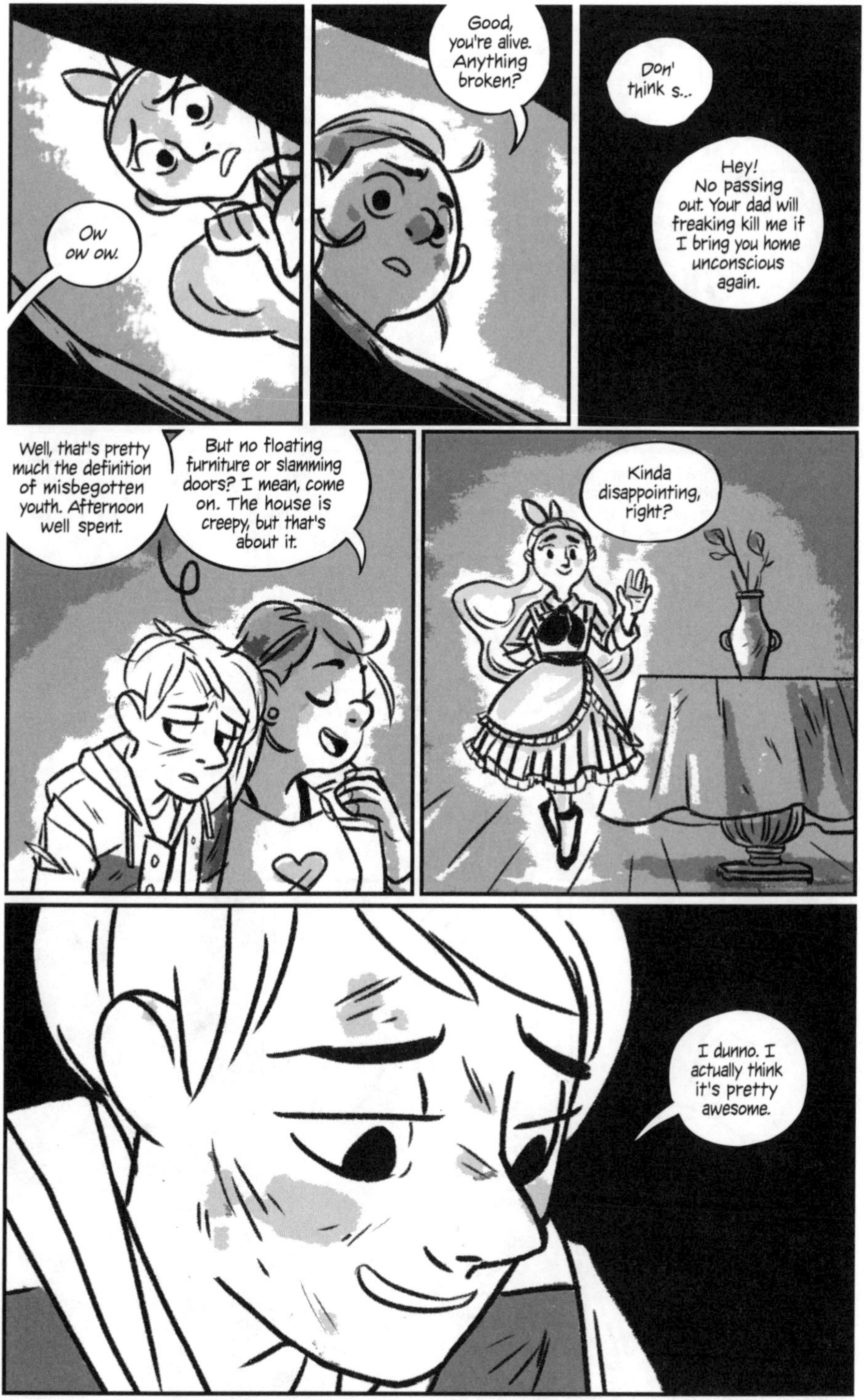
Ow
ow ow.
Good, you're alive. Anything broken?
Don' think s...
Hey! No passing out. Your dad will freaking kill me if I bring you home unconscious again.
Well, that's pretty much the definition of misbegotten youth. Afternoon well spent.
But no floating furniture or slamming doors? I mean, come on. The house is creepy, but that's about it.
Kinda disappointing, right?
I dunno. I actually think it's pretty awesome.

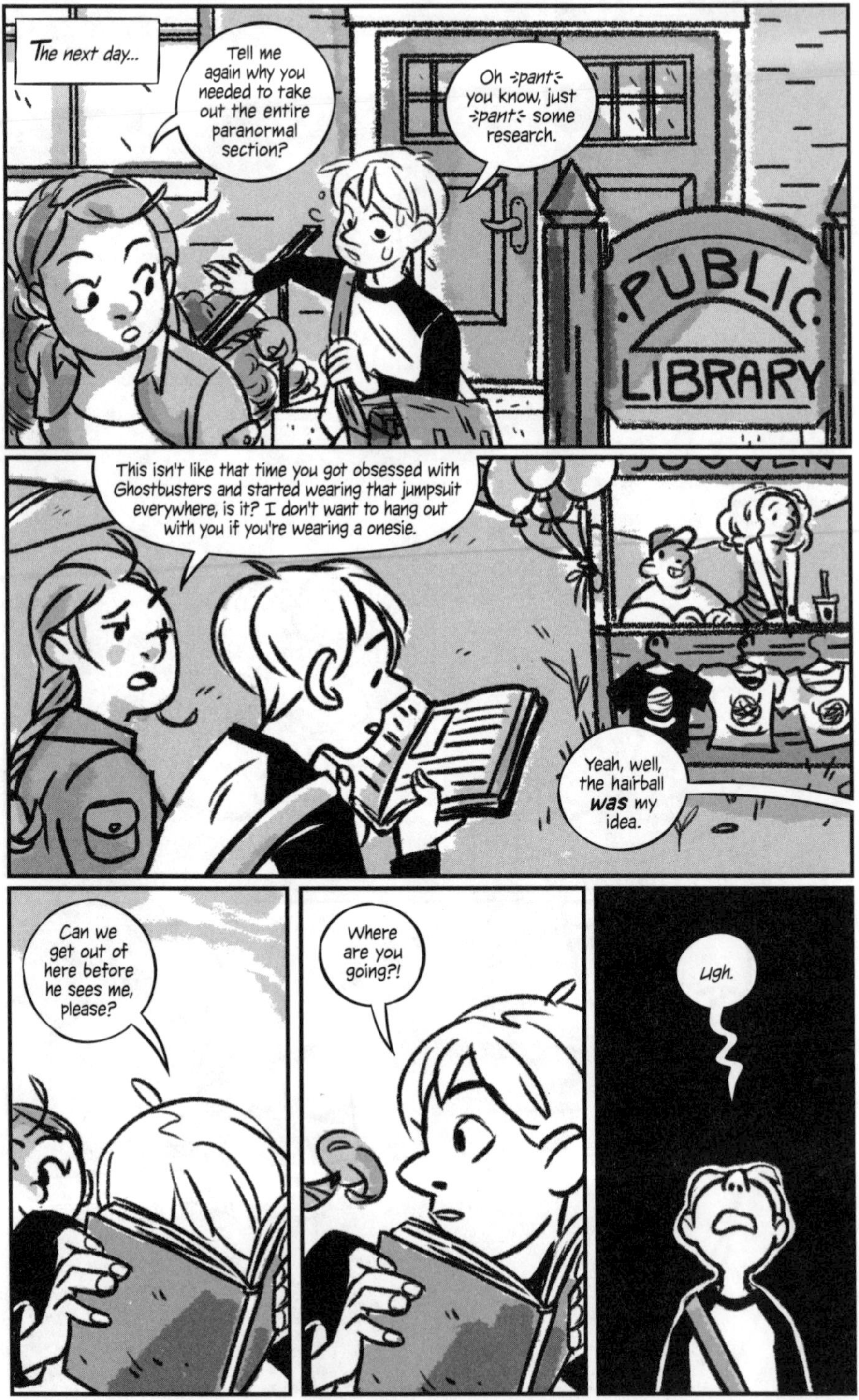
The next day...
Tell me again why you needed to take out the entire paranormal section?
Oh ⪫pant⪪ you know, just ⪫pant⪪ some research.
PUBLIC LIBRARY
This isn't like that time you got obsessed with Ghostbusters and started wearing that jumpsuit everywhere, is it? I don't want to hang out with you if you're wearing a onesie.
Yeah, well, the hairball **was** my idea.
Can we get out of here before he sees me, please?
Where are you going?!
Ugh.

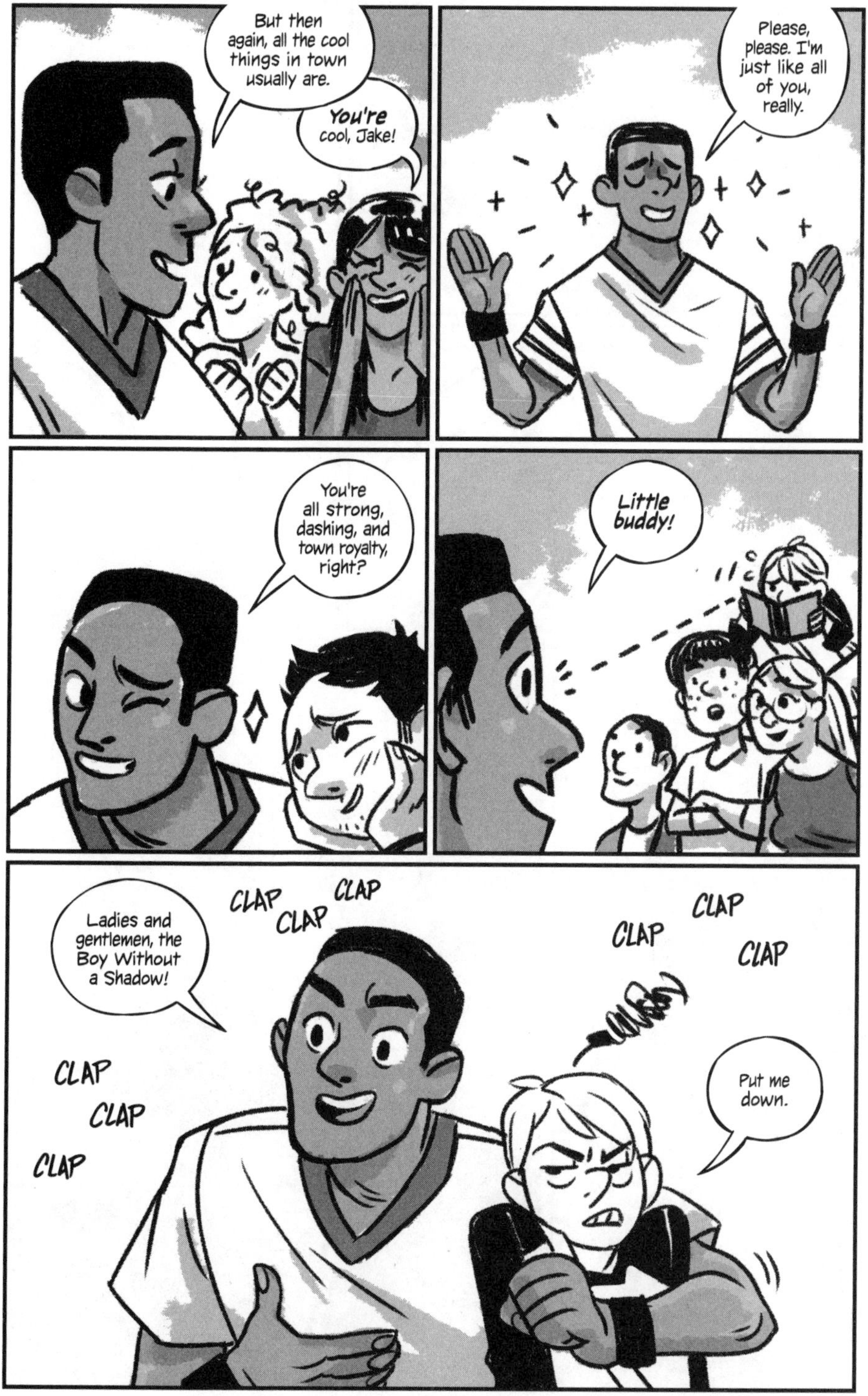

But then again, all the cool things in town usually are.
You're cool, Jake!
Please, please. I'm just like all of you, really.
You're all strong, dashing, and town royalty, right?
Little buddy!
Ladies and gentlemen, the Boy Without a Shadow!
CLAP CLAP CLAP
CLAP CLAP CLAP
Put me down.
CLAP CLAP CLAP

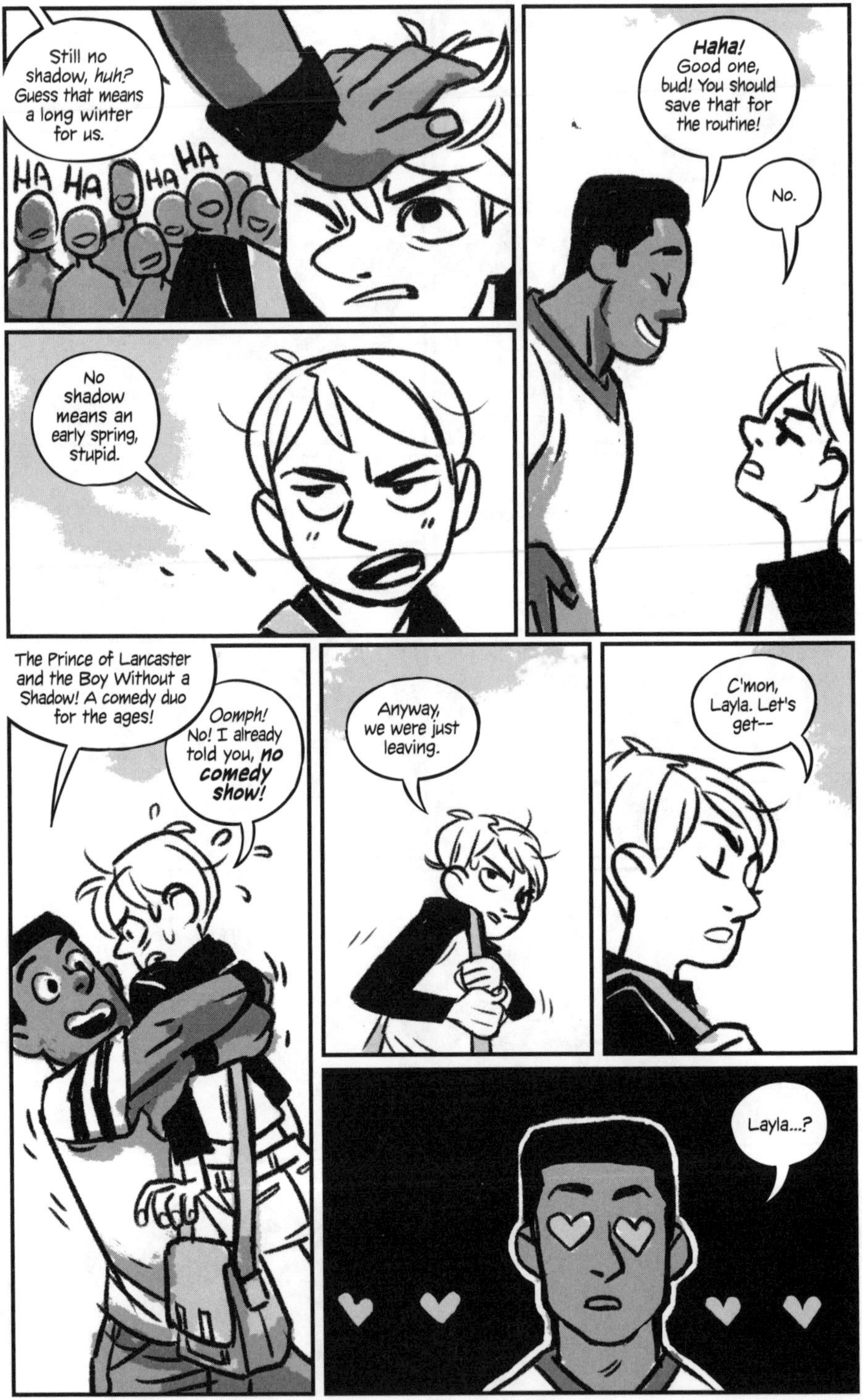
Still no shadow, *huh?* Guess that means a long winter for us.
HA HA HA HA
Haha! Good one, bud! You should save that for the routine!
No.
No shadow means an early spring, stupid.
The Prince of Lancaster and the Boy Without a Shadow! A comedy duo for the ages!
Oomph! No! I already told you, ***no comedy show!***
Anyway, we were just leaving.
C'mon, Layla. Let's get--
Layla...?

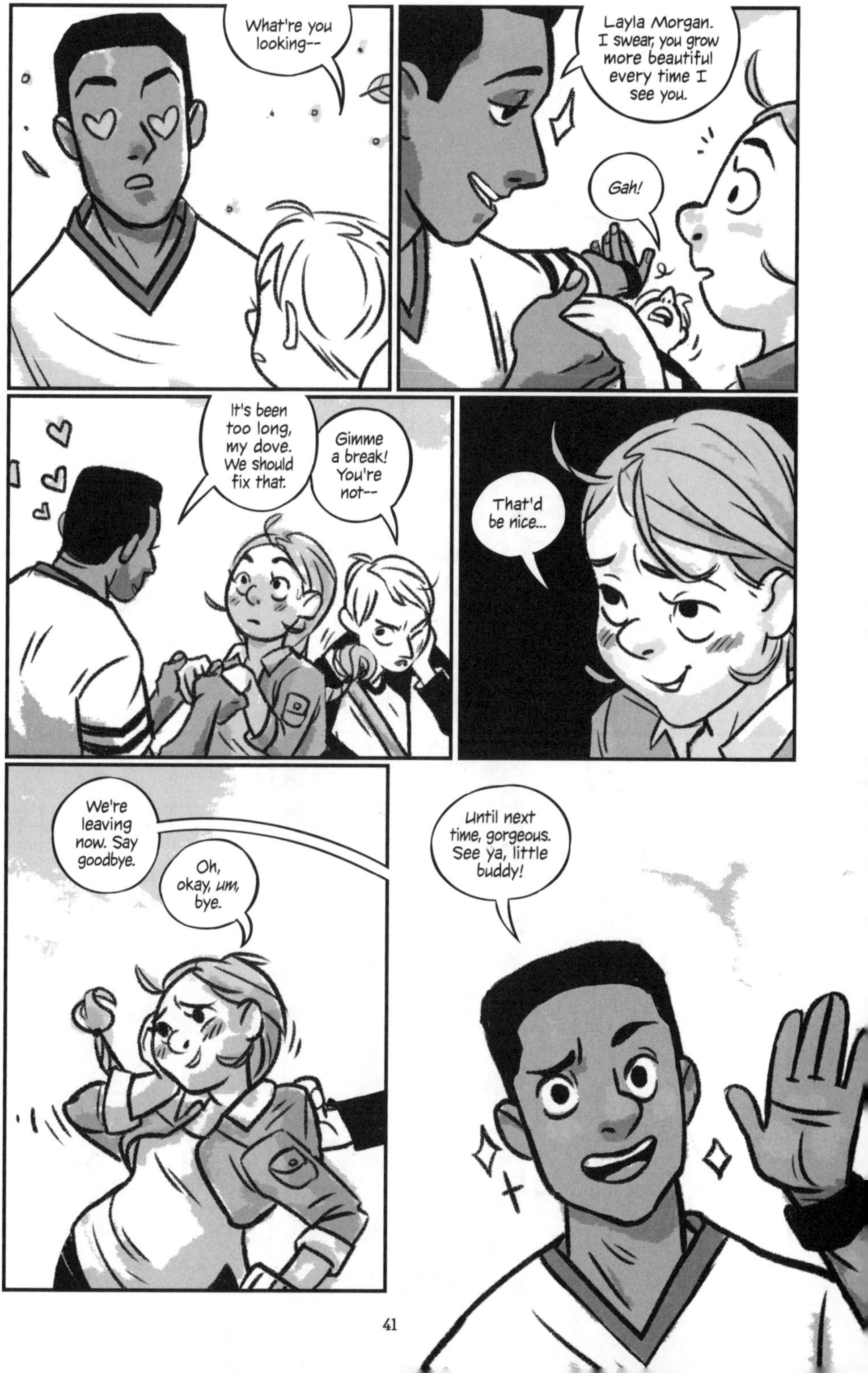
What're you looking--
Layla Morgan. I swear, you grow more beautiful every time I see you.
Gah!
It's been too long, my dove. We should fix that.
Gimme a break! You're not--
That'd be nice...
We're leaving now. Say goodbye.
Oh, okay, um, bye.
Until next time, gorgeous. See ya, little buddy!

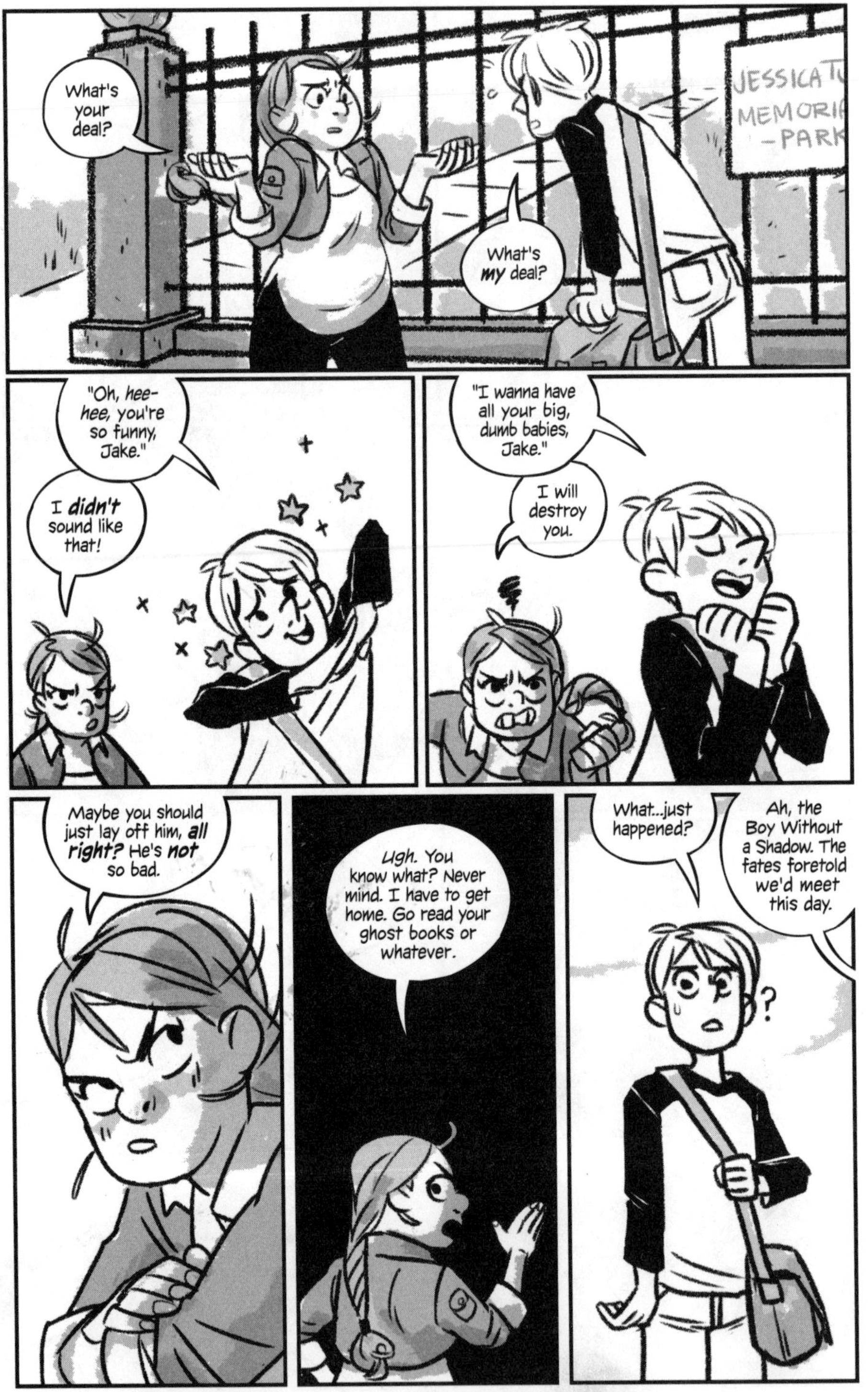
What's your deal?
What's *my* deal?
JESSICA T
MEMORIA
-PARK
"Oh, *hee-hee,* you're so funny, Jake."
I ***didn't*** sound like that!
"I wanna have all your big, dumb babies, Jake."
I will destroy you.
Maybe you should just lay off him, ***all right?*** He's ***not*** so bad.
Ugh. You know what? Never mind. I have to get home. Go read your ghost books or whatever.
What...just happened?
Ah, the Boy Without a Shadow. The fates foretold we'd meet this day.

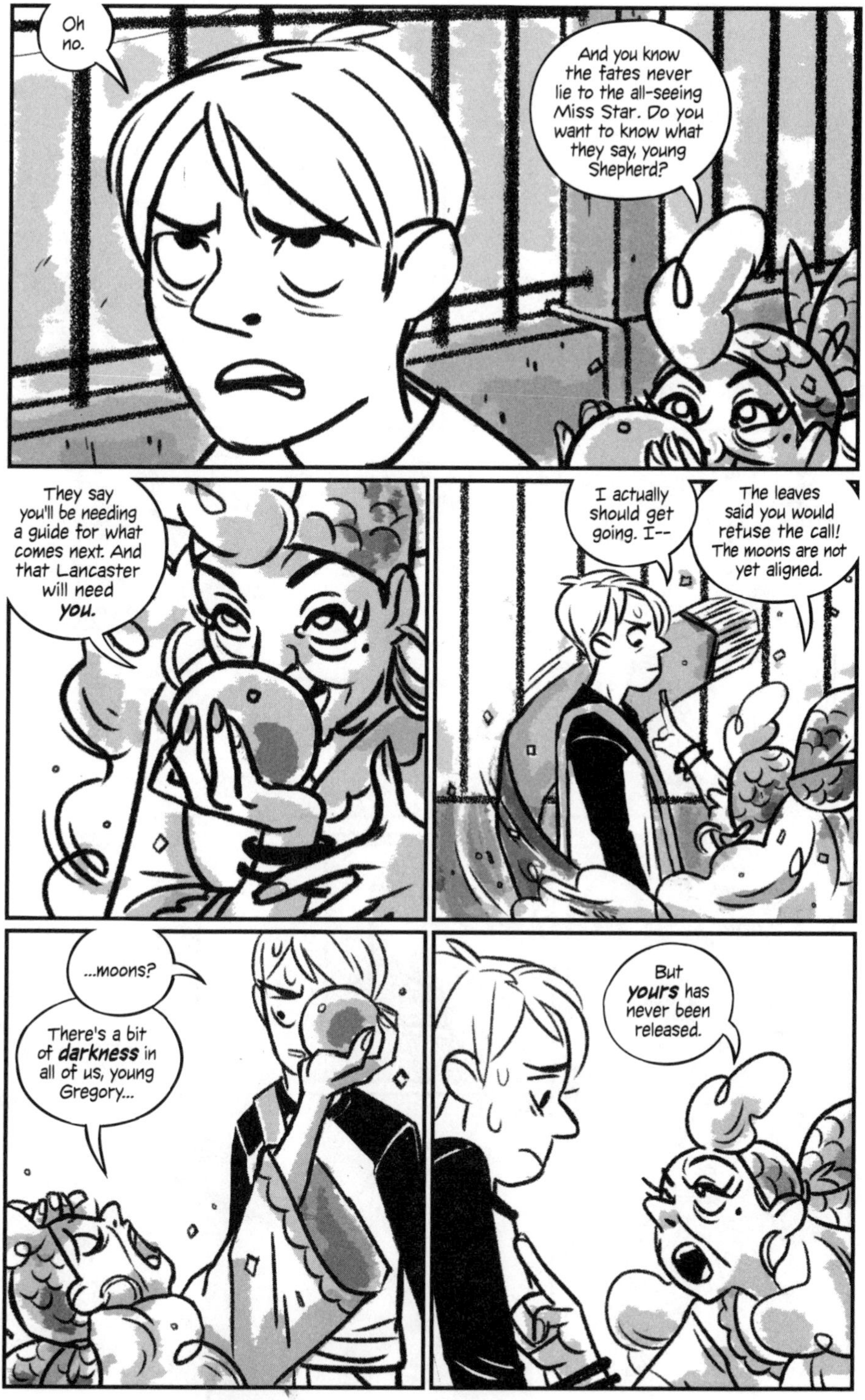
Oh no.
And you know the fates never lie to the all-seeing Miss Star. Do you want to know what they say, young Shepherd?
They say you'll be needing a guide for what comes next. And that Lancaster will need **you.**
I actually should get going. I--
The leaves said you would refuse the call! The moons are not yet aligned.
...moons?
There's a bit of **darkness** in all of us, young Gregory...
But **yours** has never been released.

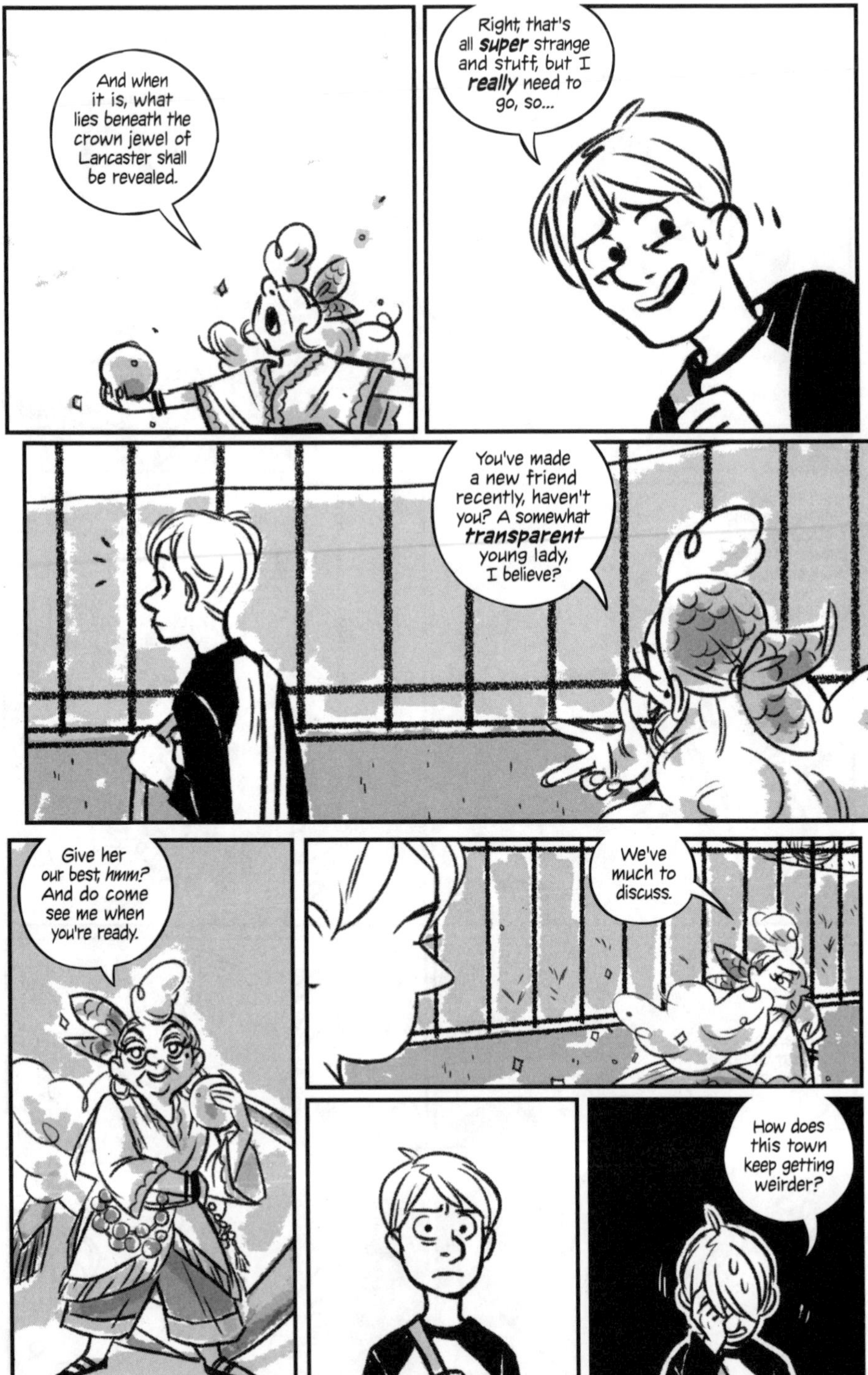
And when it is, what lies beneath the crown jewel of Lancaster shall be revealed.
Right, that's all **super** strange and stuff, but I ***really*** need to go, so...
You've made a new friend recently, haven't you? A somewhat ***transparent*** young lady, I believe?
Give her our best, *hmm?* And do come see me when you're ready.
We've much to discuss.
How does this town keep getting weirder?

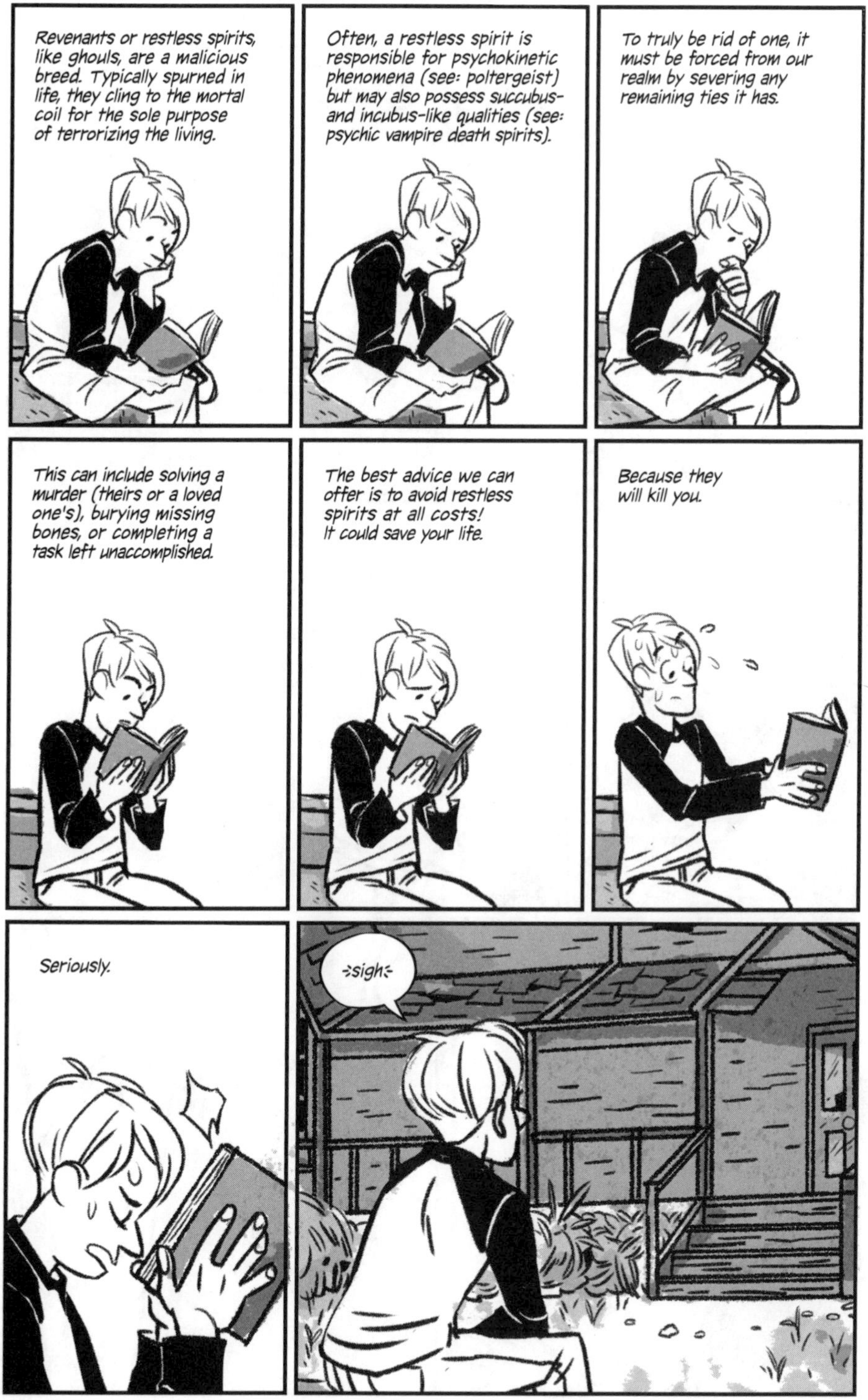
Revenants or restless spirits, like ghouls, are a malicious breed. Typically spurned in life, they cling to the mortal coil for the sole purpose of terrorizing the living.
Often, a restless spirit is responsible for psychokinetic phenomena (see: poltergeist) but may also possess succubus- and incubus-like qualities (see: psychic vampire death spirits).
To truly be rid of one, it must be forced from our realm by severing any remaining ties it has.
This can include solving a murder (theirs or a loved one's), burying missing bones, or completing a task left unaccomplished.
The best advice we can offer is to avoid restless spirits at all costs! It could save your life.
Because they will kill you.
Seriously.
sigh

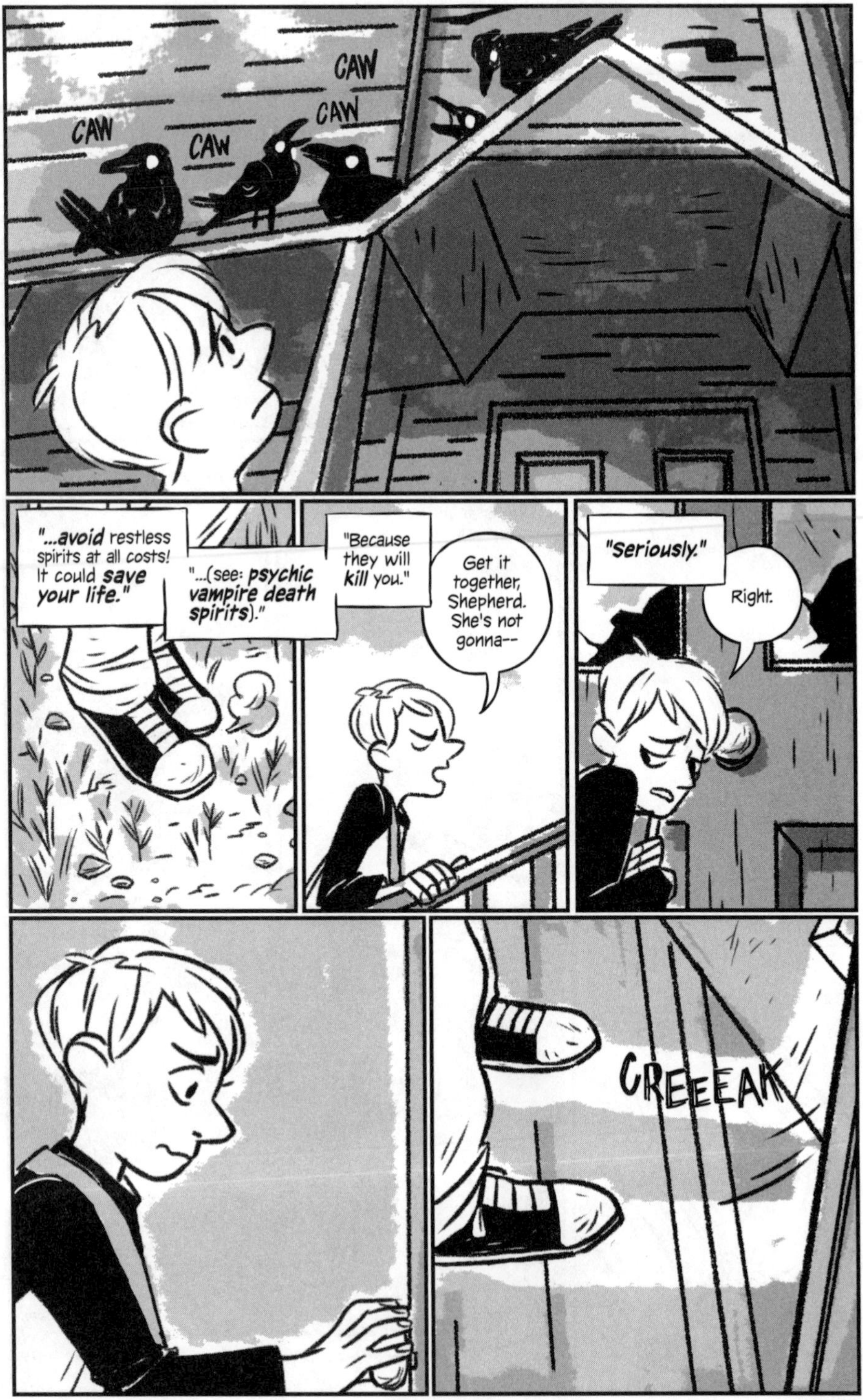
CAW
CAW
CAW
CAW
"...**avoid** restless spirits at all costs! It could **save your life.**"
"...(see: **psychic vampire death spirits**)."
"Because they will **kill** you."
Get it together, Shepherd. She's not gonna--
"**Seriously.**"
Right.
CREEEAK

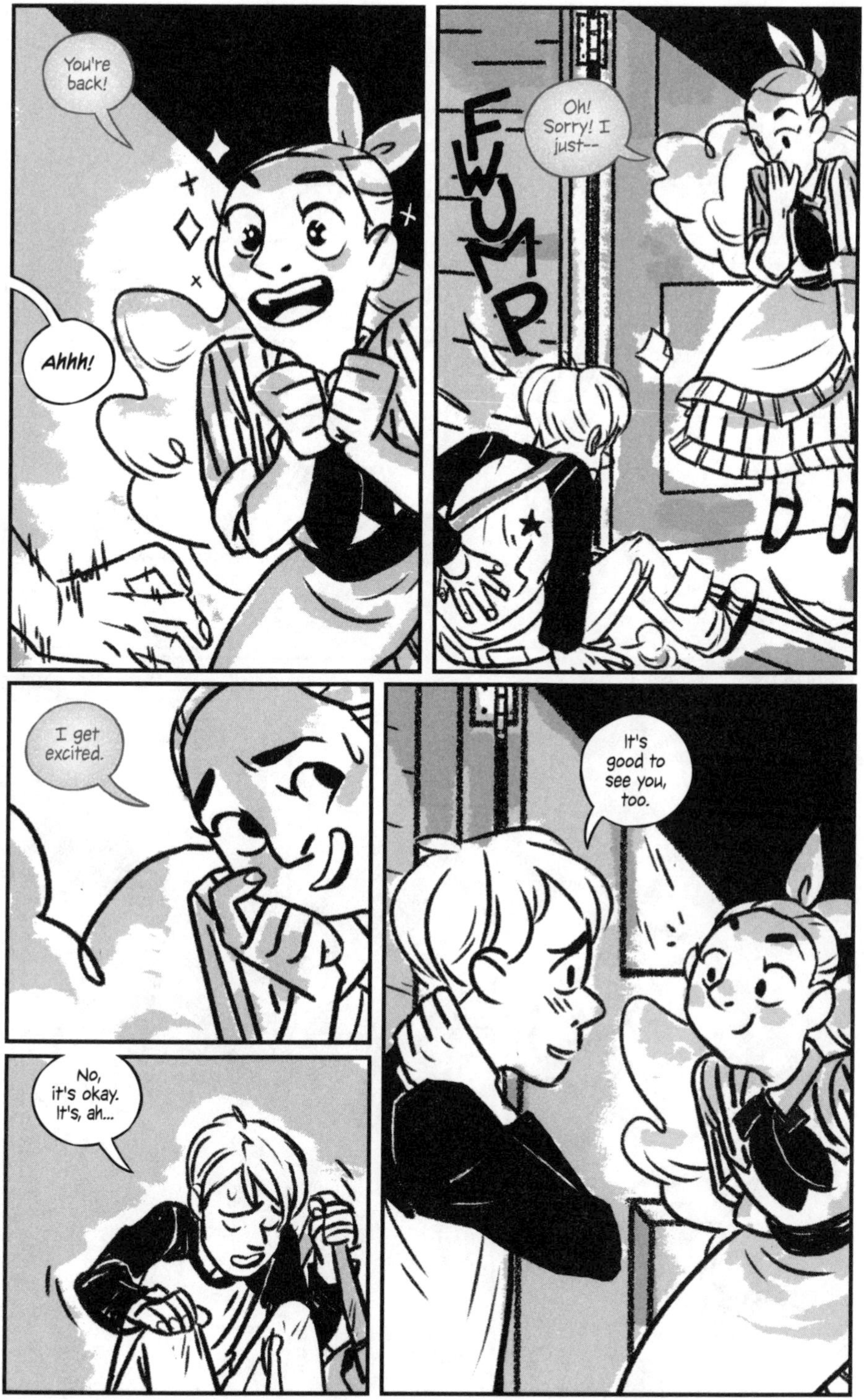

You're back!
Ahhh!
FWUMP
Oh! Sorry! I just--
I get excited.
No, it's okay. It's, ah...
It's good to see you, too.

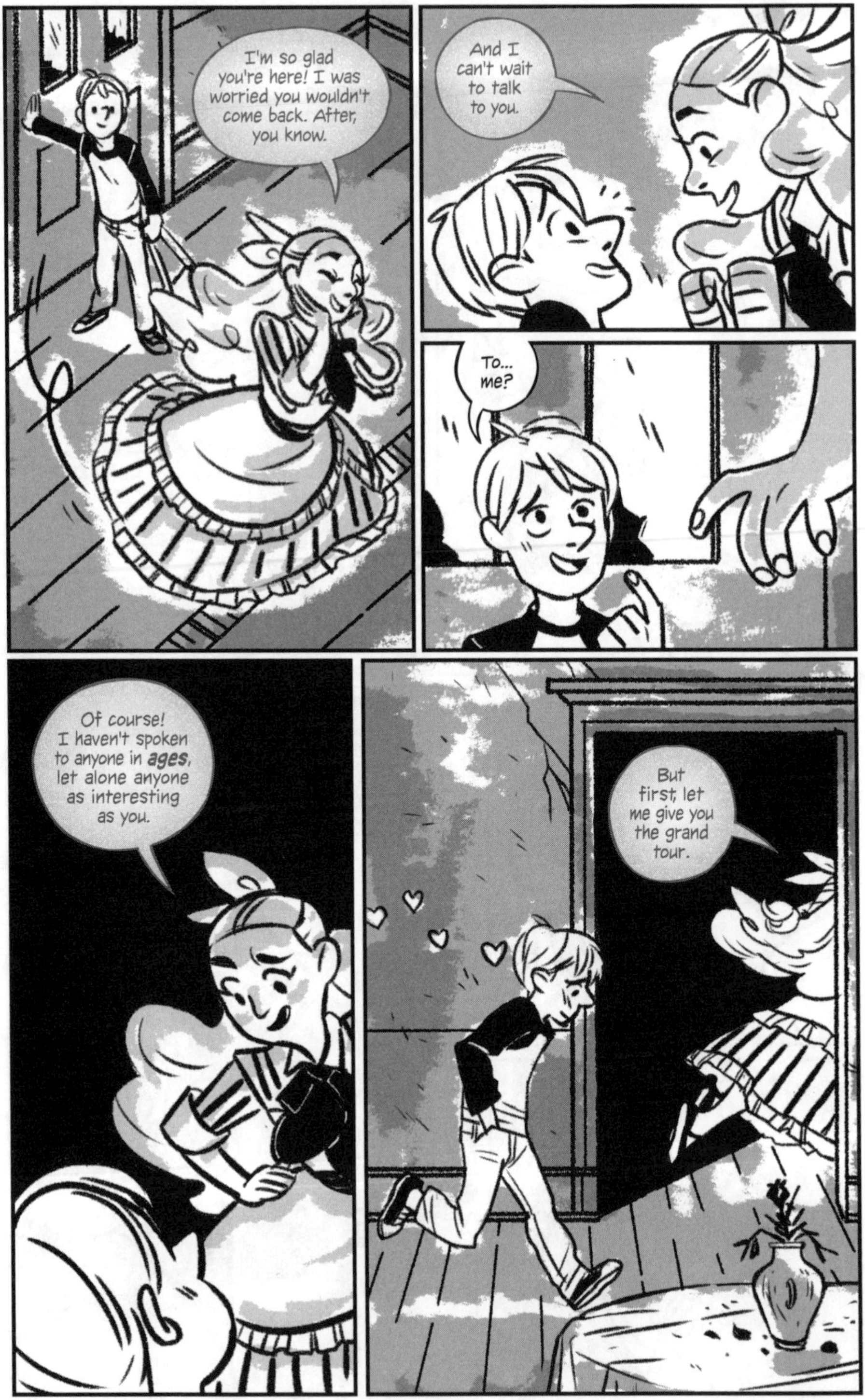
I'm so glad you're here! I was worried you wouldn't come back. After, you know.
And I can't wait to talk to you.
To... me?
Of course! I haven't spoken to anyone in **ages**, let alone anyone as interesting as you.
But first, let me give you the grand tour.

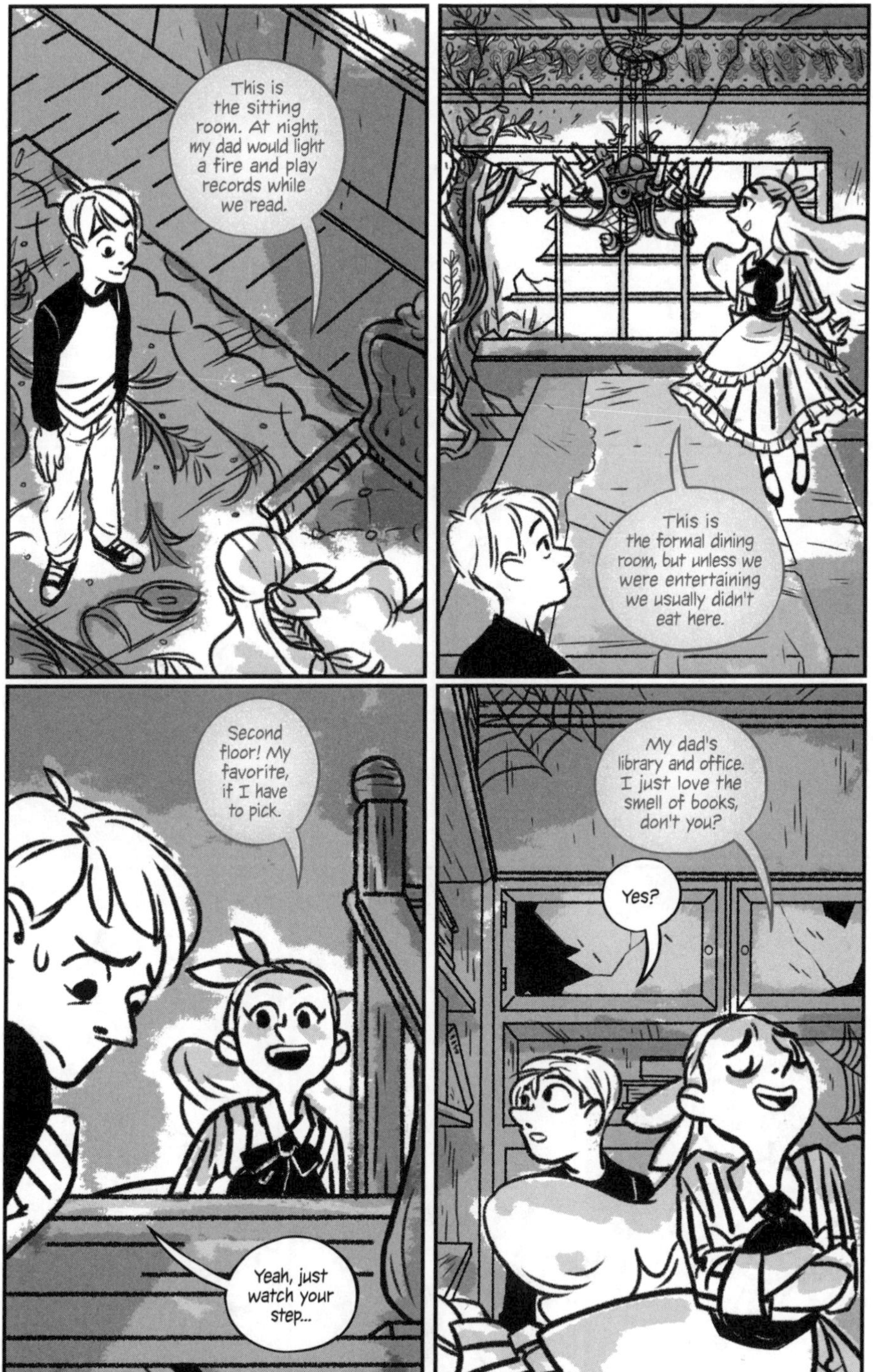
This is the sitting room. At night, my dad would light a fire and play records while we read.
This is the formal dining room, but unless we were entertaining we usually didn't eat here.
Second floor! My favorite, if I have to pick.
Yeah, just watch your step...
My dad's library and office. I just love the smell of books, don't you?
Yes?

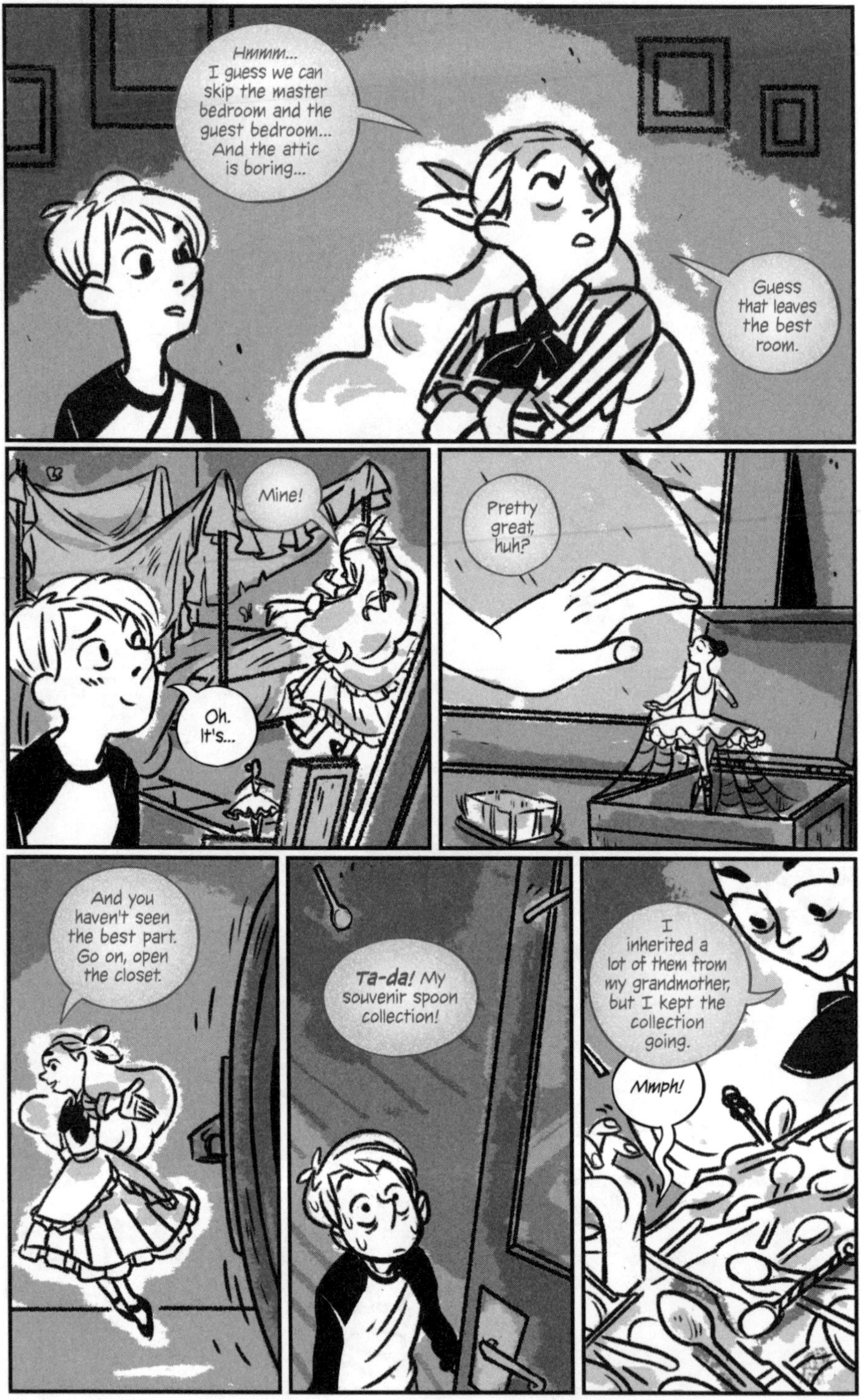
Hmmm... I guess we can skip the master bedroom and the guest bedroom... And the attic is boring...
Guess that leaves the best room.
Mine!
Oh. It's...
Pretty great, huh?
And you haven't seen the best part. Go on, open the closet.
Ta-da! My souvenir spoon collection!
I inherited a lot of them from my grandmother, but I kept the collection going.
Mmph!

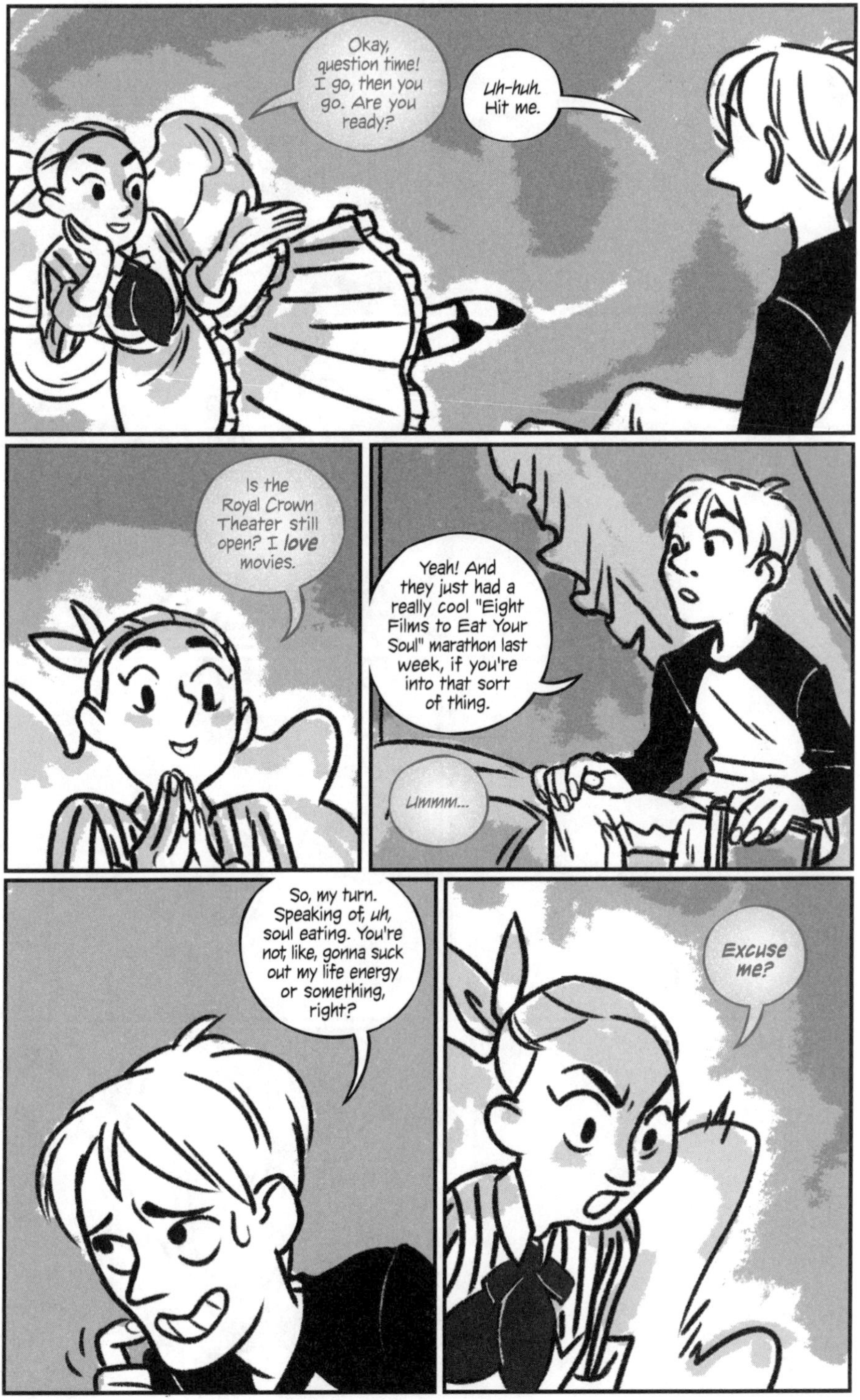
Okay, question time! I go, then you go. Are you ready?
Uh-huh. Hit me.
Is the Royal Crown Theater still open? I *love* movies.
Yeah! And they just had a really cool "Eight Films to Eat Your Soul" marathon last week, if you're into that sort of thing.
Ummm...
So, my turn. Speaking of, *uh*, soul eating. You're not like, gonna suck out my life energy or something, right?
Excuse me?

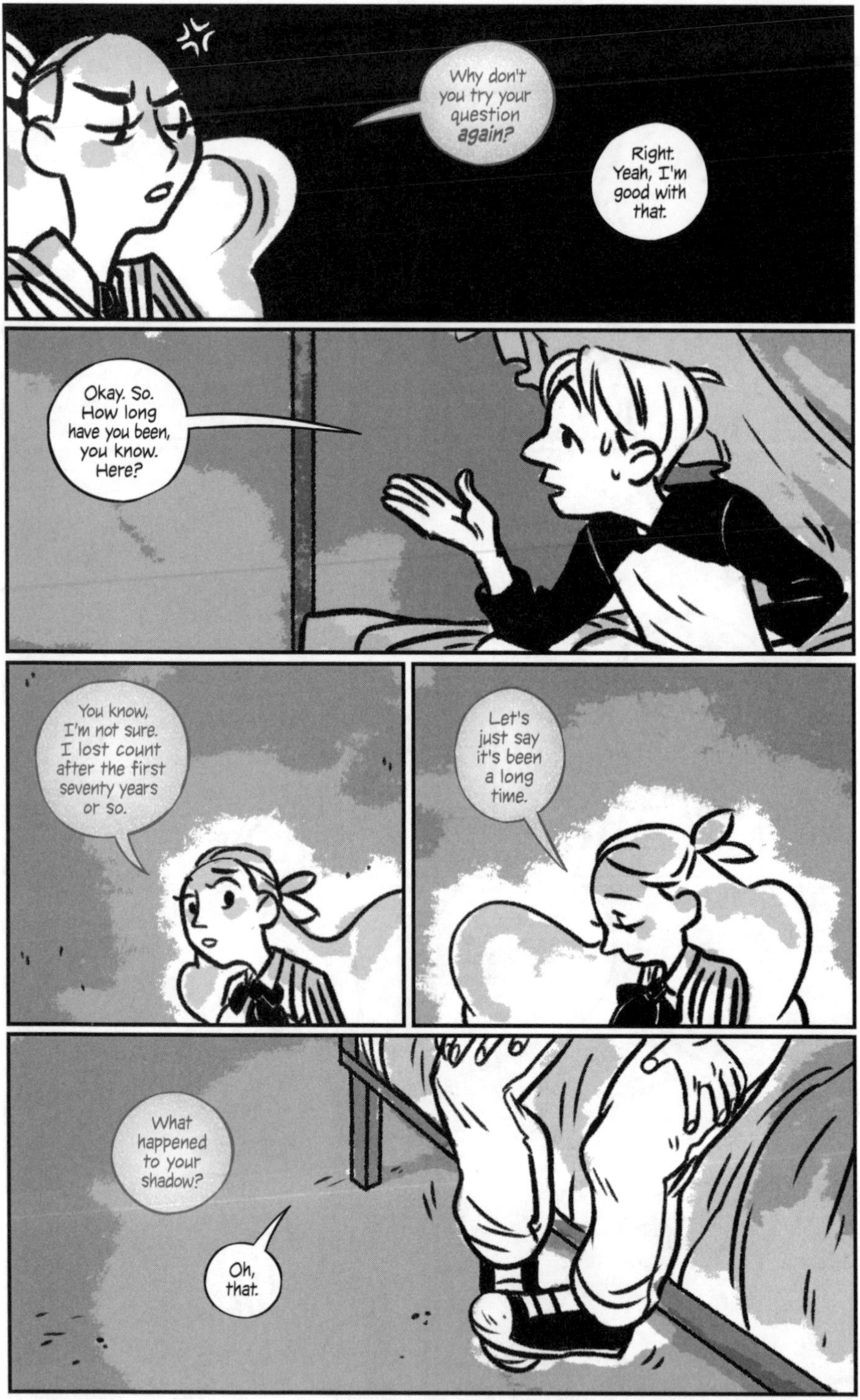
Why don't you try your question again?
Right. Yeah, I'm good with that.
Okay. So. How long have you been, you know. Here?
You know, I'm not sure. I lost count after the first seventy years or so.
Let's just say it's been a long time.
What happened to your shadow?
Oh, that.

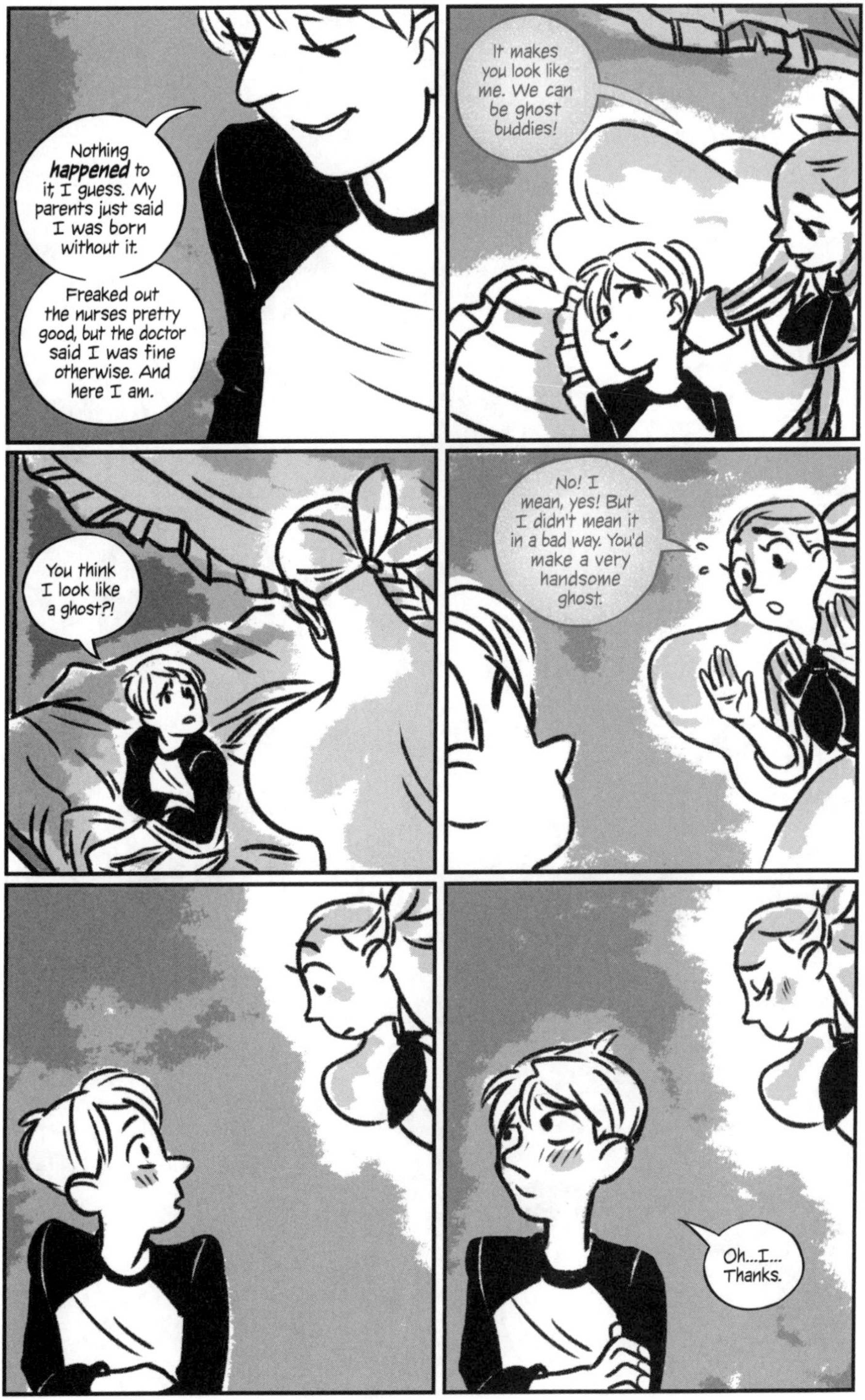
Nothing **happened** to it, I guess. My parents just said I was born without it.
Freaked out the nurses pretty good, but the doctor said I was fine otherwise. And here I am.
It makes you look like me. We can be ghost buddies!
You think I look like a ghost?!
No! I mean, yes! But I didn't mean it in a bad way. You'd make a very handsome ghost.
Oh...I... Thanks.

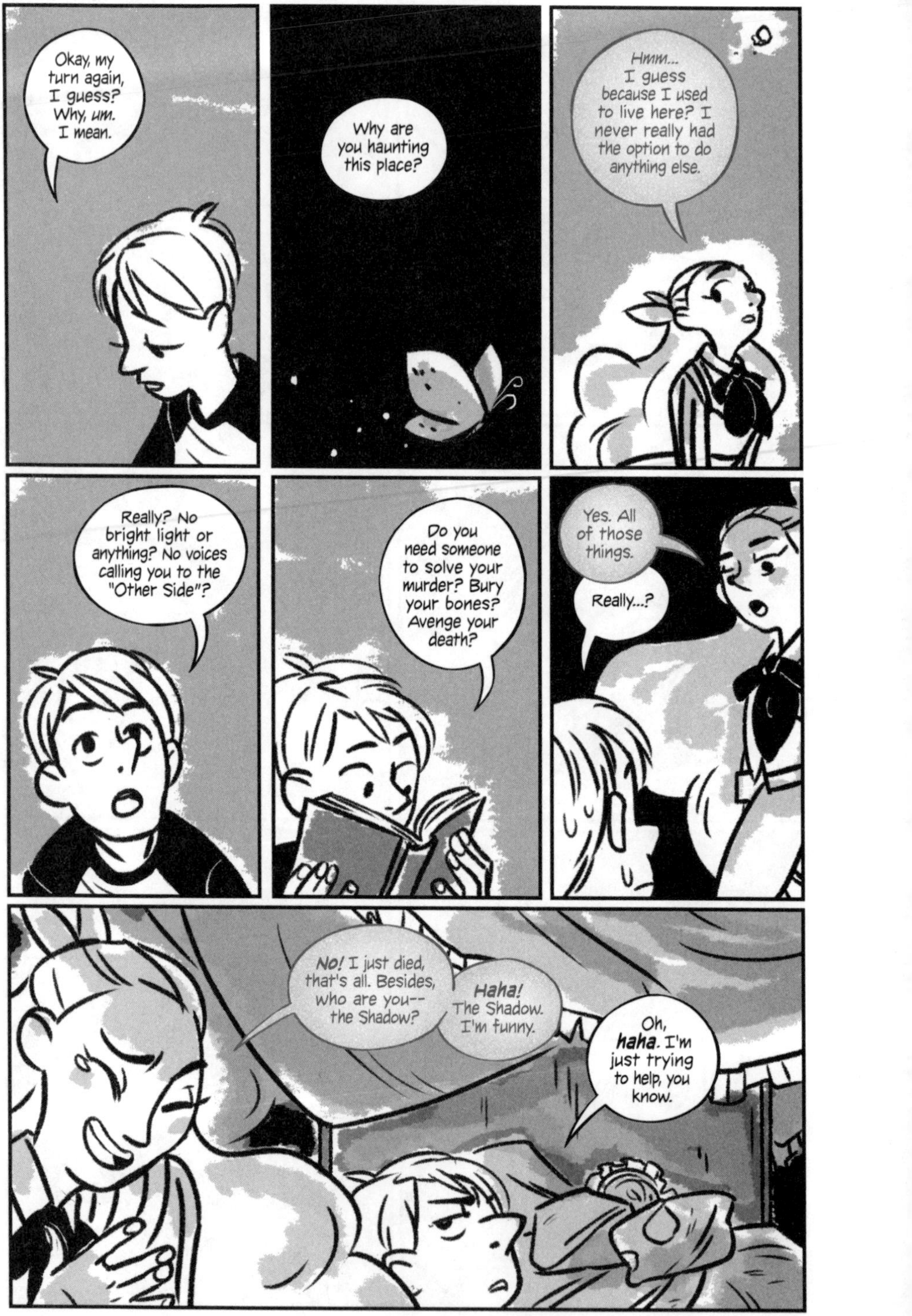
Okay, my turn again, I guess? Why, *um*. I mean.
Why are you haunting this place?
Hmm... I guess because I used to live here? I never really had the option to do anything else.
Really? No bright light or anything? No voices calling you to the "Other Side"?
Do you need someone to solve your murder? Bury your bones? Avenge your death?
Yes. All of those things.
Really...?
No! I just died, that's all. Besides, who are you-- the Shadow?
Haha! The Shadow. I'm funny.
Oh, **haha**. I'm just trying to help, you know.

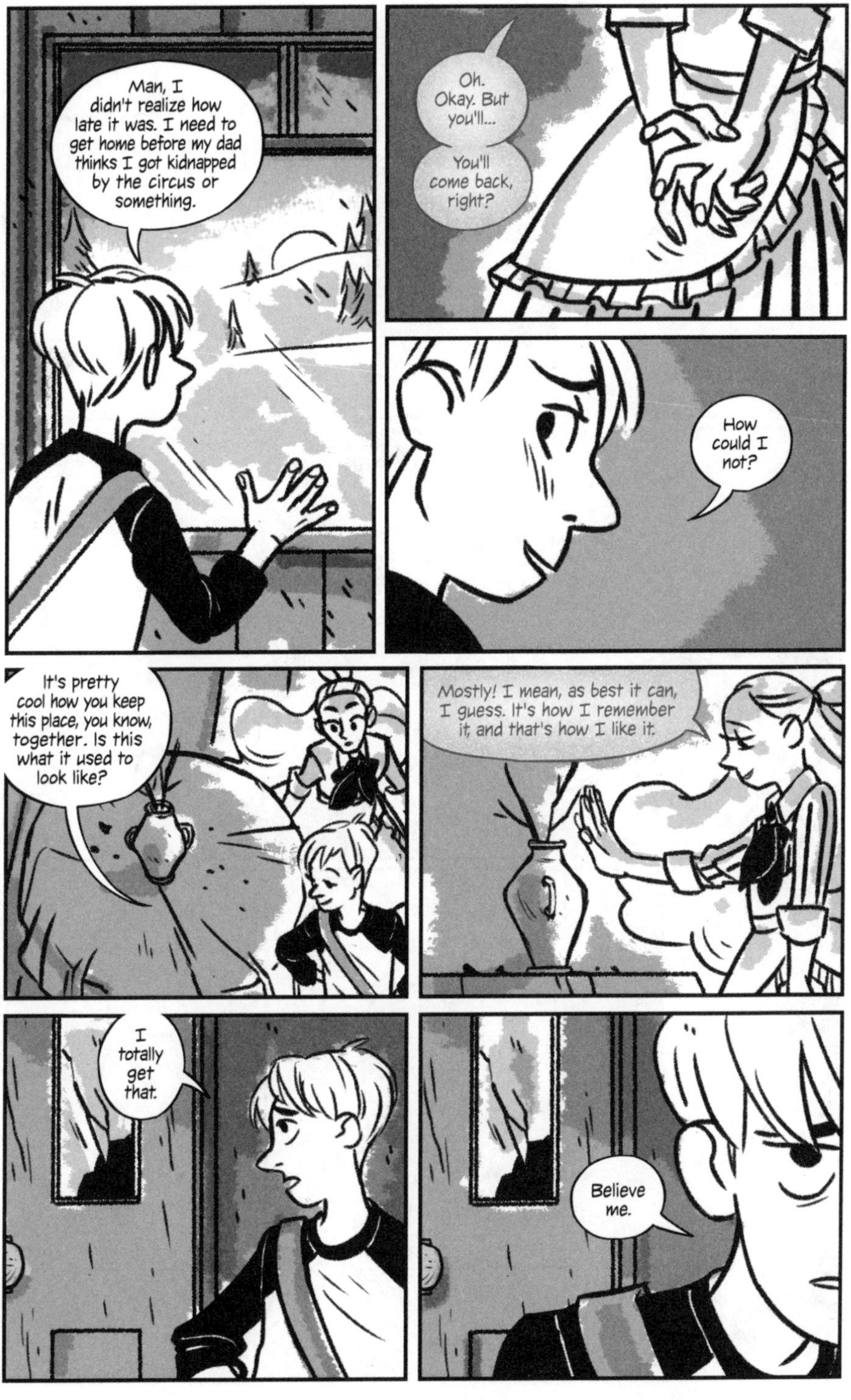
Man, I didn't realize how late it was. I need to get home before my dad thinks I got kidnapped by the circus or something.
Oh. Okay. But you'll...
You'll come back, right?
How could I not?
It's pretty cool how you keep this place, you know, together. Is this what it used to look like?
Mostly! I mean, as best it can, I guess. It's how I remember it, and that's how I like it.
I totally get that.
Believe me.

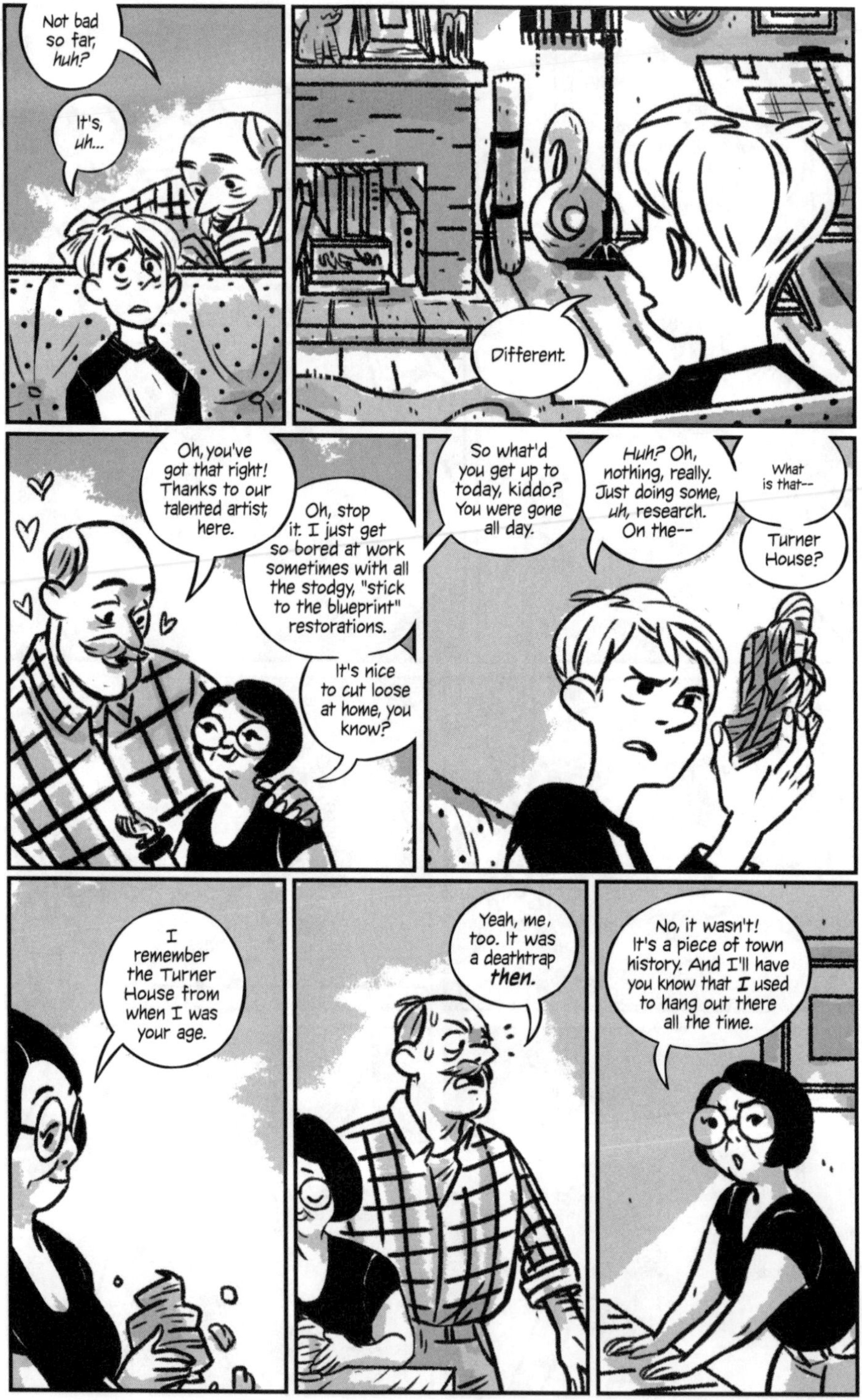

Not bad so far, *huh?*
It's, *uh...*
Different.
Oh, you've got that right! Thanks to our talented artist, here.
Oh, stop it. I just get so bored at work sometimes with all the stodgy, "stick to the blueprint" restorations.
It's nice to cut loose at home, you know?
So what'd you get up to today, kiddo? You were gone all day.
Huh? Oh, nothing, really. Just doing some, *uh,* research. On the--
What is that--
Turner House?
I remember the Turner House from when I was your age.
Yeah, me, too. It was a deathtrap ***then.***
No, it wasn't! It's a piece of town history. And I'll have you know that ***I*** used to hang out there all the time.

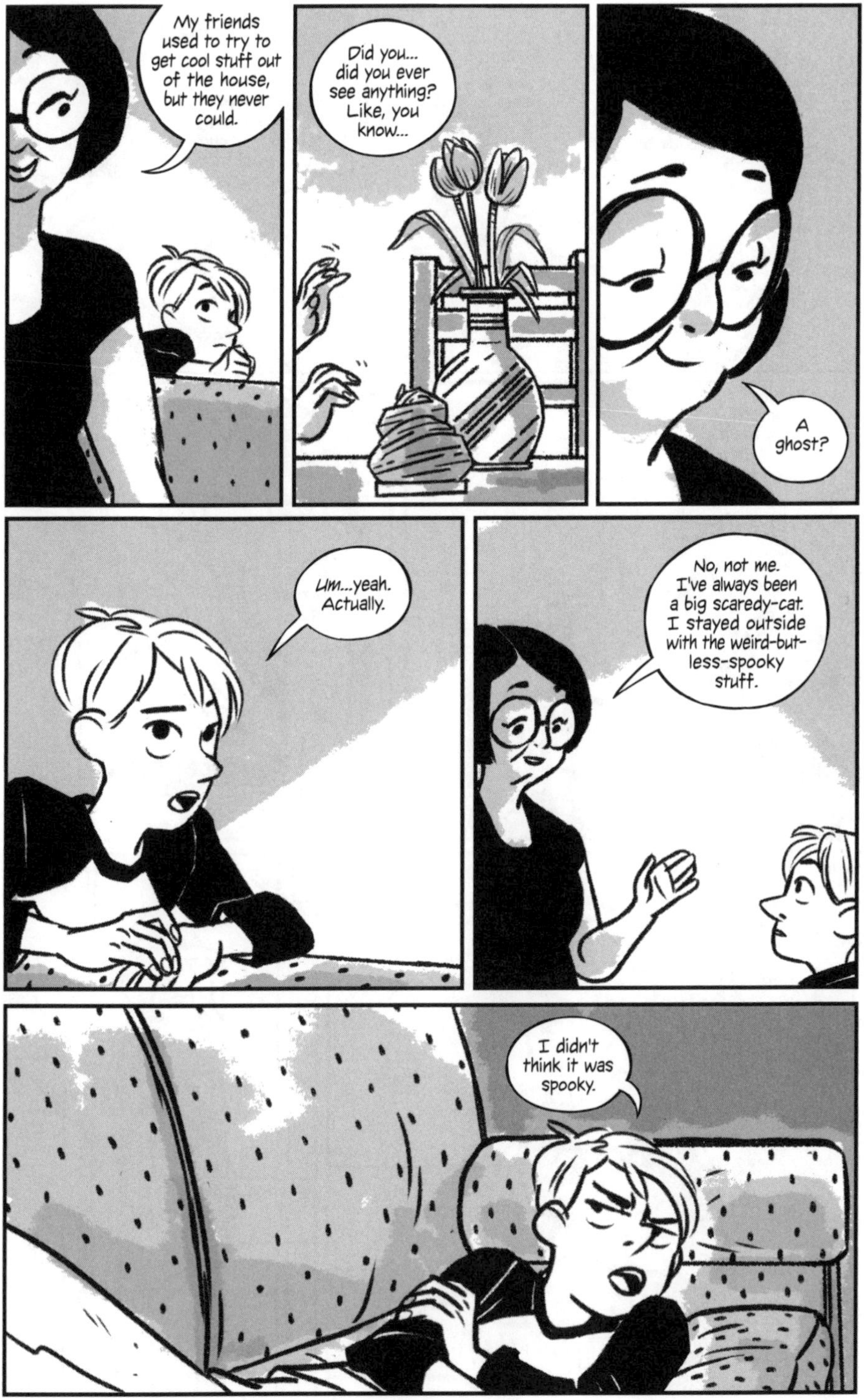
My friends used to try to get cool stuff out of the house, but they never could.
Did you... did you ever see anything? Like, you know...
A ghost?
Um...yeah. Actually.
No, not me. I've always been a big scaredy-cat. I stayed outside with the weird-but-less-spooky stuff.
I didn't think it was spooky.

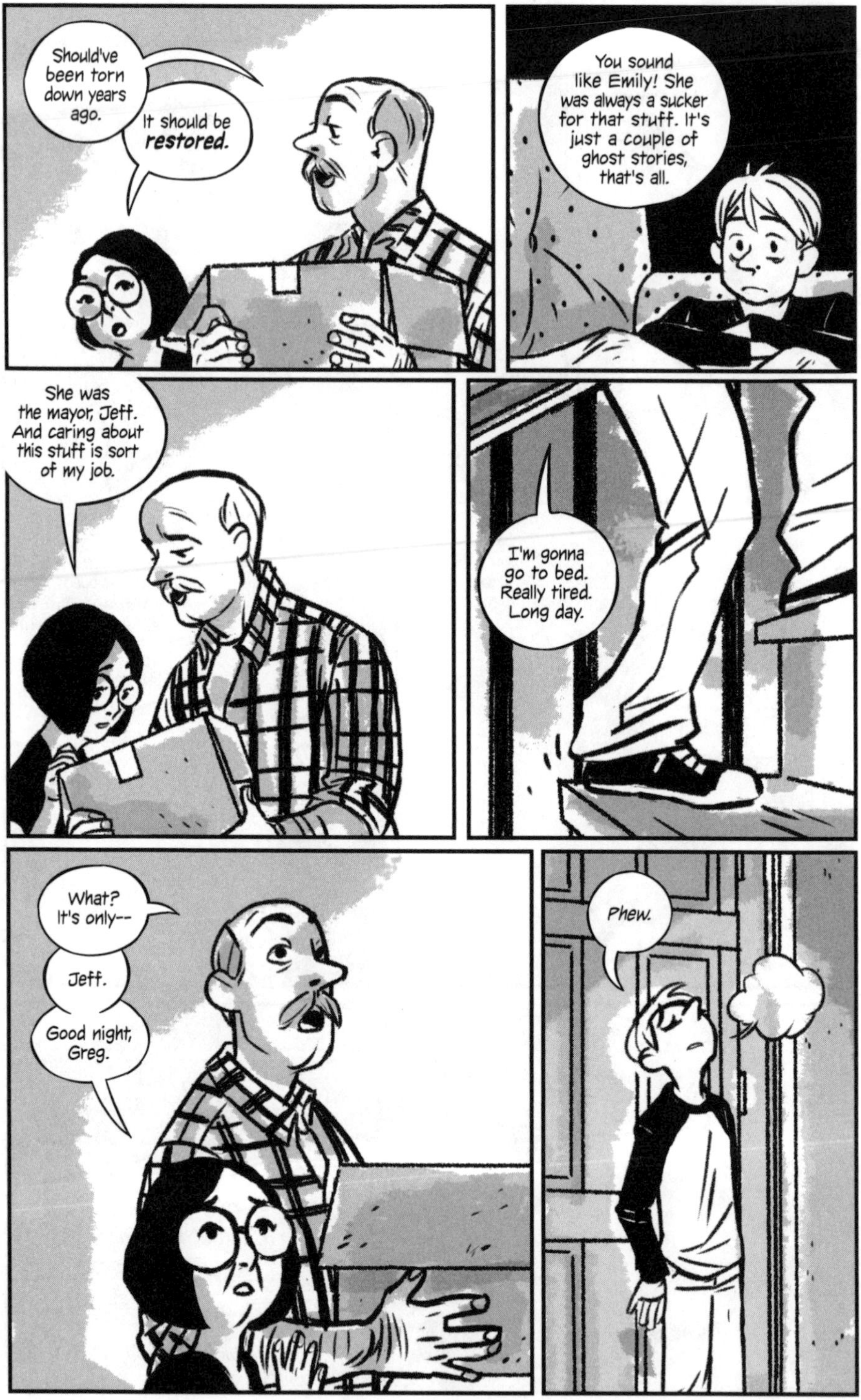
Should've been torn down years ago.
It should be **restored.**
You sound like Emily! She was always a sucker for that stuff. It's just a couple of ghost stories, that's all.
She was the mayor, Jeff. And caring about this stuff is sort of my job.
I'm gonna go to bed. Really tired. Long day.
What? It's only--
Jeff.
Good night, Greg.
Phew.

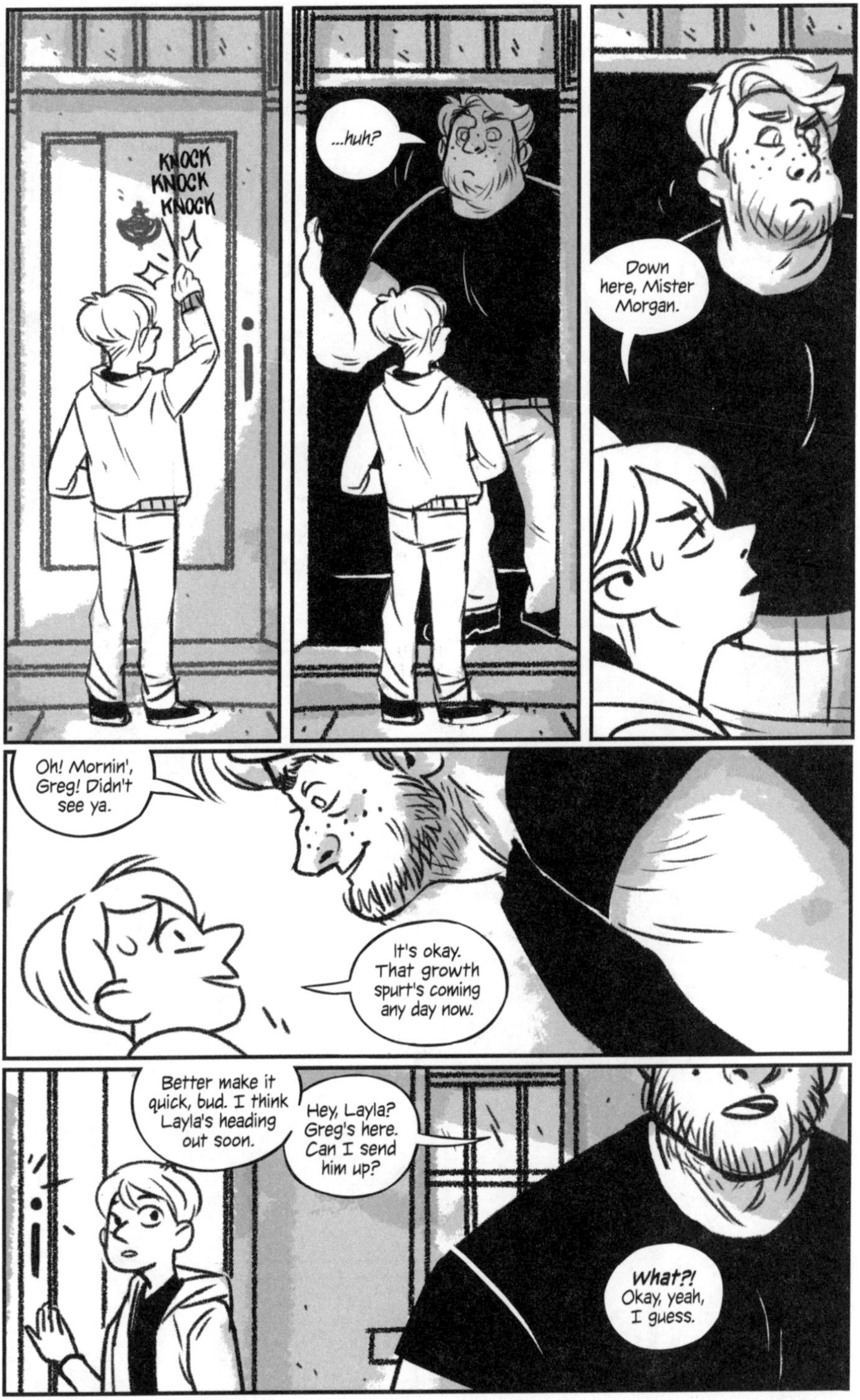
KNOCK
KNOCK
KNOCK
...huh?
Down here, Mister Morgan.
Oh! Mornin', Greg! Didn't see ya.
It's okay. That growth spurt's coming any day now.
Better make it quick, bud. I think Layla's heading out soon.
Hey, Layla? Greg's here. Can I send him up?
What?! Okay, yeah, I guess.

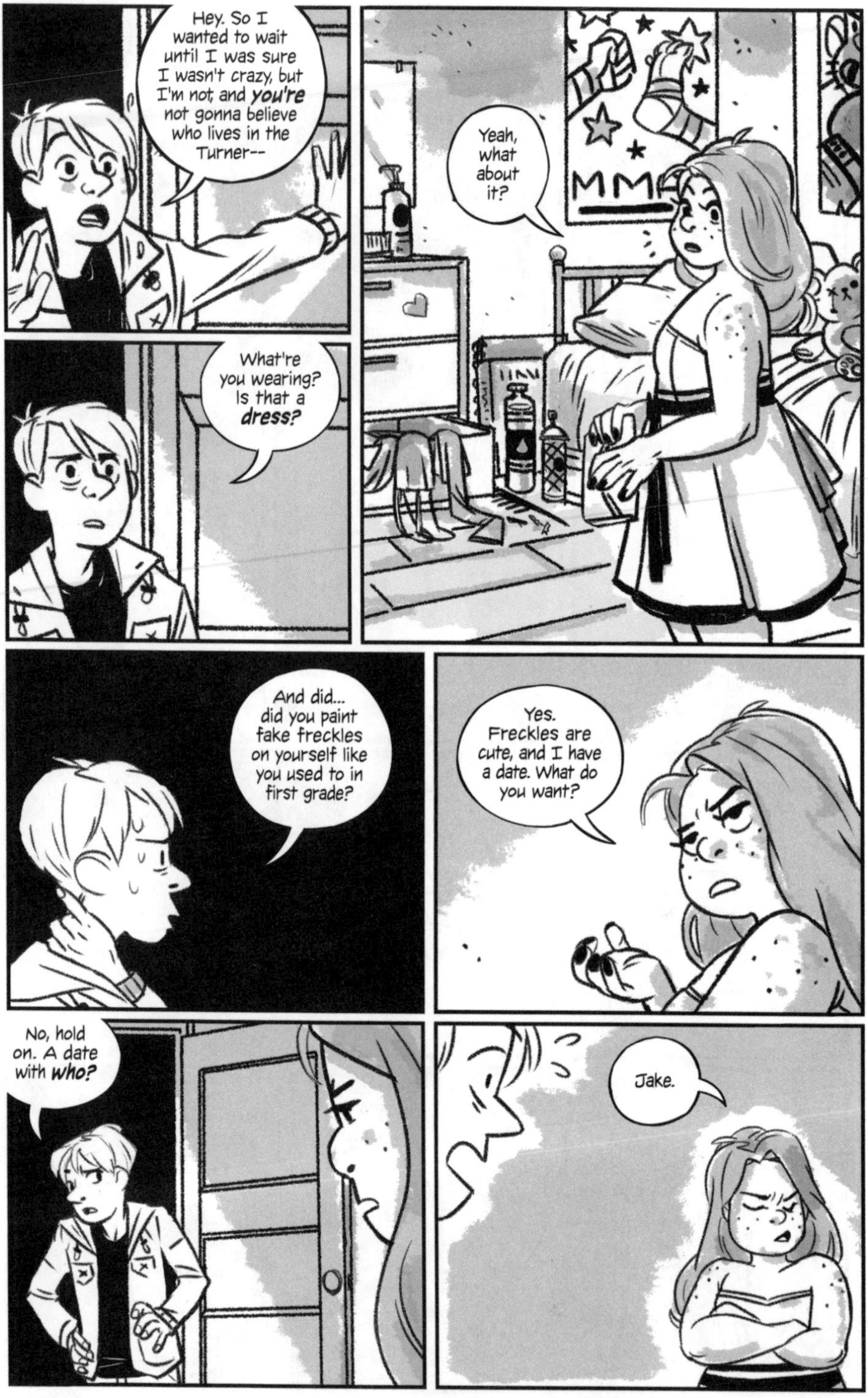

Hey. So I wanted to wait until I was sure I wasn't crazy, but I'm not, and ***you're*** not gonna believe who lives in the Turner--
Yeah, what about it?
What're you wearing? Is that a ***dress?***
And did... did you paint fake freckles on yourself like you used to in first grade?
Yes. Freckles are cute, and I have a date. What do you want?
No, hold on. A date with ***who?***
Jake.

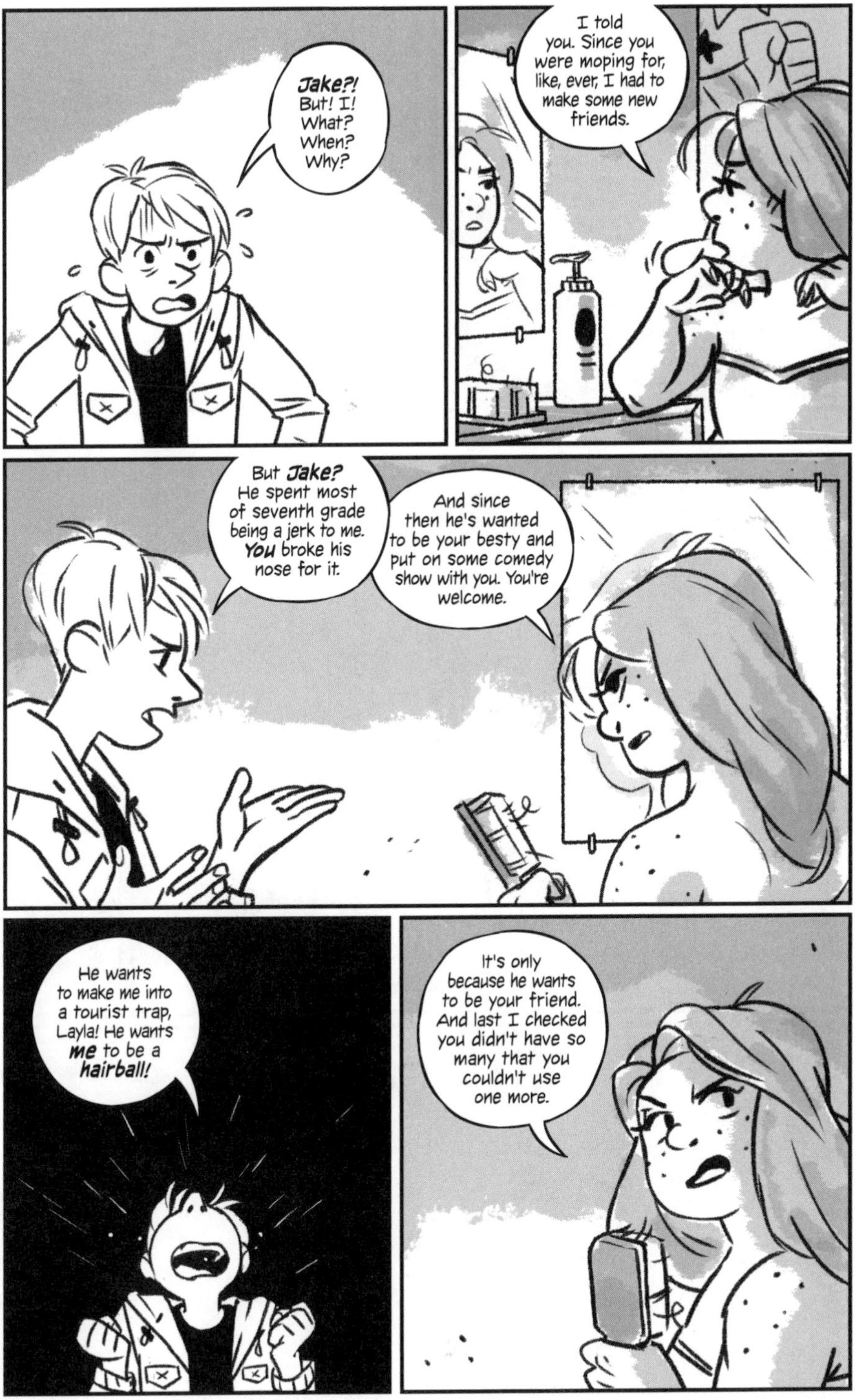

Jake?! But! I! What? When? Why?
I told you. Since you were moping for, like, ever, I had to make some new friends.
But Jake? He spent most of seventh grade being a jerk to me. You broke his nose for it.
And since then he's wanted to be your besty and put on some comedy show with you. You're welcome.
He wants to make me into a tourist trap, Layla! He wants me to be a hairball!
It's only because he wants to be your friend. And last I checked you didn't have so many that you couldn't use one more.

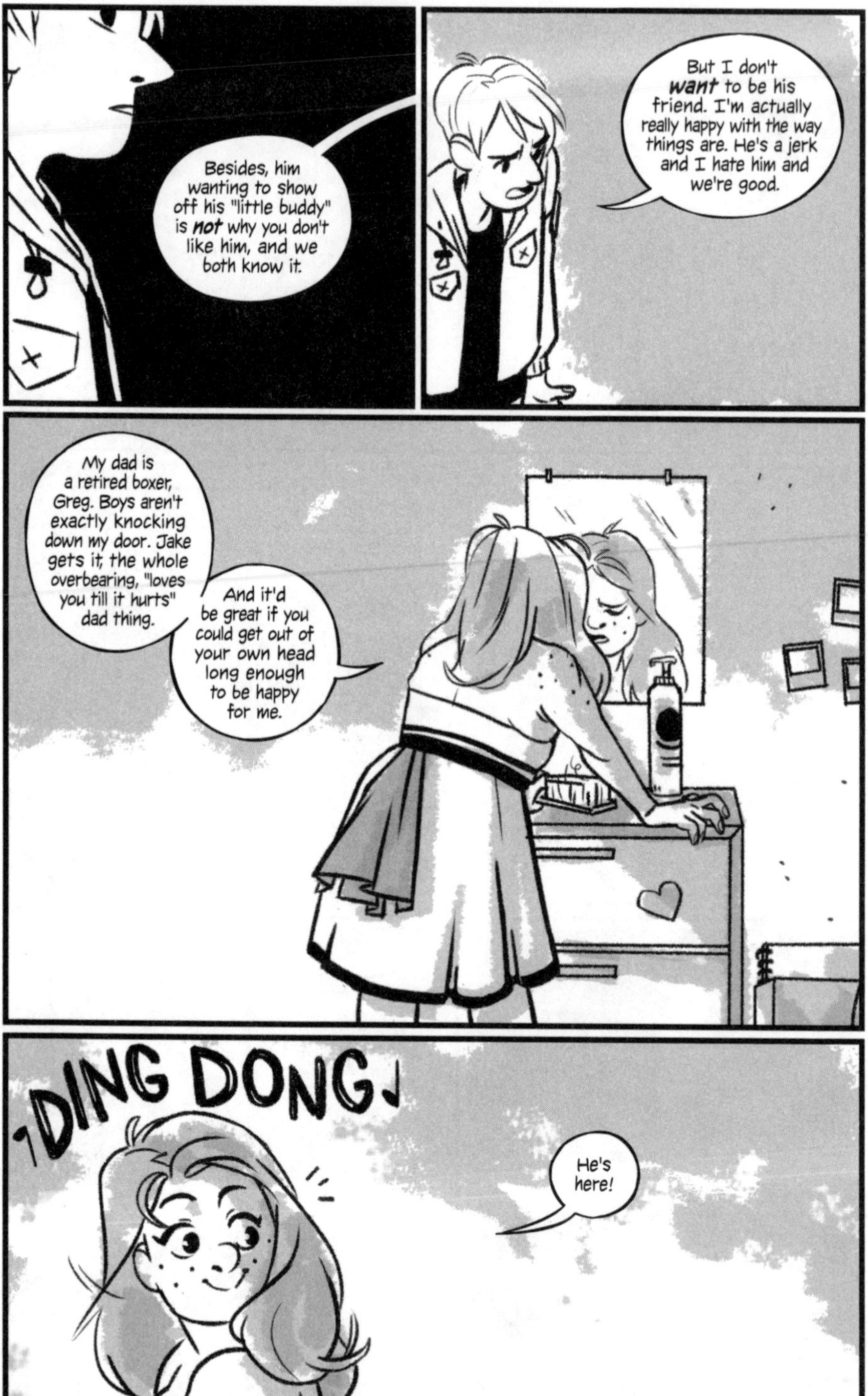
Besides, him wanting to show off his "little buddy" is **not** why you don't like him, and we both know it.
But I don't **want** to be his friend. I'm actually really happy with the way things are. He's a jerk and I hate him and we're good.
My dad is a retired boxer, Greg. Boys aren't exactly knocking down my door. Jake gets it, the whole overbearing, "loves you till it hurts" dad thing.
And it'd be great if you could get out of your own head long enough to be happy for me.
DING DONG
He's here!

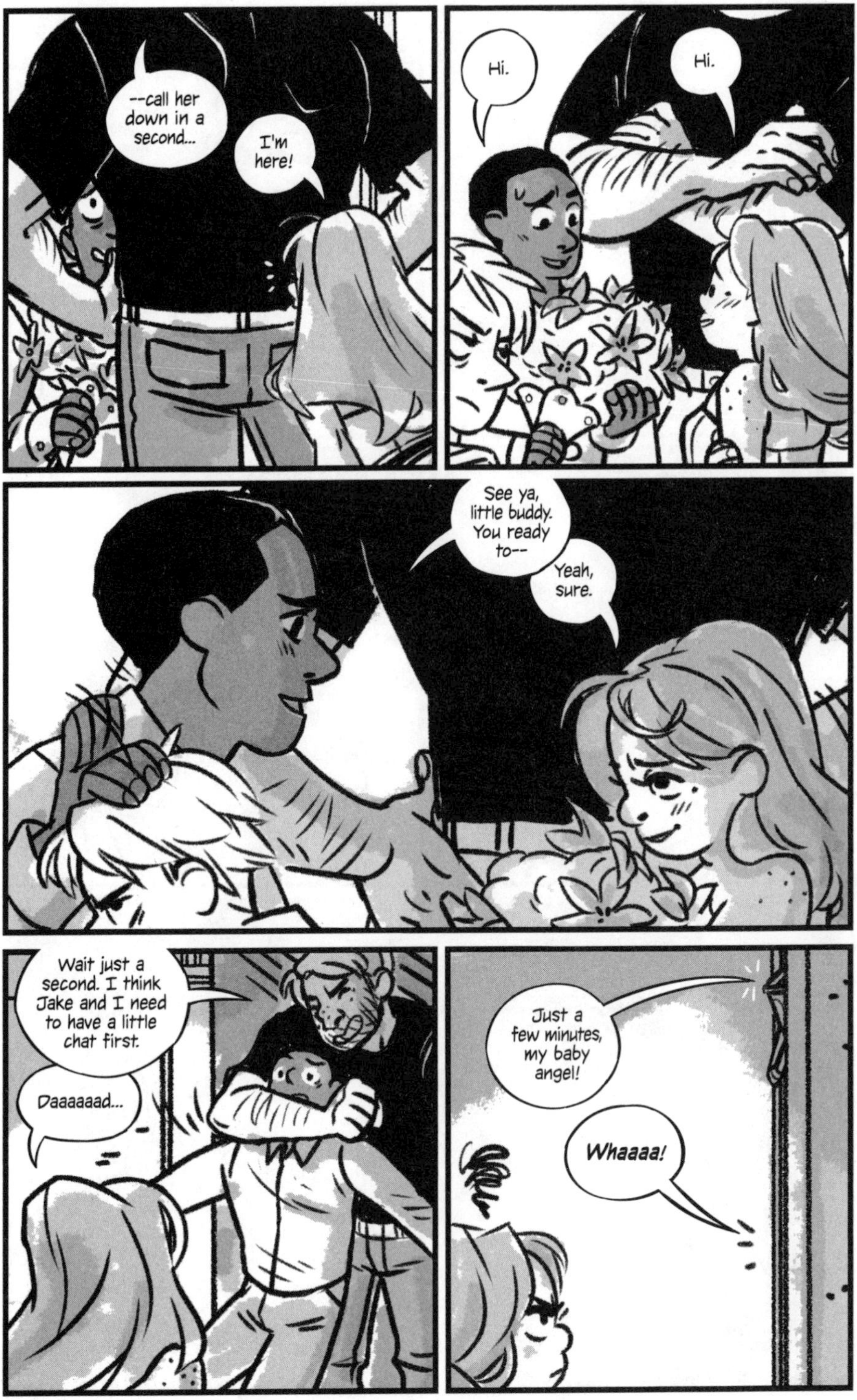
--call her down in a second...
I'm here!
Hi.
Hi.
See ya, little buddy. You ready to--
Yeah, sure.
Wait just a second. I think Jake and I need to have a little chat first.
Daaaaaad...
Just a few minutes, my baby angel!
Whaaaa!

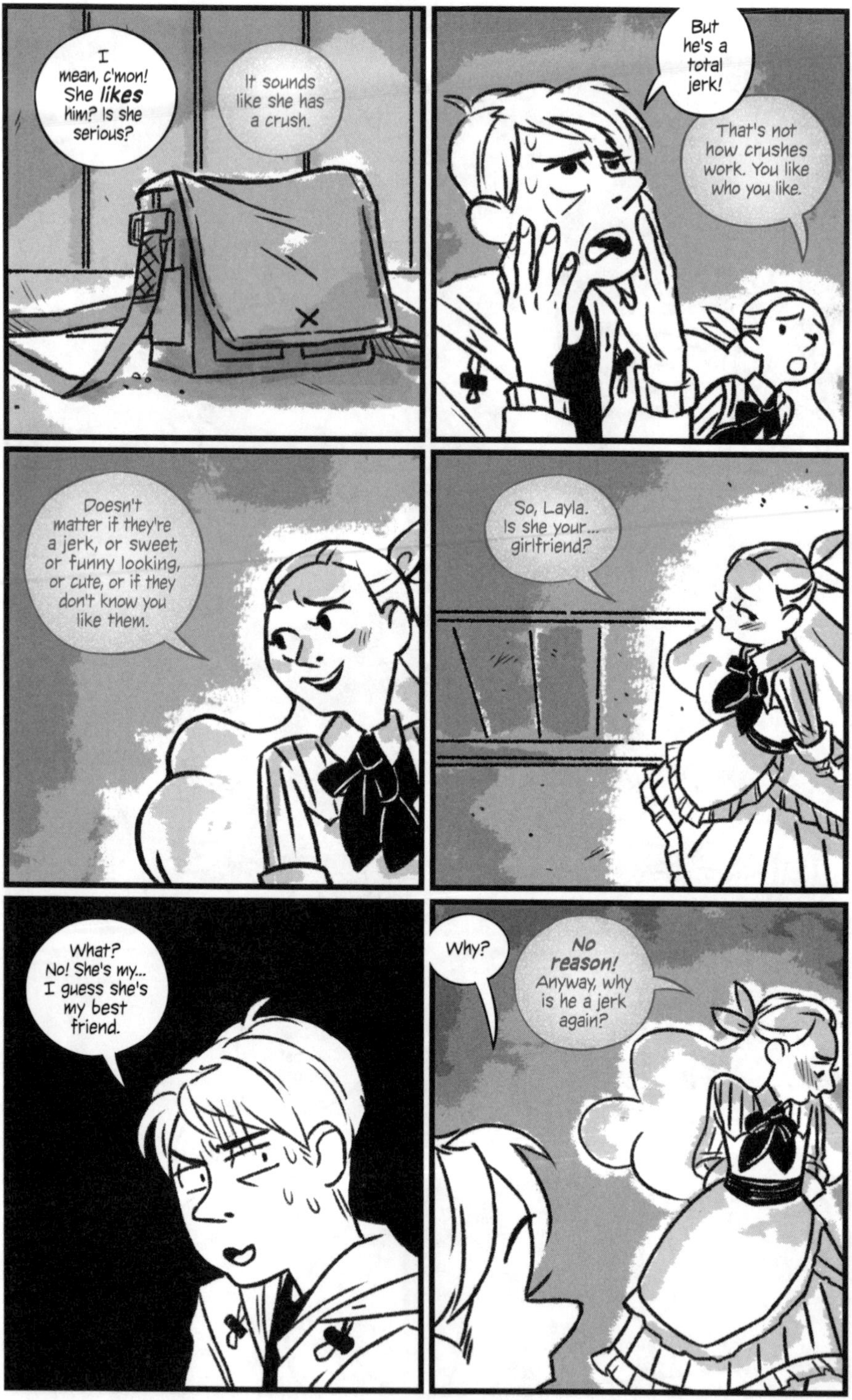
I mean, c'mon! She ***likes*** him? Is she serious?
It sounds like she has a crush.
But he's a total jerk!
That's not how crushes work. You like who you like.
Doesn't matter if they're a jerk, or sweet, or funny looking, or cute, or if they don't know you like them.
So, Layla. Is she your... girlfriend?
What? No! She's my... I guess she's my best friend.
Why?
No reason! Anyway, why is he a jerk again?

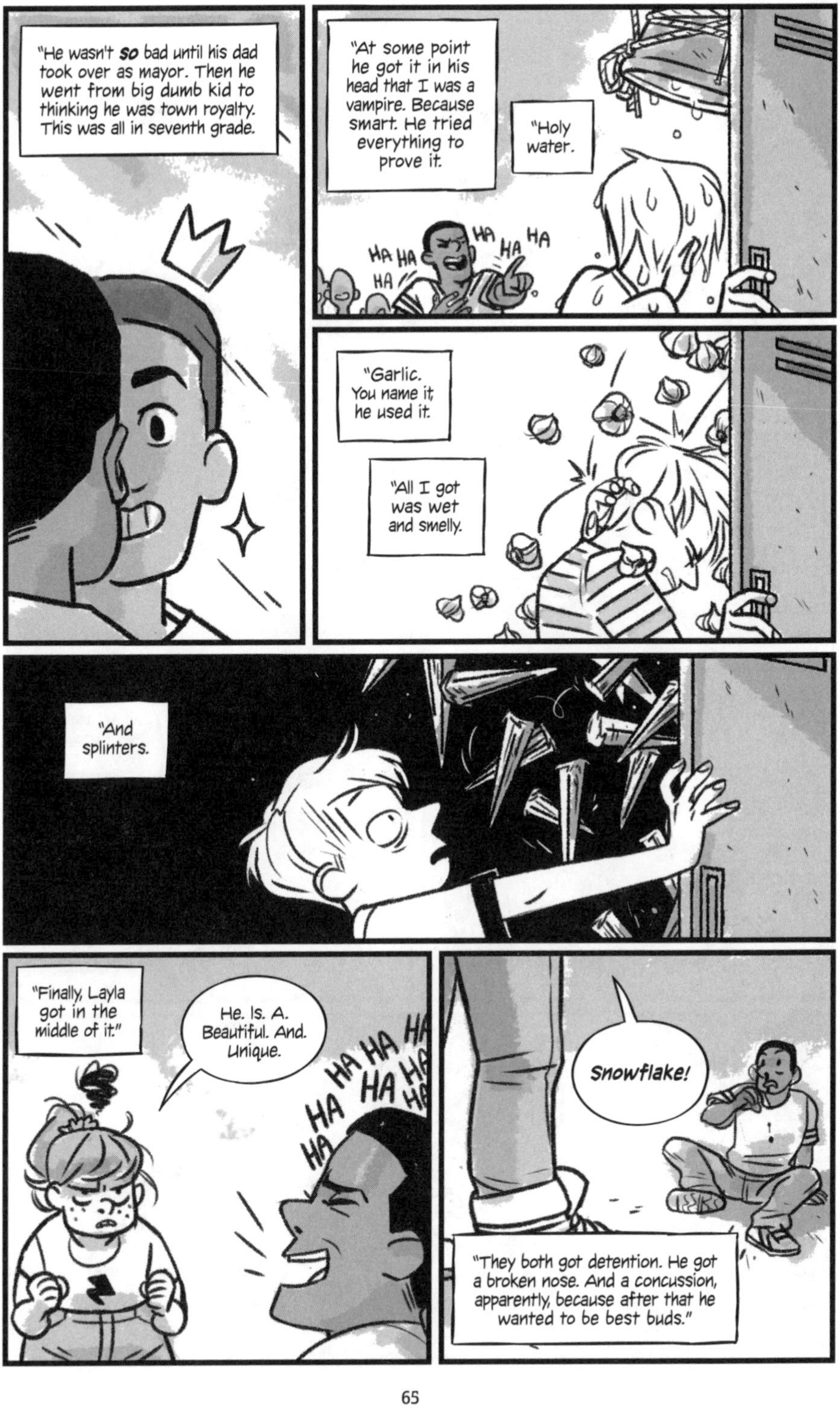
"He wasn't **so** bad until his dad took over as mayor. Then he went from big dumb kid to thinking he was town royalty. This was all in seventh grade.
"At some point he got it in his head that I was a vampire. Because smart. He tried everything to prove it.
"Holy water.
HA HA HA HA HA HA
"Garlic. You name it, he used it.
"All I got was wet and smelly.
"And splinters.
"Finally, Layla got in the middle of it."
He. Is. A. Beautiful. And. Unique.
HA HA HA HA HA HA HA HA
Snowflake!
"They both got detention. He got a broken nose. And a concussion, apparently, because after that he wanted to be best buds."

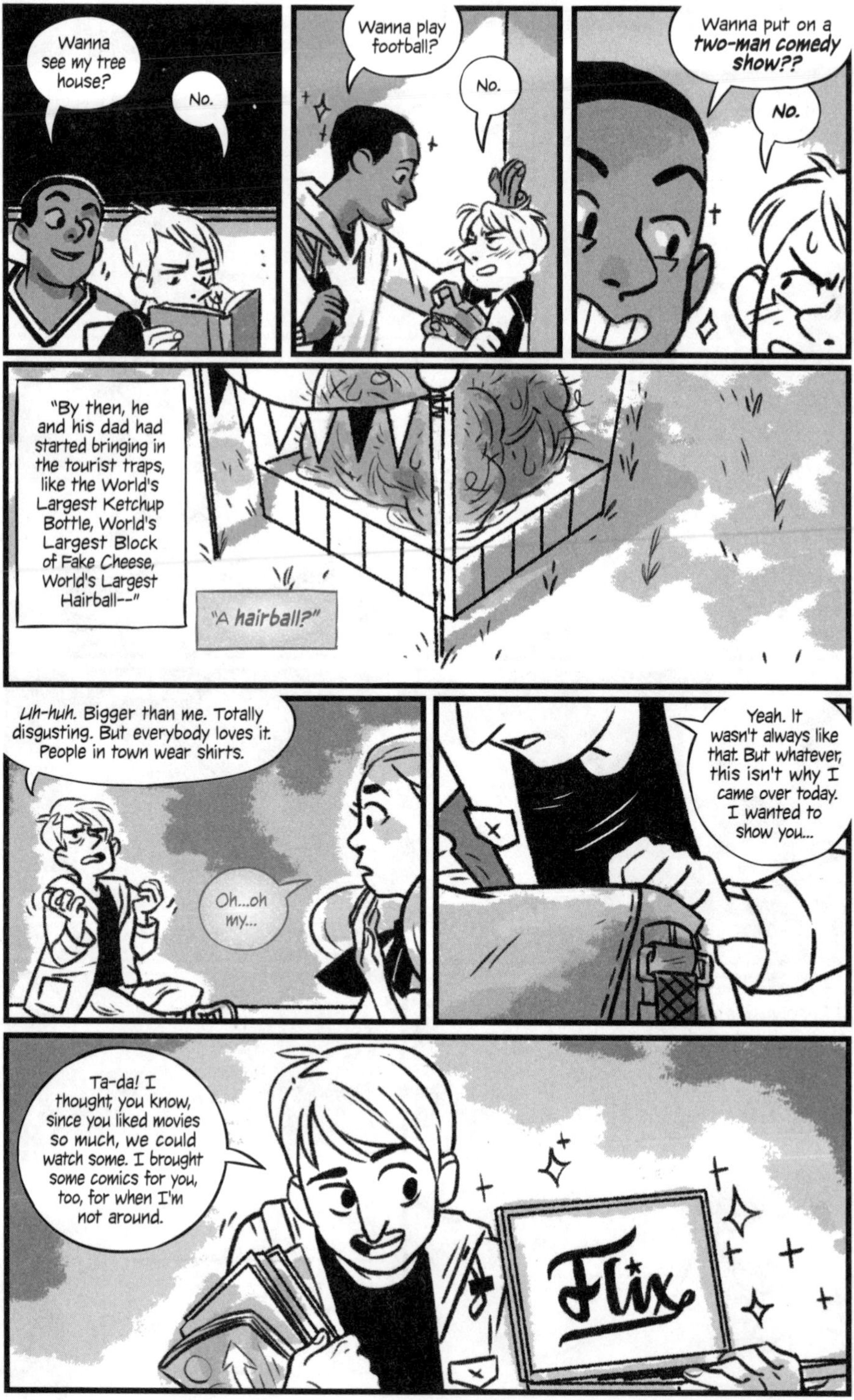
Wanna see my tree house?
No.
Wanna play football?
No.
Wanna put on a *two-man comedy show??*
No.
"By then, he and his dad had started bringing in the tourist traps, like the World's Largest Ketchup Bottle, World's Largest Block of Fake Cheese, World's Largest Hairball--"
"A *hairball?*"
Uh-huh. Bigger than me. Totally disgusting. But everybody loves it. People in town wear shirts.
Oh...oh my...
Yeah. It wasn't always like that. But whatever, this isn't why I came over today. I wanted to show you...
Ta-da! I thought, you know, since you liked movies so much, we could watch some. I brought some comics for you, too, for when I'm not around.
Flix

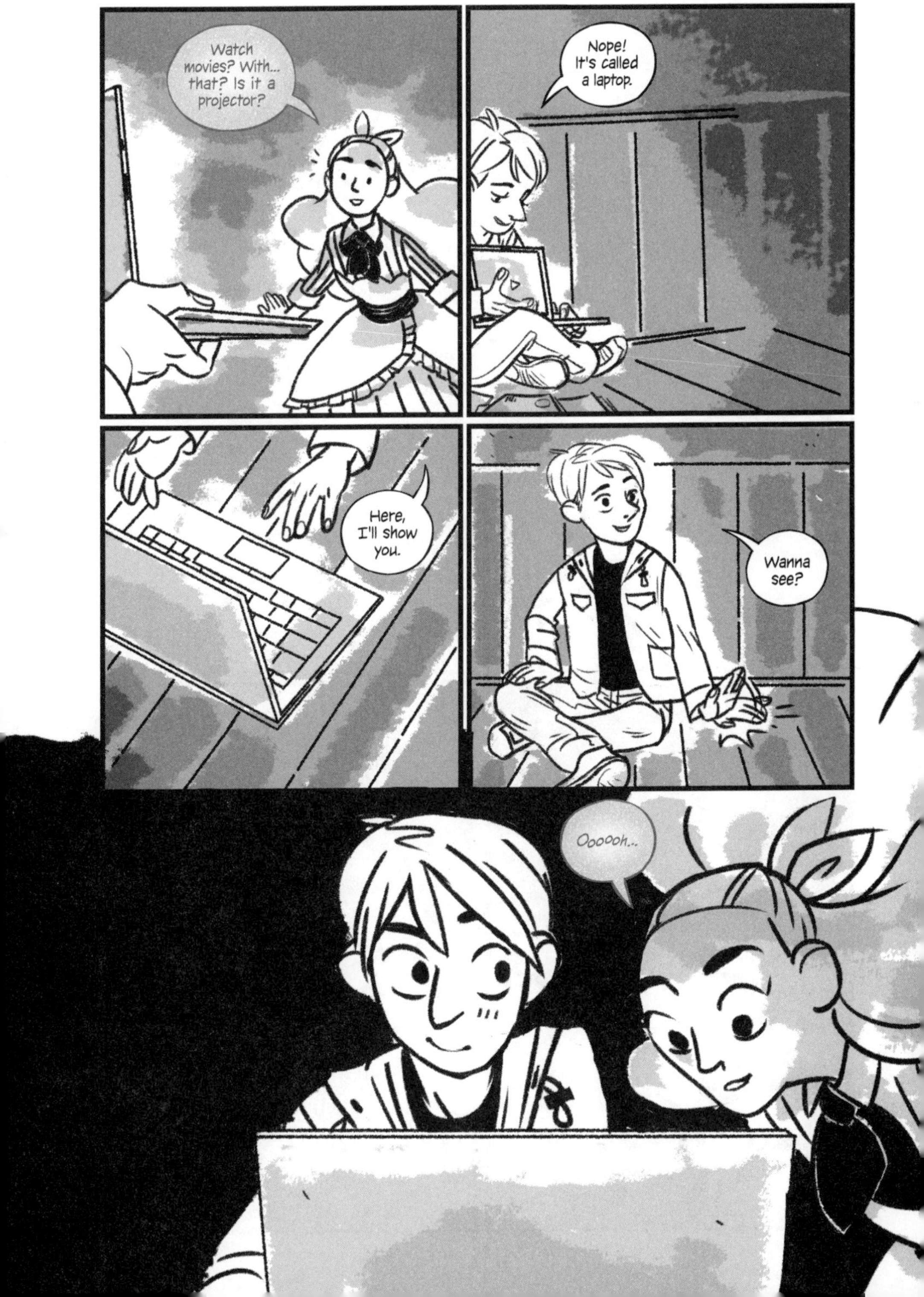

Watch movies? With... that? Is it a projector?
Nope! It's called a laptop.
Here, I'll show you.
Wanna see?
Oooooh...

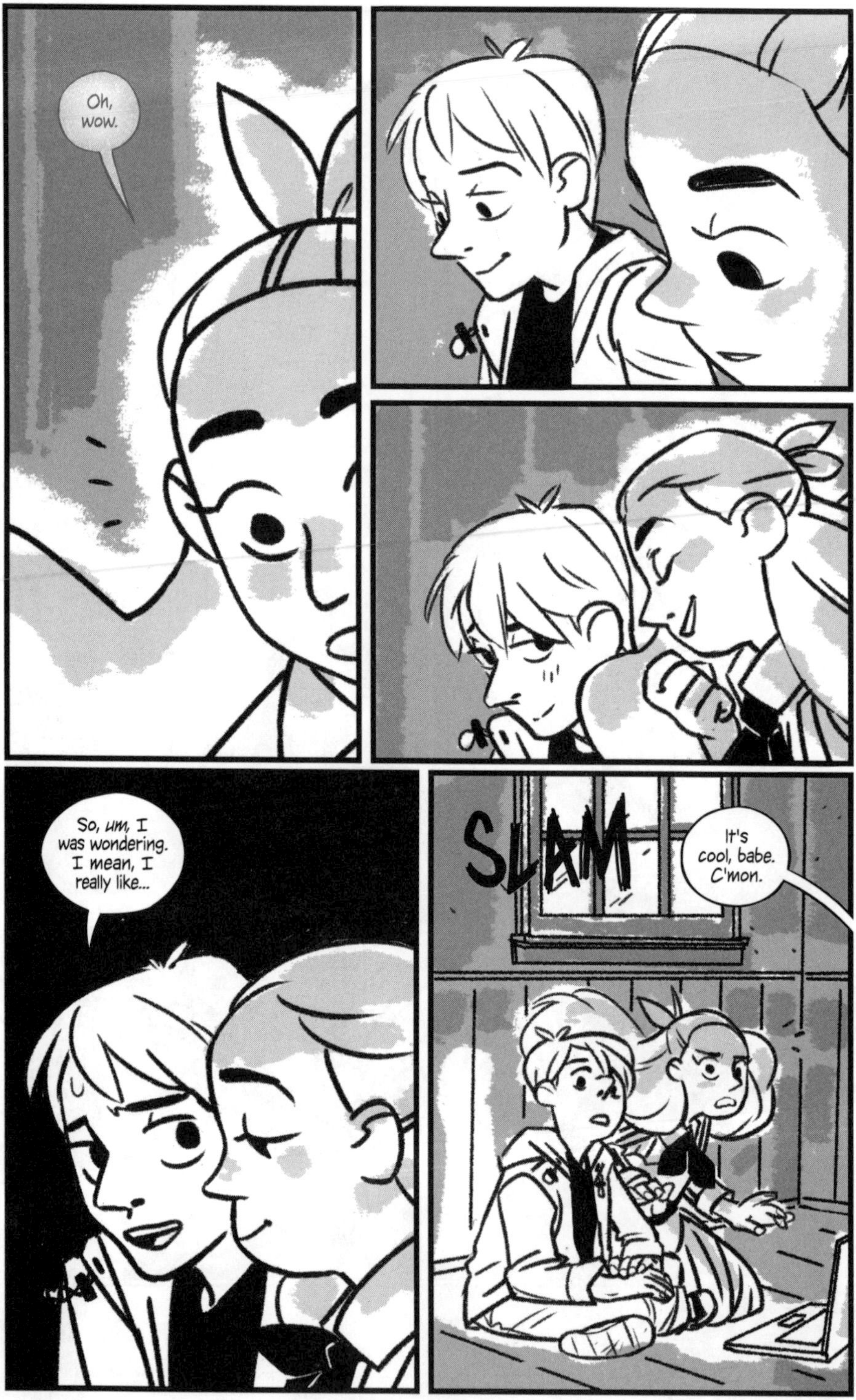
Oh, wow.
So, um, I was wondering. I mean, I really like...
SLAM
It's cool, babe. C'mon.

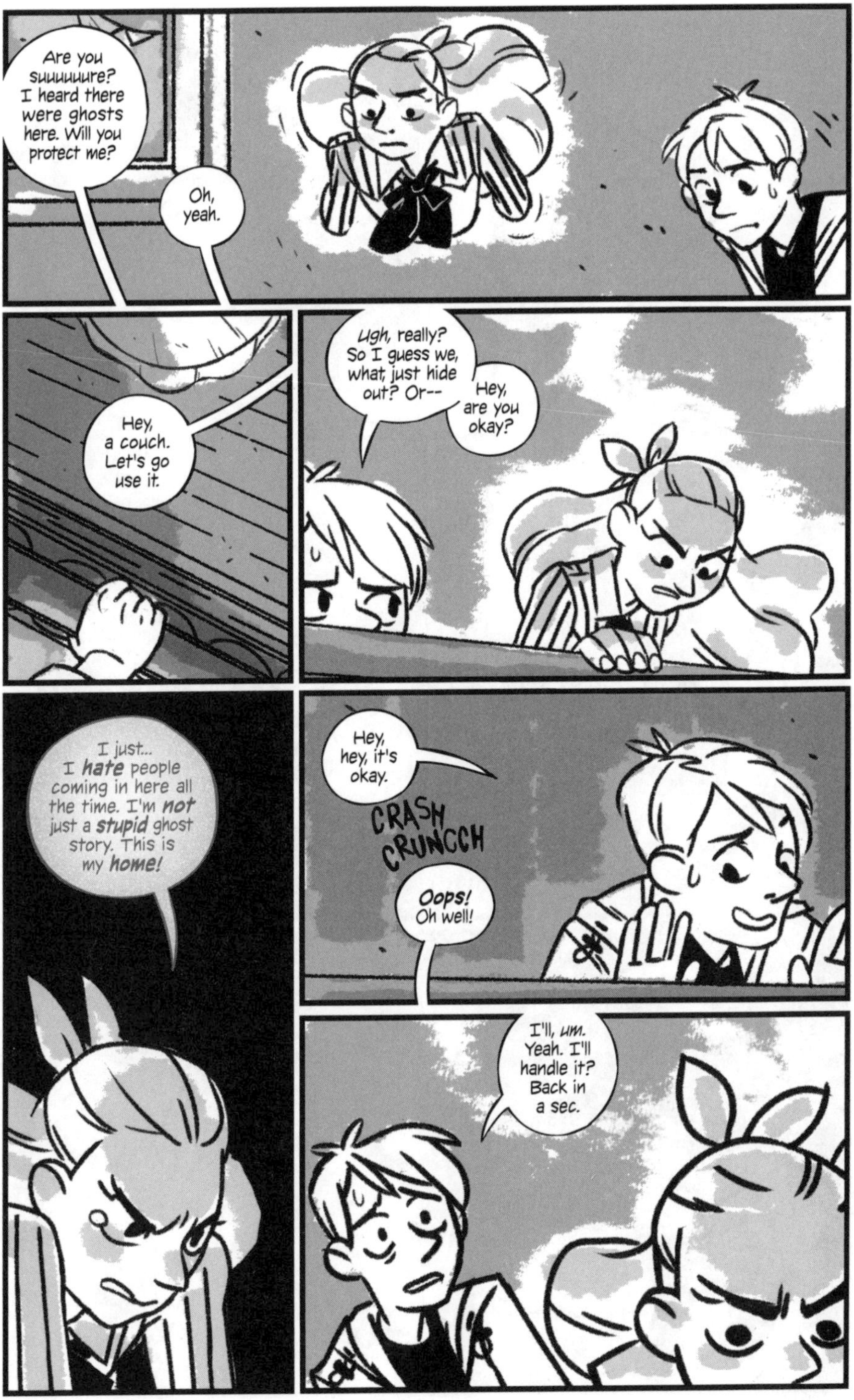
Are you suuuuuure? I heard there were ghosts here. Will you protect me?
Oh, yeah.
Hey, a couch. Let's go use it.
Ugh, really? So I guess we, what, just hide out? Or--
Hey, are you okay?
I just... I hate people coming in here all the time. I'm not just a stupid ghost story. This is my home!
Hey, hey, it's okay.
CRASH
CRUNCCH
Oops! Oh well!
I'll, um. Yeah. I'll handle it? Back in a sec.

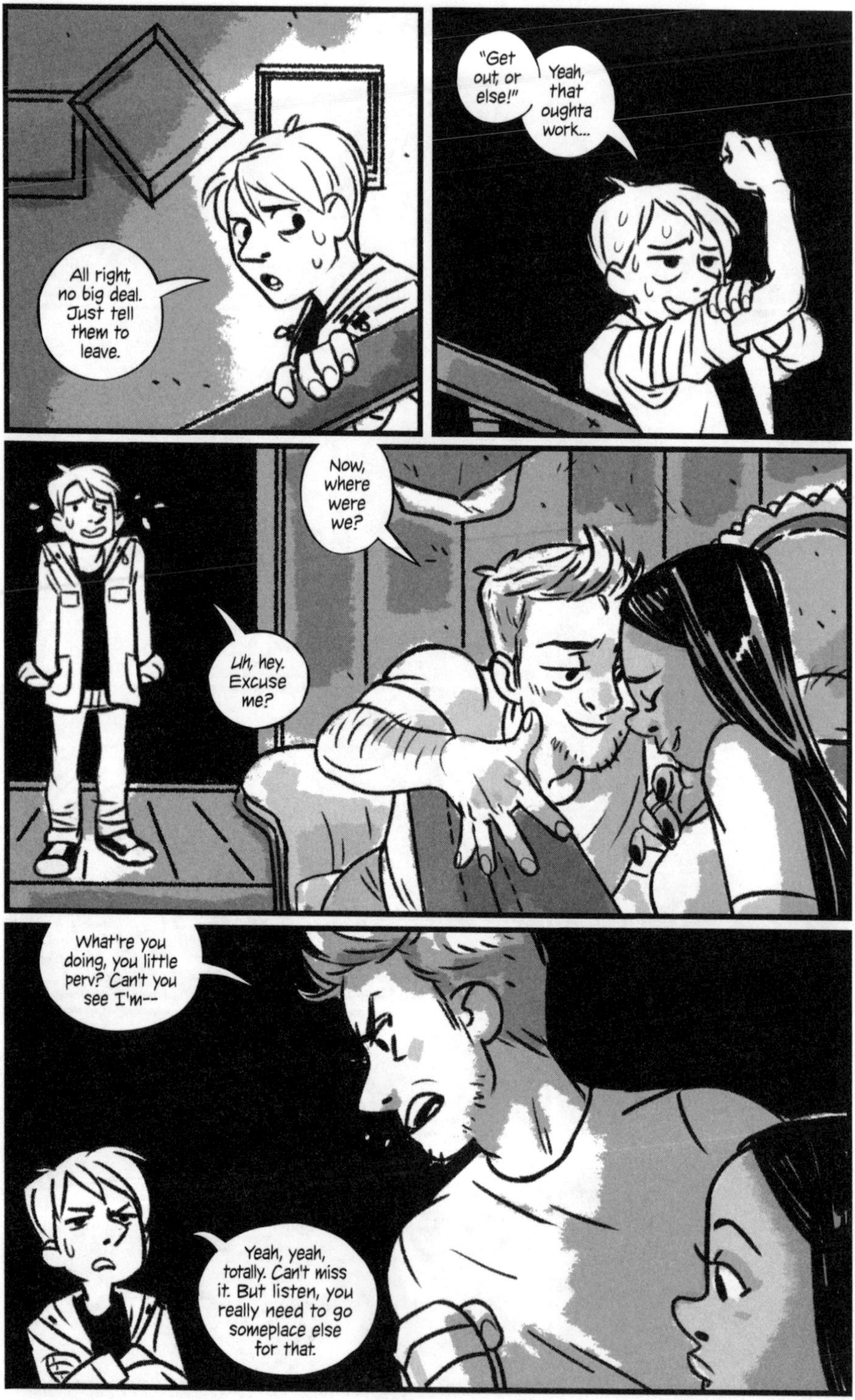
All right, no big deal. Just tell them to leave.
"Get out, or else!"
Yeah, that oughta work...
Now, where were we?
Uh, hey. Excuse me?
What're you doing, you little perv? Can't you see I'm--
Yeah, yeah, totally. Can't miss it. But listen, you really need to go someplace else for that.

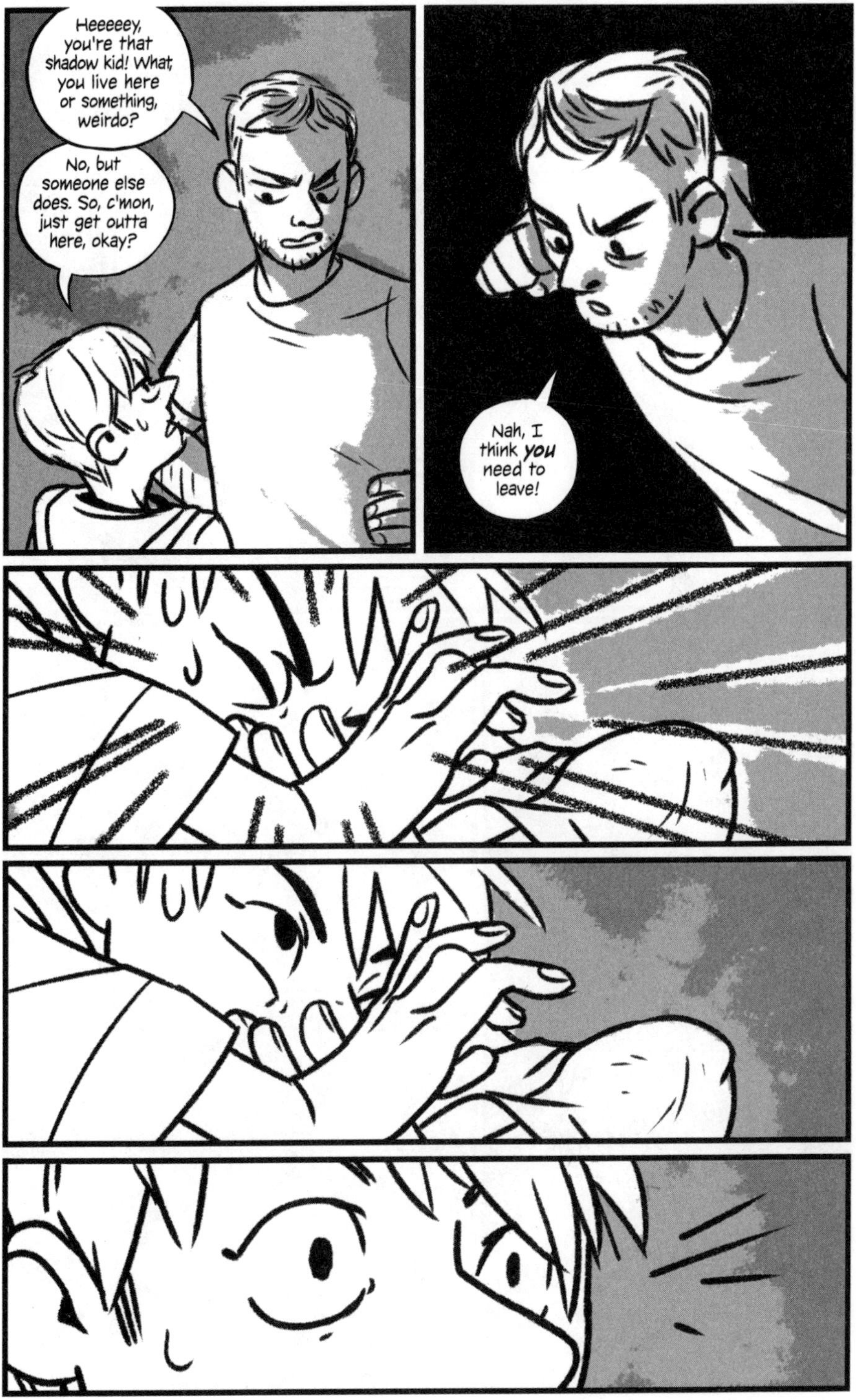
Heeeeey, you're that shadow kid! What, you live here or something, weirdo?
No, but someone else does. So, c'mon, just get outta here, okay?
Nah, I think *you* need to leave!

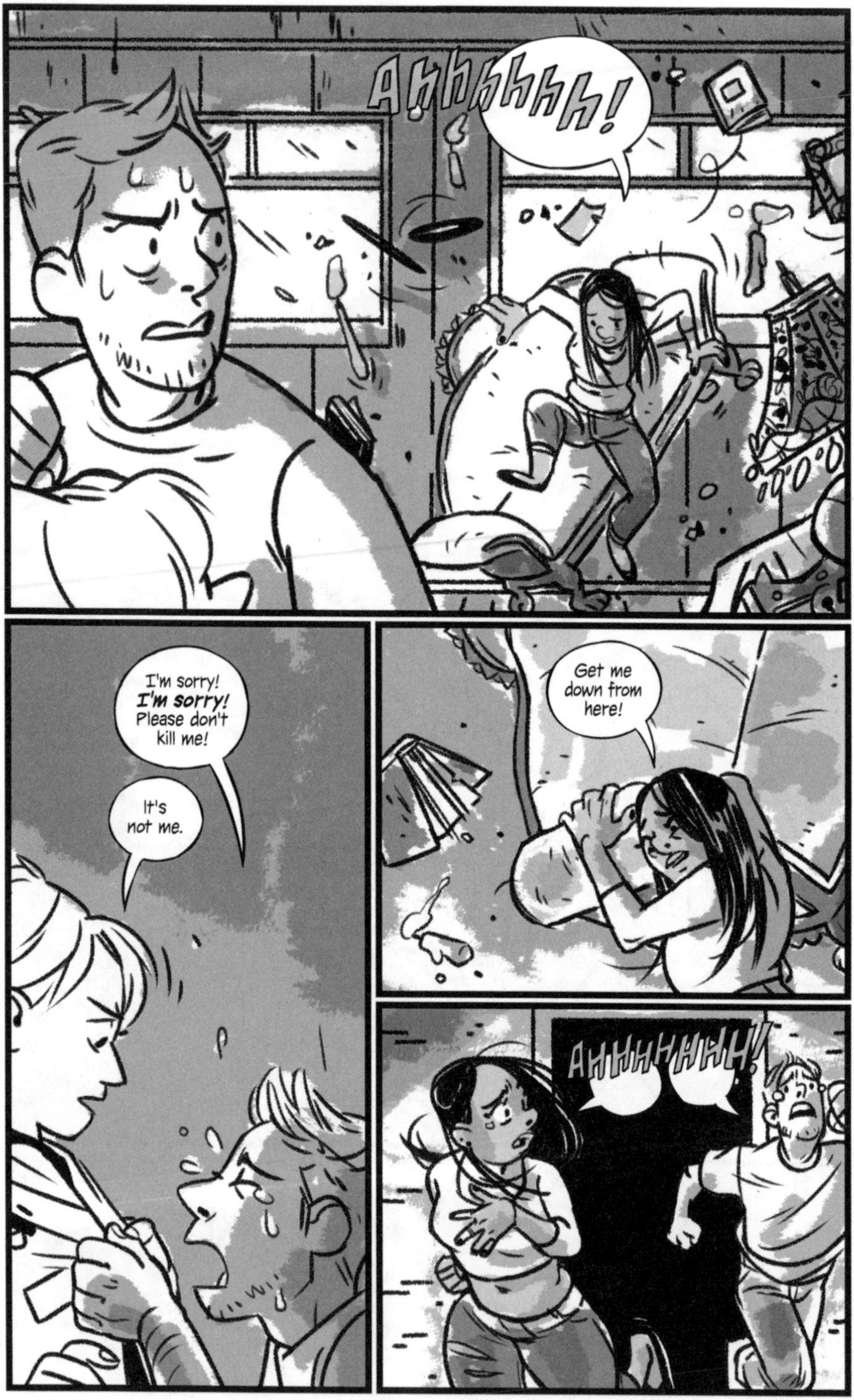
Ahhhhhh!
I'm sorry! **I'm sorry!** Please don't kill me!
It's not me.
Get me down from here!
AHHHHHHH!

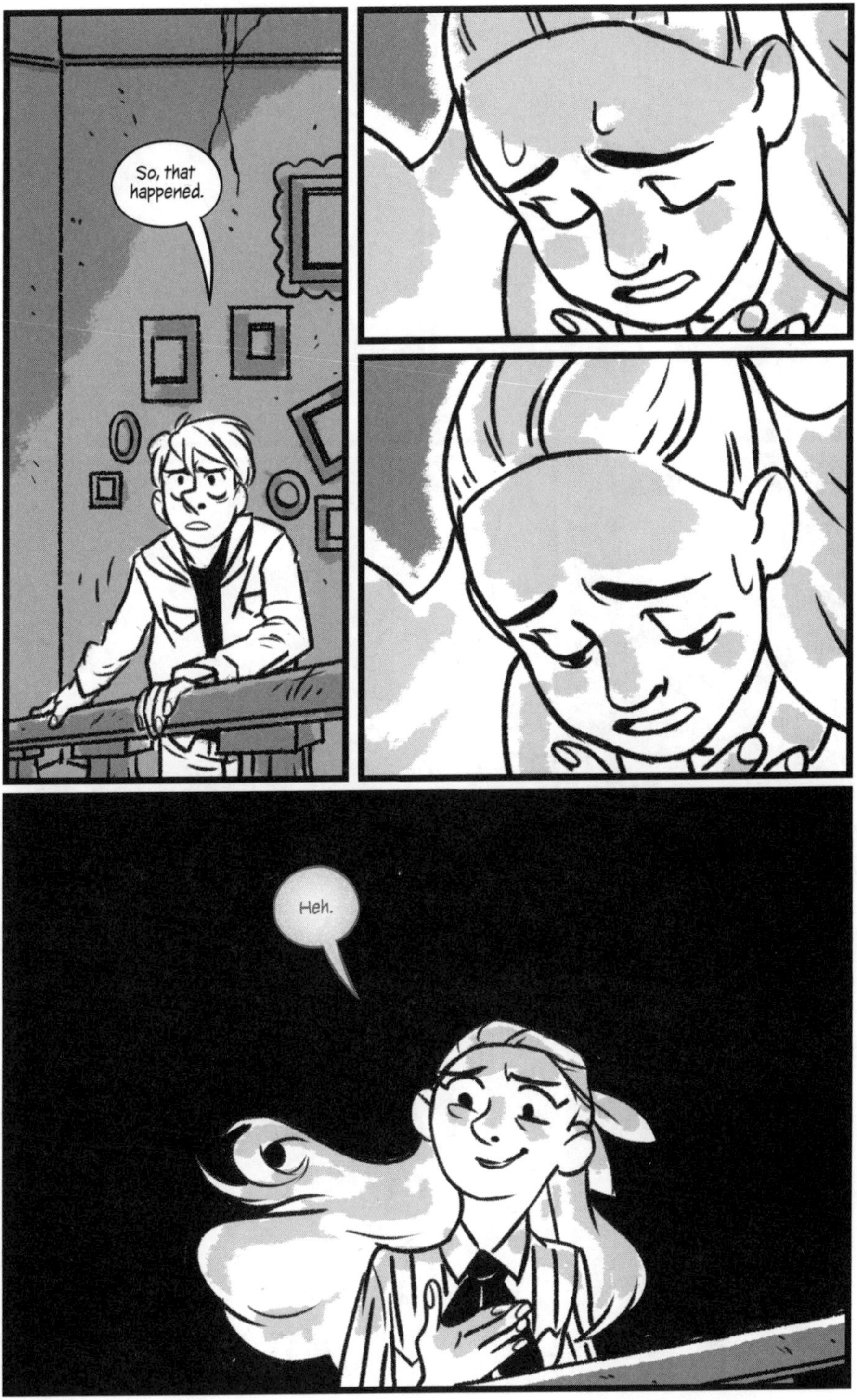
So, that happened.
Heh.

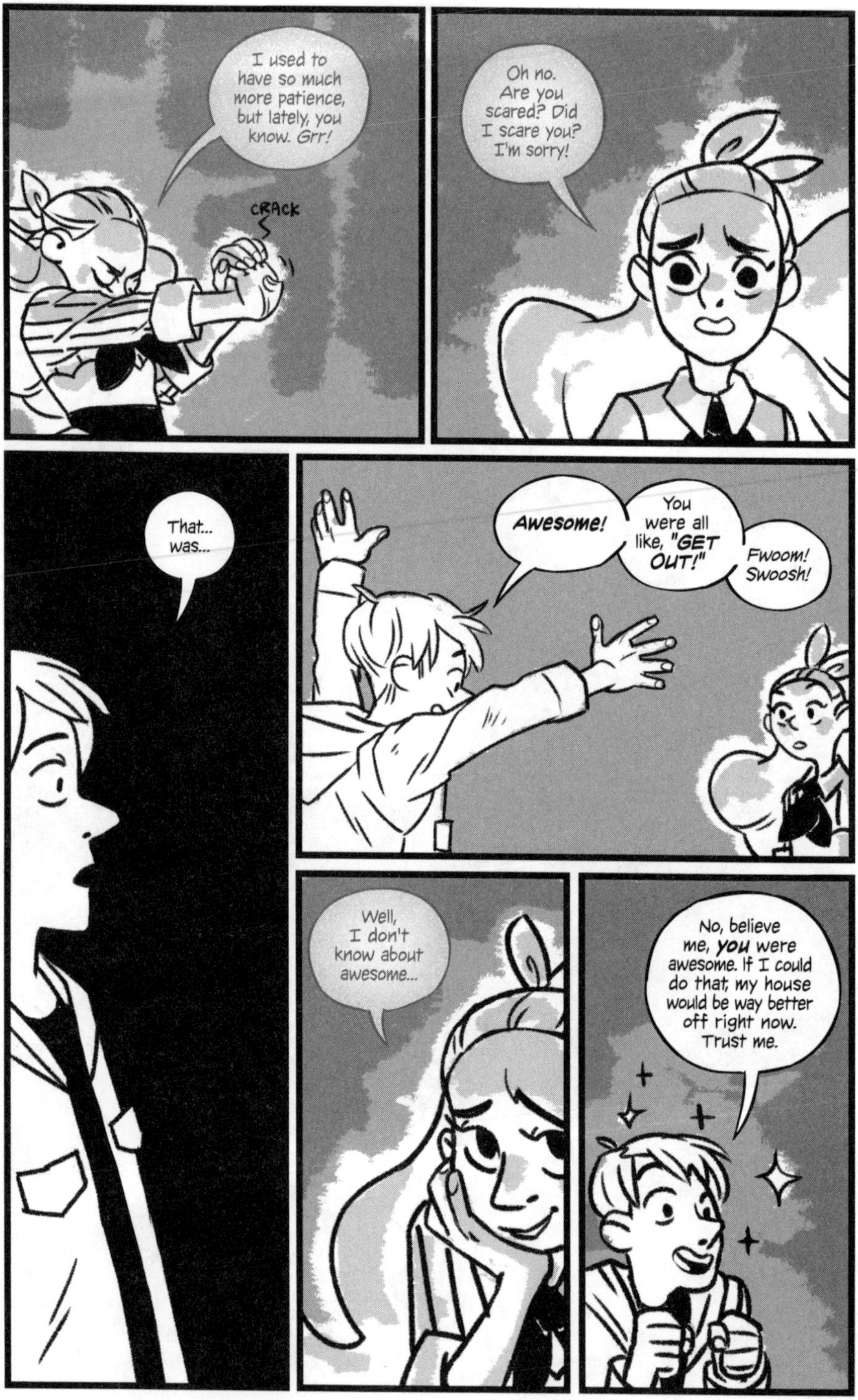

I used to have so much more patience, but lately, you know. Grr!
CRACK
Oh no. Are you scared? Did I scare you? I'm sorry!
That... was...
Awesome!
You were all like, "GET OUT!"
Fwoom! Swoosh!
Well, I don't know about awesome...
No, believe me, you were awesome. If I could do that, my house would be way better off right now. Trust me.

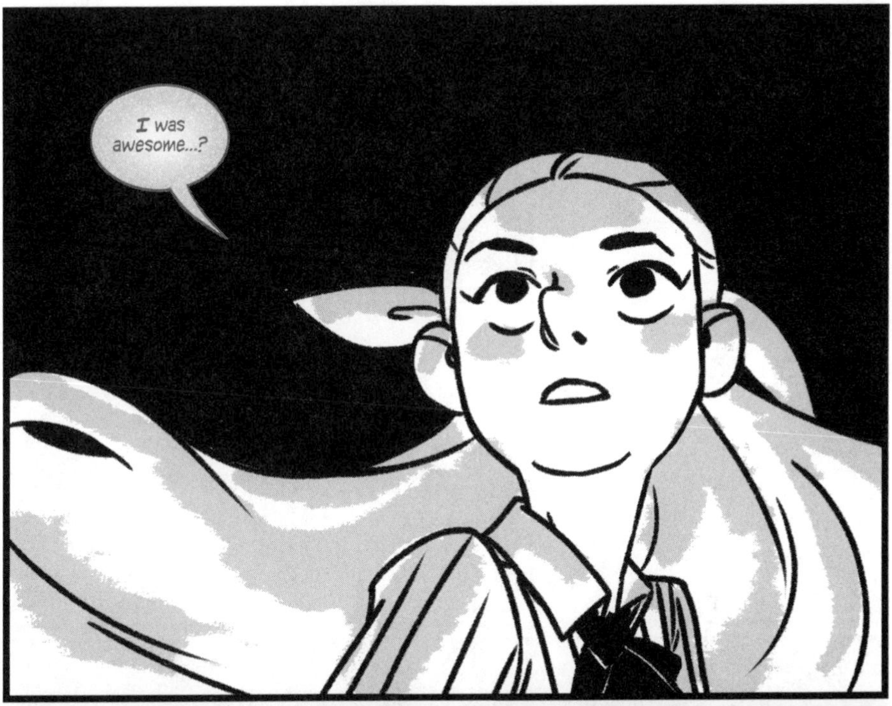
I was awesome...?

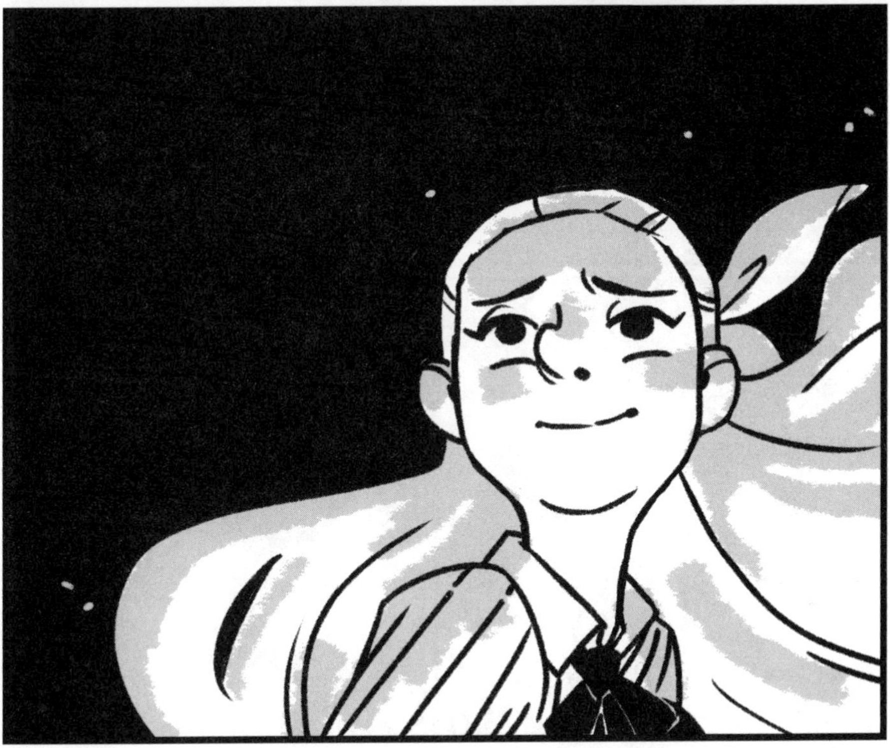

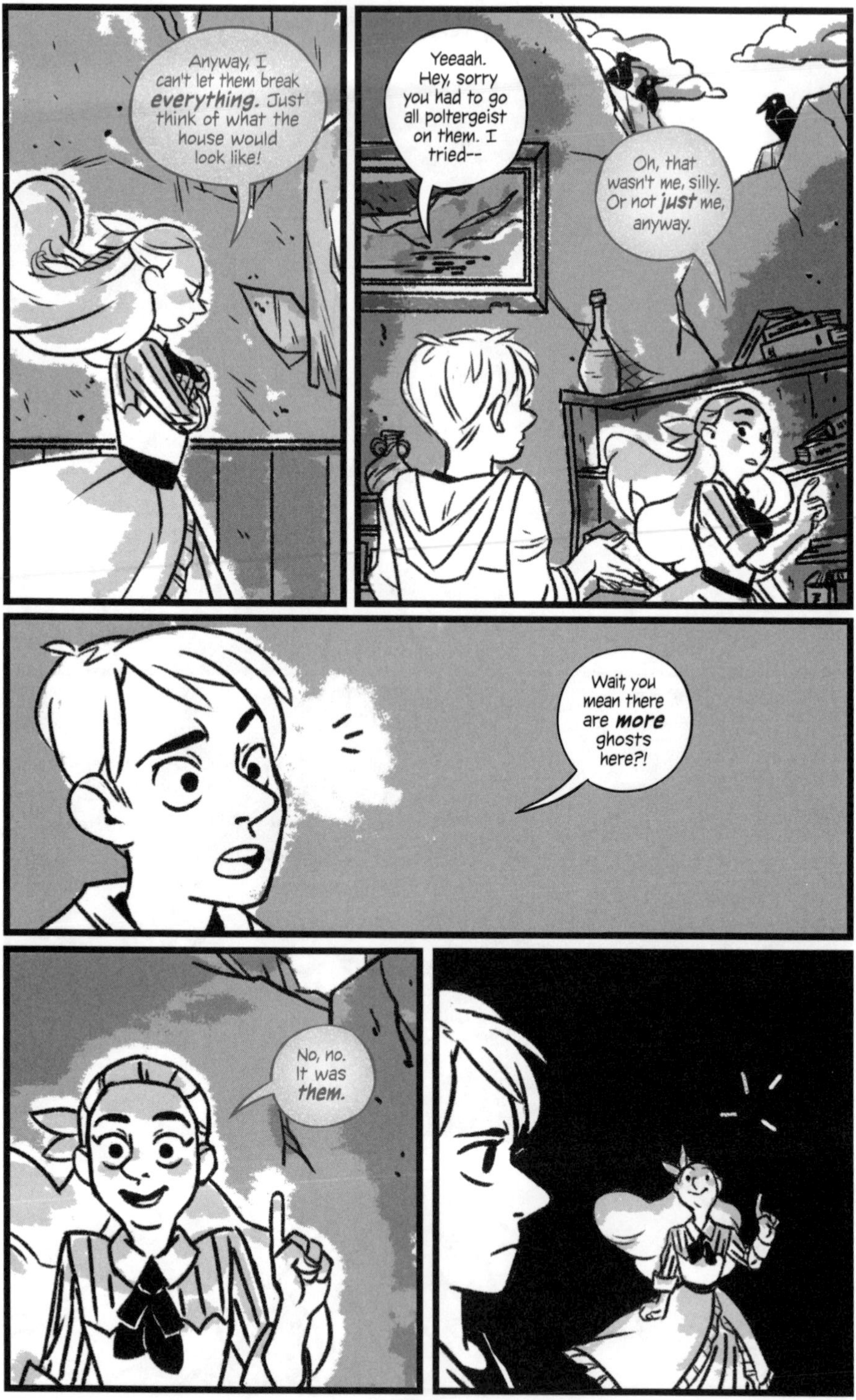
Anyway, I can't let them break ***everything.*** Just think of what the house would look like!
Yeeaah. Hey, sorry you had to go all poltergeist on them. I tried--
Oh, that wasn't me, silly. Or not ***just*** me, anyway.
Wait, you mean there are ***more*** ghosts here?!
No, no. It was ***them.***

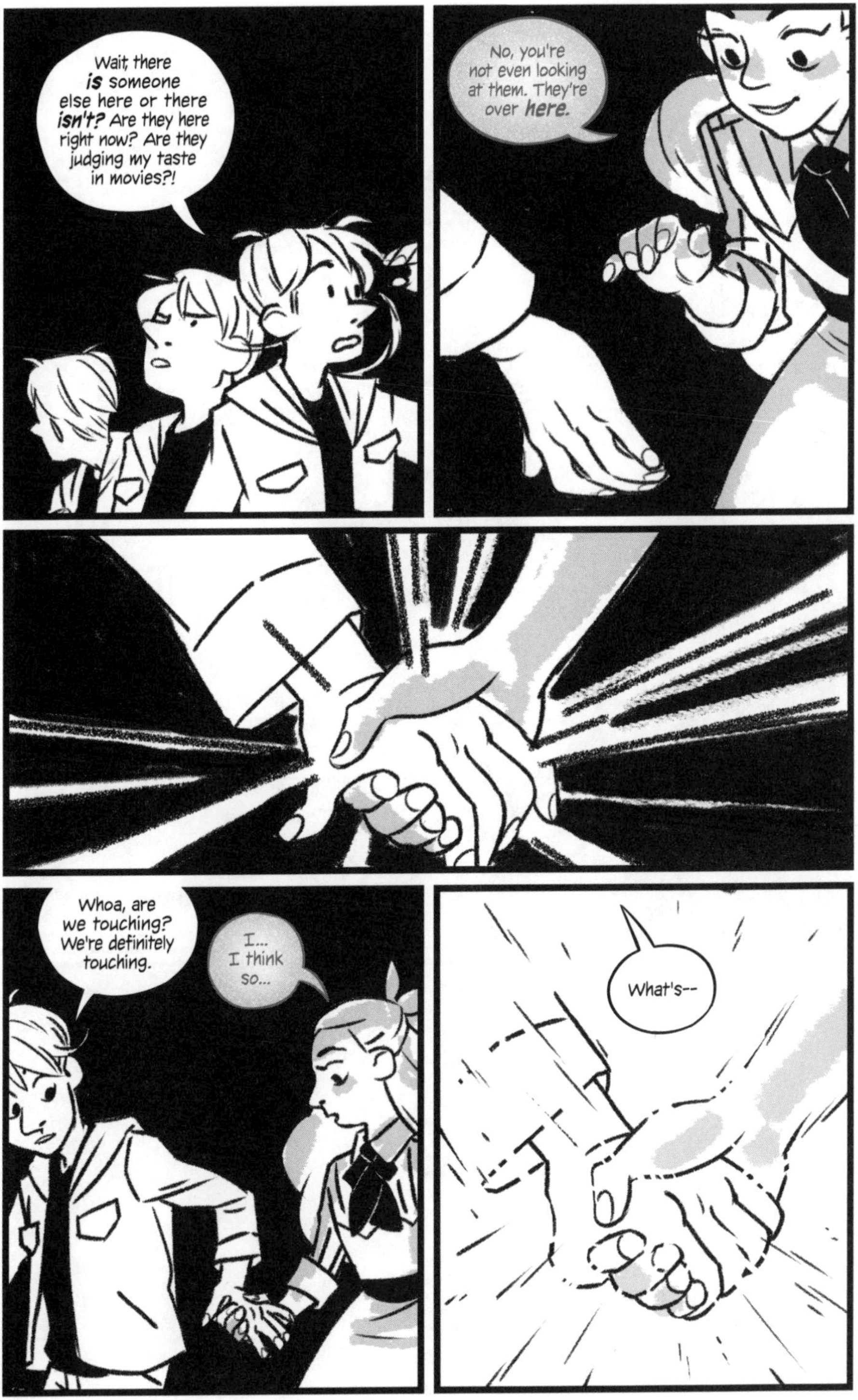
Wait, there is someone else here or there isn't? Are they here right now? Are they judging my taste in movies?!
No, you're not even looking at them. They're over here.
Whoa, are we touching? We're definitely touching.
I... I think so...
What's--

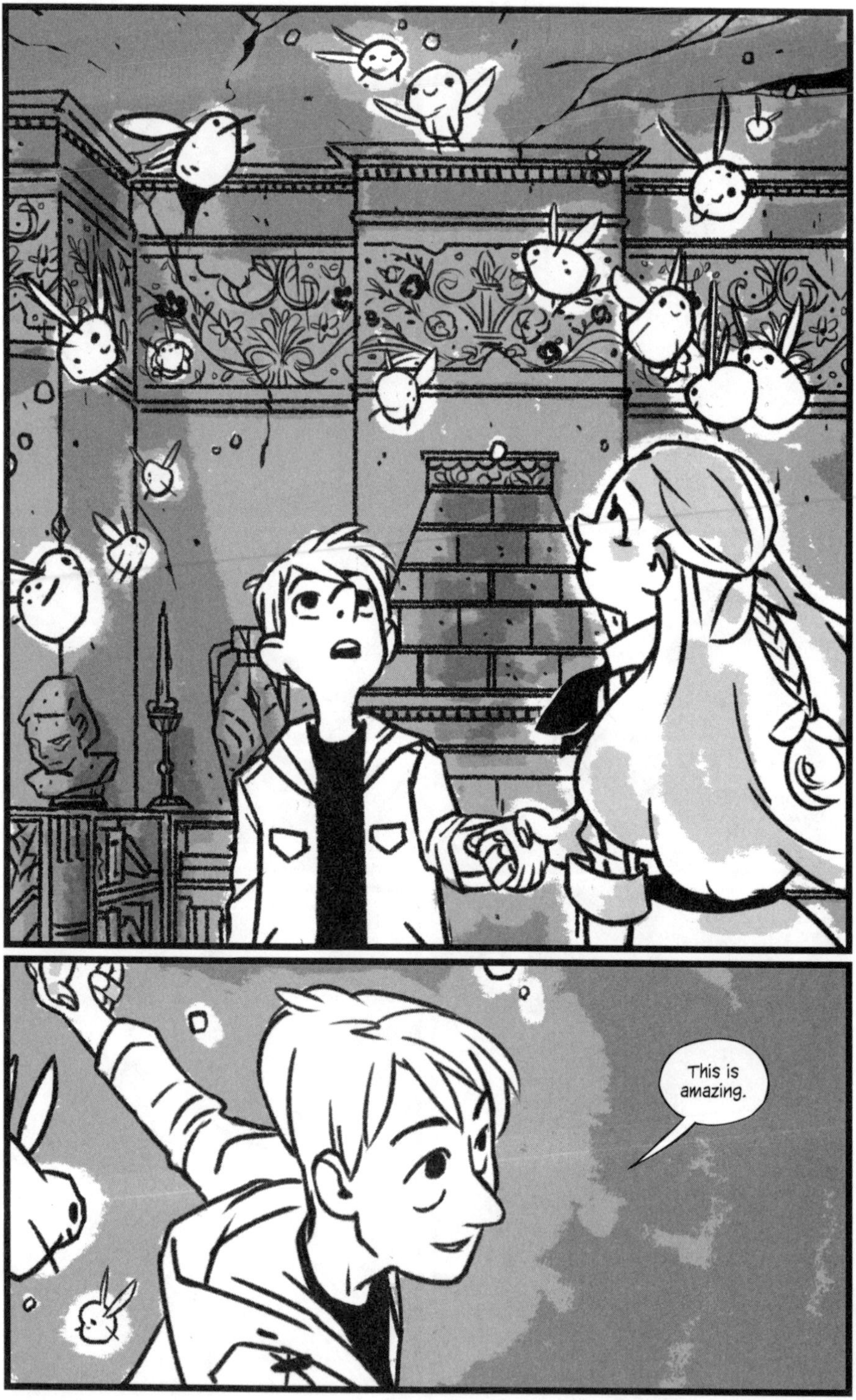
This is amazing.

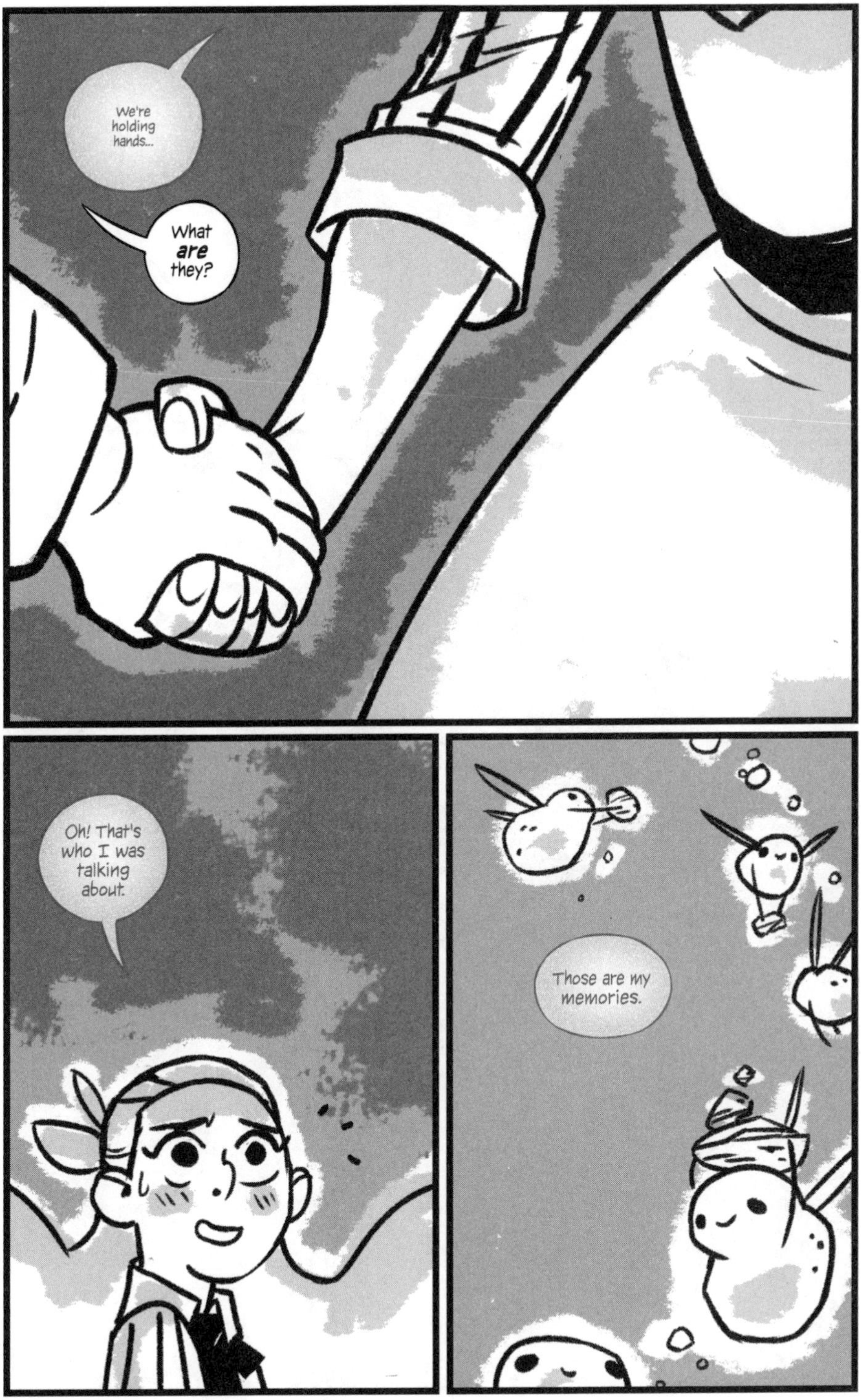
We're holding hands...
What **are** they?
Oh! That's who I was talking about.
Those are my memories.

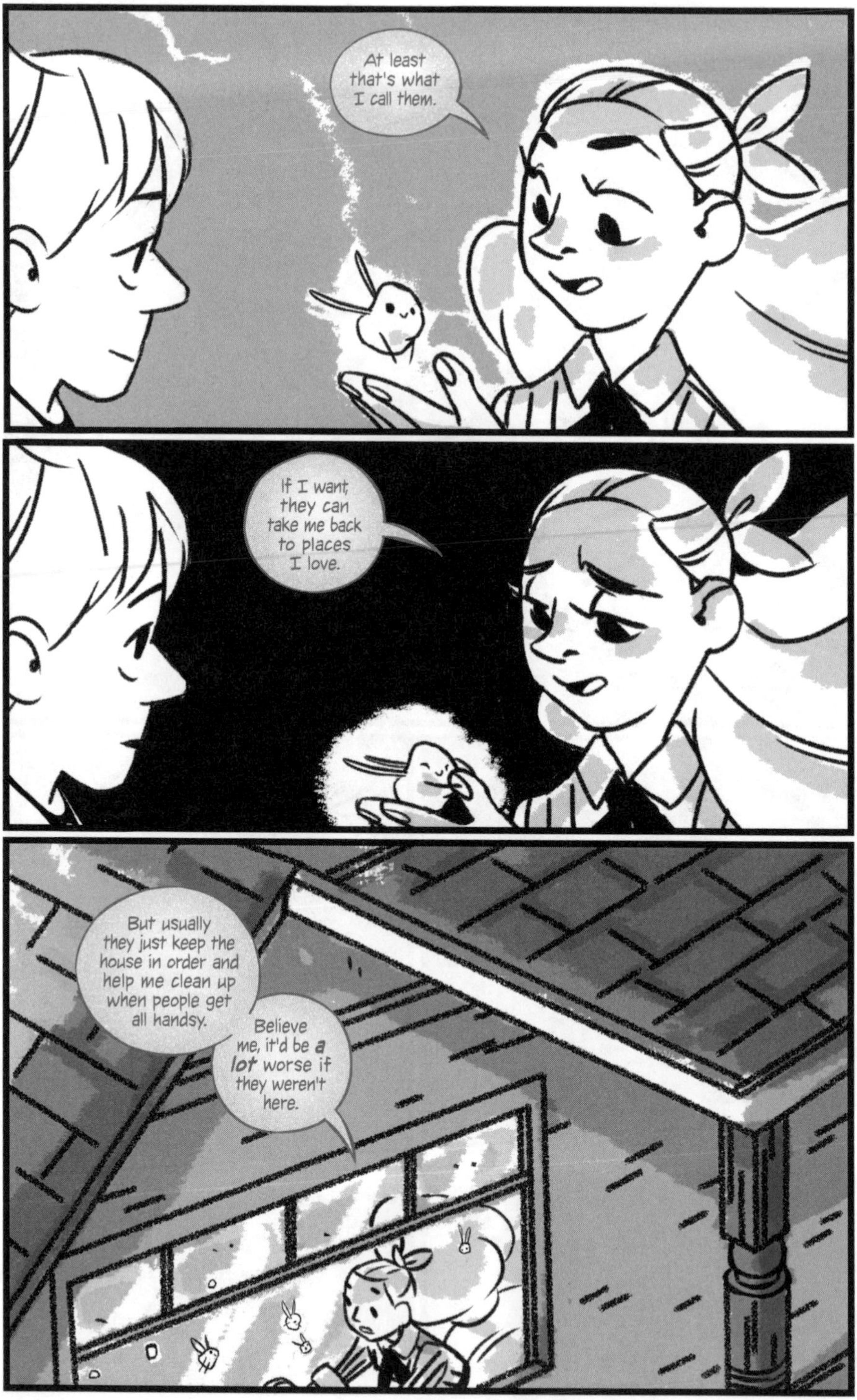
At least that's what I call them.
If I want, they can take me back to places I love.
But usually they just keep the house in order and help me clean up when people get all handsy.
Believe me, it'd be **a lot** worse if they weren't here.

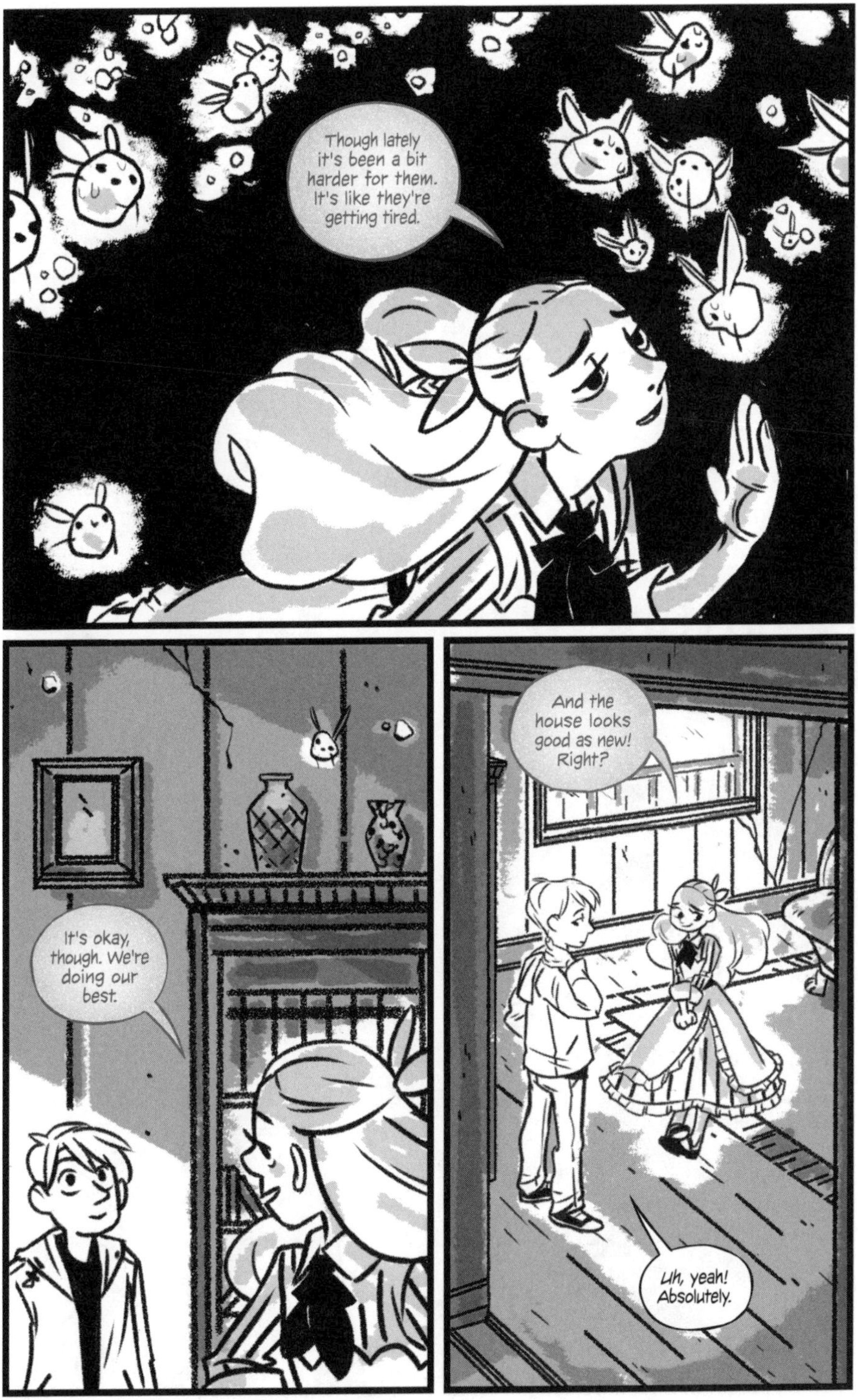
Though lately it's been a bit harder for them. It's like they're getting tired.
It's okay, though. We're doing our best.
And the house looks good as new! Right?
Uh, yeah! Absolutely.

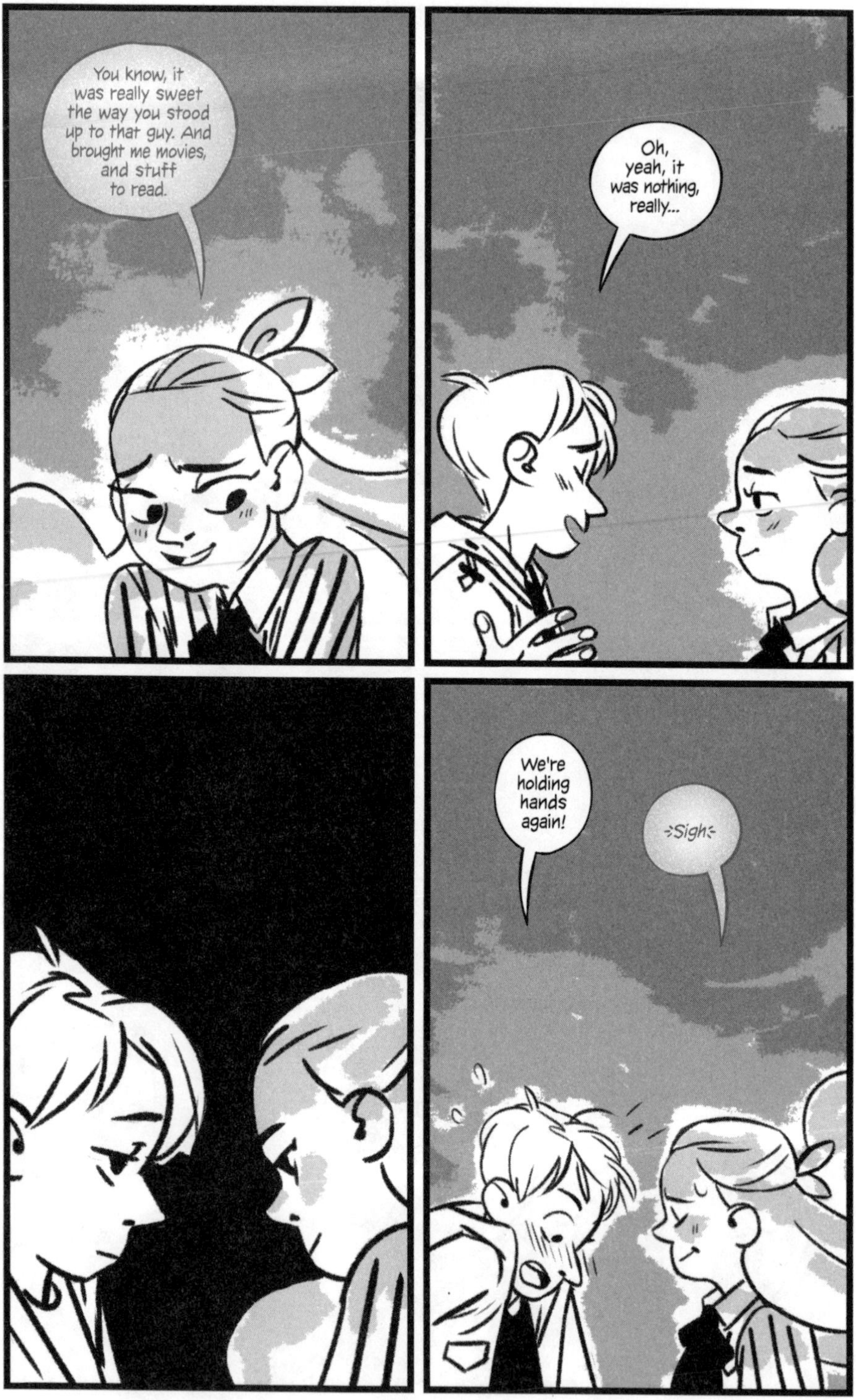
You know, it was really sweet the way you stood up to that guy. And brought me movies, and stuff to read.
Oh, yeah, it was nothing, really...
We're holding hands again!
Sigh

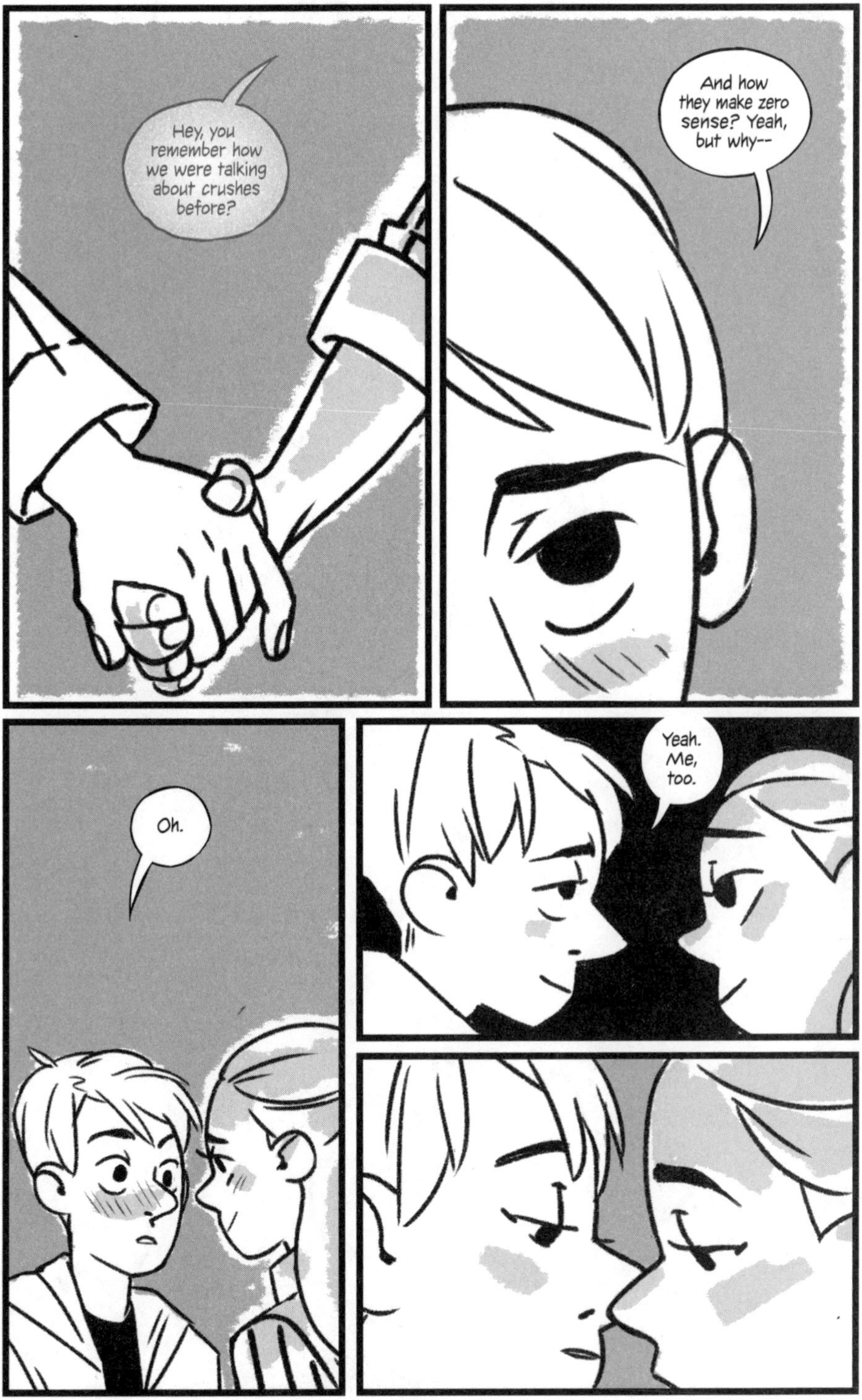
Hey, you remember how we were talking about crushes before?
And how they make zero sense? Yeah, but why--
Oh.
Yeah. Me, too.

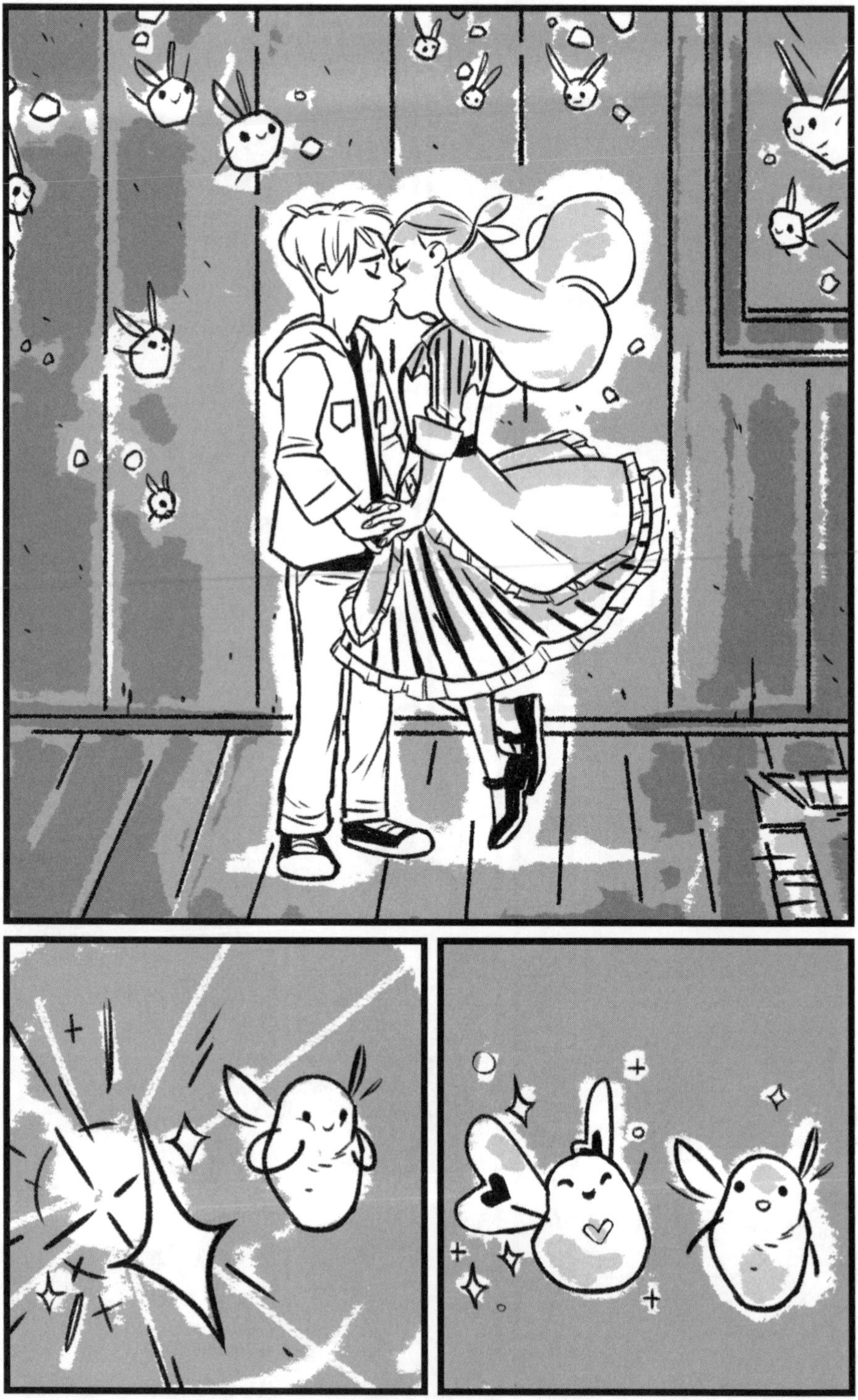

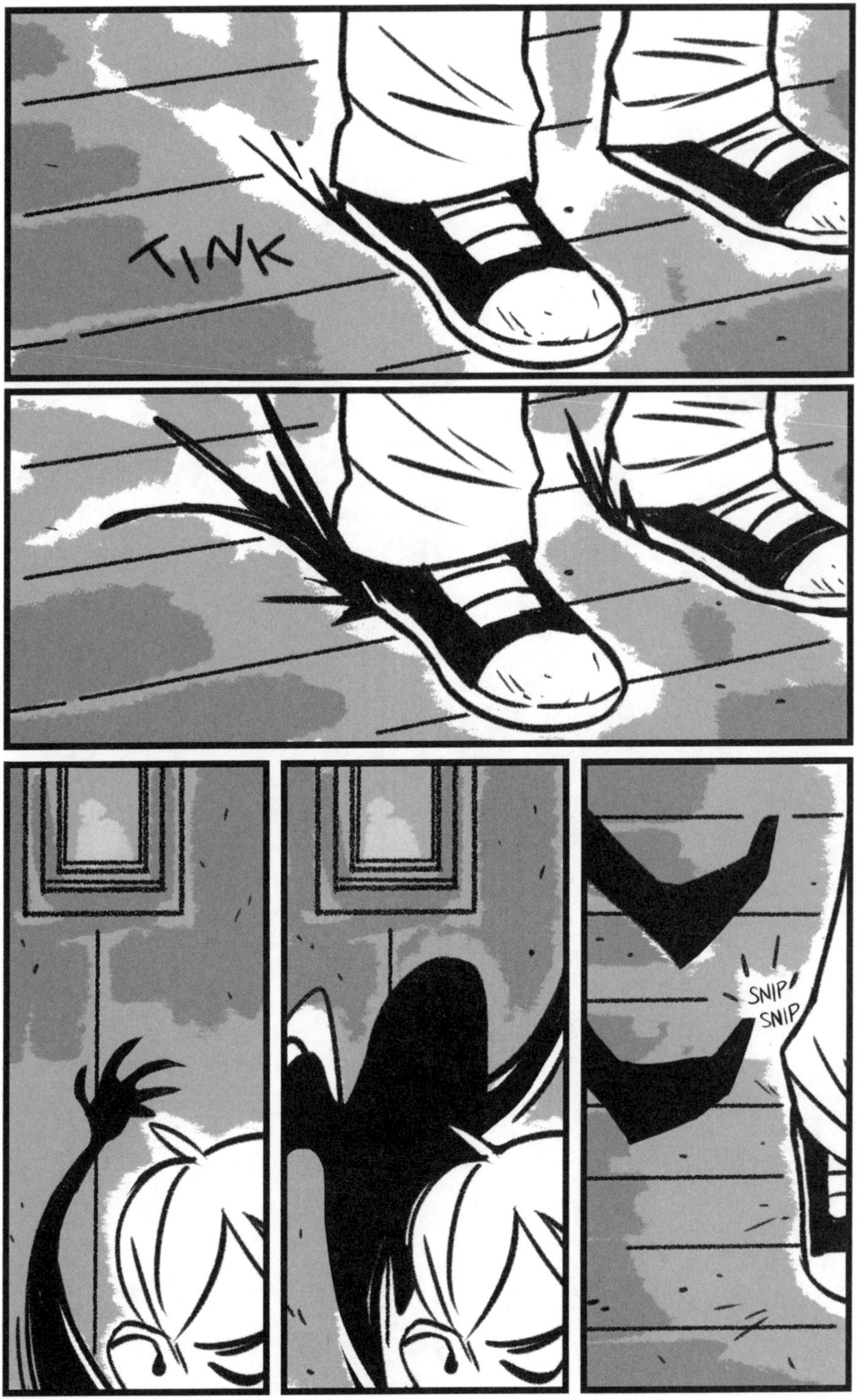
TINK
SNIP
SNIP

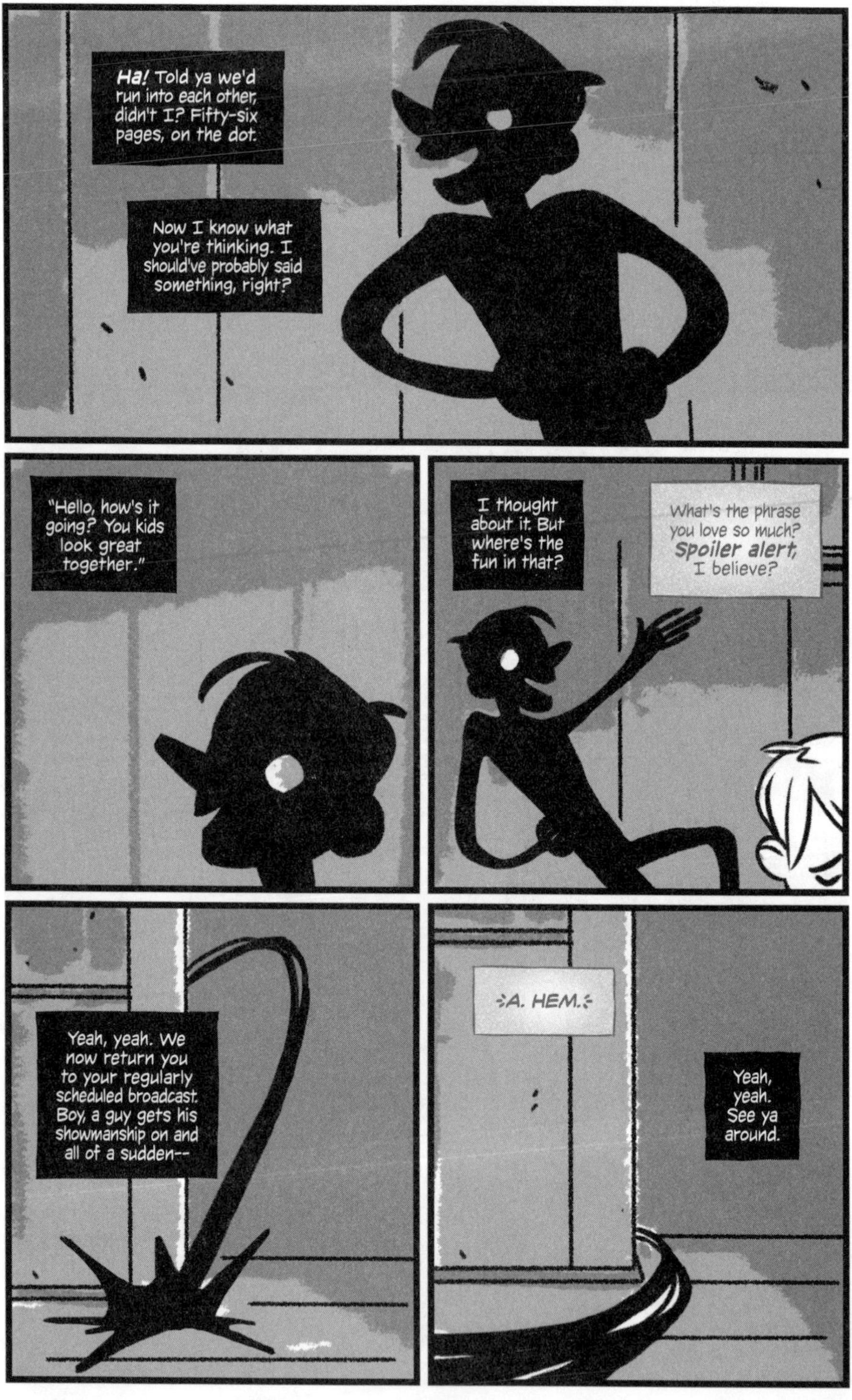

Ha! Told ya we'd run into each other, didn't I? Fifty-six pages, on the dot.
Now I know what you're thinking. I should've probably said something, right?
"Hello, how's it going? You kids look great together."
I thought about it. But where's the fun in that?
What's the phrase you love so much? Spoiler alert, I believe?
Yeah, yeah. We now return you to your regularly scheduled broadcast. Boy, a guy gets his showmanship on and all of a sudden--
A. HEM.
Yeah, yeah. See ya around.

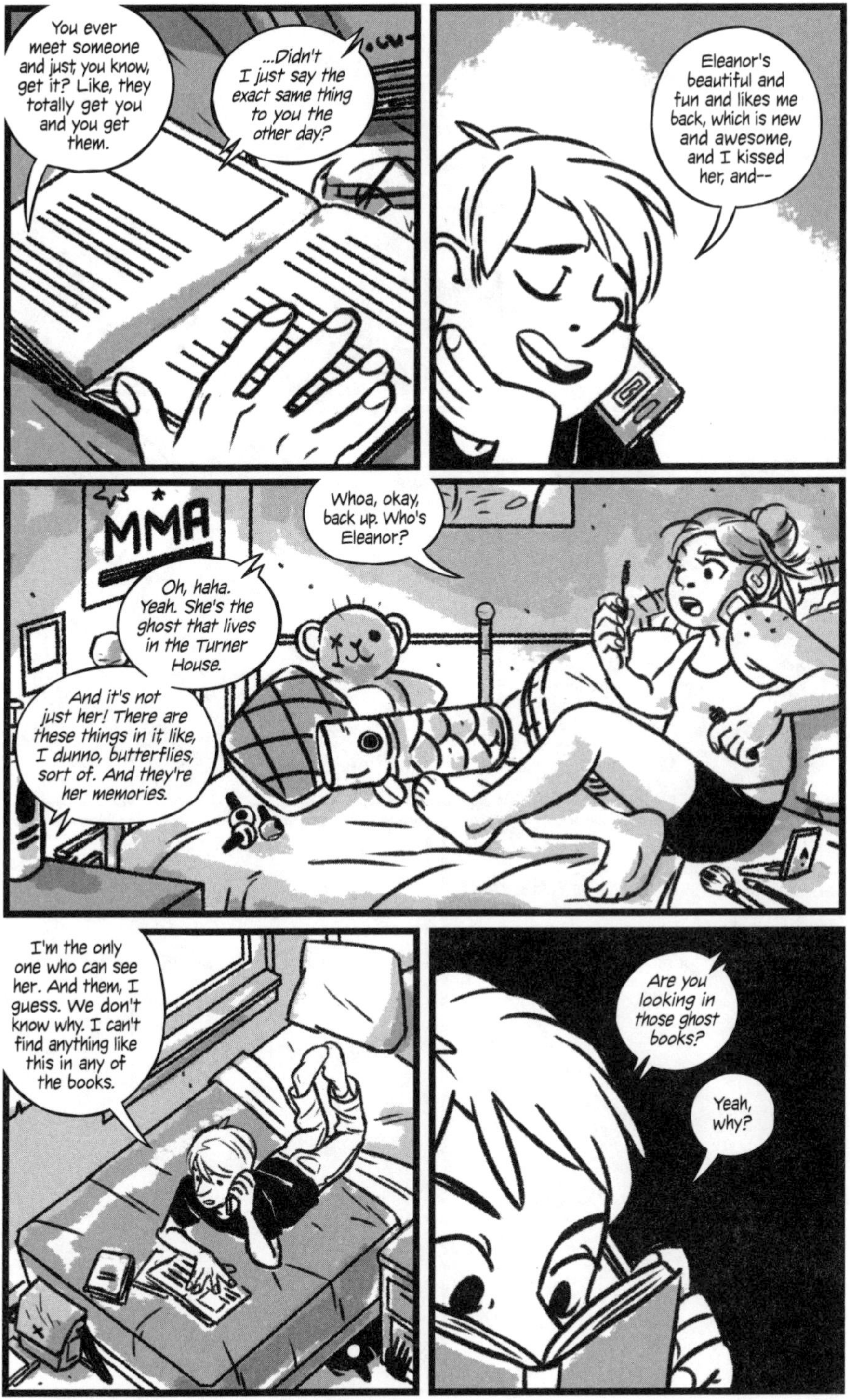
You ever meet someone and just, you know, get it? Like, they totally get you and you get them.
...Didn't I just say the exact same thing to you the other day?
Eleanor's beautiful and fun and likes me back, which is new and awesome, and I kissed her, and--
MMA
Whoa, okay, back up. Who's Eleanor?
Oh, haha. Yeah. She's the ghost that lives in the Turner House.
And it's not just her! There are these things in it like, I dunno, butterflies, sort of. And they're her memories.
I'm the only one who can see her. And them, I guess. We don't know why. I can't find anything like this in any of the books.
Are you looking in those ghost books?
Yeah, why?

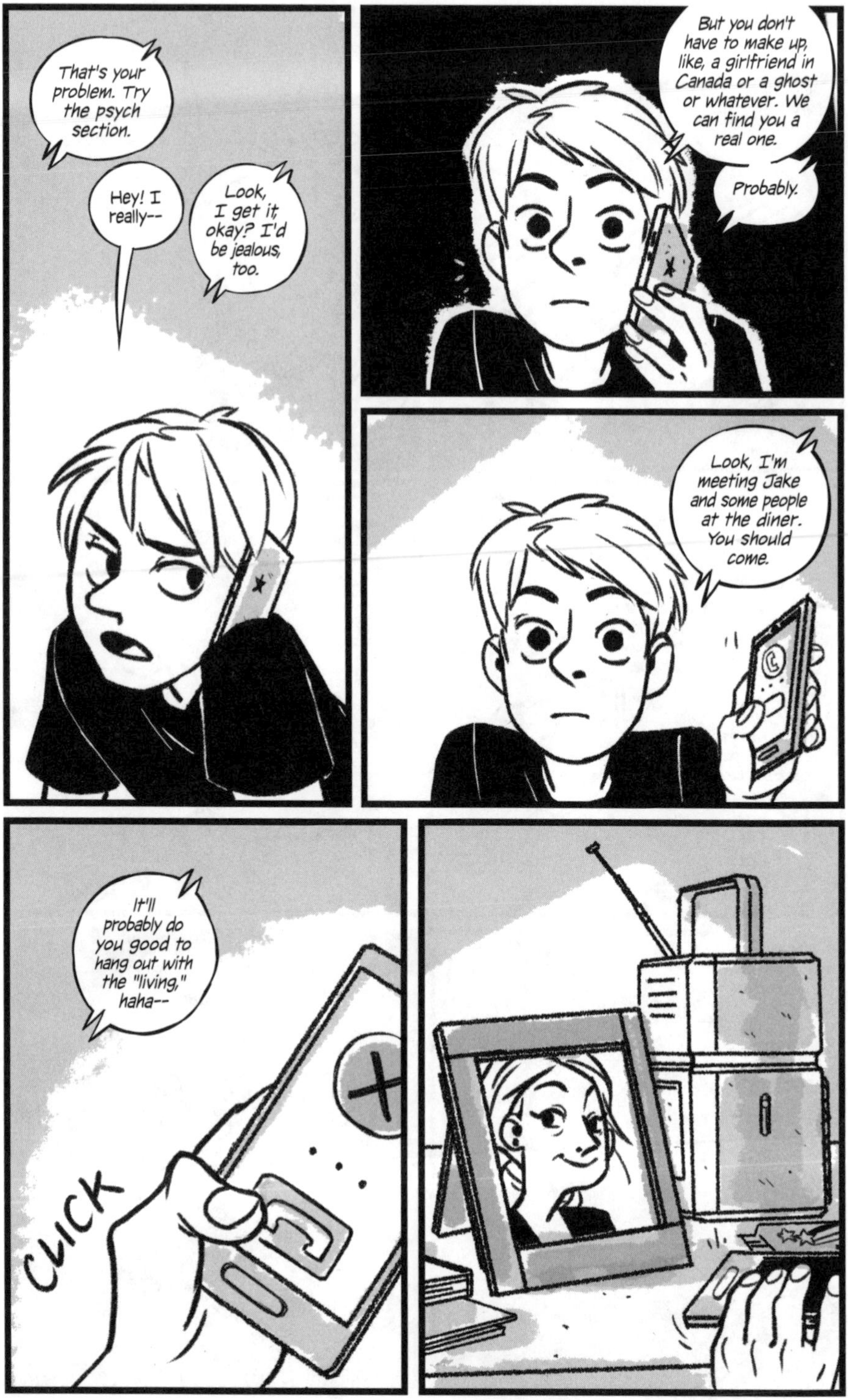
That's your problem. Try the psych section.
Hey! I really--
Look, I get it okay? I'd be jealous, too.
But you don't have to make up, like, a girlfriend in Canada or a ghost or whatever. We can find you a real one.
Probably.
Look, I'm meeting Jake and some people at the diner. You should come.
It'll probably do you good to hang out with the "living," haha--
CLICK

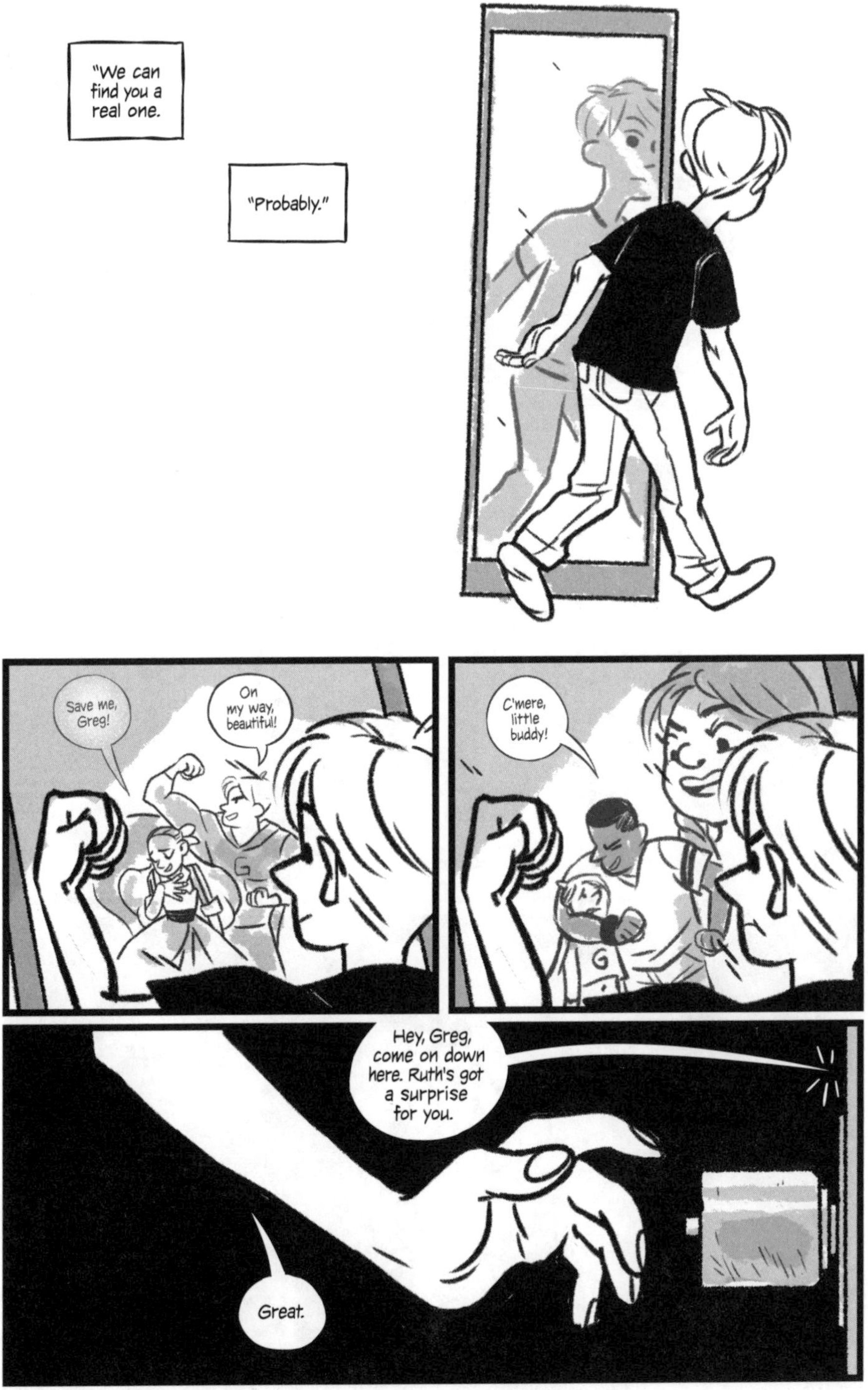
"We can find you a real one.
"Probably."
Save me, Greg!
On my way, beautiful!
C'mere, little buddy!
Hey, Greg, come on down here. Ruth's got a surprise for you.
Great.

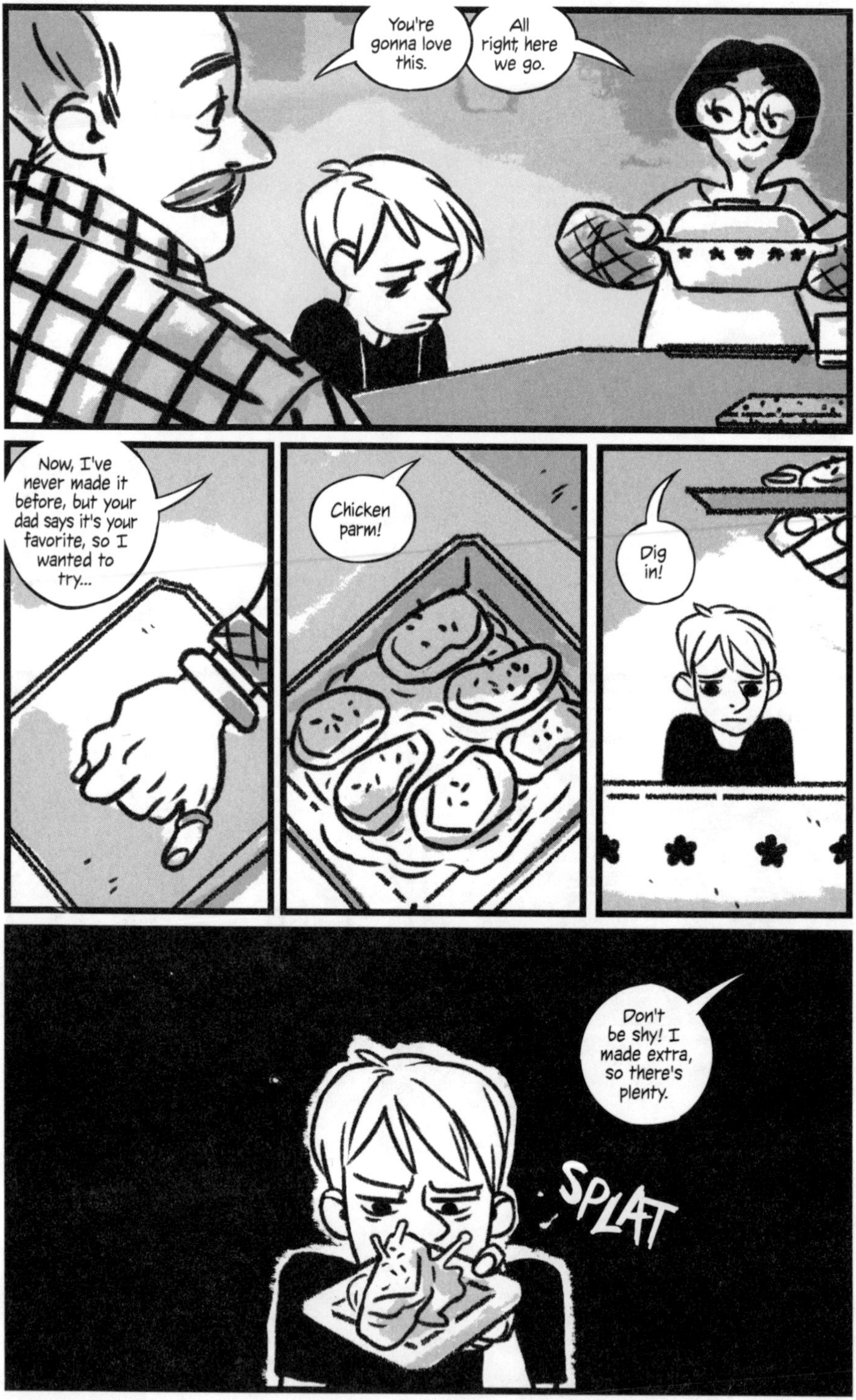
You're gonna love this.
All right, here we go.
Now, I've never made it before, but your dad says it's your favorite, so I wanted to try...
Chicken parm!
Dig in!
Don't be shy! I made extra, so there's plenty.
SPLAT

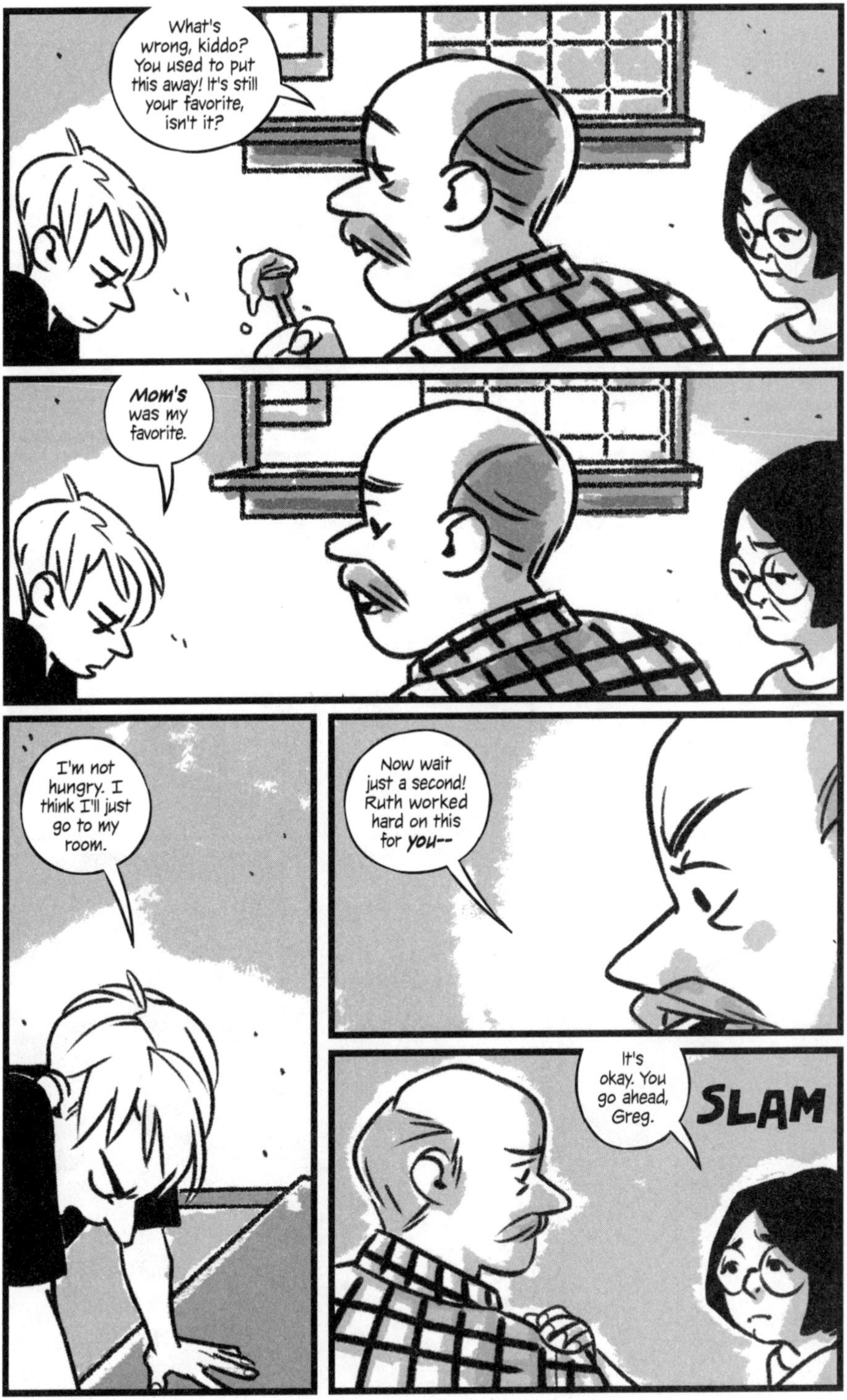
What's wrong, kiddo? You used to put this away! It's still your favorite, isn't it?
Mom's was my favorite.
I'm not hungry. I think I'll just go to my room.
Now wait just a second! Ruth worked hard on this for you--
It's okay. You go ahead, Greg.
SLAM

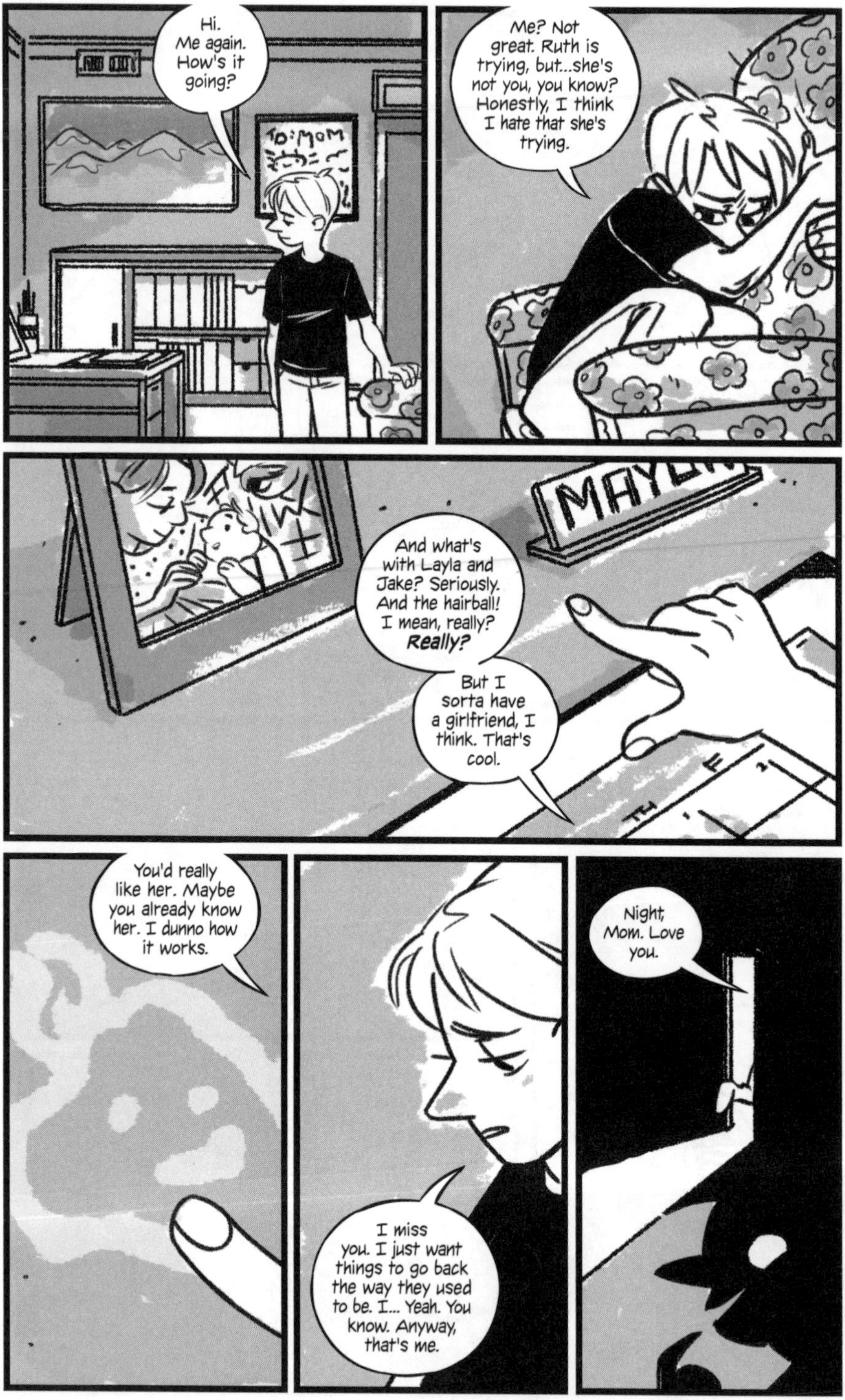
Hi.
Me again.
How's it going?
TO: MOM
Me? Not great. Ruth is trying, but...she's not you, you know? Honestly, I think I hate that she's trying.
MAYL
And what's with Layla and Jake? Seriously. And the hairball! I mean, really? ***Really?***
But I sorta have a girlfriend, I think. That's cool.
You'd really like her. Maybe you already know her. I dunno how it works.
I miss you. I just want things to go back the way they used to be. I... Yeah. You know. Anyway, that's me.
Night, Mom. Love you.

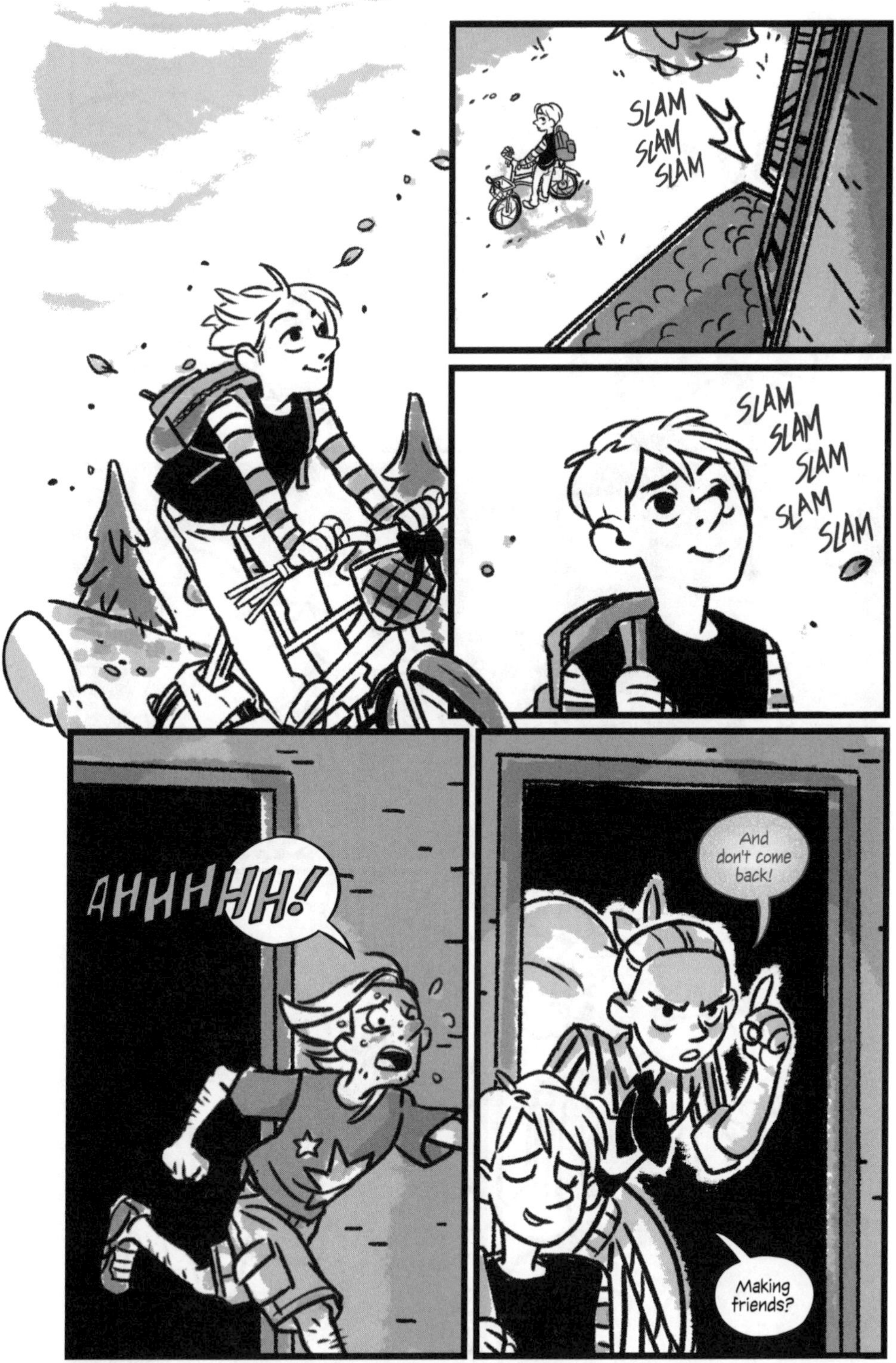

SLAM
SLAM
SLAM
SLAM
SLAM
SLAM
SLAM
SLAM
AHHHHHH!
And don't come back!
Making friends?

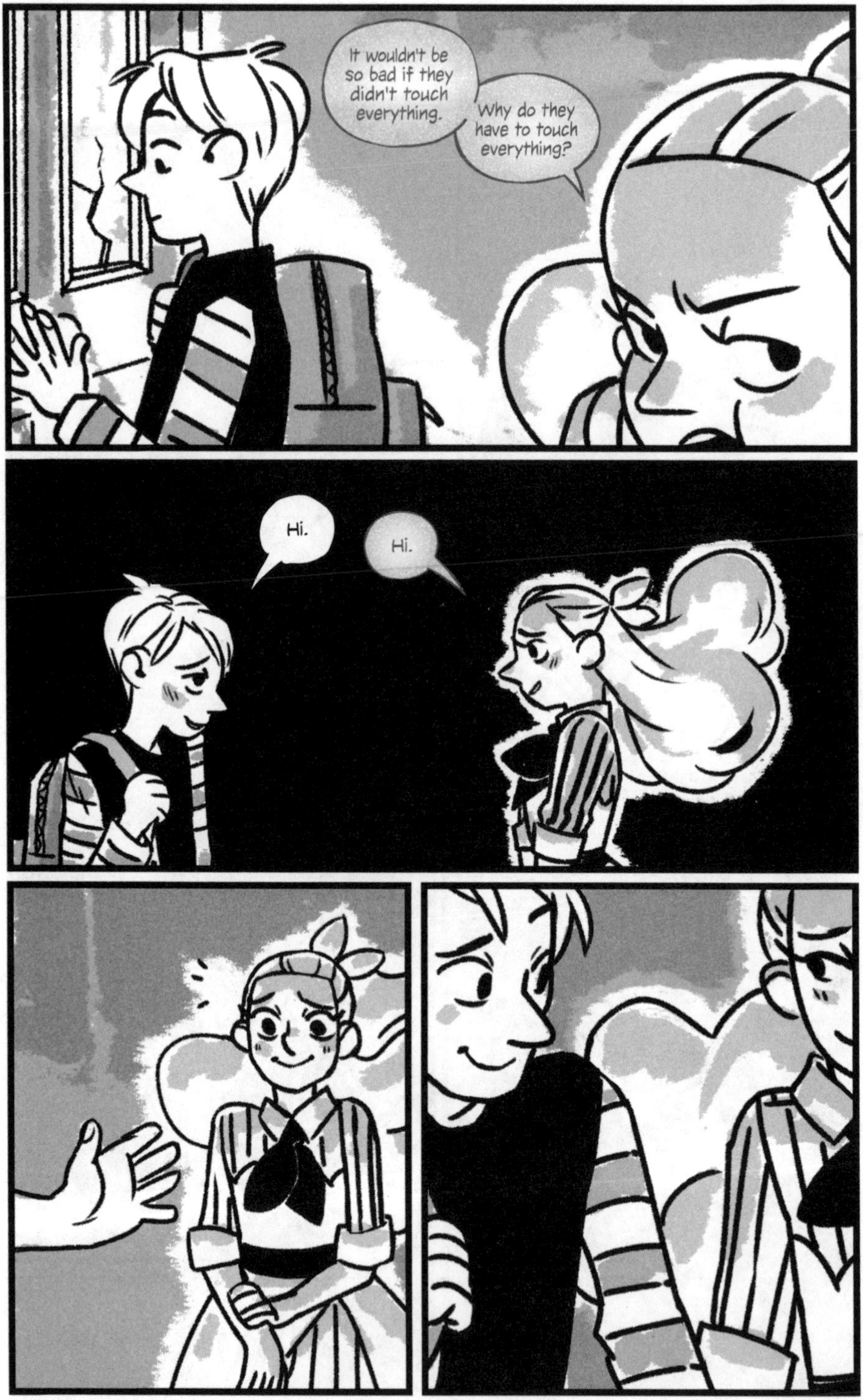

It wouldn't be so bad if they didn't touch everything.
Why do they have to touch everything?
Hi.
Hi.

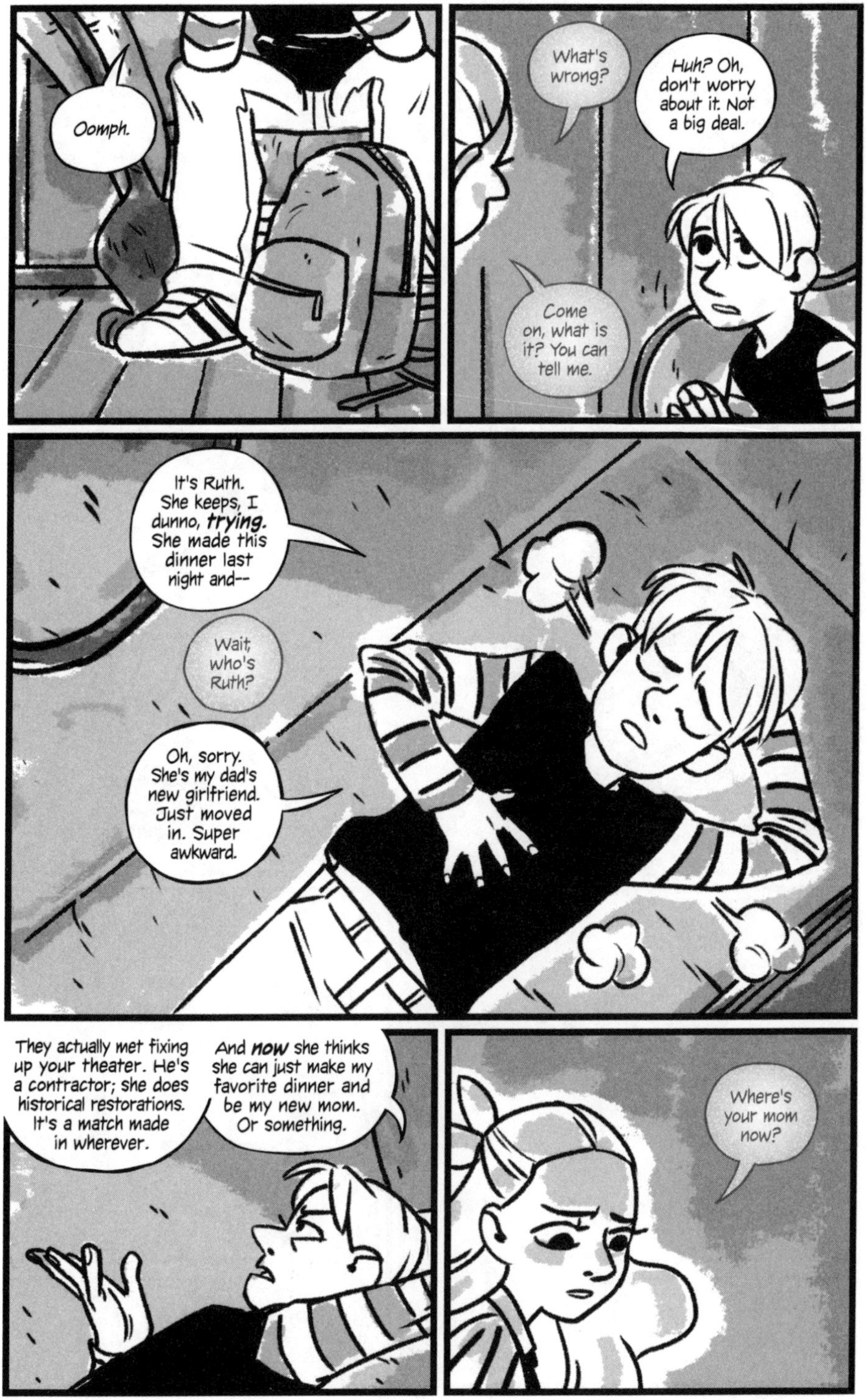
Oomph.
What's wrong?
Huh? Oh, don't worry about it. Not a big deal.
Come on, what is it? You can tell me.
It's Ruth. She keeps, I dunno, **trying.** She made this dinner last night and--
Wait, who's Ruth?
Oh, sorry. She's my dad's new girlfriend. Just moved in. Super awkward.
They actually met fixing up your theater. He's a contractor; she does historical restorations. It's a match made in wherever.
And **now** she thinks she can just make my favorite dinner and be my new mom. Or something.
Where's your mom now?

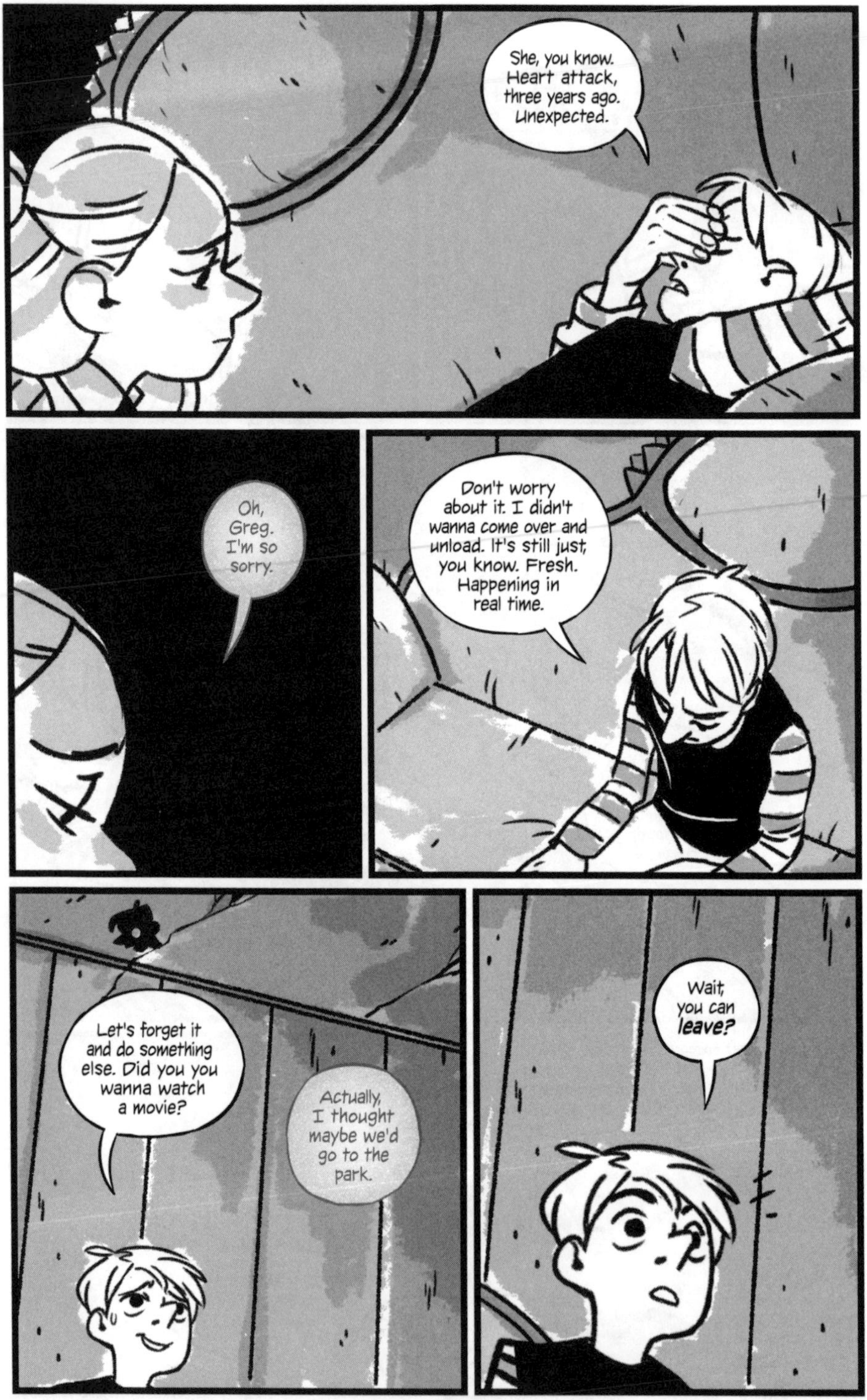
She, you know. Heart attack, three years ago. Unexpected.
Oh, Greg. I'm so sorry.
Don't worry about it. I didn't wanna come over and unload. It's still just, you know. Fresh. Happening in real time.
Let's forget it and do something else. Did you you wanna watch a movie?
Actually, I thought maybe we'd go to the park.
Wait, you can ***leave?***

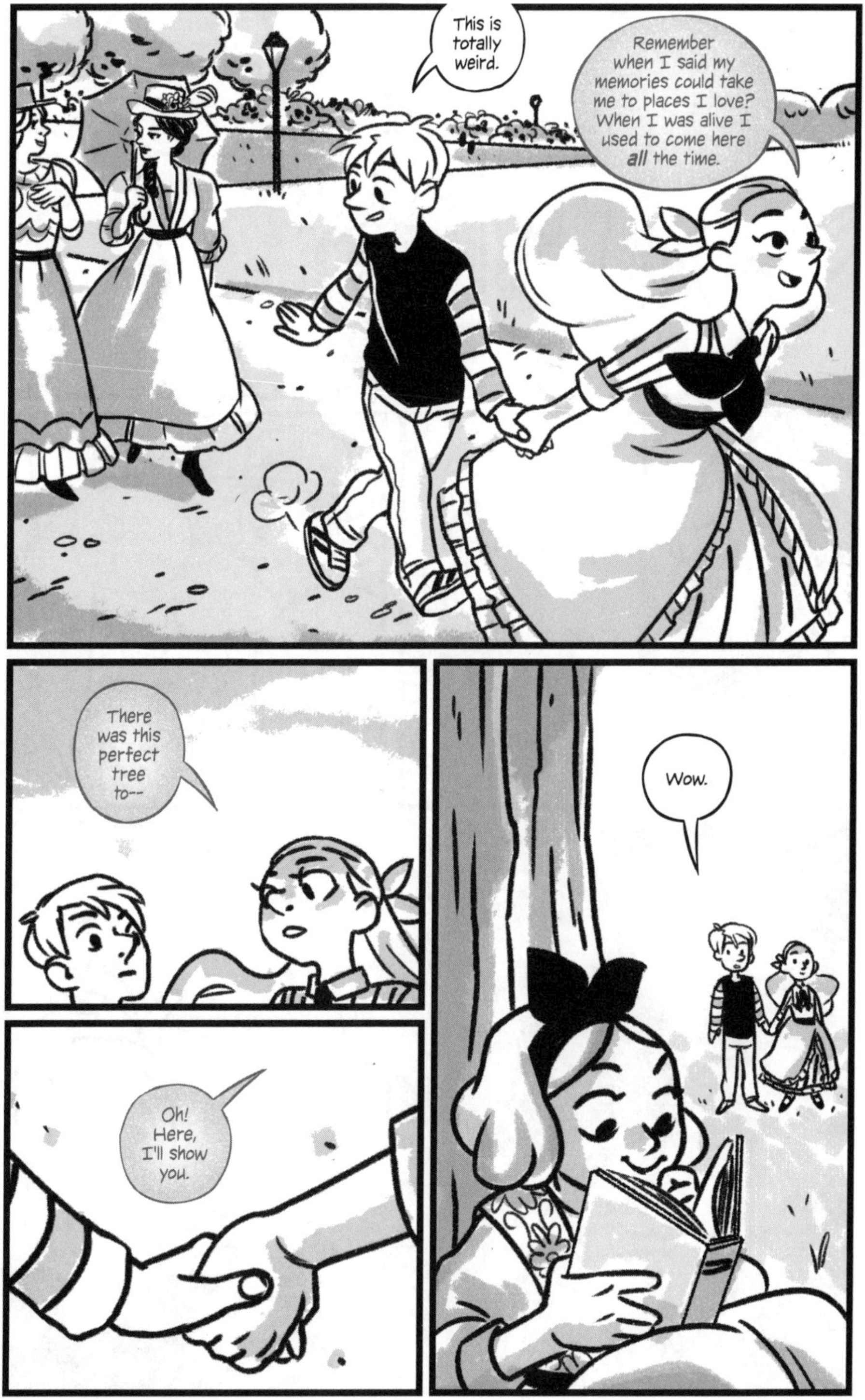
This is totally weird.
Remember when I said my memories could take me to places I love? When I was alive I used to come here *all* the time.
There was this perfect tree to--
Oh! Here, I'll show you.
Wow.

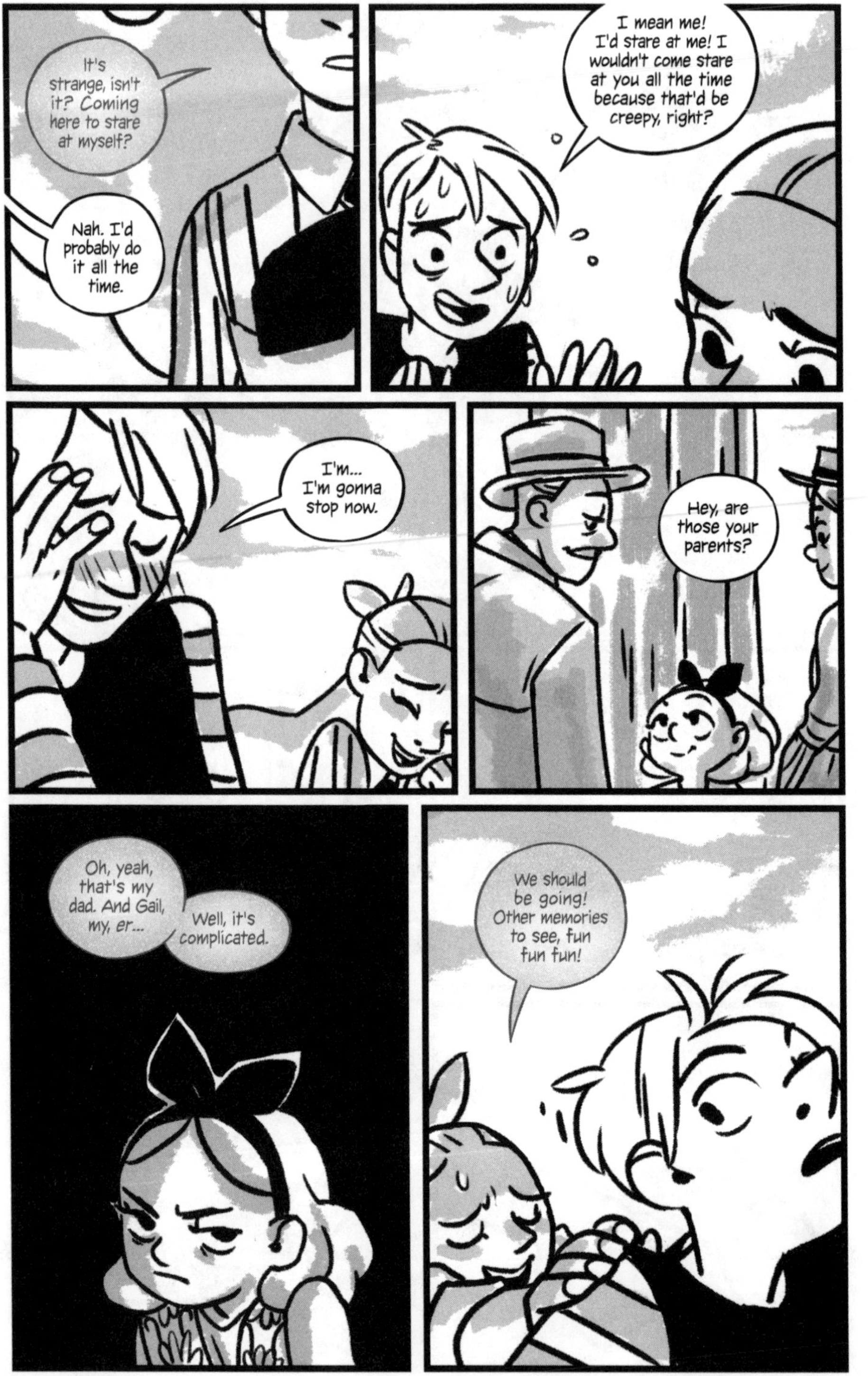
It's strange, isn't it? Coming here to stare at myself?
Nah. I'd probably do it all the time.
I mean me! I'd stare at me! I wouldn't come stare at you all the time because that'd be creepy, right?
I'm... I'm gonna stop now.
Hey, are those your parents?
Oh, yeah, that's my dad. And Gail, my, er...
Well, it's complicated.
We should be going! Other memories to see, fun fun fun!

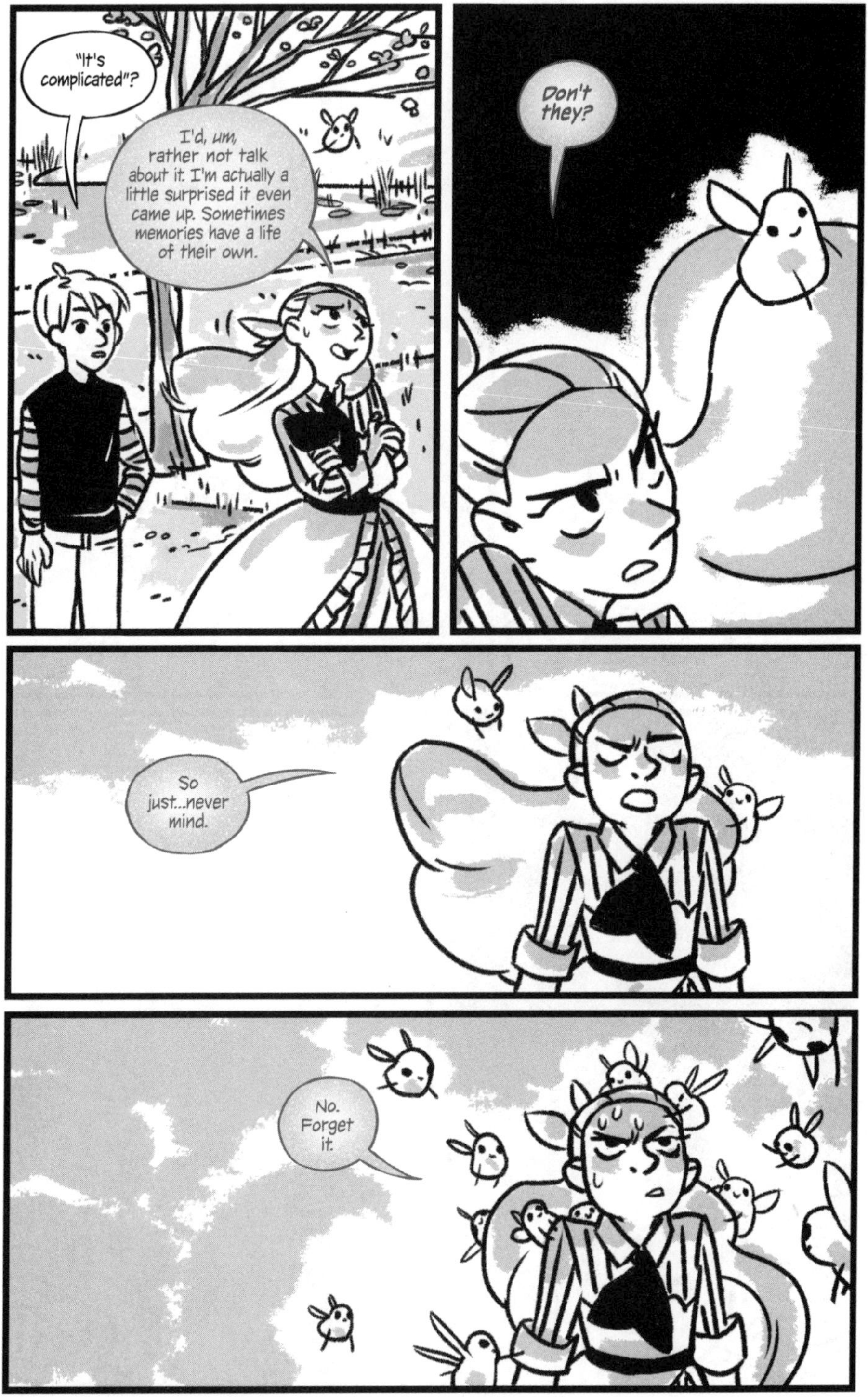
"It's complicated"?
I'd, um, rather not talk about it. I'm actually a little surprised it even came up. Sometimes memories have a life of their own.
Don't they?
So just...never mind.
No. Forget it.

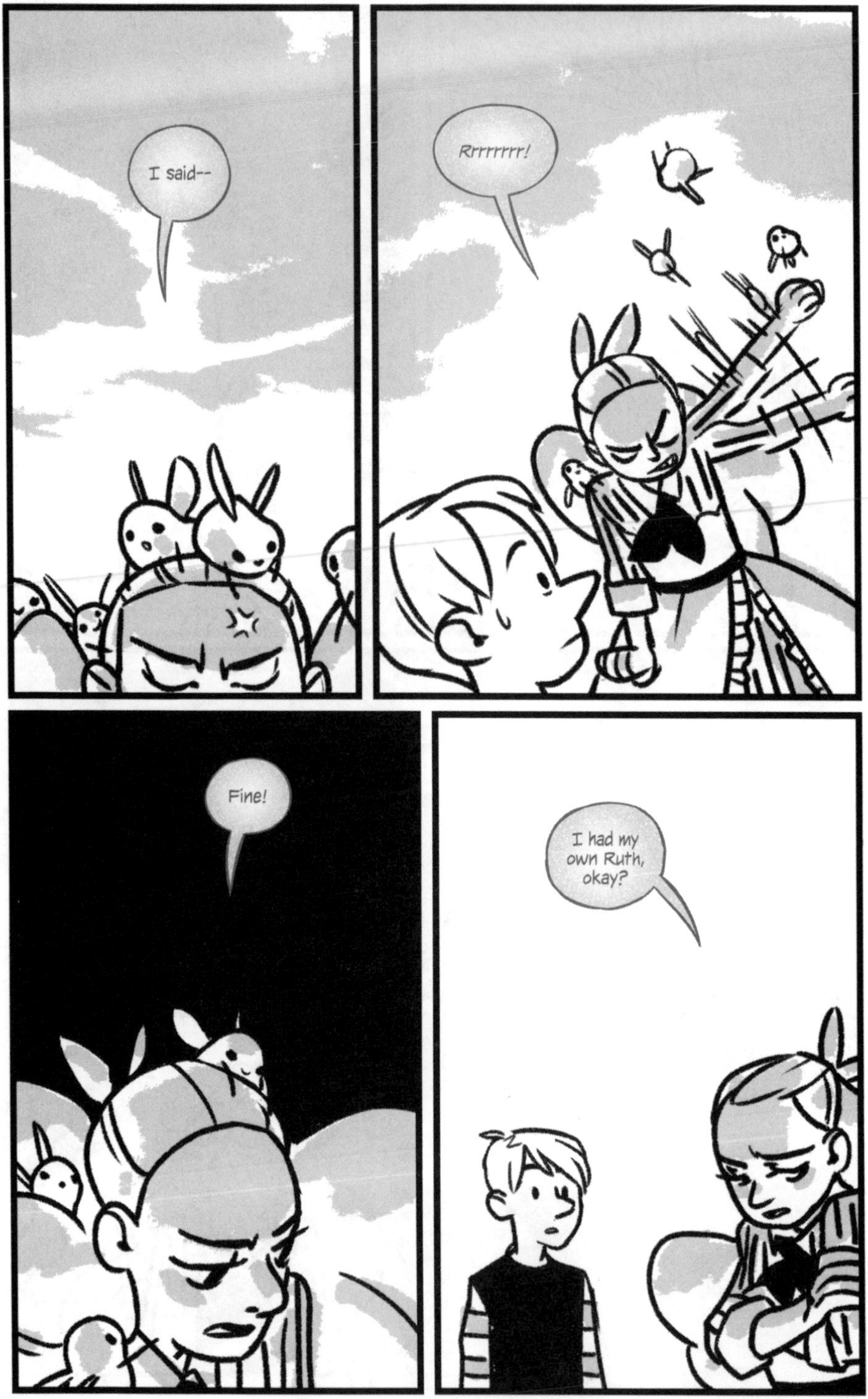
I said--
Rrrrrrrr!
Fine!
I had my own Ruth, okay?

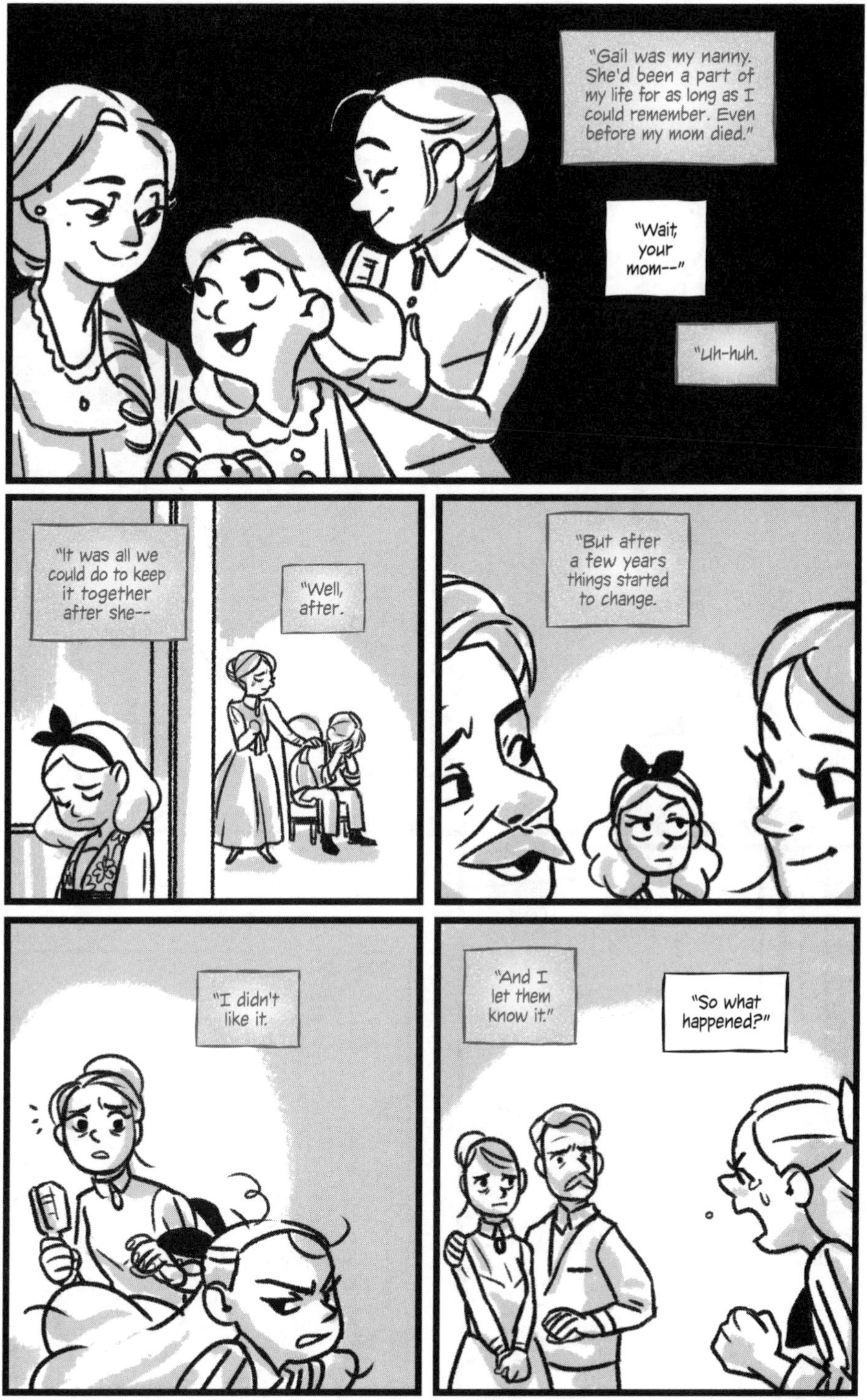
"Gail was my nanny. She'd been a part of my life for as long as I could remember. Even before my mom died."
"Wait, your mom--"
"Uh-huh.
"It was all we could do to keep it together after she--
"Well, after.
"But after a few years things started to change.
"I didn't like it.
"And I let them know it."
"So what happened?"

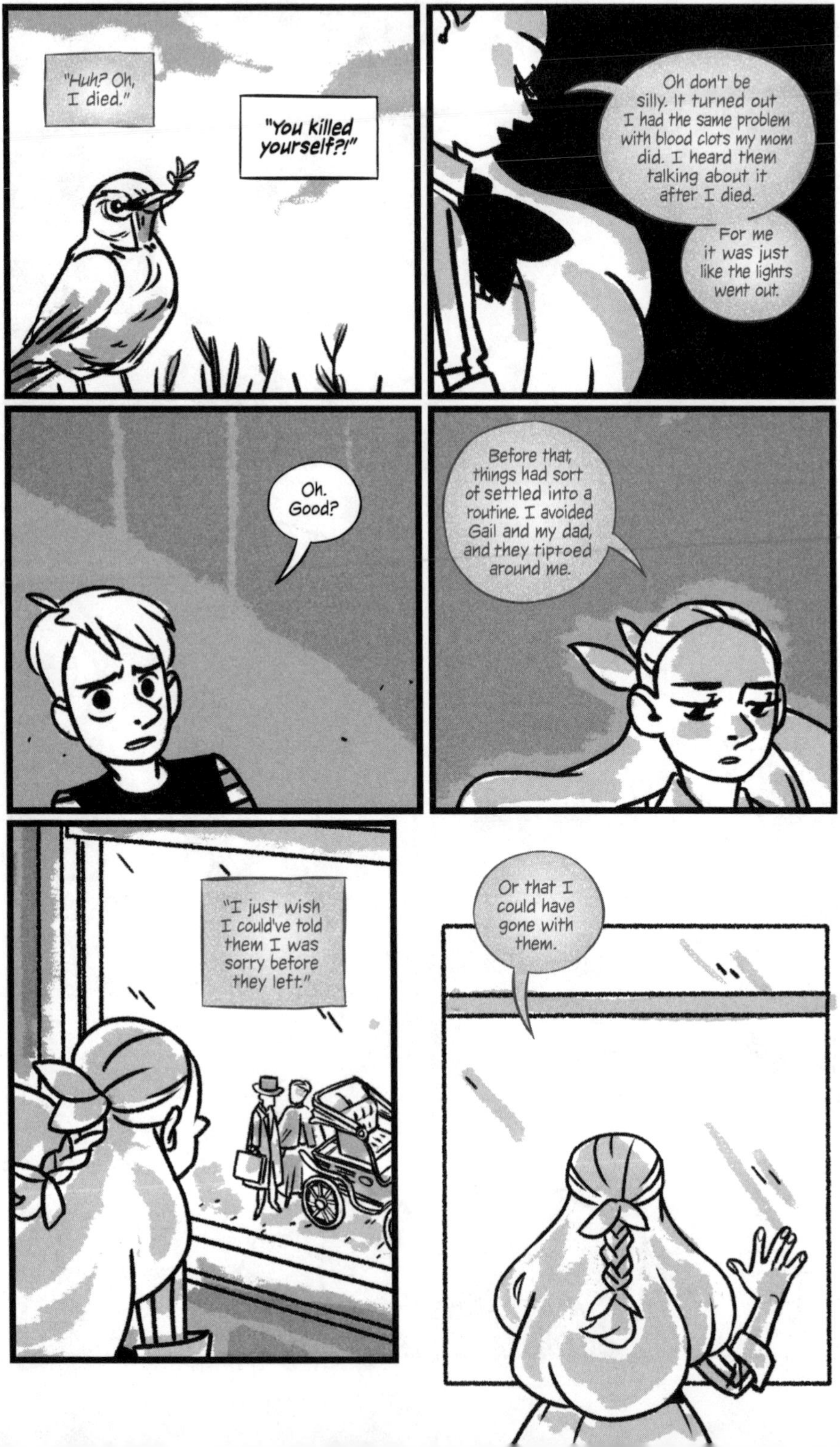
"Huh? Oh, I died."
"You killed yourself?!"
Oh don't be silly. It turned out I had the same problem with blood clots my mom did. I heard them talking about it after I died.
For me it was just like the lights went out.
Oh. Good?
Before that, things had sort of settled into a routine. I avoided Gail and my dad, and they tiptoed around me.
"I just wish I could've told them I was sorry before they left."
Or that I could have gone with them.

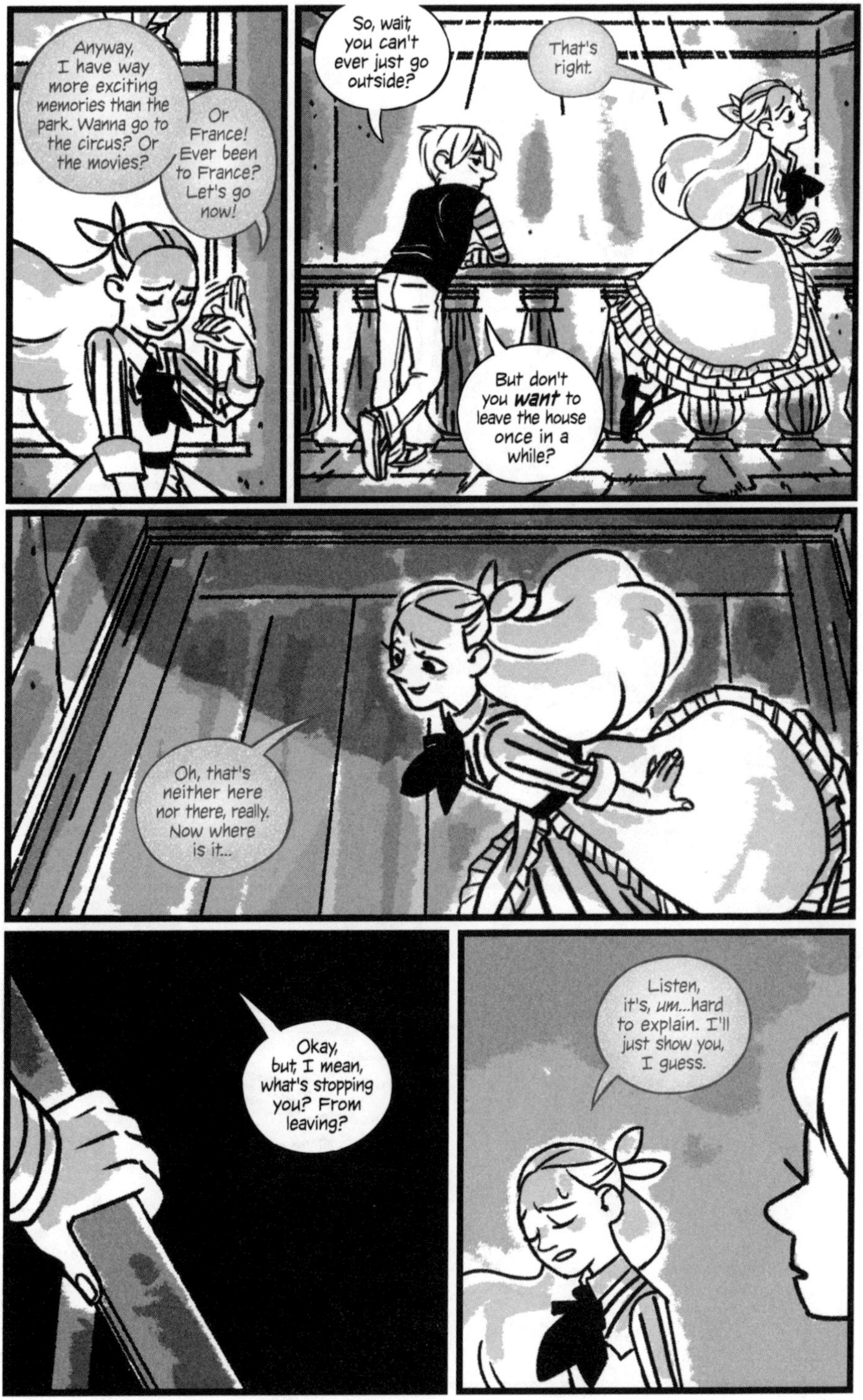
Anyway, I have way more exciting memories than the park. Wanna go to the circus? Or the movies?
Or France! Ever been to France? Let's go now!
So, wait, you can't ever just go outside?
That's right.
But don't you *want* to leave the house once in a while?
Oh, that's neither here nor there, really. Now where is it...
Okay, but, I mean, what's stopping you? From leaving?
Listen, it's, *um*...hard to explain. I'll just show you, I guess.

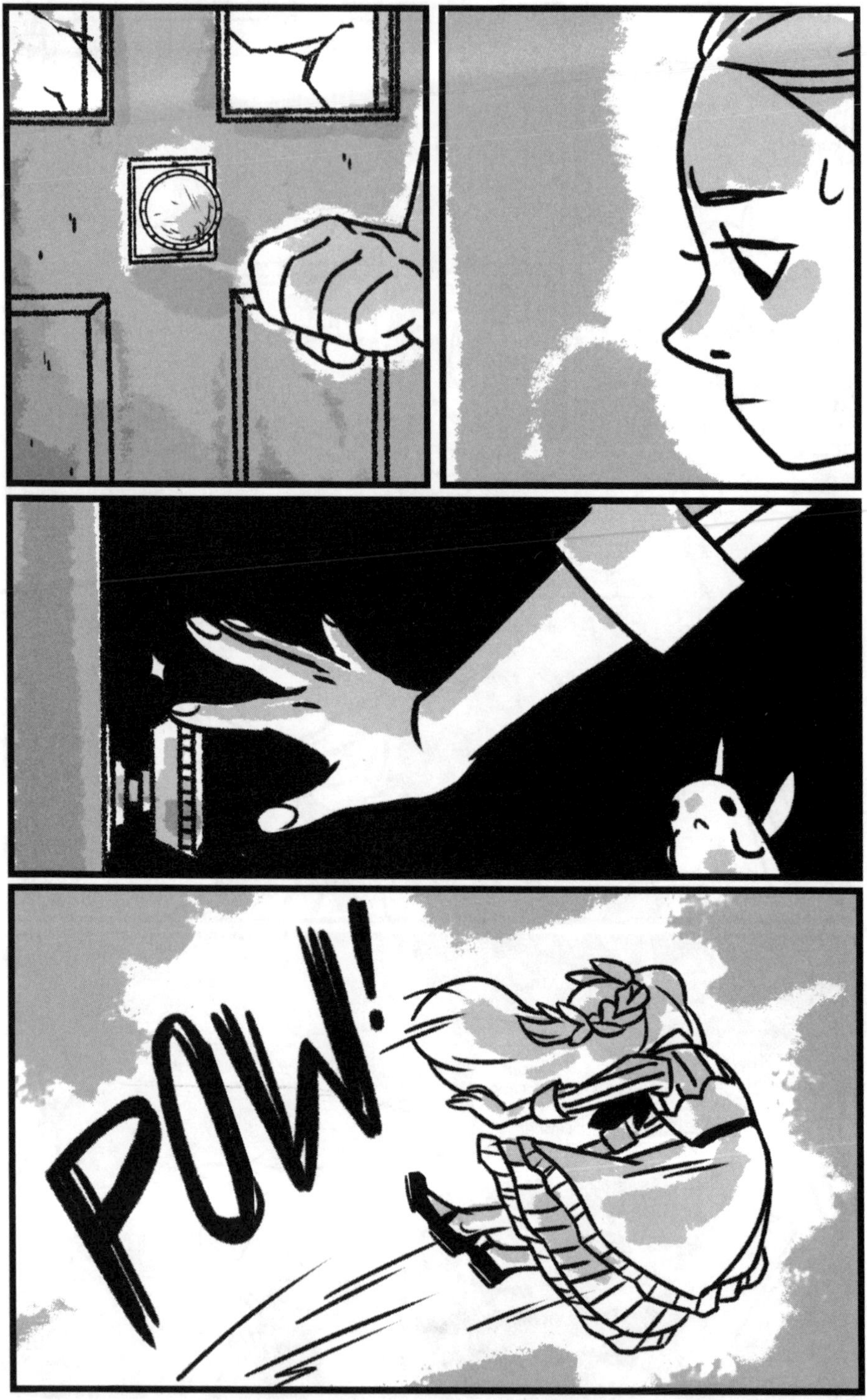
POW!

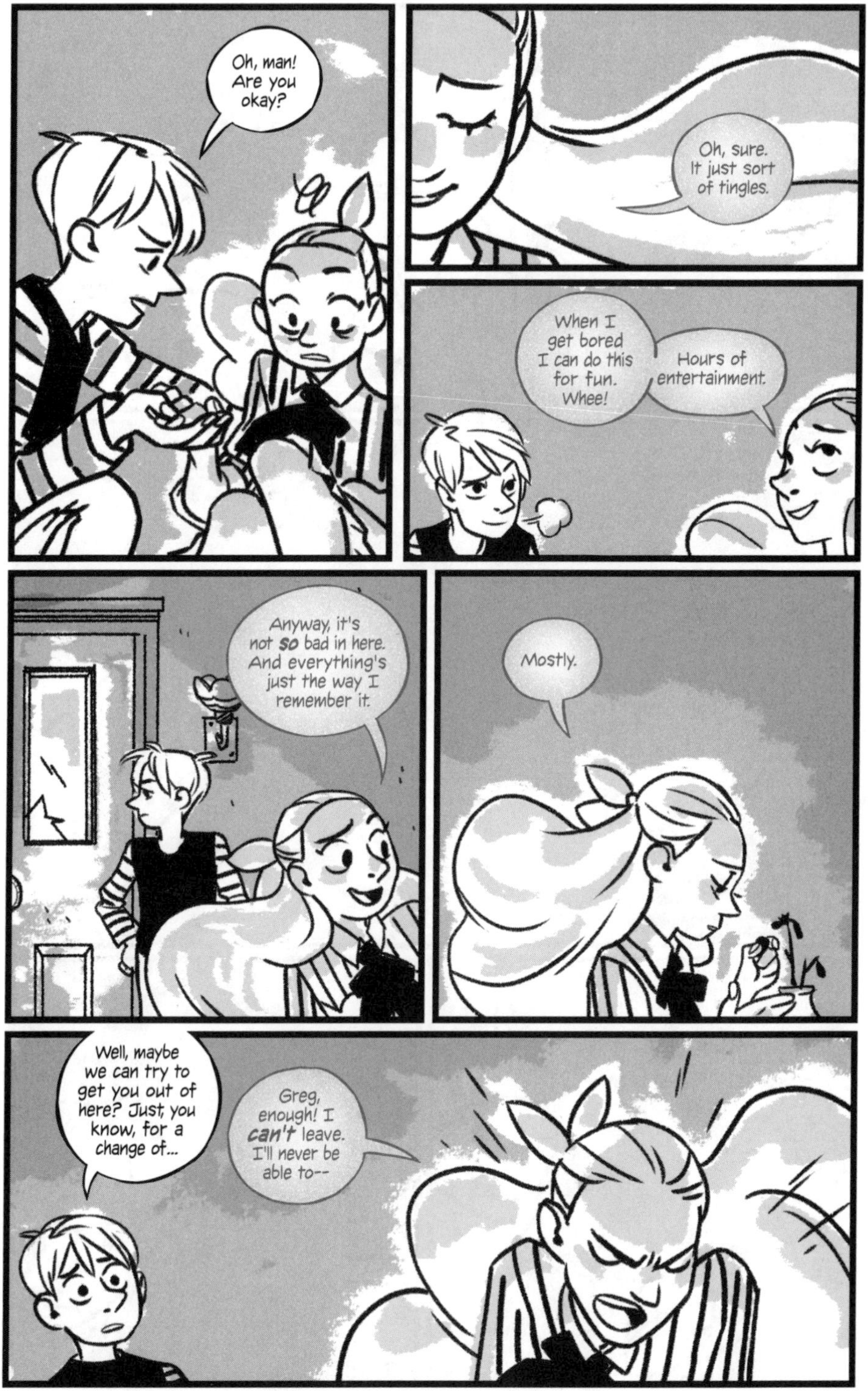
Oh, man! Are you okay?
Oh, sure. It just sort of tingles.
When I get bored I can do this for fun. Whee!
Hours of entertainment.
Anyway, it's not **so** bad in here. And everything's just the way I remember it.
Mostly.
Well, maybe we can try to get you out of here? Just, you know, for a change of...
Greg, enough! I **can't** leave. I'll never be able to--

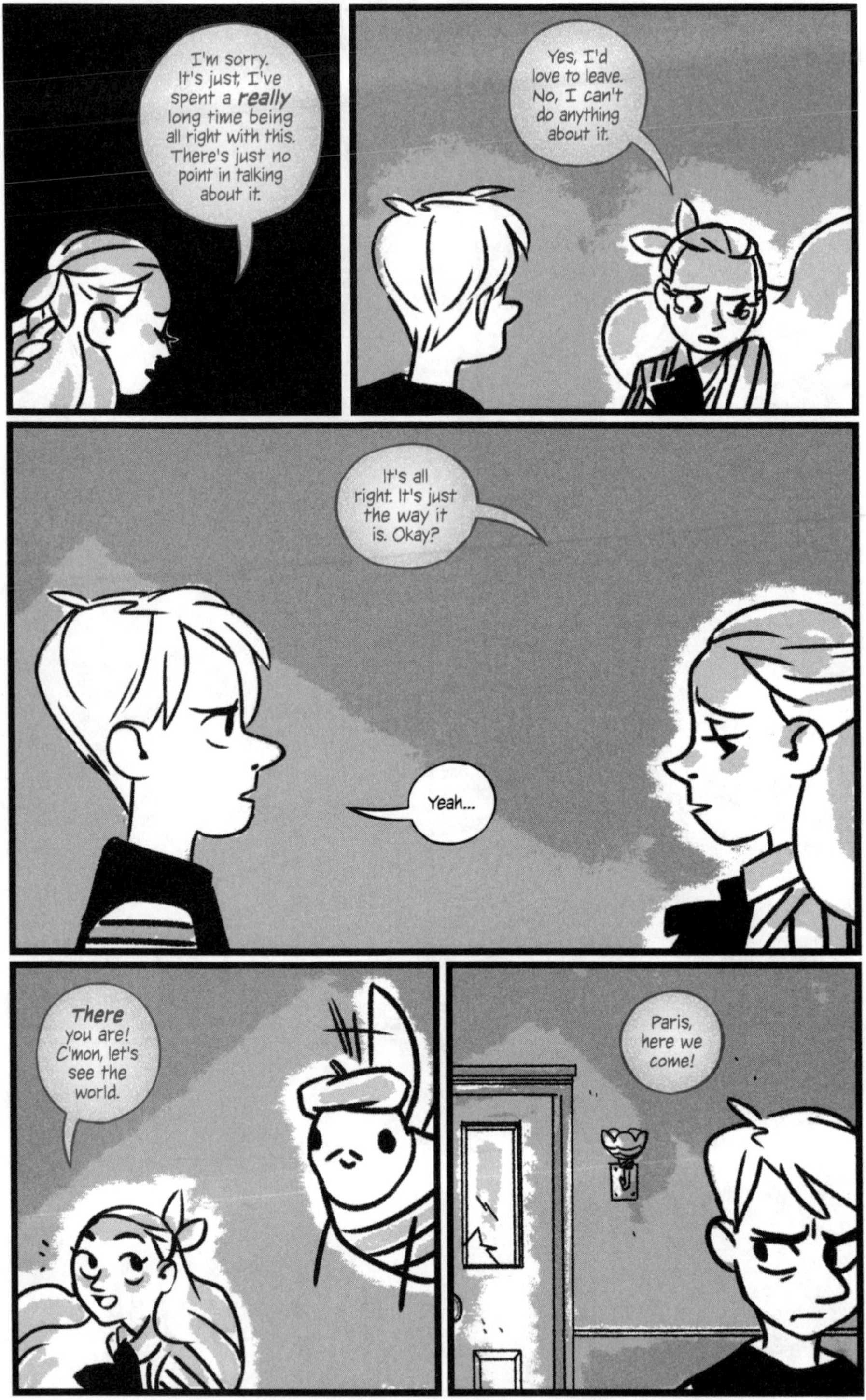
I'm sorry. It's just, I've spent a really long time being all right with this. There's just no point in talking about it.
Yes, I'd love to leave. No, I can't do anything about it.
It's all right. It's just the way it is. Okay?
Yeah...
There you are! C'mon, let's see the world.
Paris, here we come!

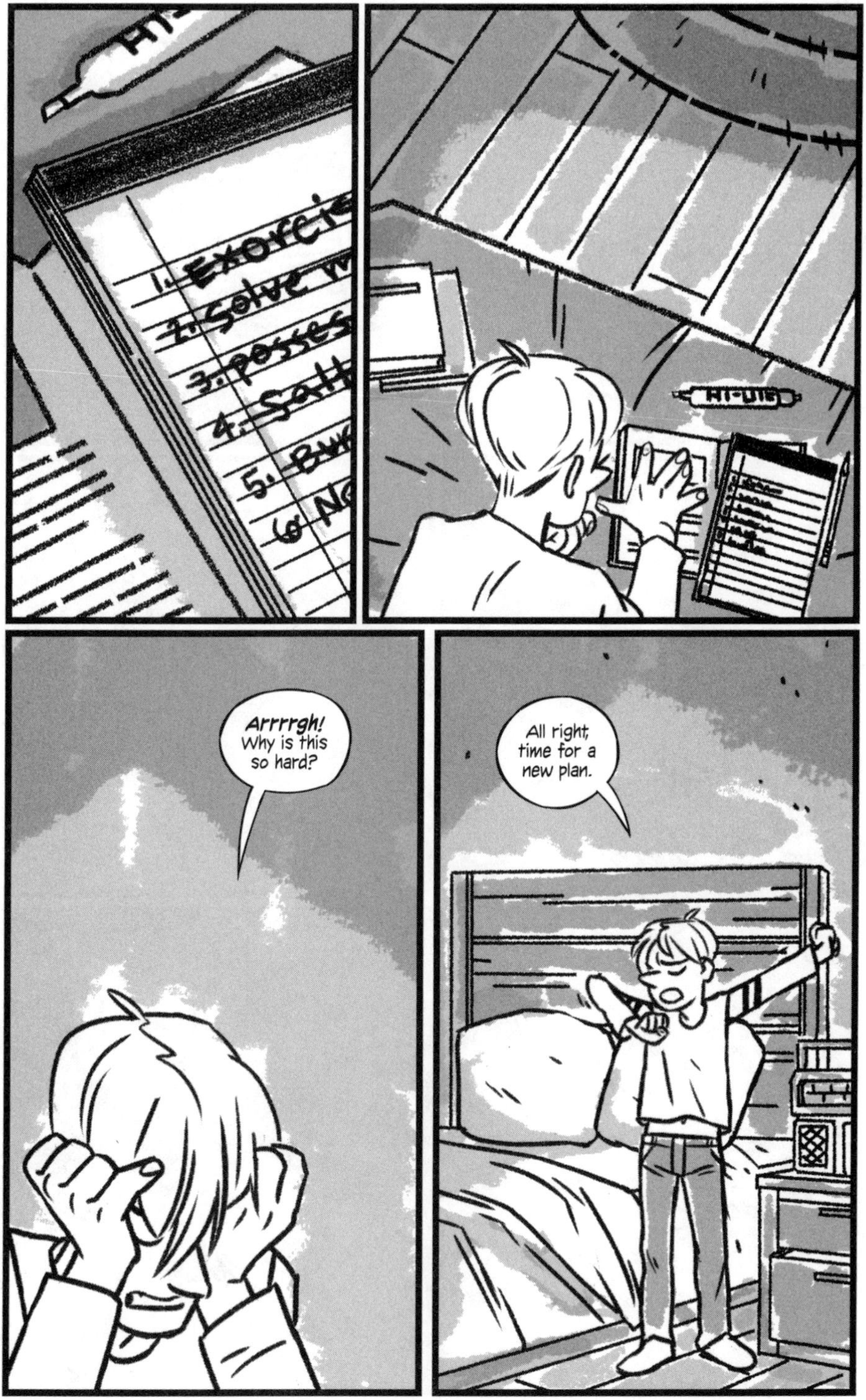
Arrrrgh! Why is this so hard?
All right, time for a new plan.

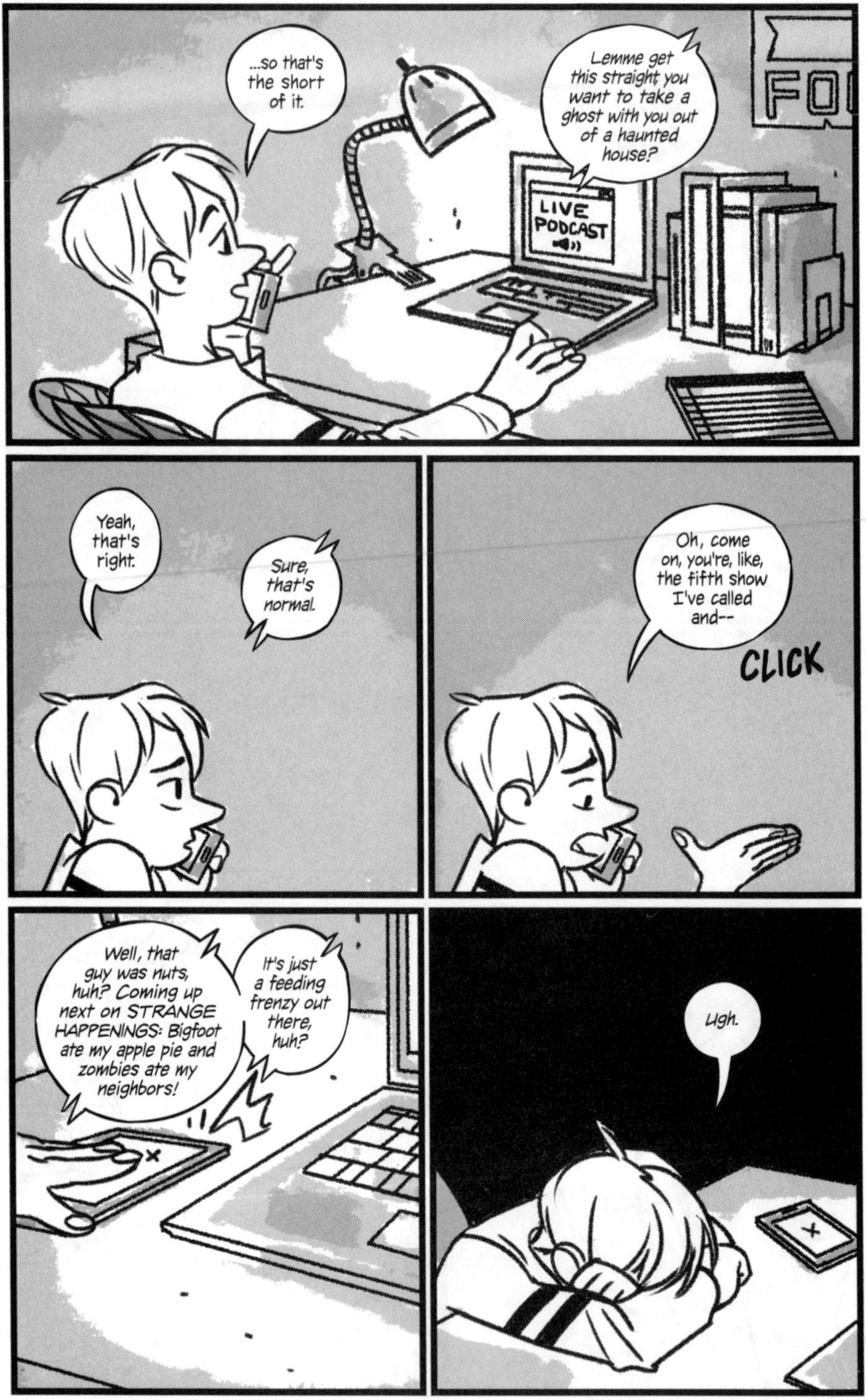

...so that's the short of it.
Lemme get this straight, you want to take a ghost with you out of a haunted house?
LIVE PODCAST
Yeah, that's right.
Sure, that's normal.
Oh, come on, you're, like, the fifth show I've called and--
CLICK
Well, that guy was nuts, huh? Coming up next on STRANGE HAPPENINGS: Bigfoot ate my apple pie and zombies ate my neighbors!
It's just a feeding frenzy out there, huh?
Ugh.

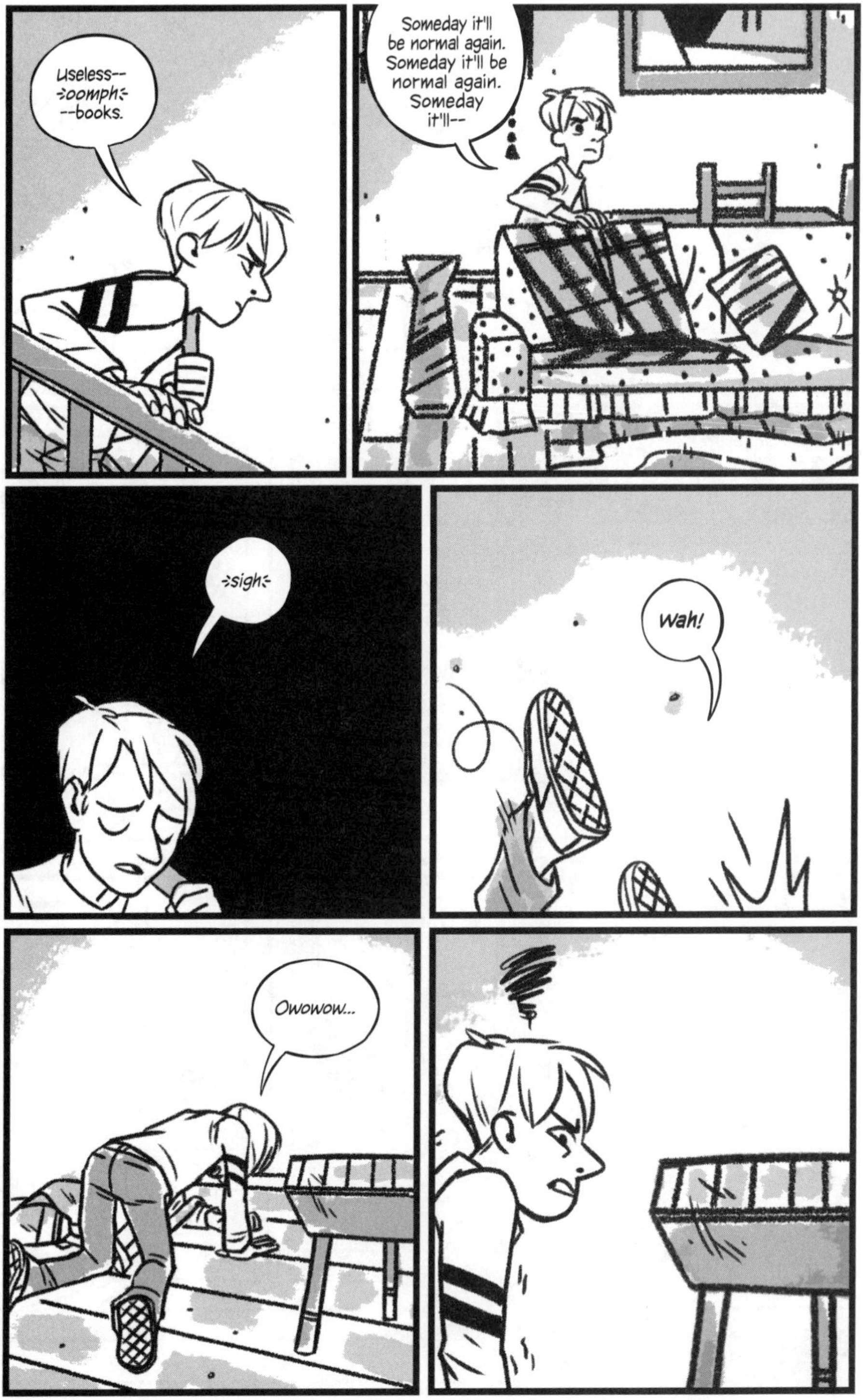
Useless--
≈oomph≈
--books.
Someday it'll be normal again. Someday it'll be normal again. Someday it'll--
≈sigh≈
Wah!
Owowow...

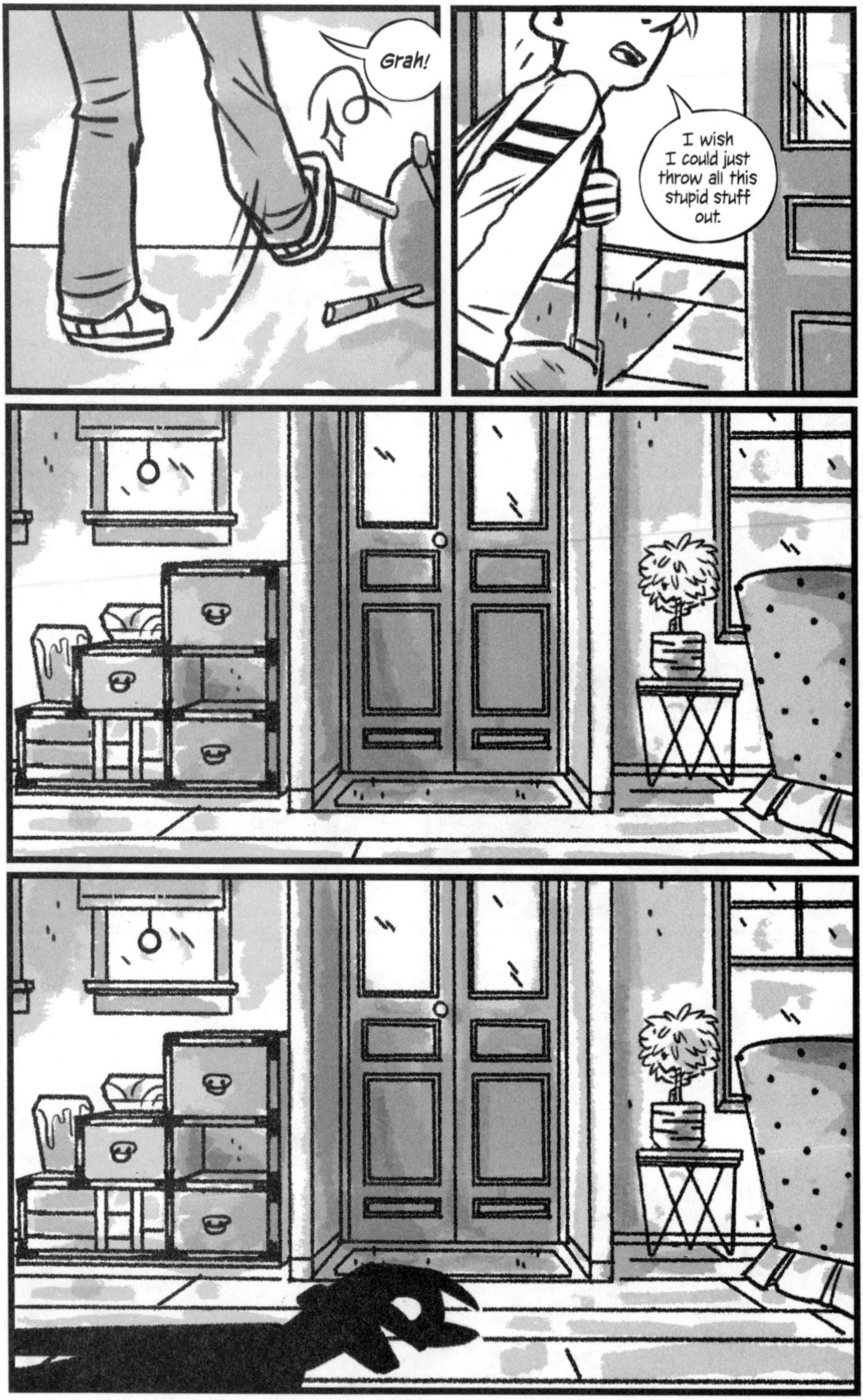
Grah!
I wish I could just throw all this stupid stuff out.

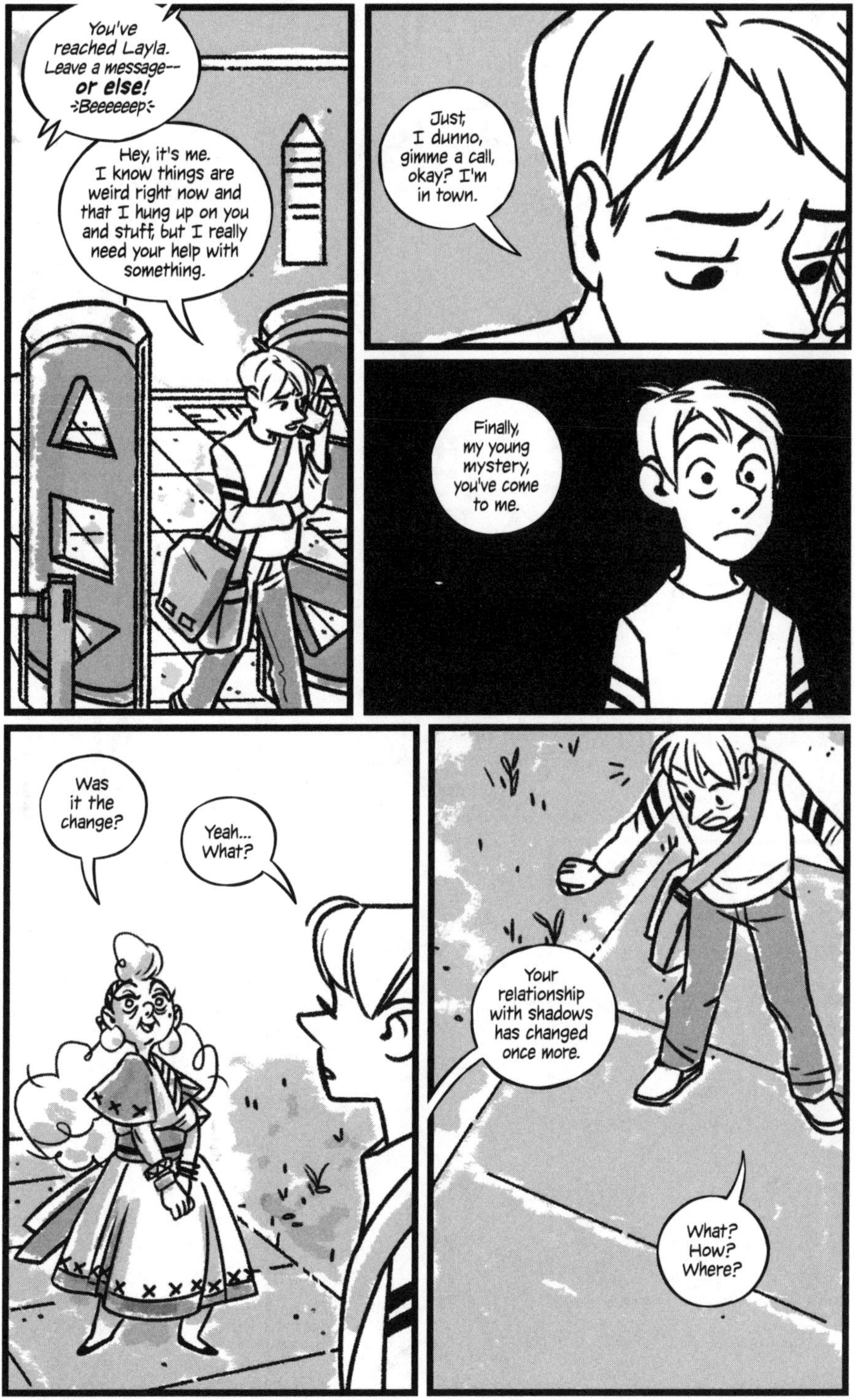
You've reached Layla. Leave a message-- or else! ⁓Beeeeeep⁓
Hey, it's me. I know things are weird right now and that I hung up on you and stuff, but I really need your help with something.
Just, I dunno, gimme a call, okay? I'm in town.
Finally, my young mystery, you've come to me.
Was it the change?
Yeah... What?
Your relationship with shadows has changed once more.
What? How? Where?

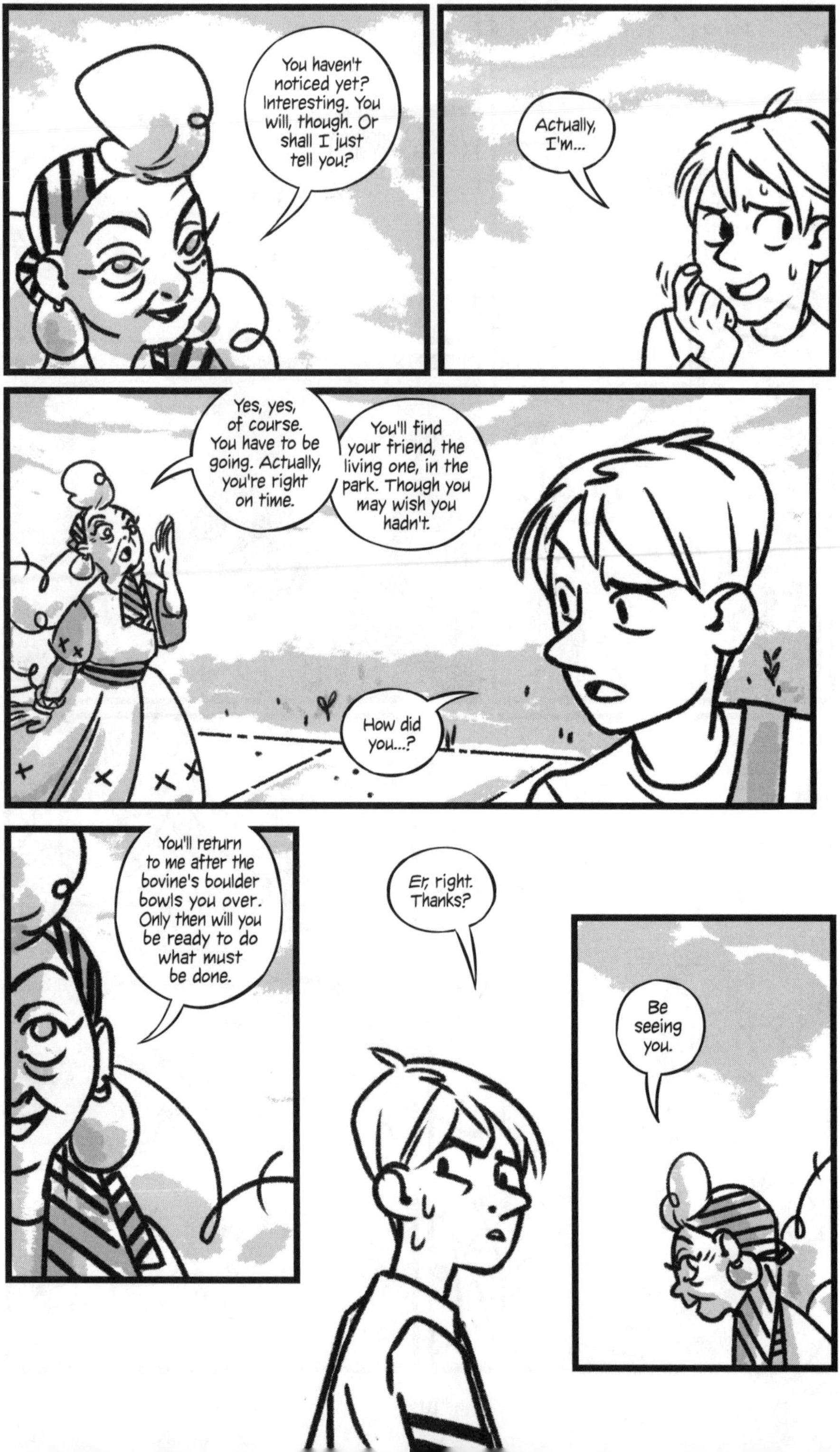

You haven't noticed yet? Interesting. You will, though. Or shall I just tell you?
Actually, I'm...
Yes, yes, of course. You have to be going. Actually, you're right on time.
You'll find your friend, the living one, in the park. Though you may wish you hadn't.
How did you...?
You'll return to me after the bovine's boulder bowls you over. Only then will you be ready to do what must be done.
Er, right. Thanks?
Be seeing you.

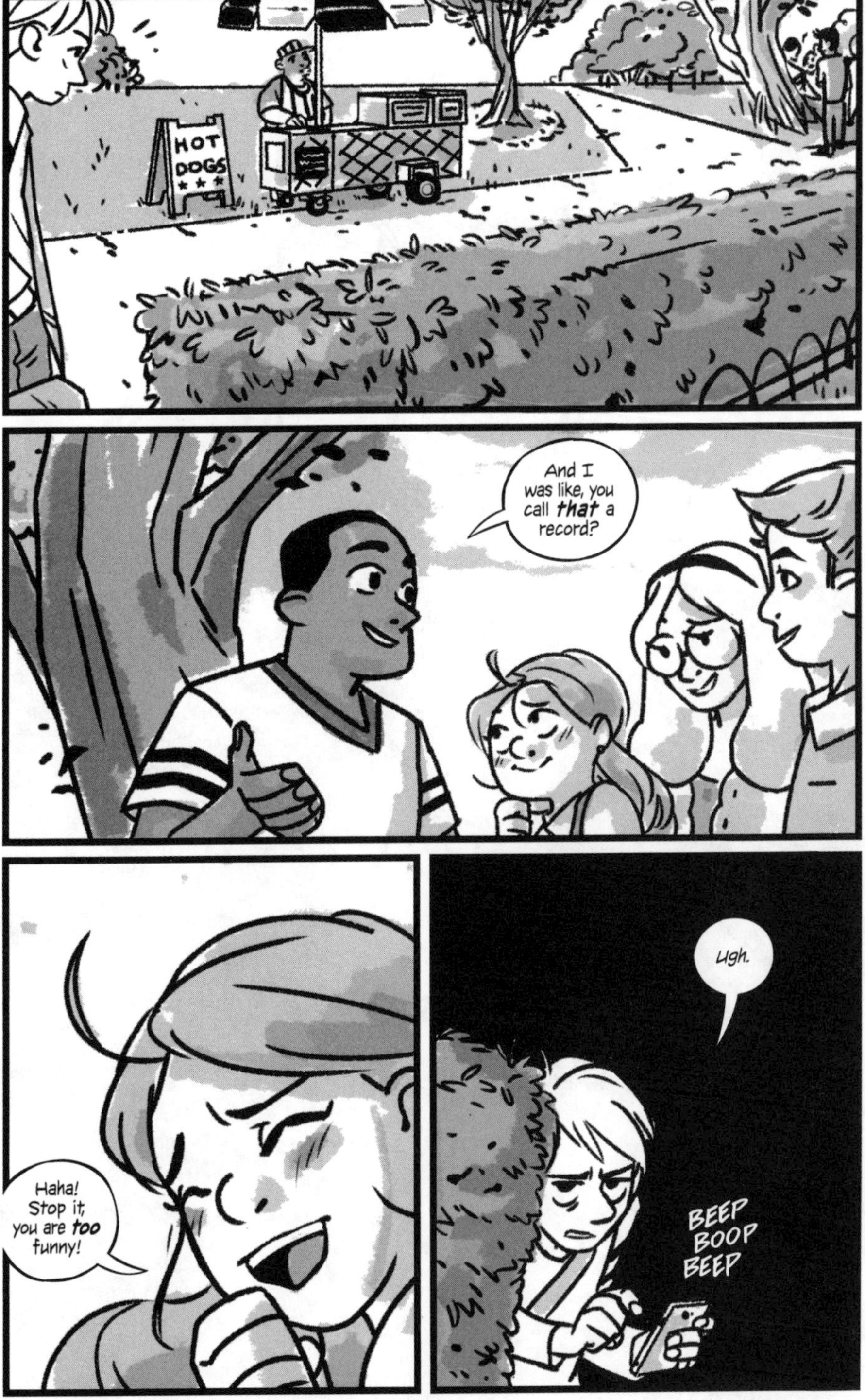
HOT DOGS
And I was like, you call **that** a record?
Haha! Stop it, you are **too** funny!
Ugh.
BEEP BOOP BEEP

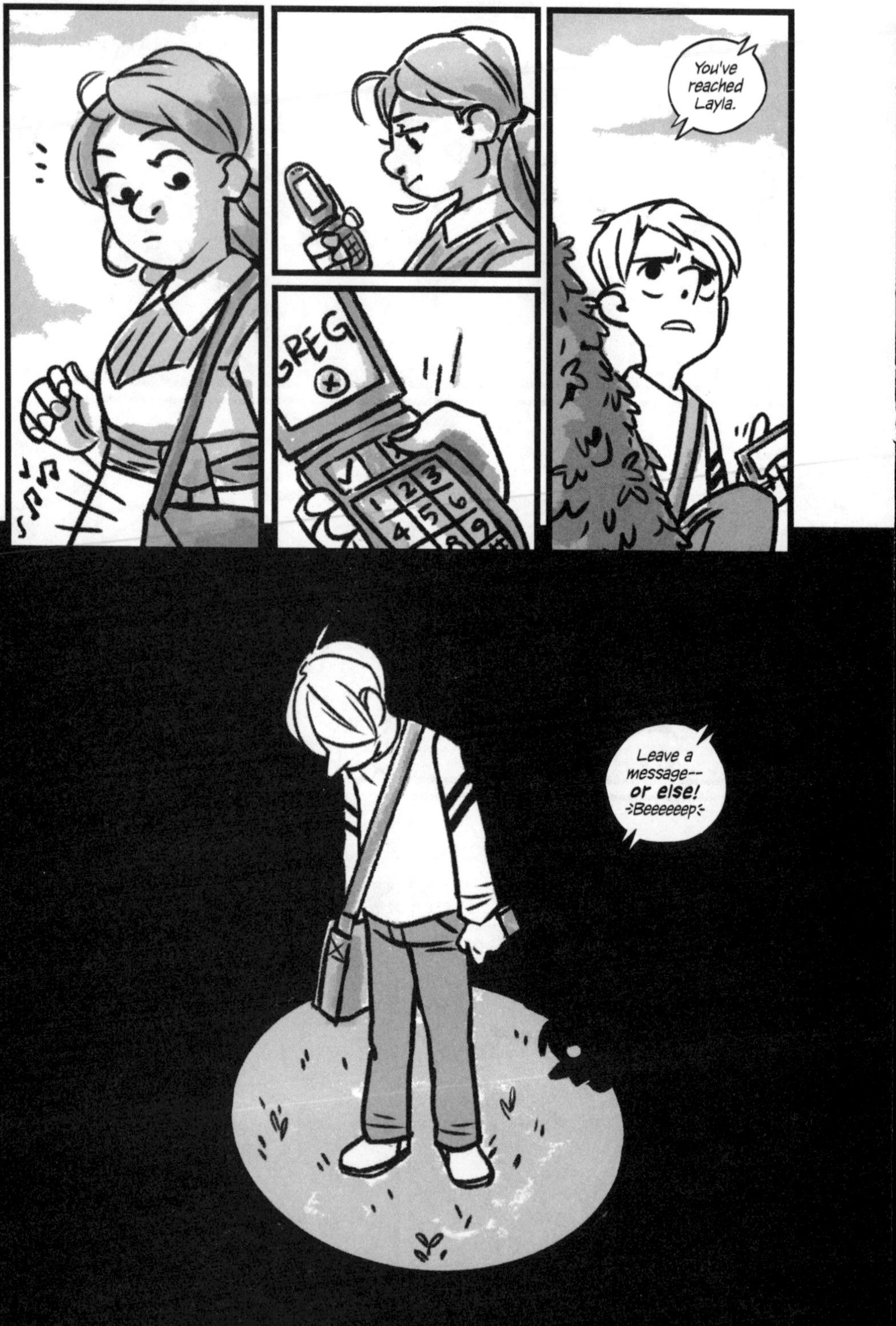
GREG
You've reached Layla.
Leave a message-- **or else!**
-Beeeeeep-

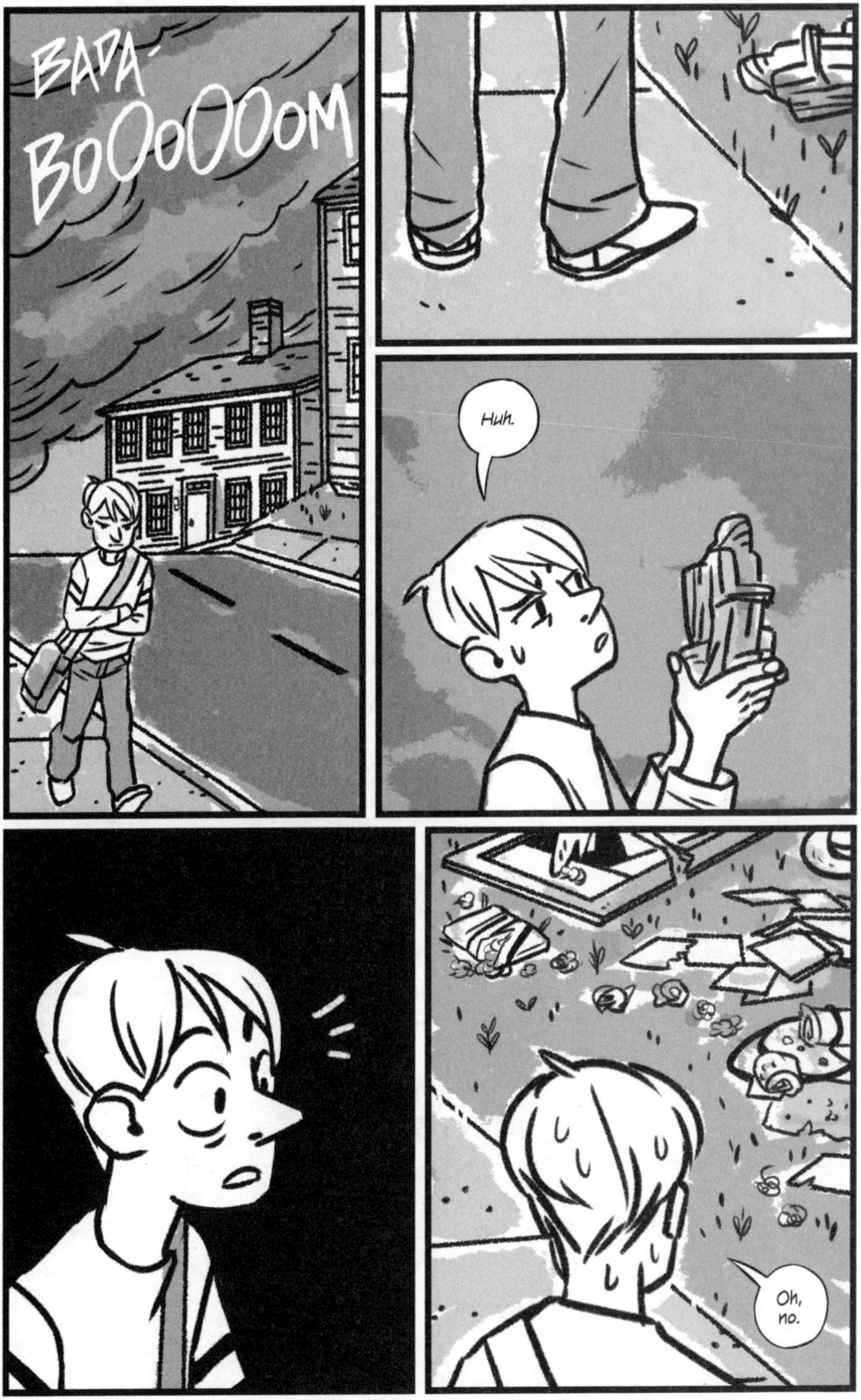
BADA-
BOOoOOOM
Huh.
Oh,
no.

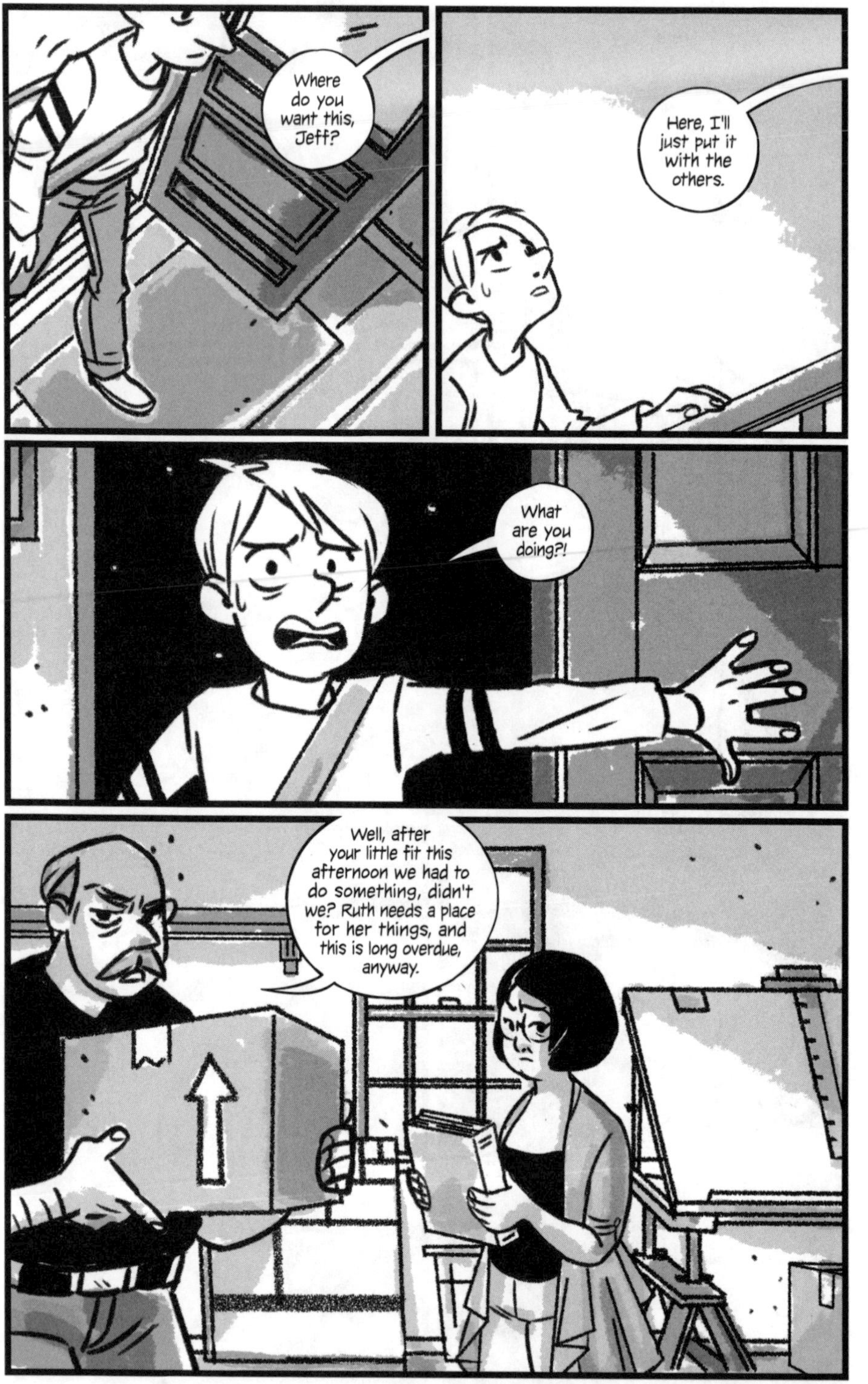
Where do you want this, Jeff?
Here, I'll just put it with the others.
What are you doing?!
Well, after your little fit this afternoon we had to do something, didn't we? Ruth needs a place for her things, and this is long overdue, anyway.

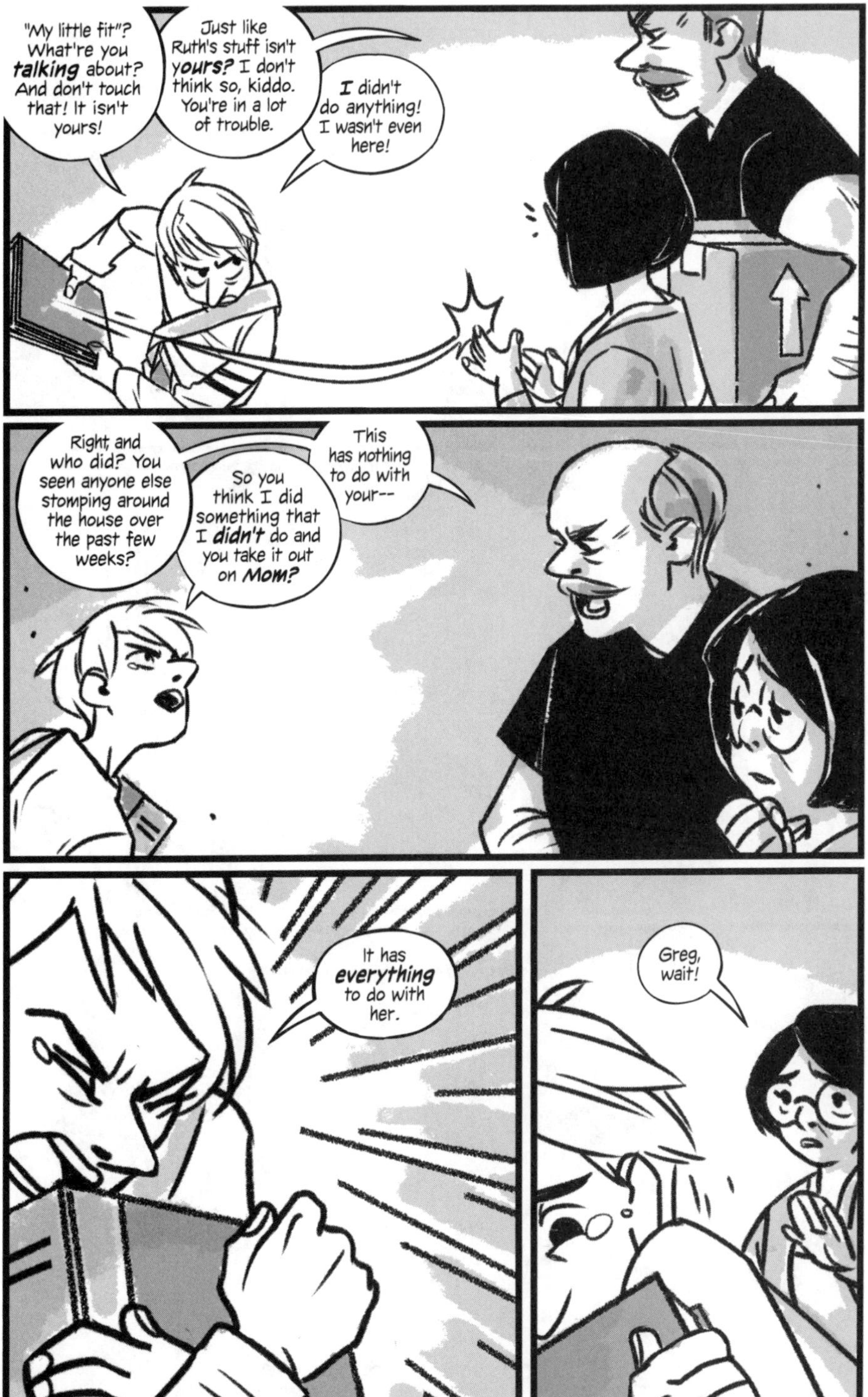
"My little fit"? What're you *talking* about? And don't touch that! It isn't yours!
Just like Ruth's stuff isn't y*ours?* I don't think so, kiddo. You're in a lot of trouble.
I didn't do anything! I wasn't even here!
Right, and who did? You seen anyone else stomping around the house over the past few weeks?
So you think I did something that I *didn't* do and you take it out on *Mom?*
This has nothing to do with your--
It has *everything* to do with her.
Greg, wait!

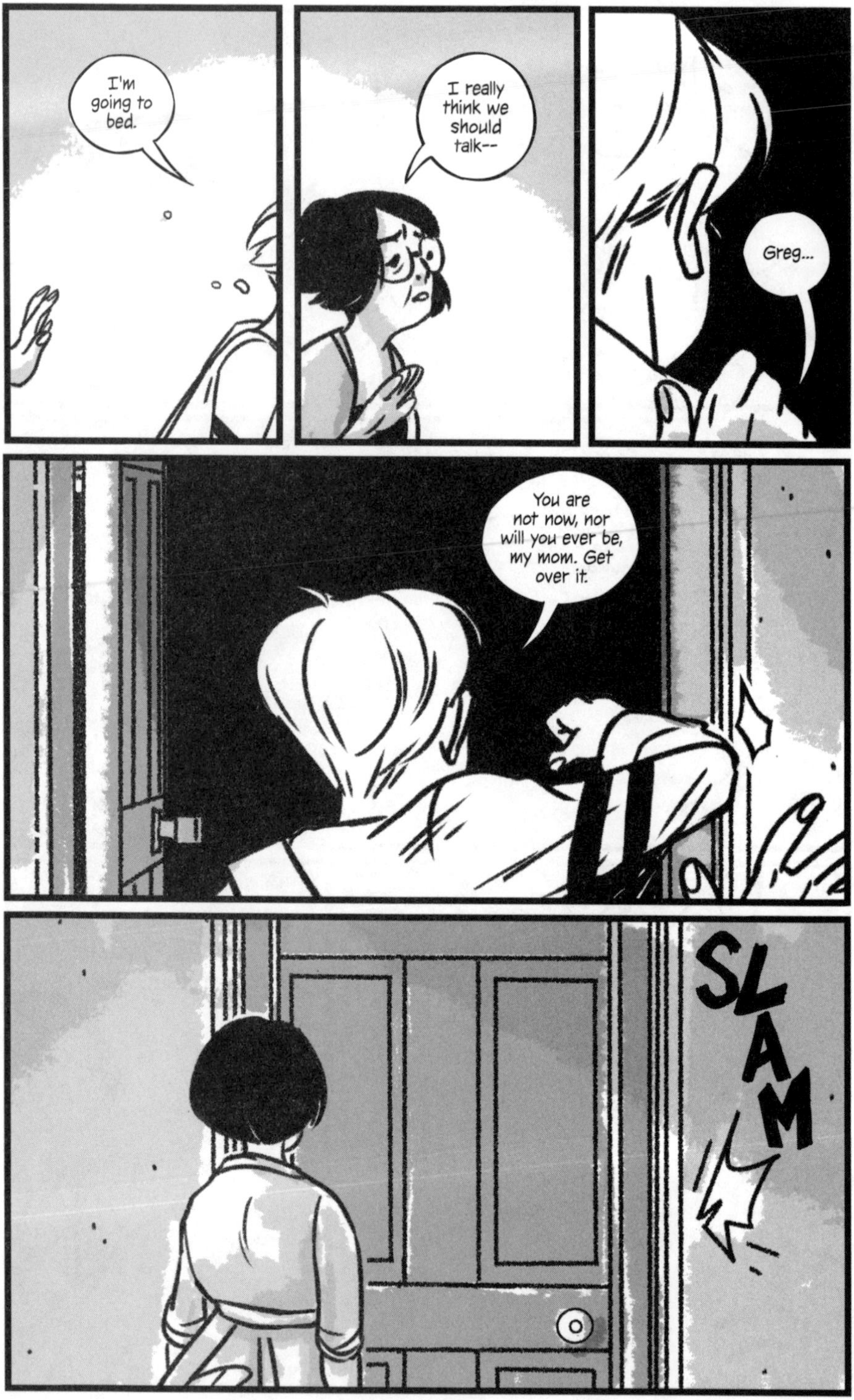
I'm going to bed.
I really think we should talk--
Greg...
You are not now, nor will you ever be, my mom. Get over it.
SLAM

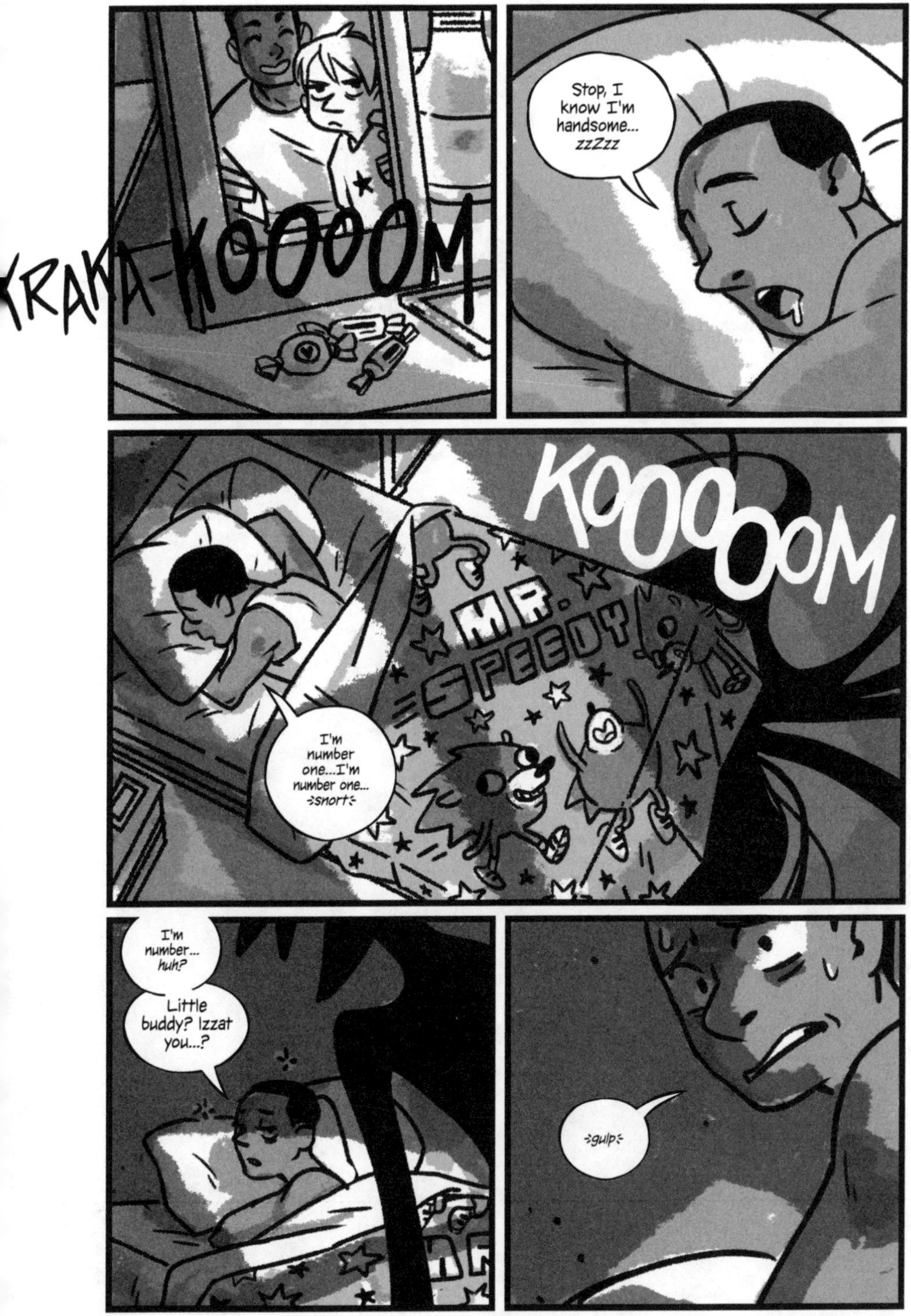
KRAKA-KOOOOM
Stop, I know I'm handsome... zzZzz
KOOOOOOM
MR. SPEEDY
I'm number one...I'm number one... ⩫snort⩪
I'm number... huh?
Little buddy? Izzat you...?
⩫gulp⩪

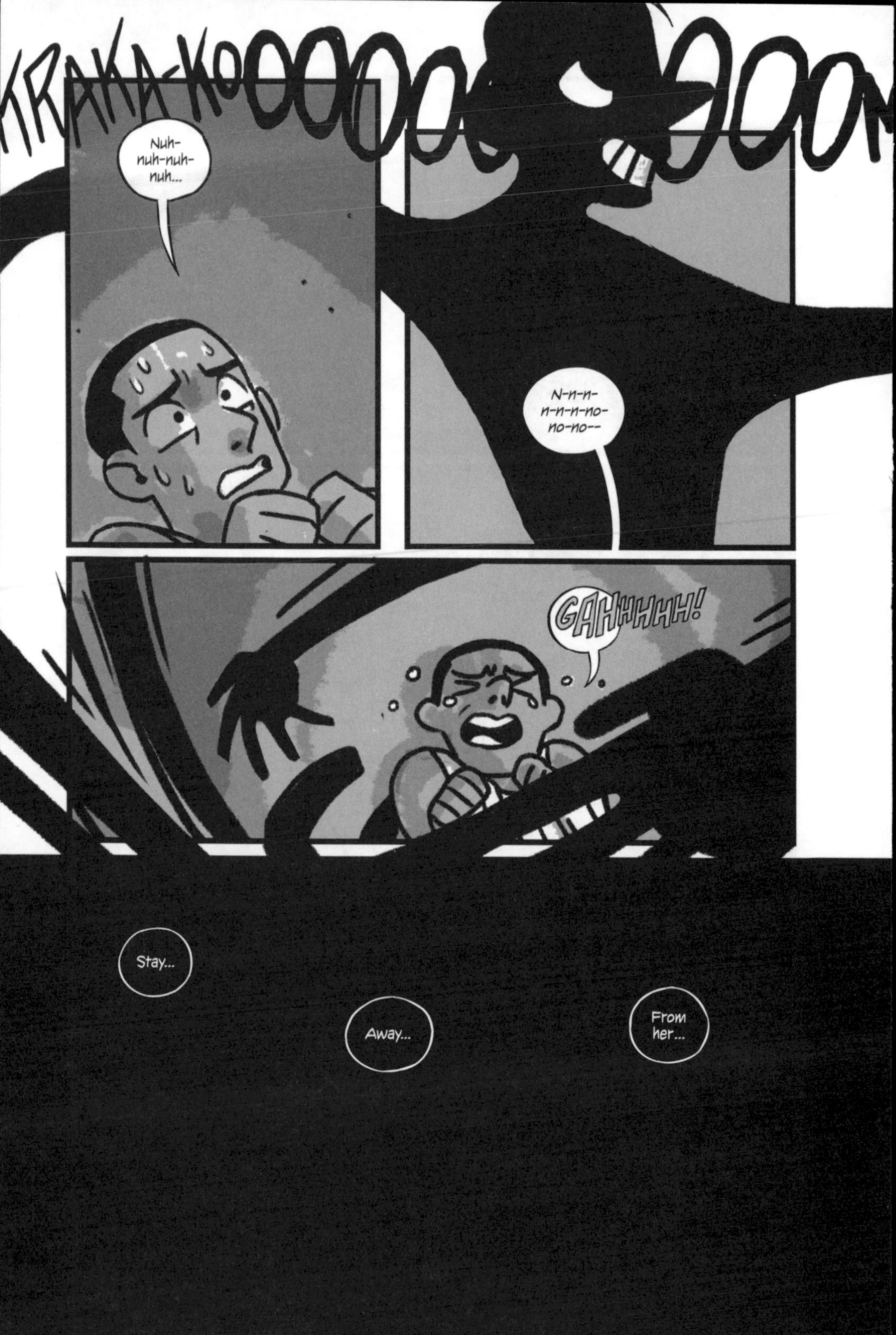
KRAKA-KOOOOOOOOOOOM
Nuh-nuh-nuh-nuh...
N-n-n-n-n-n-no-no-no--
GAHHHHH!
Stay...
Away...
From her...

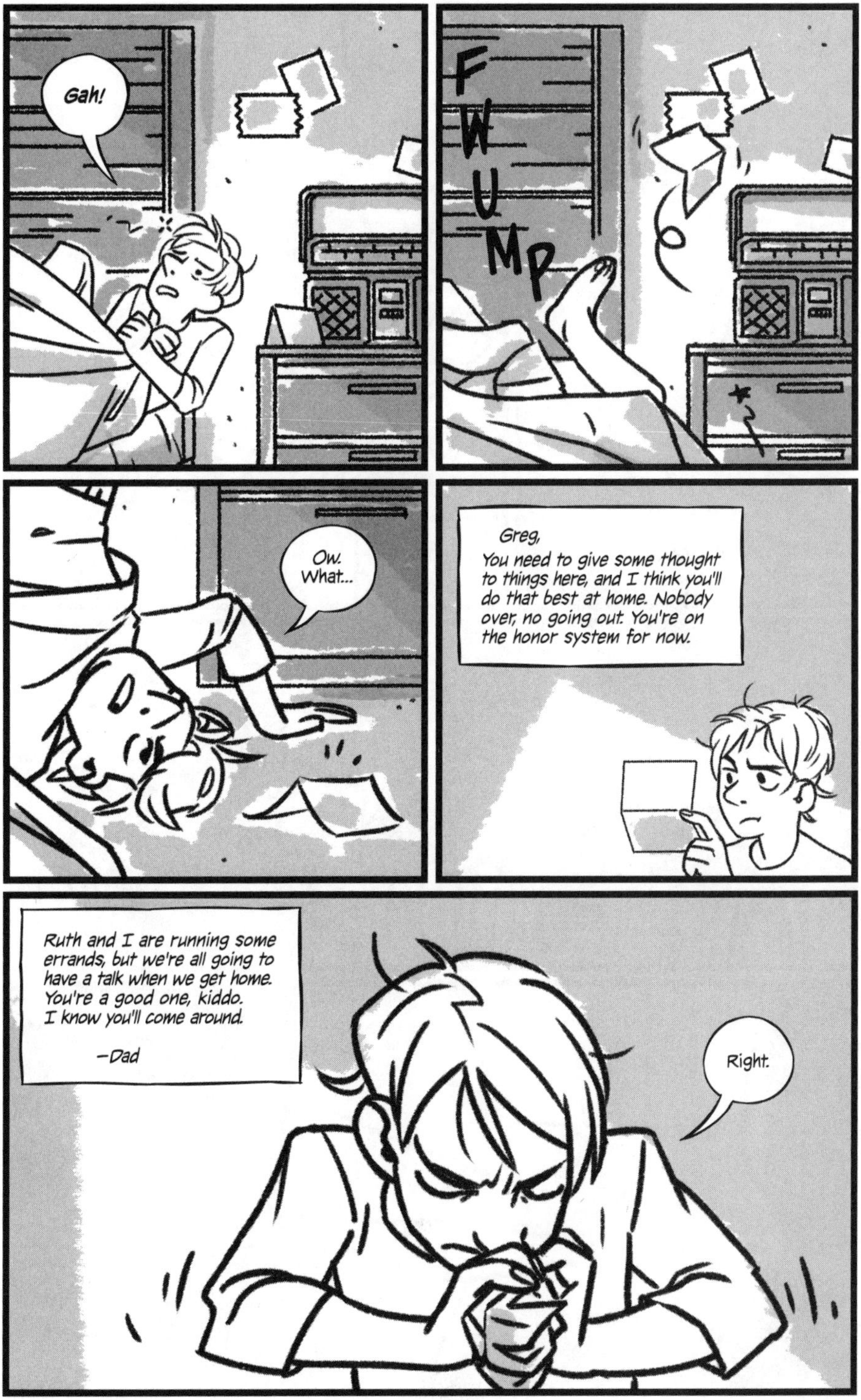
Gah!
FWUMP
Ow. What...
Greg,
You need to give some thought to things here, and I think you'll do that best at home. Nobody over, no going out. You're on the honor system for now.
Ruth and I are running some errands, but we're all going to have a talk when we get home. You're a good one, kiddo. I know you'll come around.
—Dad
Right.

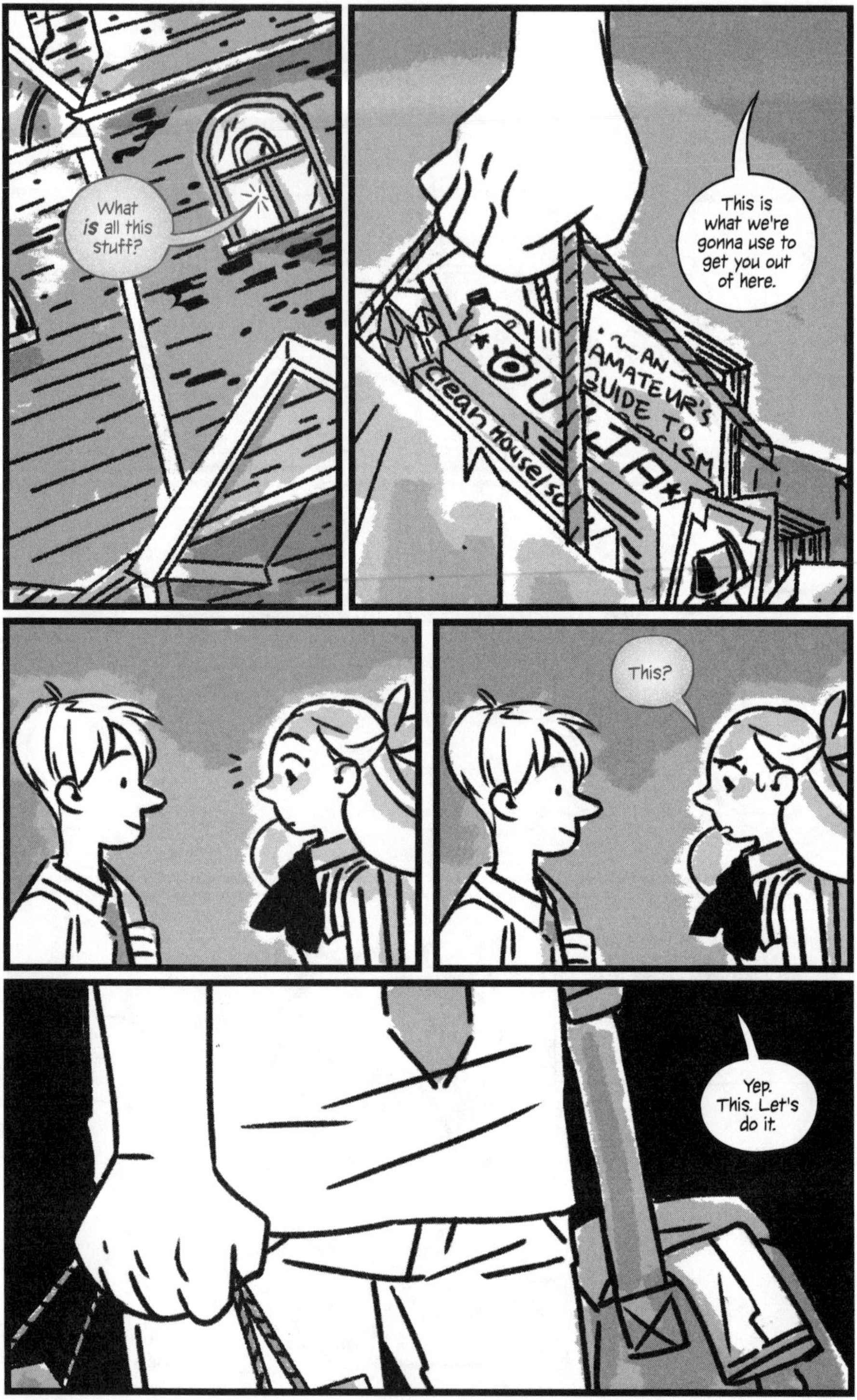

What is all this stuff?
This is what we're gonna use to get you out of here.
AN AMATEUR'S GUIDE TO
This?
Yep. This. Let's do it.

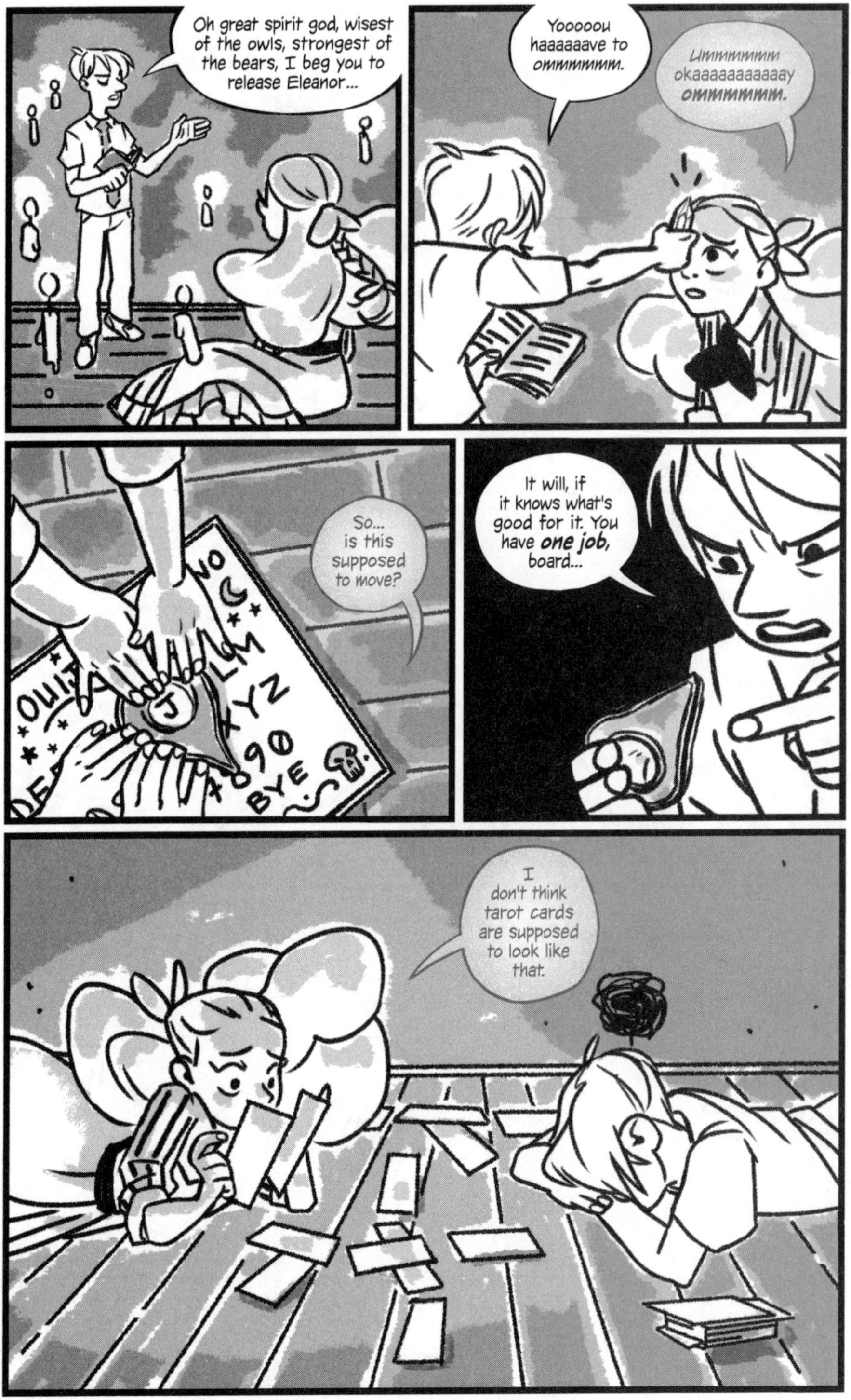
Oh great spirit god, wisest of the owls, strongest of the bears, I beg you to release Eleanor...
Yoooooou haaaaaave to *ommmmmm.*
Ummmmmm okaaaaaaaaaaay ***ommmmmm.***
So... is this supposed to move?
OUIJA
NO
LM
XYZ
90
BYE
It will, if it knows what's good for it. You have ***one job,*** board...
I don't think tarot cards are supposed to look like that.

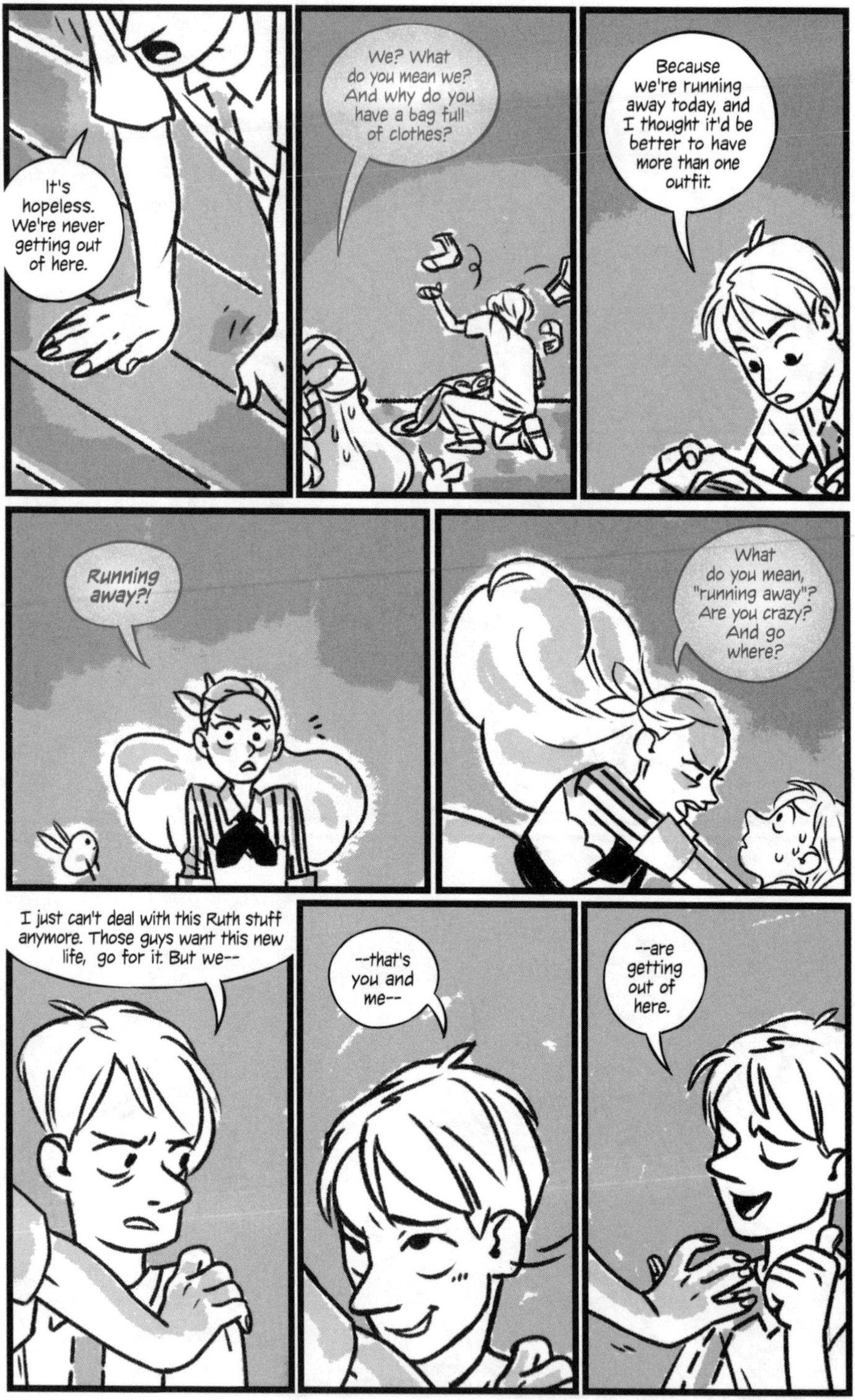
It's hopeless. We're never getting out of here.
We? What do you mean we? And why do you have a bag full of clothes?
Because we're running away today, and I thought it'd be better to have more than one outfit.
Running away?!
What do you mean, "running away"? Are you crazy? And go where?
I just can't deal with this Ruth stuff anymore. Those guys want this new life, go for it. But we--
--that's you and me--
--are getting out of here.

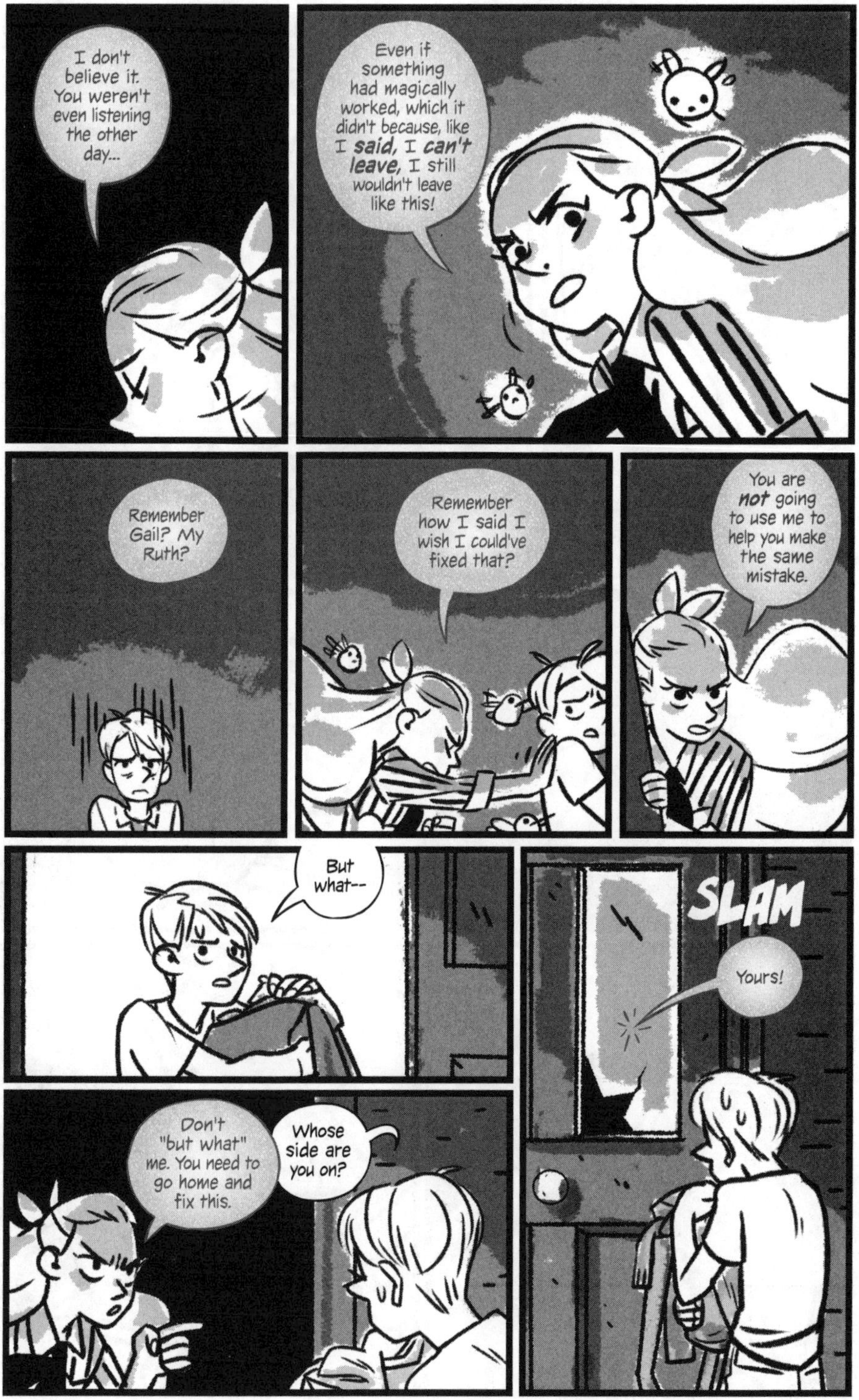
I don't believe it. You weren't even listening the other day...
Even if something had magically worked, which it didn't because, like I **said,** I **can't leave,** I still wouldn't leave like this!
Remember Gail? My Ruth?
Remember how I said I wish I could've fixed that?
You are **not** going to use me to help you make the same mistake.
But what--
Don't "but what" me. You need to go home and fix this.
Whose side are you on?
SLAM
Yours!

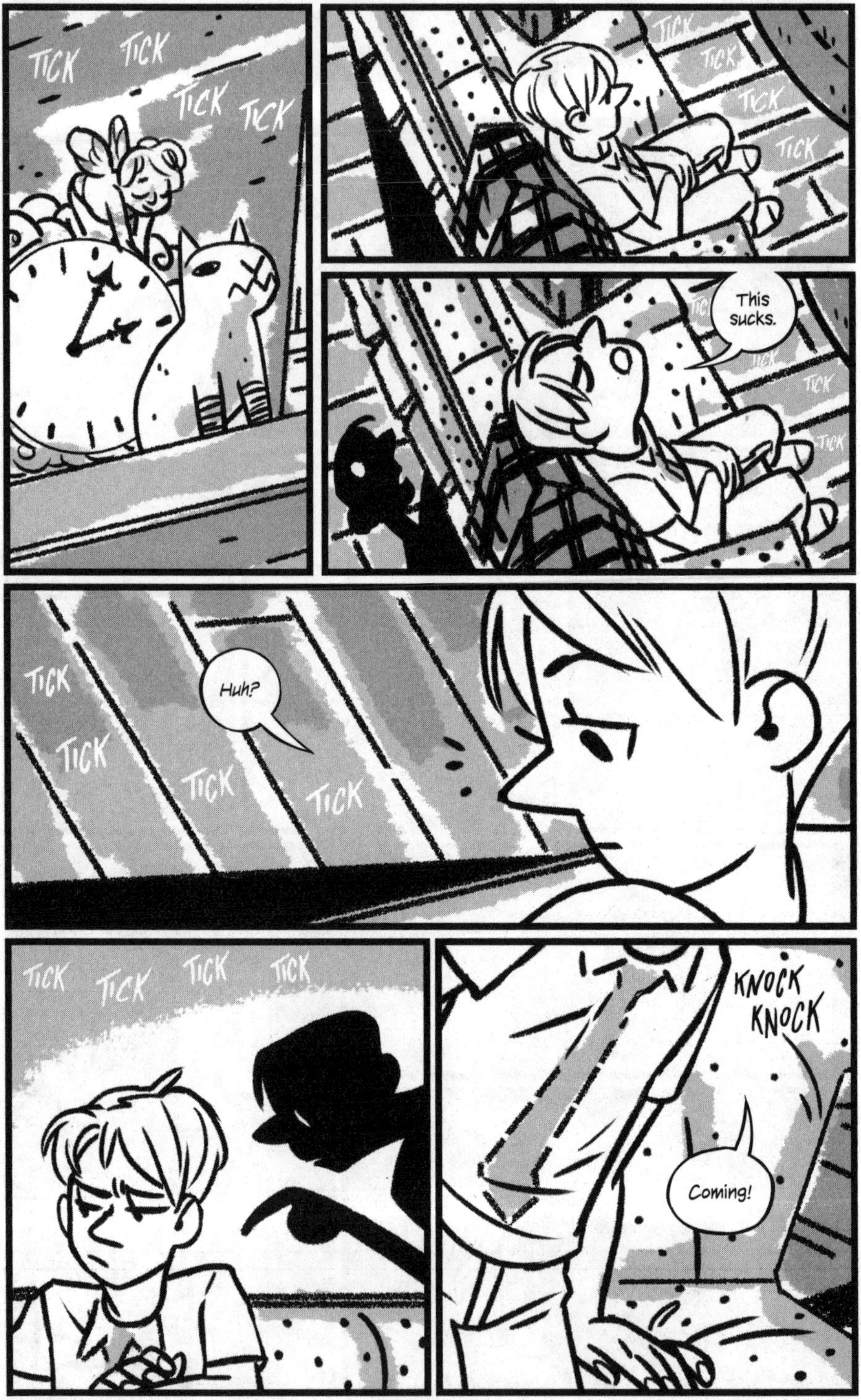
TICK
TICK
TICK
TICK
TICK
TICK
TICK
TICK
This sucks.
TICK
TICK
Huh?
TICK
TICK
TICK
TICK
TICK
TICK
TICK
TICK
KNOCK KNOCK
Coming!

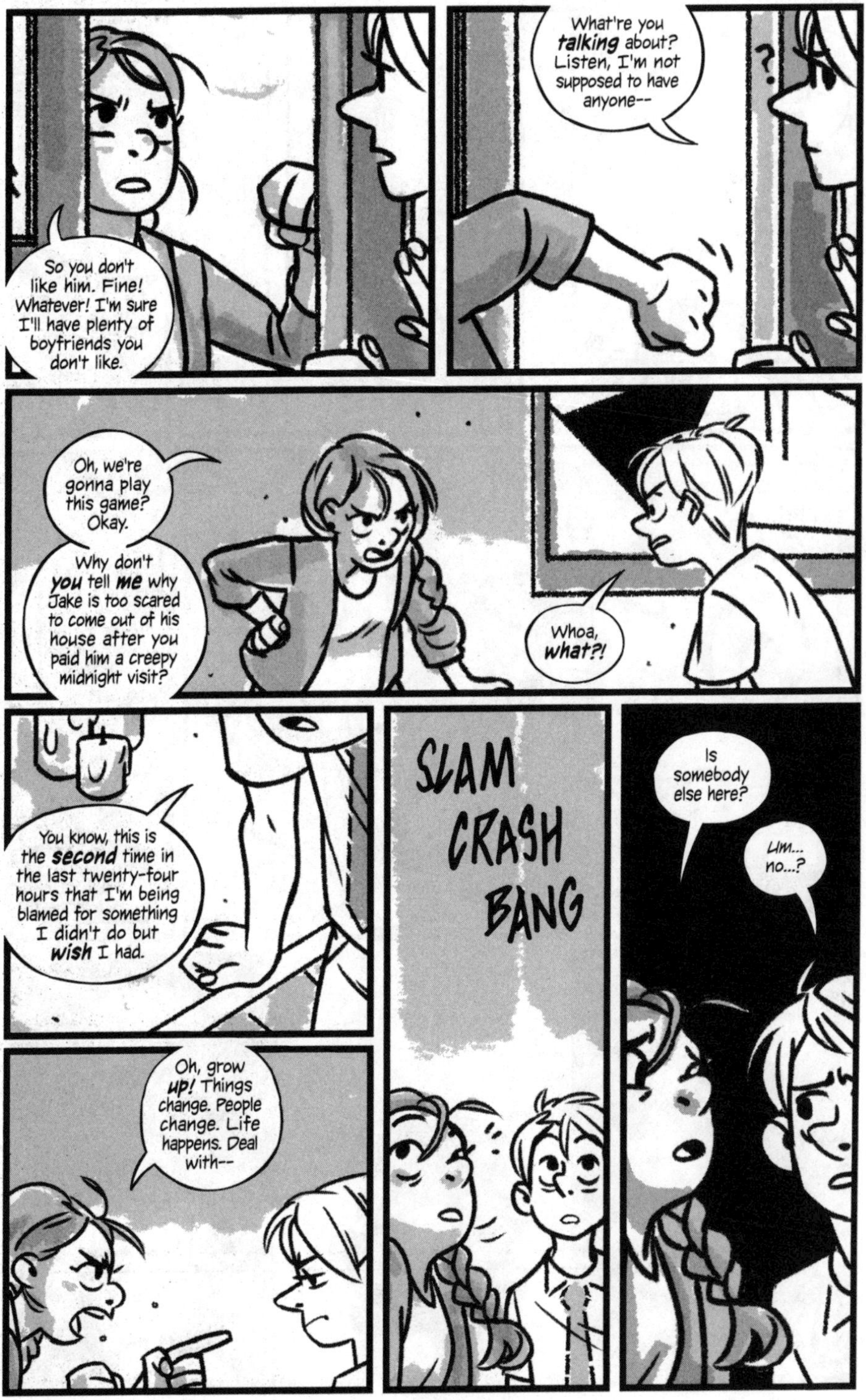
So you don't like him. Fine! Whatever! I'm sure I'll have plenty of boyfriends you don't like.
What're you talking about? Listen, I'm not supposed to have anyone--
?
Oh, we're gonna play this game? Okay.
Why don't you tell me why Jake is too scared to come out of his house after you paid him a creepy midnight visit?
Whoa, what?!
You know, this is the second time in the last twenty-four hours that I'm being blamed for something I didn't do but wish I had.
Oh, grow up! Things change. People change. Life happens. Deal with--
SLAM
CRASH
BANG
Is somebody else here?
Um... no...?

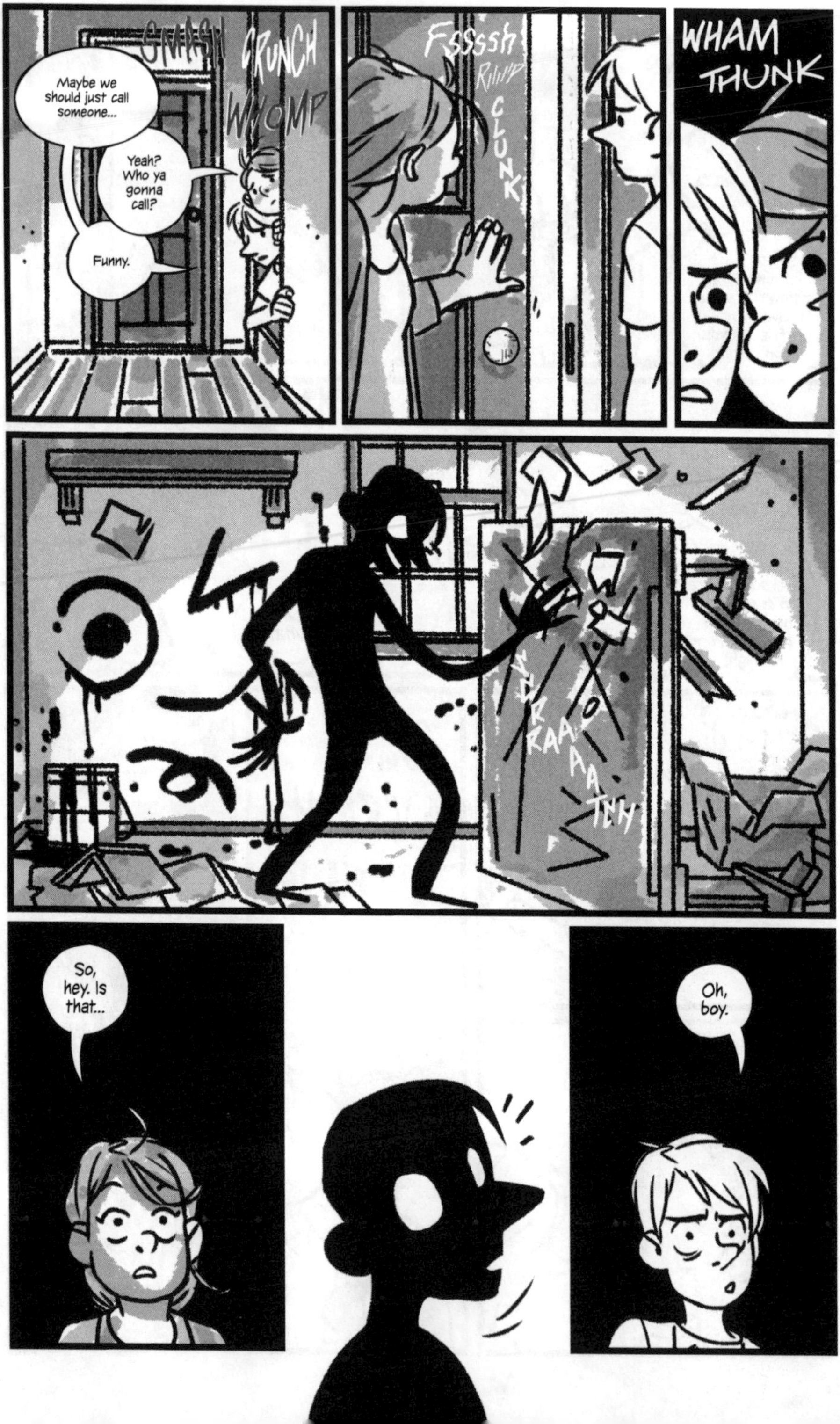
SMASH CRUNCH WHOMP
Maybe we should just call someone...
Yeah? Who ya gonna call?
Funny.
Fssssh
CLUNK
WHAM
THUNK
SCRAAAATCH
So, hey. Is that...
Oh, boy.

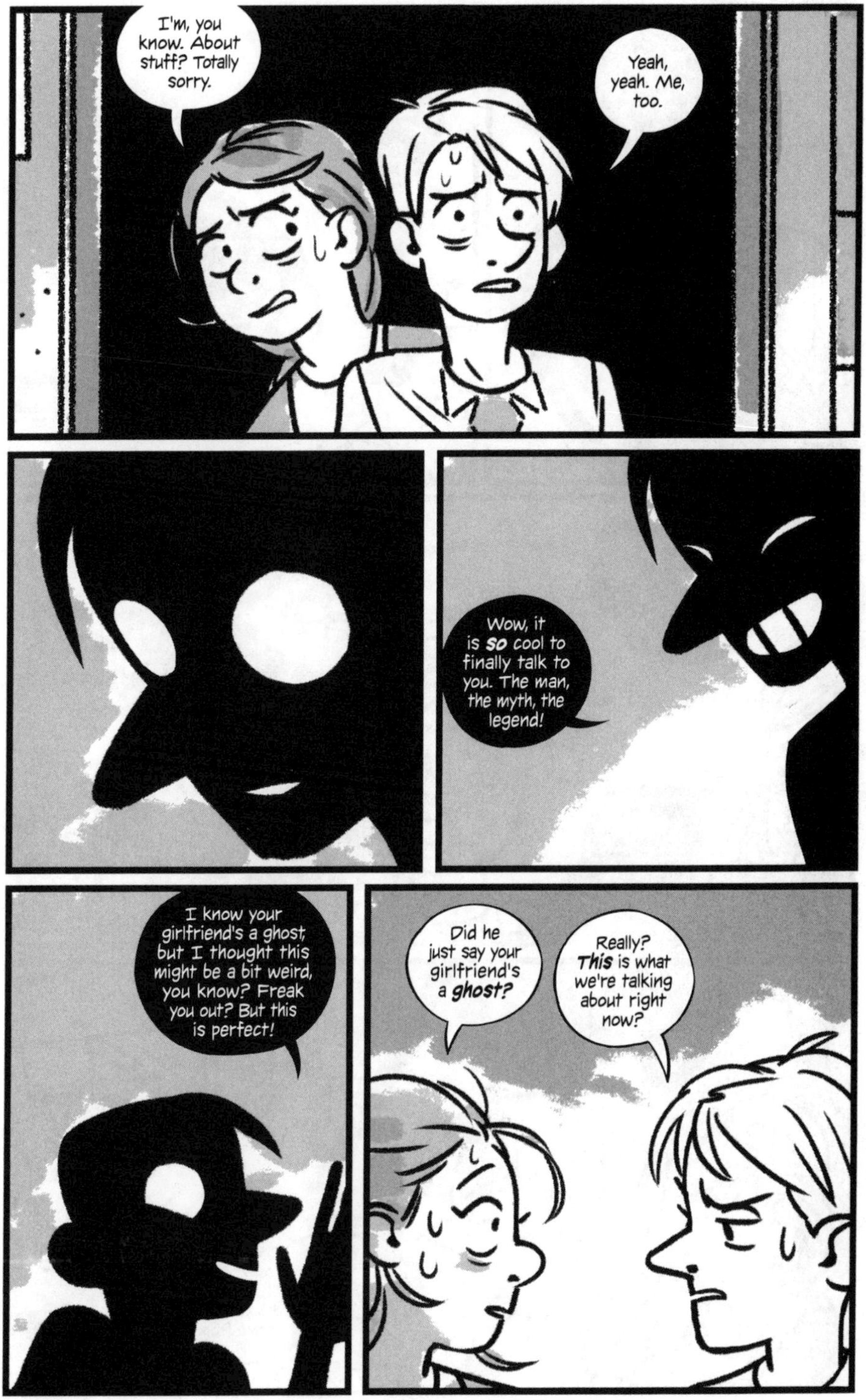
I'm, you know. About stuff? Totally sorry.
Yeah, yeah. Me, too.
Wow, it is **so** cool to finally talk to you. The man, the myth, the legend!
I know your girlfriend's a ghost, but I thought this might be a bit weird, you know? Freak you out? But this is perfect!
Did he just say your girlfriend's a ***ghost?***
Really? ***This*** is what we're talking about right now?

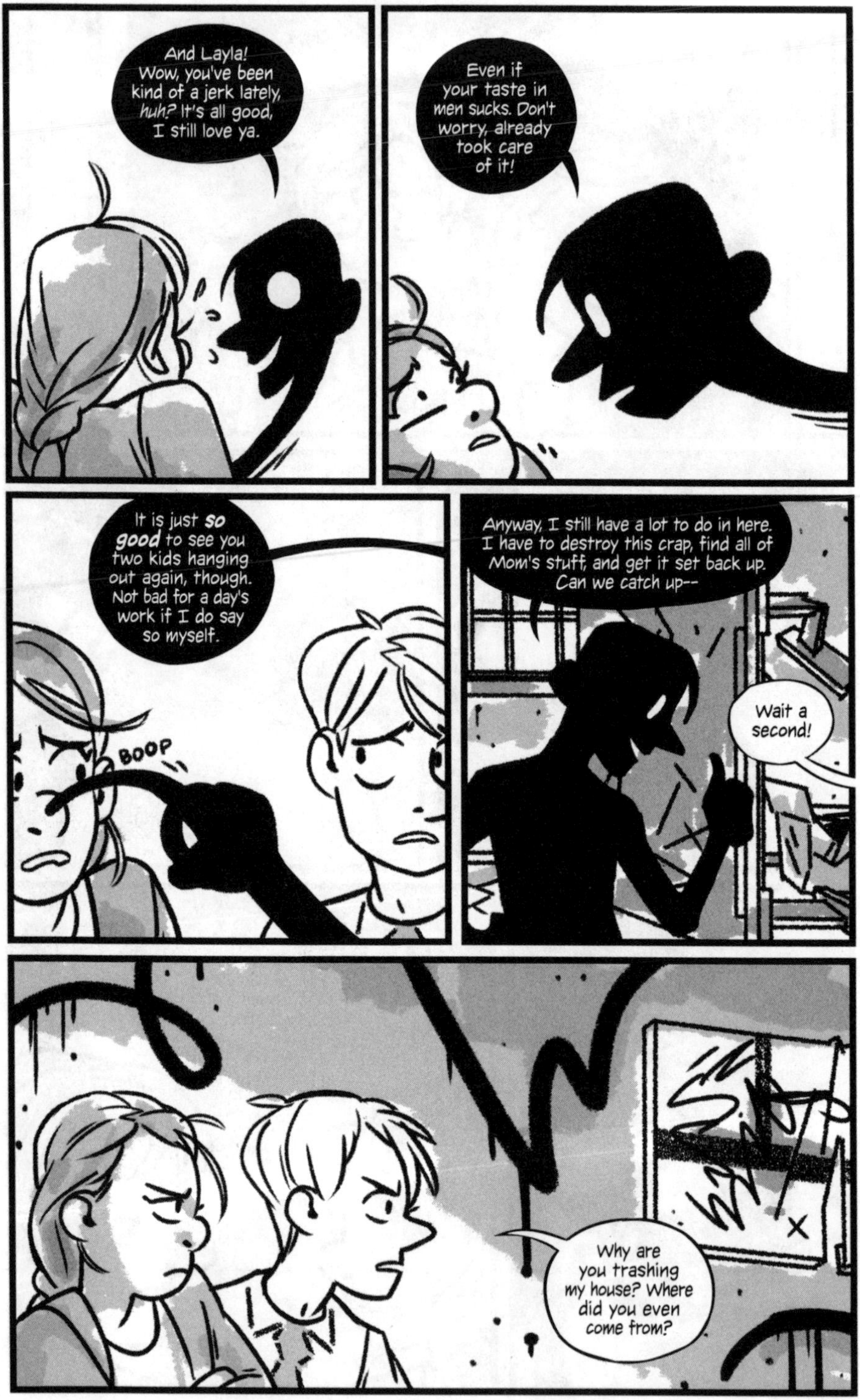
And Layla! Wow, you've been kind of a jerk lately, *huh?* It's all good, I still love ya.
Even if your taste in men sucks. Don't worry, already took care of it!
It is just **so good** to see you two kids hanging out again, though. Not bad for a day's work if I do say so myself.
BOOP
Anyway, I still have a lot to do in here. I have to destroy this crap, find all of Mom's stuff, and get it set back up. Can we catch up--
Wait a second!
Why are you trashing my house? Where did you even come from?

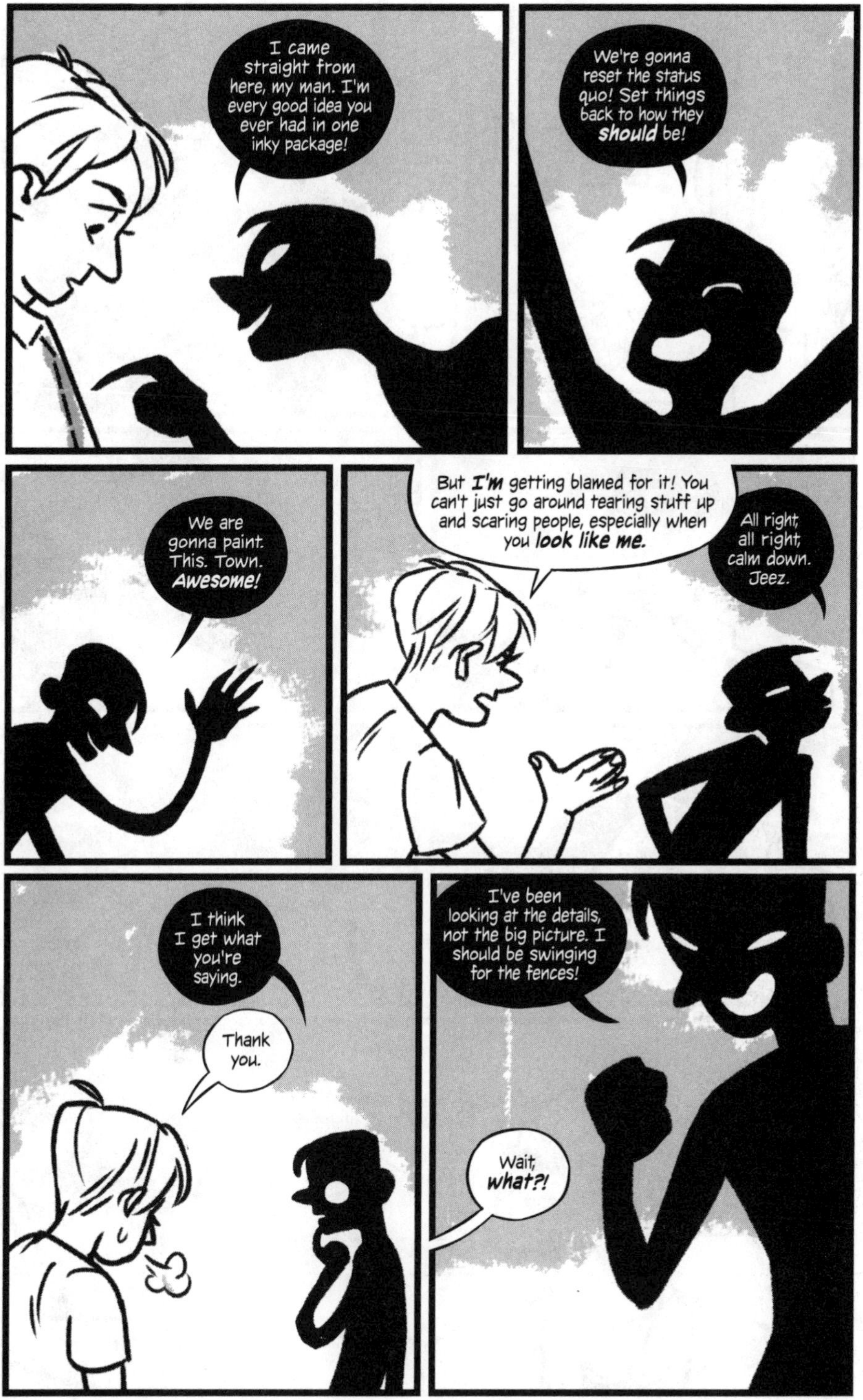
I came straight from here, my man. I'm every good idea you ever had in one inky package!
We're gonna reset the status quo! Set things back to how they **should** be!
We are gonna paint. This. Town. ***Awesome!***
But ***I'm*** getting blamed for it! You can't just go around tearing stuff up and scaring people, especially when you ***look like me.***
All right, all right, calm down. Jeez.
I think I get what you're saying.
Thank you.
I've been looking at the details, not the big picture. I should be swinging for the fences!
Wait, ***what?!***

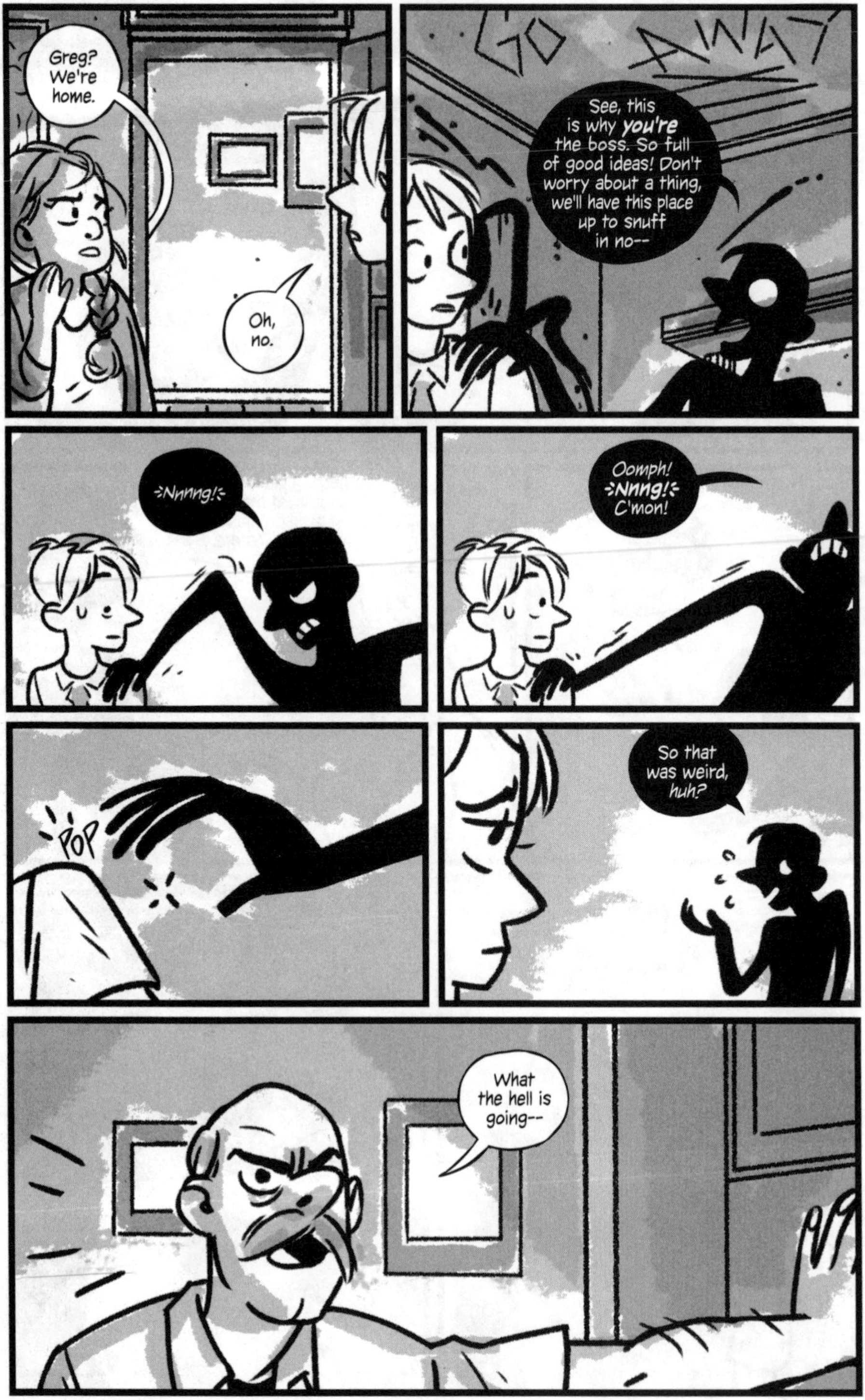
Greg? We're home.
Oh, no.
GO AWAY
See, this is why **you're** the boss. So full of good ideas! Don't worry about a thing, we'll have this place up to snuff in no--
Nnnng!
Oomph! **Nnng!** C'mon!
POP
So that was weird, huh?
What the hell is going--

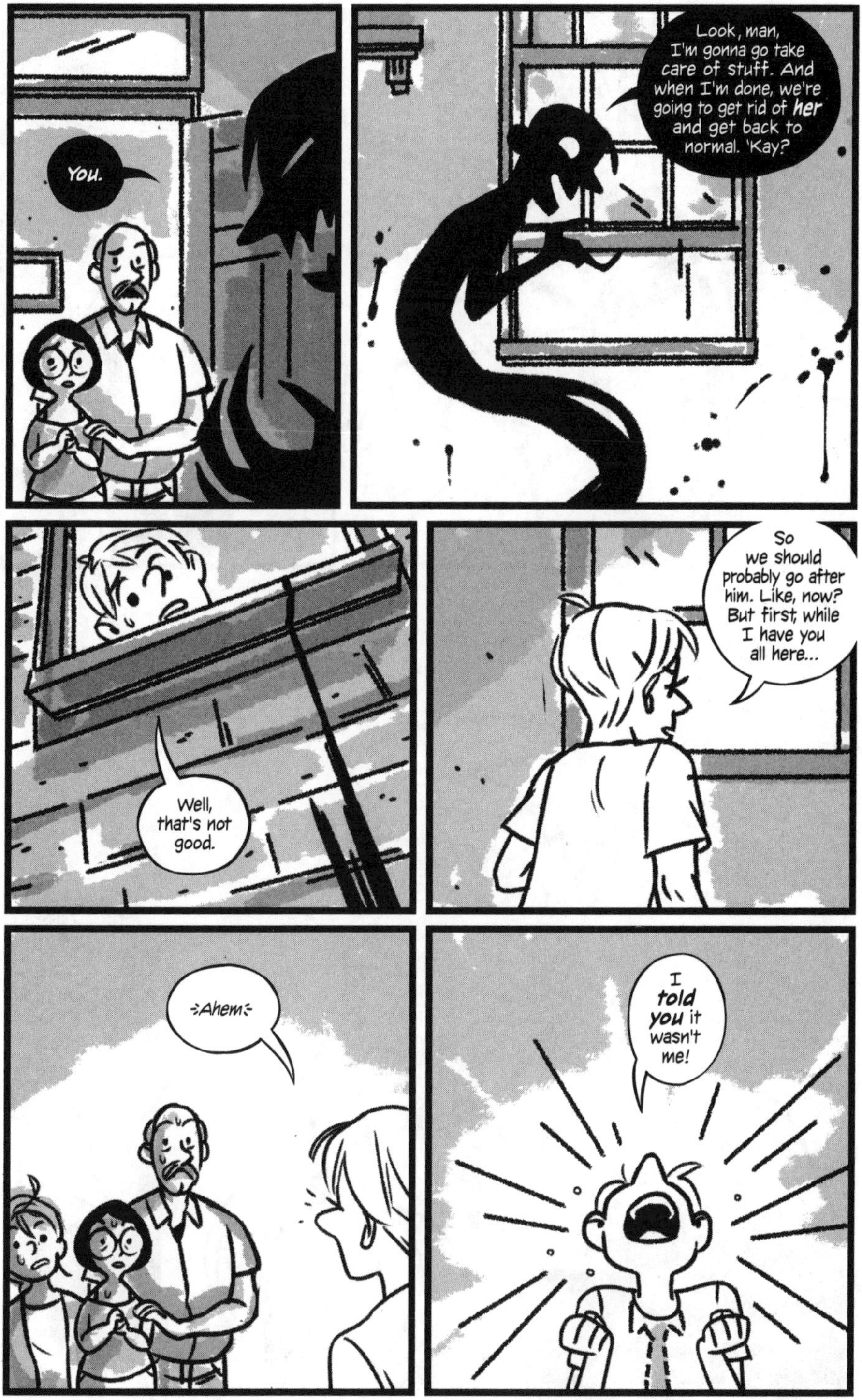
You.
Look, man, I'm gonna go take care of stuff. And when I'm done, we're going to get rid of **her** and get back to normal. 'Kay?
Well, that's not good.
So we should probably go after him. Like, now? But first, while I have you all here...
Ahem
I **told you** it wasn't me!

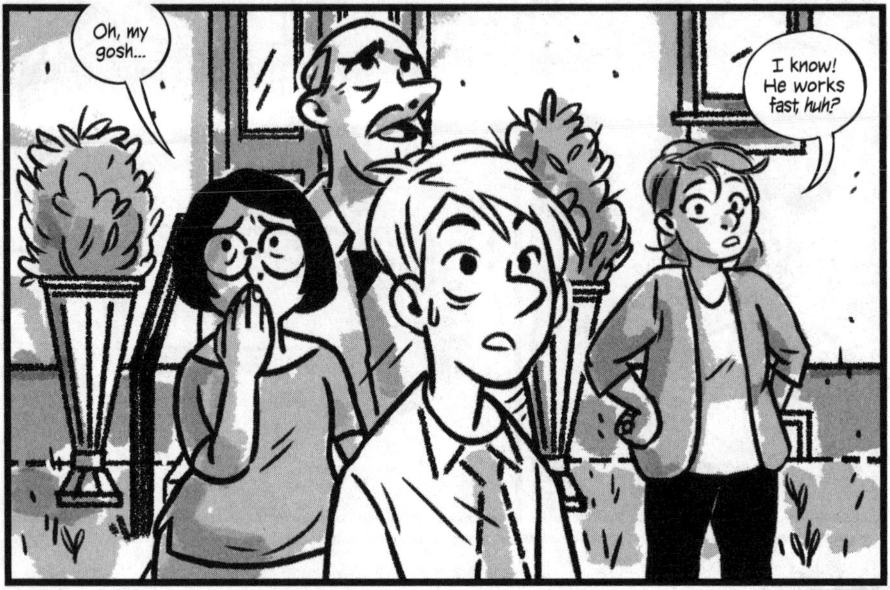
Oh, my gosh...
I know! He works fast, huh?

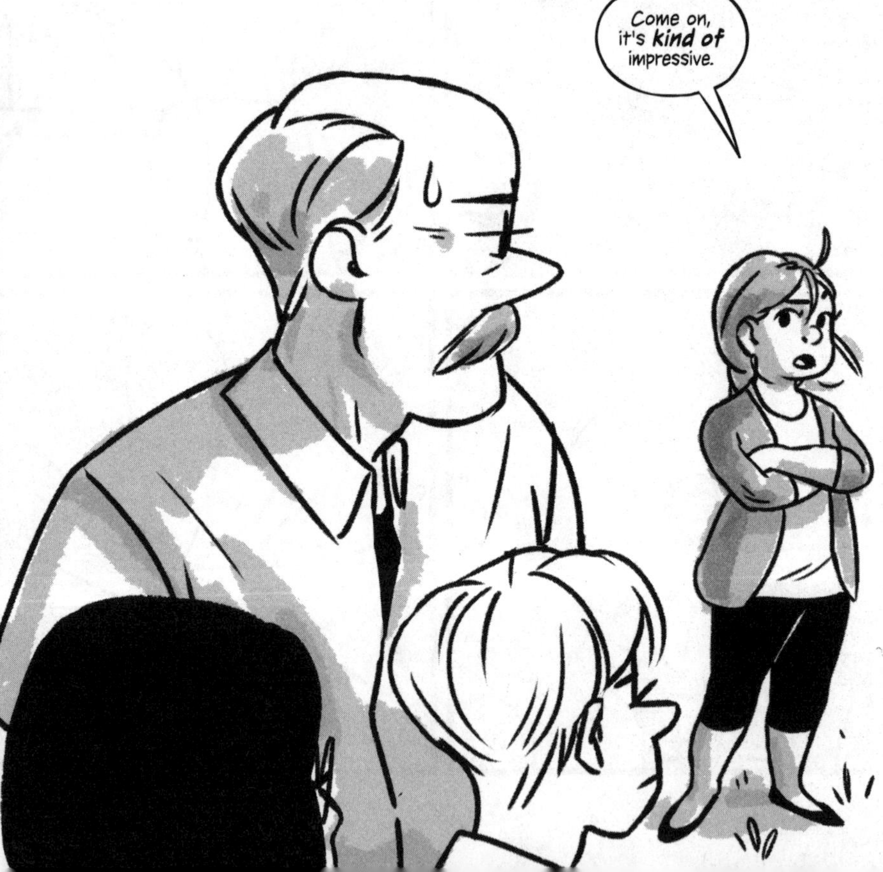
Come on, it's **kind of** impressive.

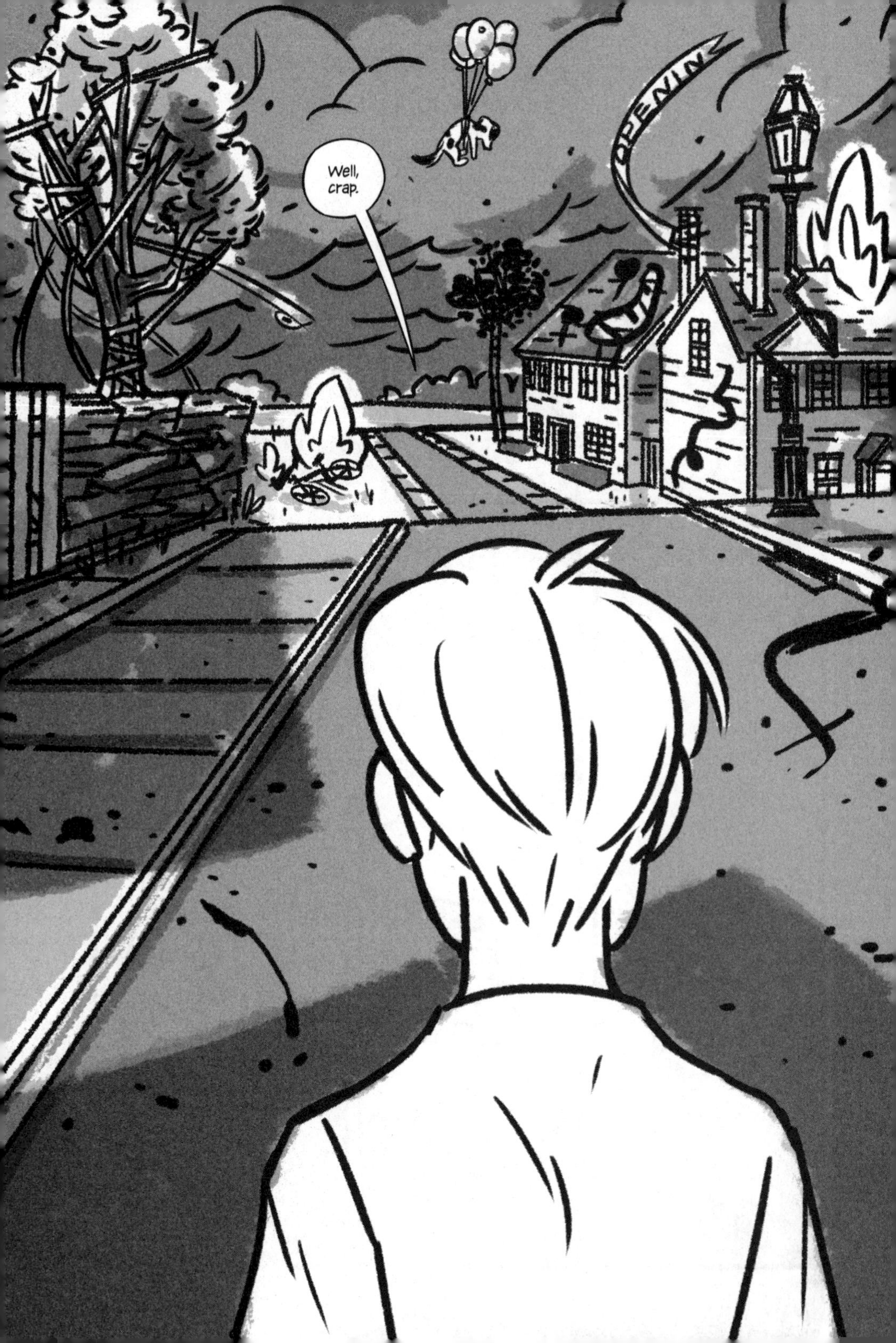
Well, crap.

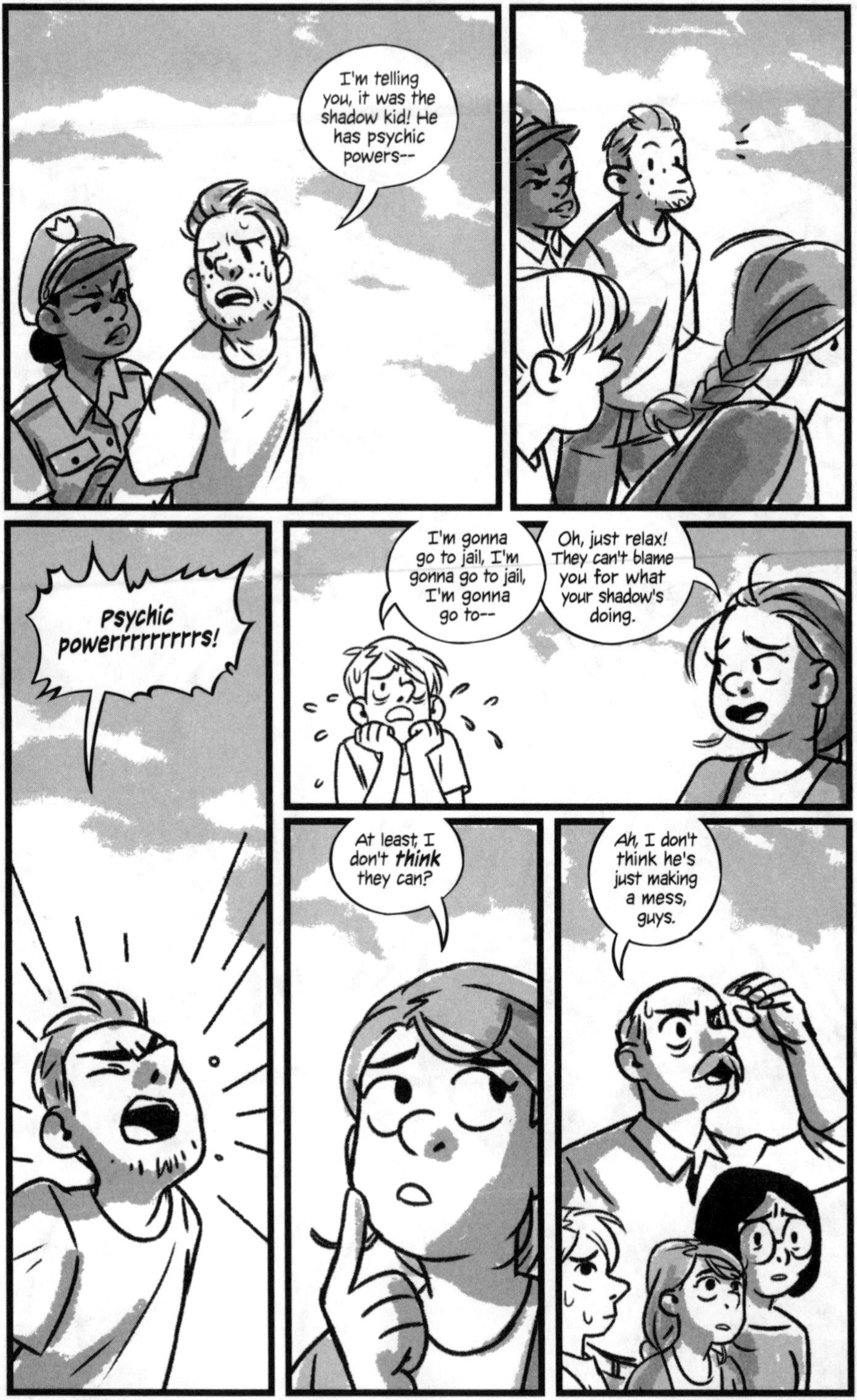
I'm telling you, it was the shadow kid! He has psychic powers--
Psychic powerrrrrrrrrs!
I'm gonna go to jail, I'm gonna go to jail, I'm gonna go to--
Oh, just relax! They can't blame you for what your shadow's doing.
At least, I don't *think* they can?
Ah, I don't think he's just making a mess, guys.

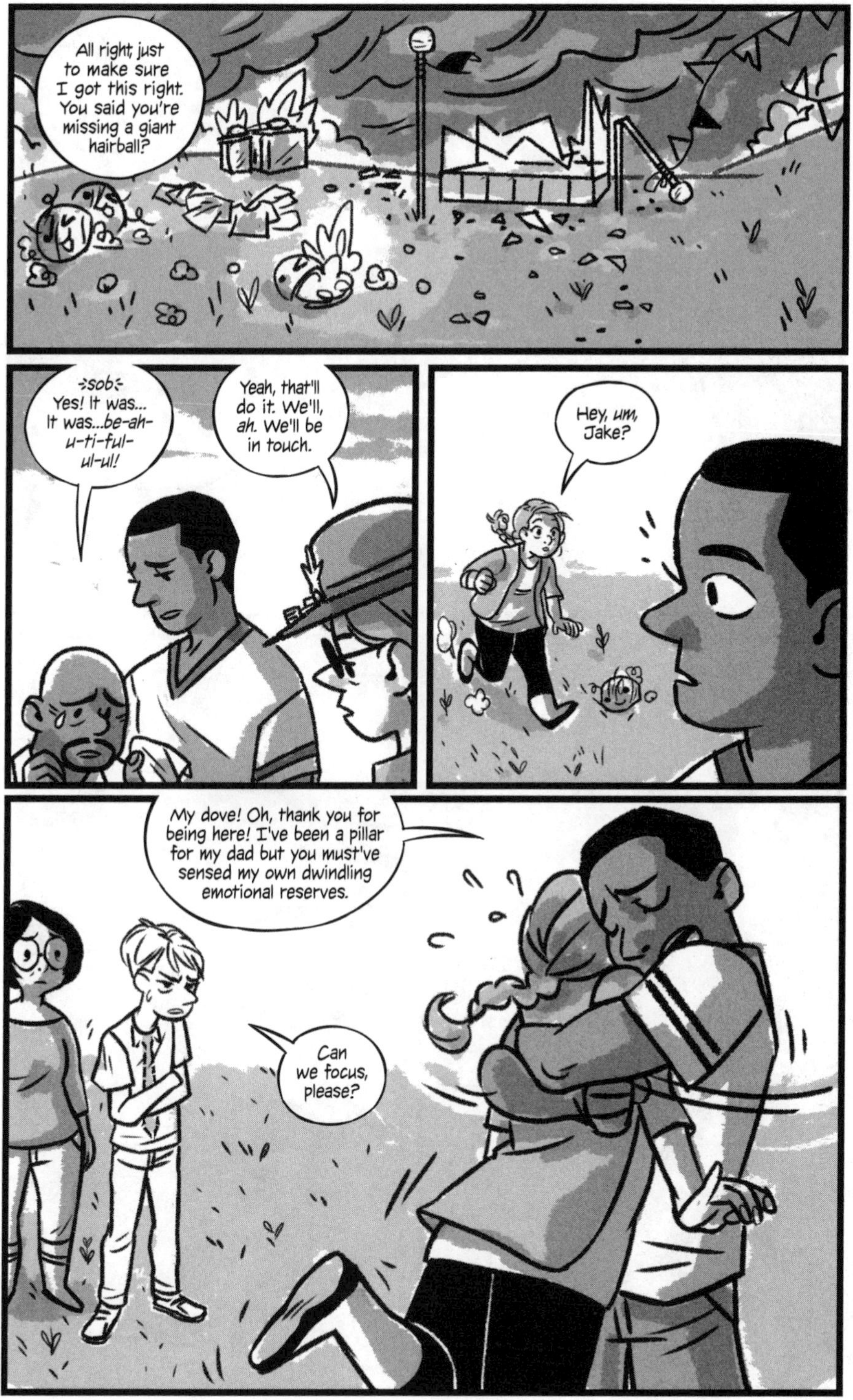
All right, just to make sure I got this right. You said you're missing a giant hairball?
-sob- Yes! It was... It was...be-ah-u-ti-ful-ul-ul!
Yeah, that'll do it. We'll, ah. We'll be in touch.
Hey, um, Jake?
My dove! Oh, thank you for being here! I've been a pillar for my dad but you must've sensed my own dwindling emotional reserves.
Can we focus, please?

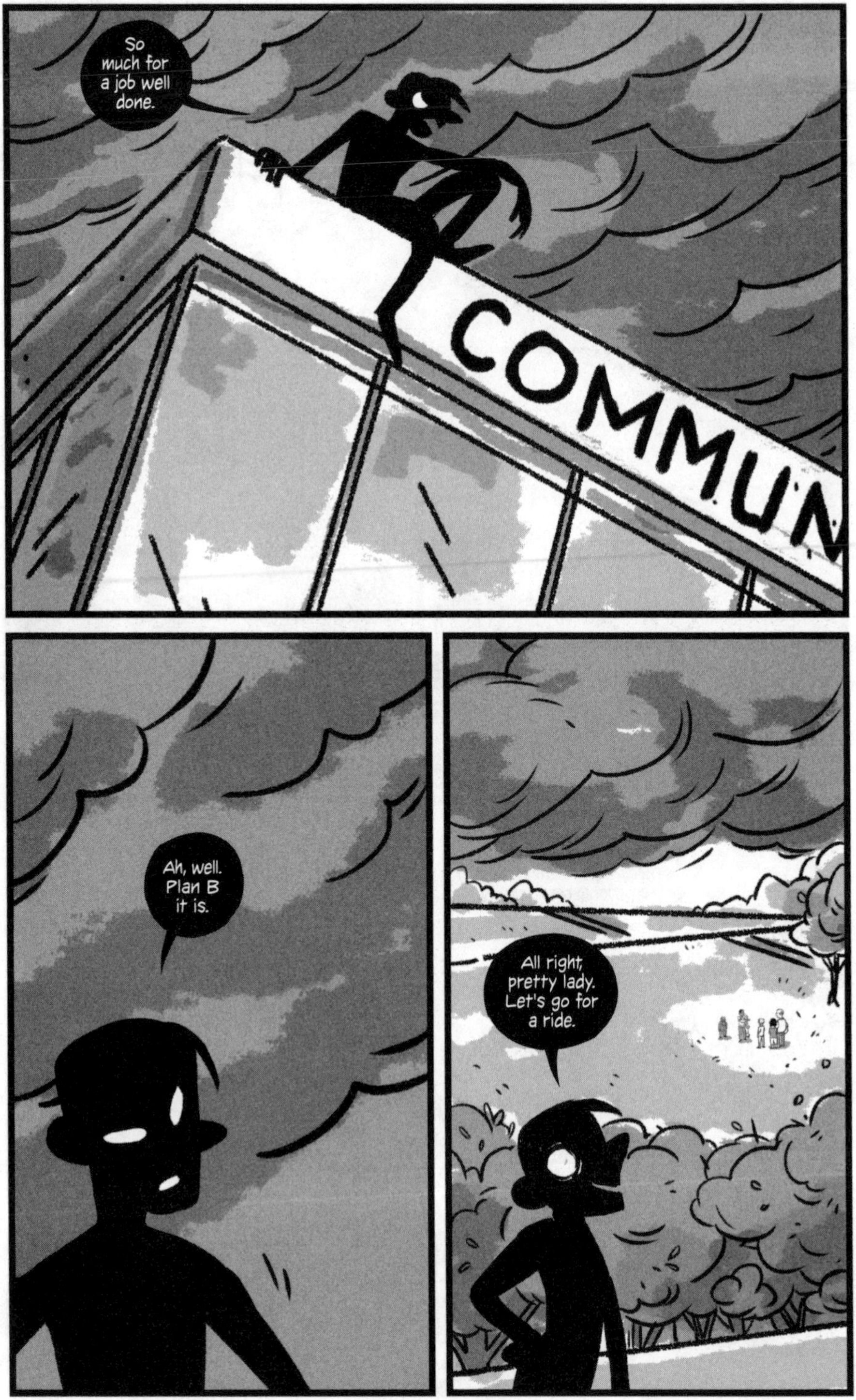
So much for a job well done.
COMMUN
Ah, well. Plan B it is.
All right, pretty lady. Let's go for a ride.

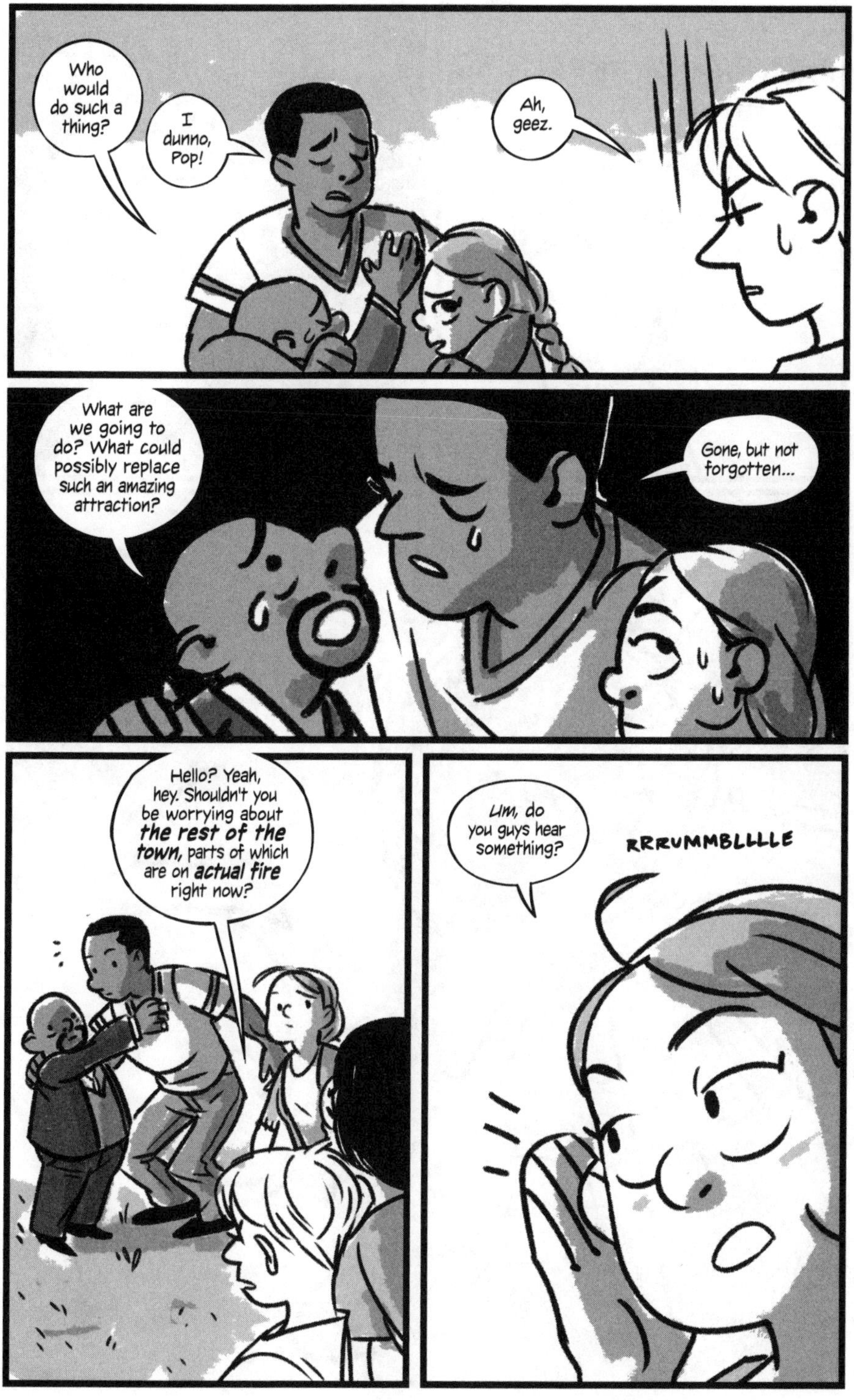
Who would do such a thing?
I dunno, Pop!
Ah, geez.
What are we going to do? What could possibly replace such an amazing attraction?
Gone, but not forgotten...
Hello? Yeah, hey. Shouldn't you be worrying about **the rest of the town,** parts of which are on **actual fire** right now?
Um, do you guys hear something?
RRRUMMBLLLLE

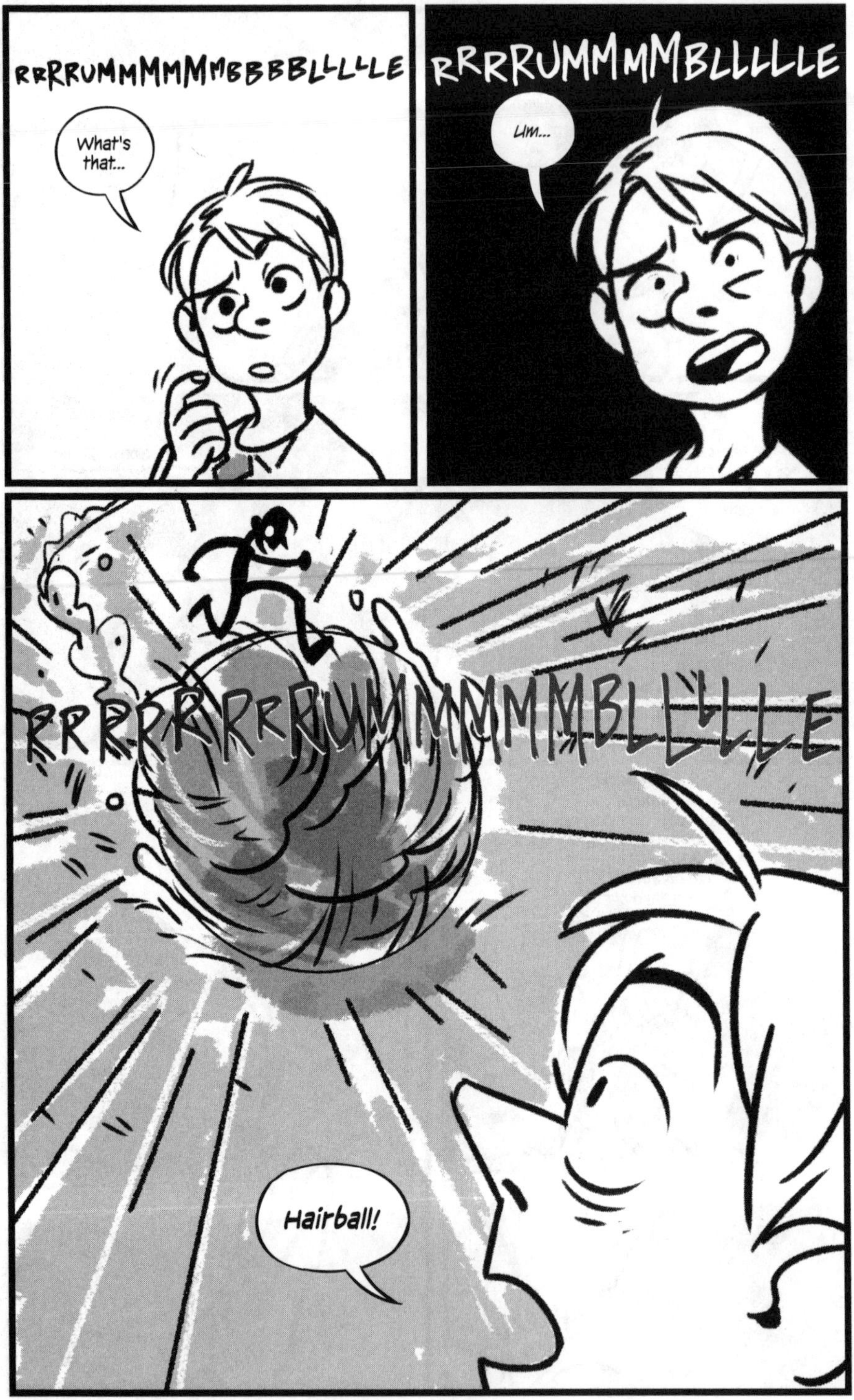
RRRRUMMMMMMMBBBBLLLLLE
What's that...
RRRRUMMMMMBLLLLLE
Um...
RRRRRRRRRUMMMMMMMBLLLLLE
Hairball!

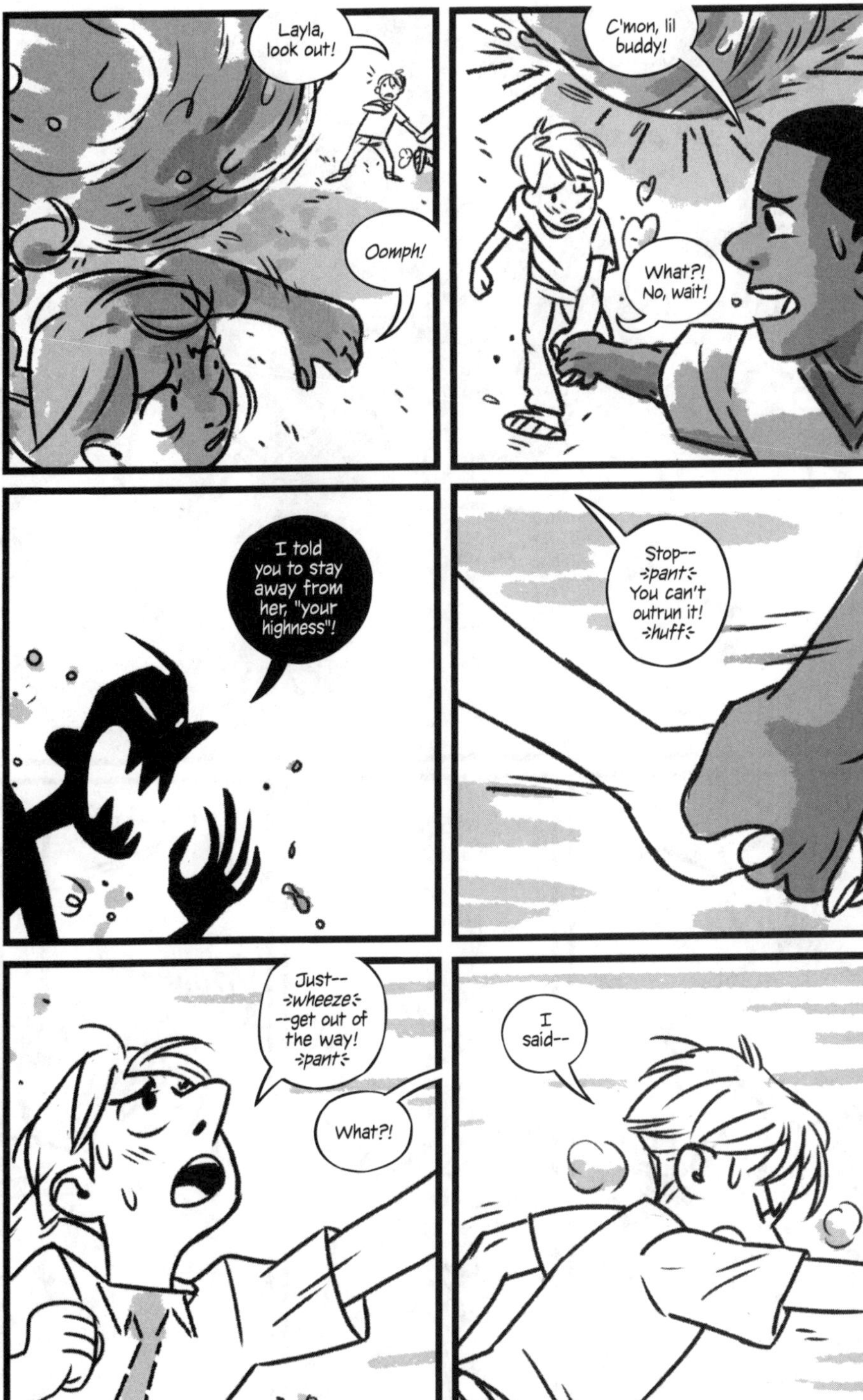
Layla, look out!
Oomph!
C'mon, lil buddy!
What?! No, wait!
I told you to stay away from her, "your highness"!
Stop-- *pant* You can't outrun it! *huff*
Just-- *wheeze* --get out of the way! *pant*
What?!
I said--

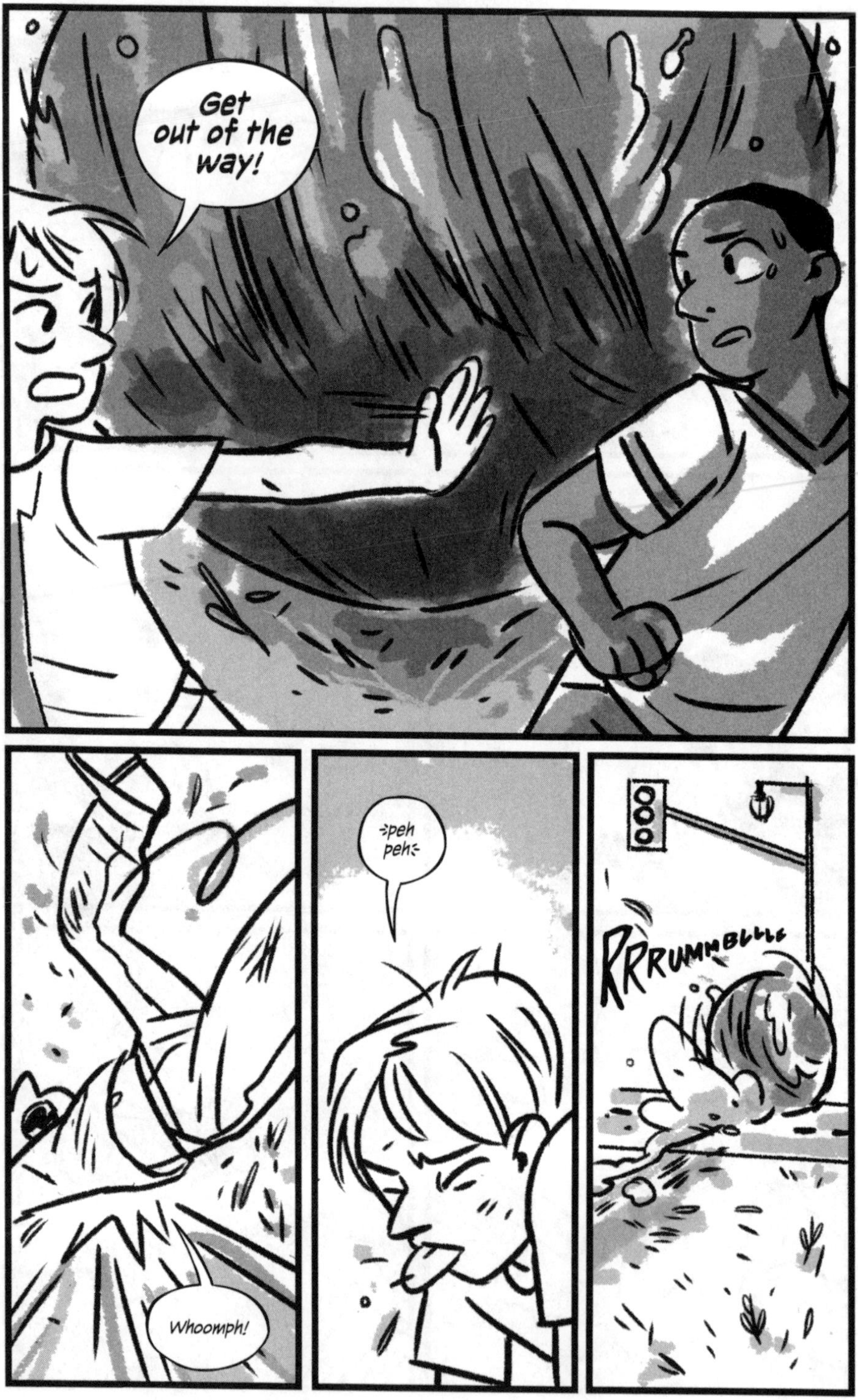
Get out of the way!
Whoomph!
peh peh
RRRUMMBLLLL

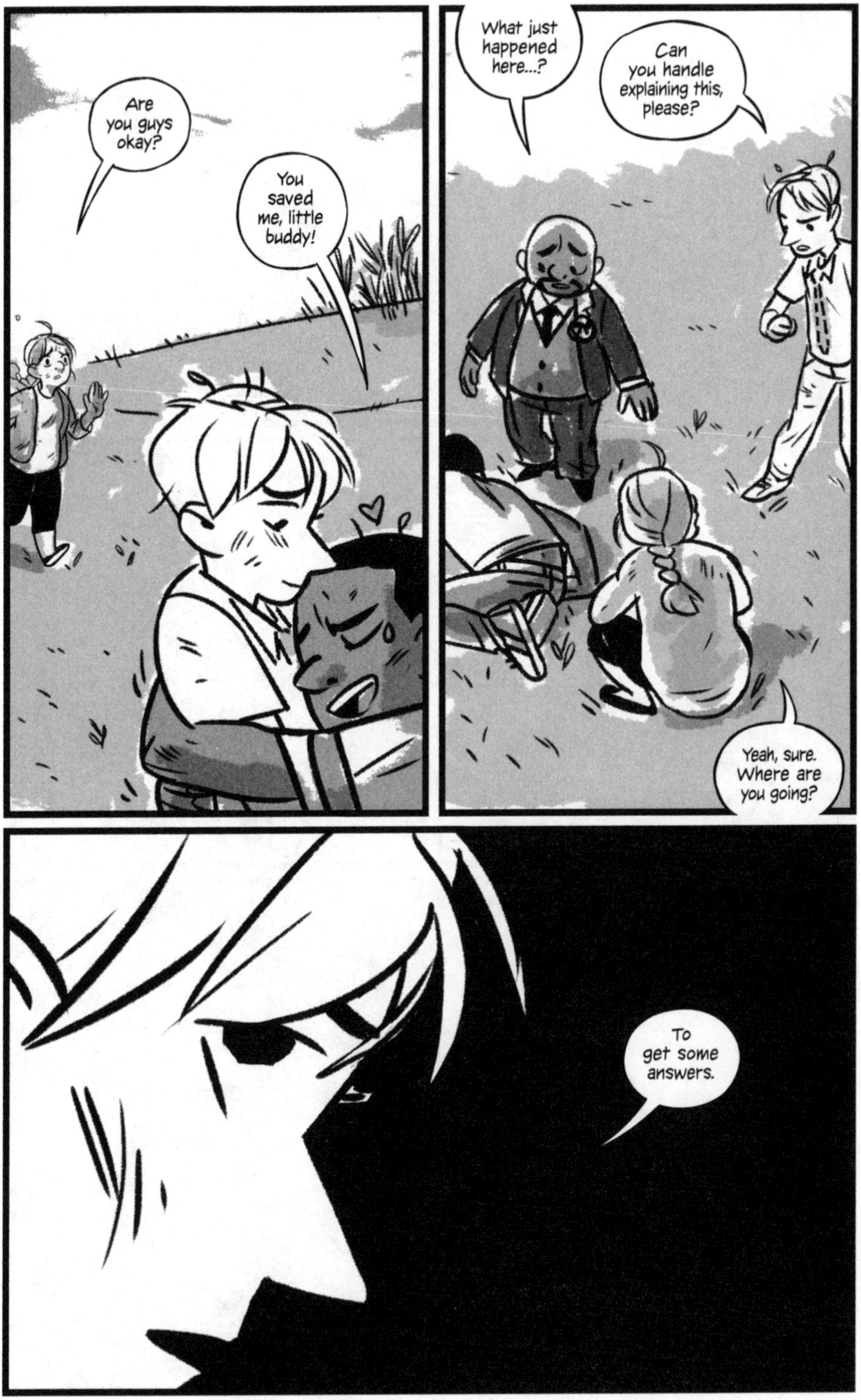
Are you guys okay?
You saved me, little buddy!
What just happened here...?
Can you handle explaining this, please?
Yeah, sure. Where are you going?
To get some answers.

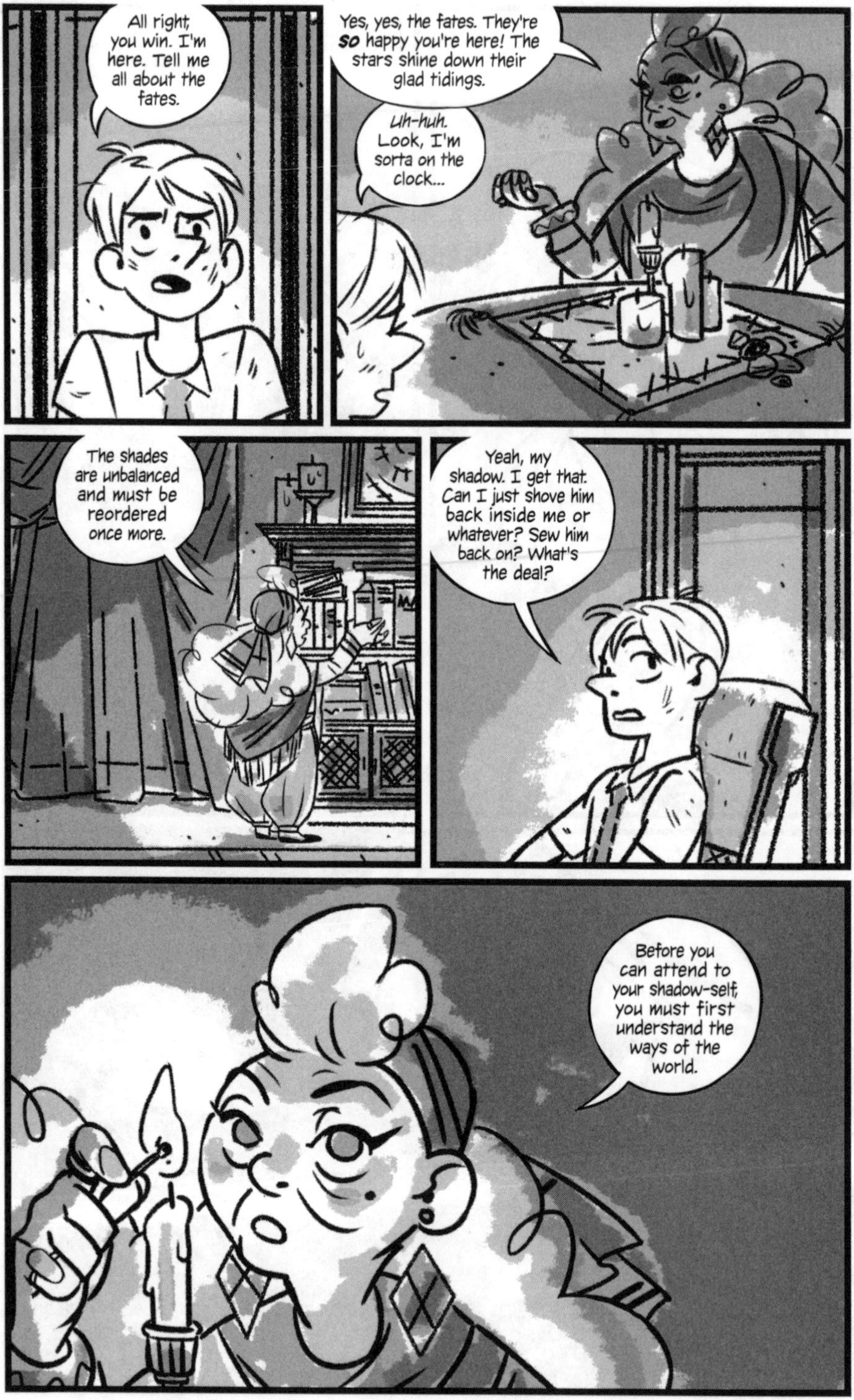
All right, you win. I'm here. Tell me all about the fates.
Yes, yes, the fates. They're **SO** happy you're here! The stars shine down their glad tidings.
Uh-huh. Look, I'm sorta on the clock...
The shades are unbalanced and must be reordered once more.
Yeah, my shadow. I get that. Can I just shove him back inside me or whatever? Sew him back on? What's the deal?
Before you can attend to your shadow-self, you must first understand the ways of the world.

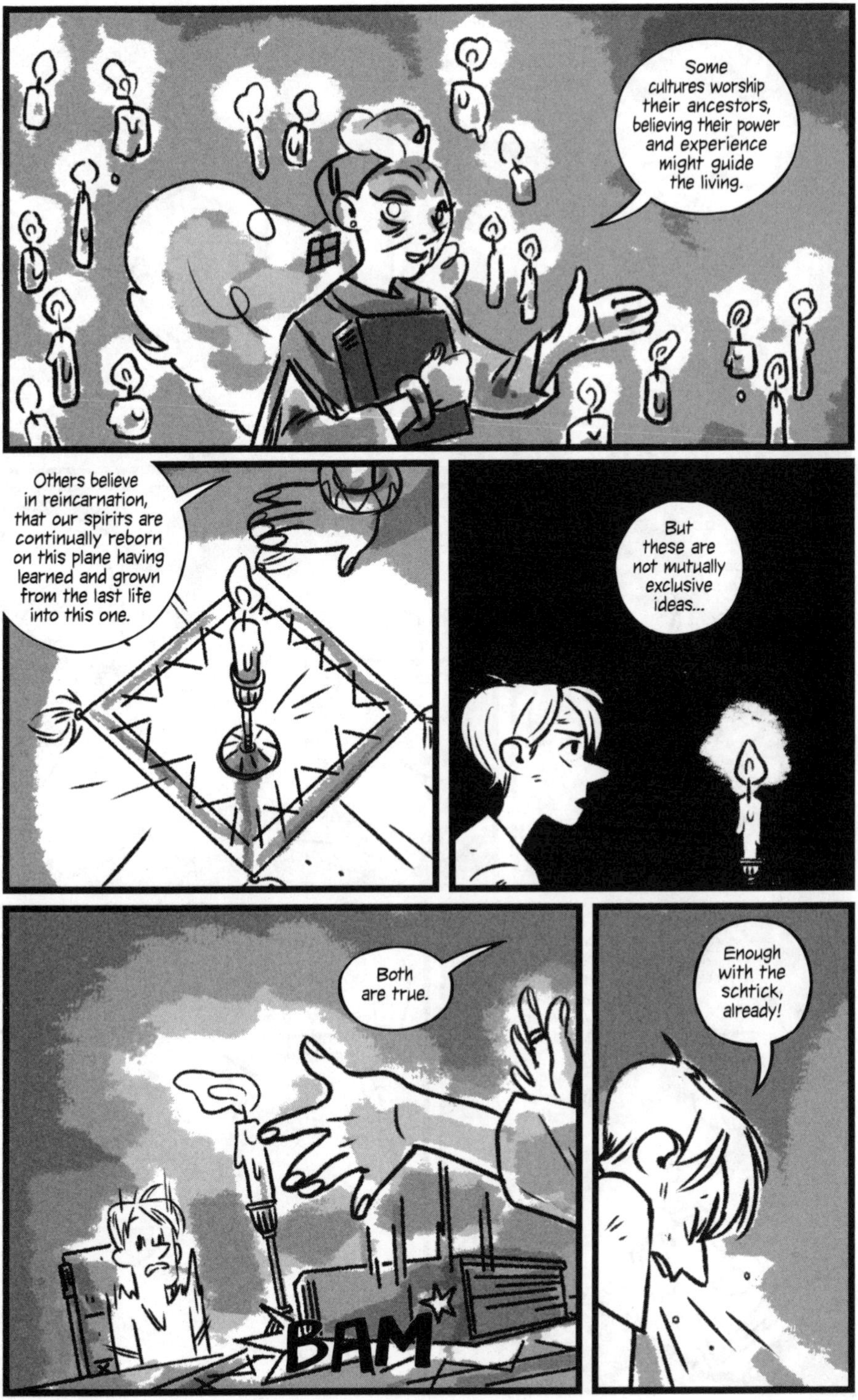
Some cultures worship their ancestors, believing their power and experience might guide the living.
Others believe in reincarnation, that our spirits are continually reborn on this plane having learned and grown from the last life into this one.
But these are not mutually exclusive ideas...
Both are true.
BAM
Enough with the schtick, already!

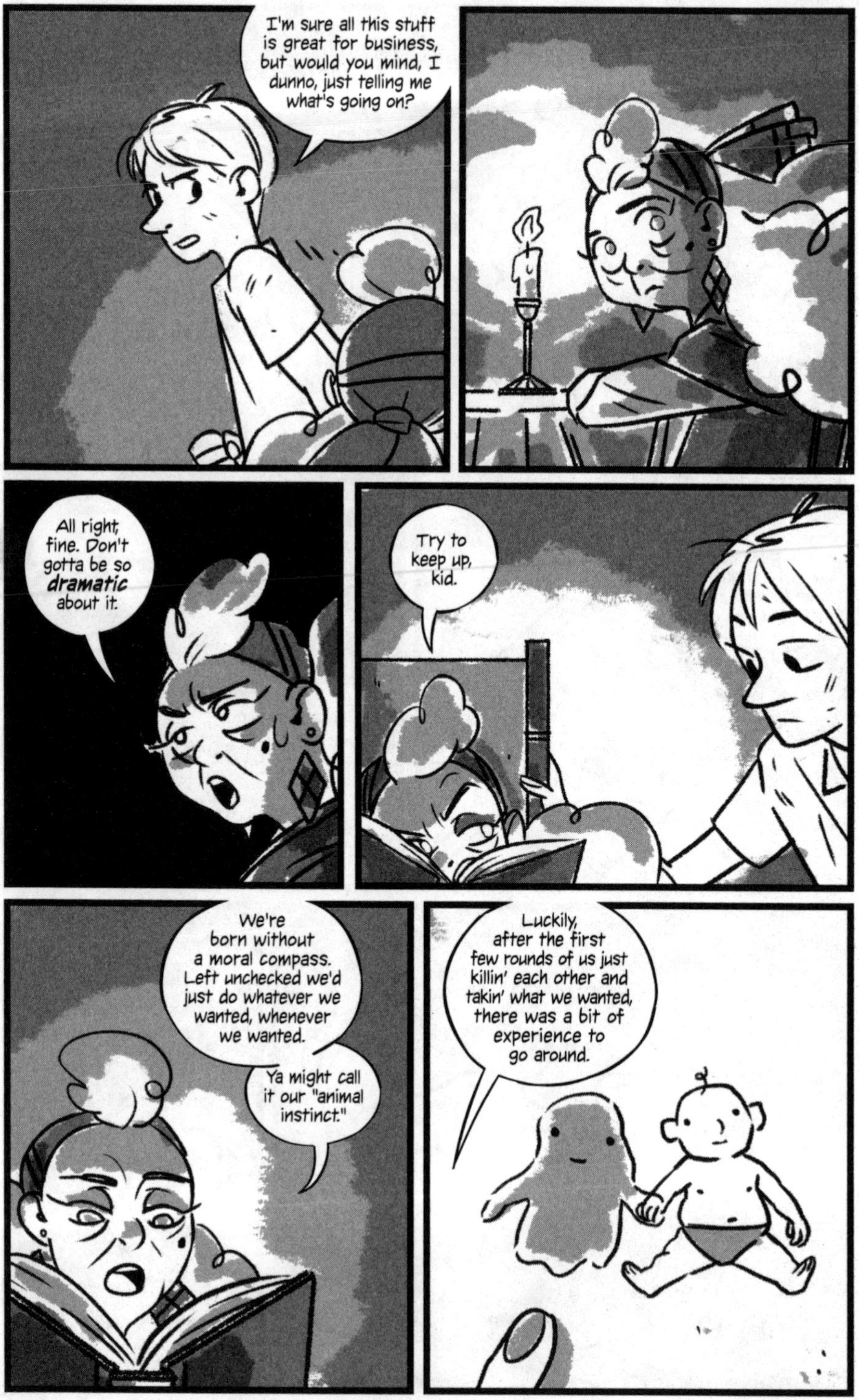
I'm sure all this stuff is great for business, but would you mind, I dunno, just telling me what's going on?
All right, fine. Don't gotta be so **dramatic** about it.
Try to keep up, kid.
We're born without a moral compass. Left unchecked we'd just do whatever we wanted, whenever we wanted.
Ya might call it our "animal instinct."
Luckily, after the first few rounds of us just killin' each other and takin' what we wanted, there was a bit of experience to go around.

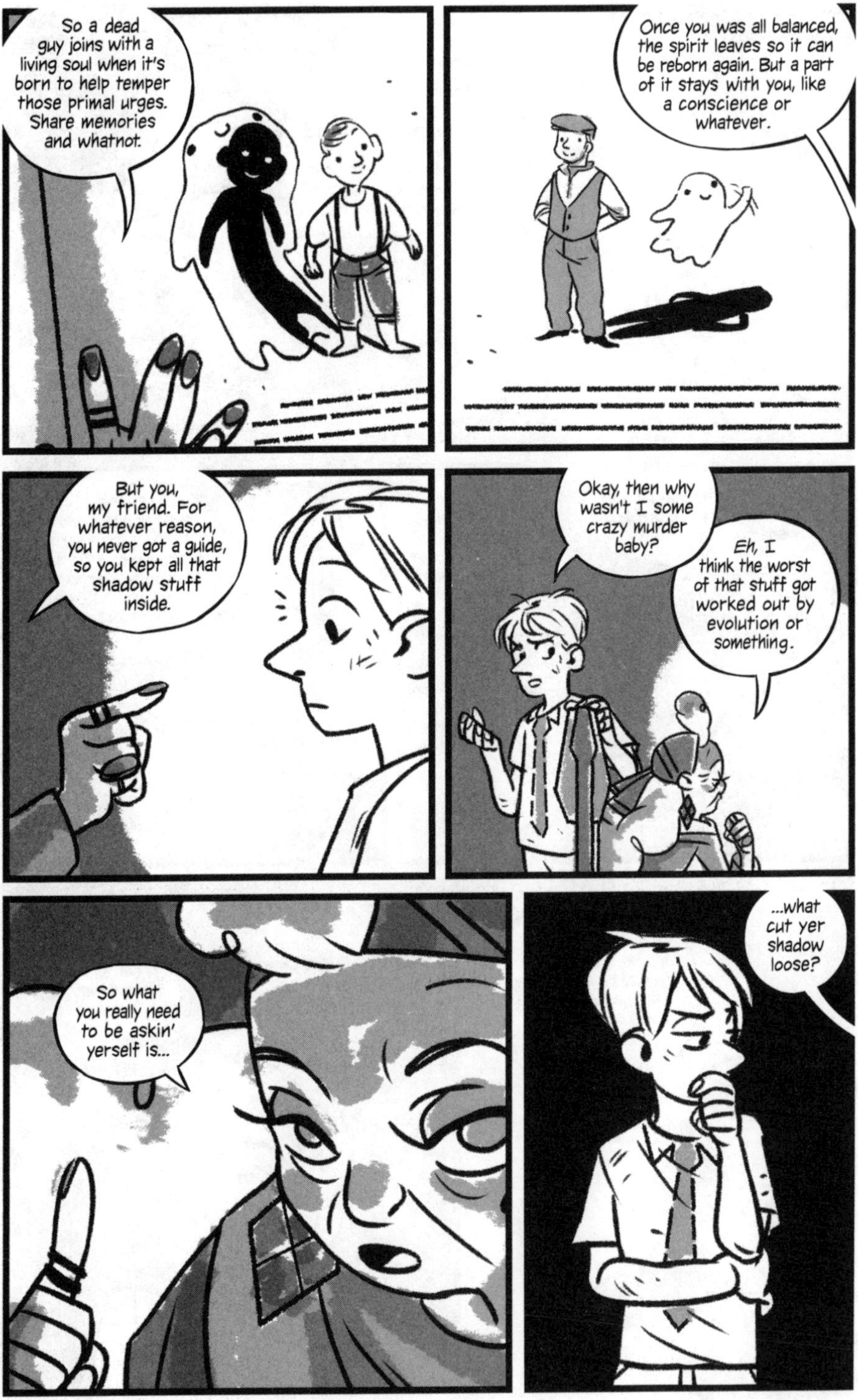
So a dead guy joins with a living soul when it's born to help temper those primal urges. Share memories and whatnot.
Once you was all balanced, the spirit leaves so it can be reborn again. But a part of it stays with you, like a conscience or whatever.
But you, my friend. For whatever reason, you never got a guide, so you kept all that shadow stuff inside.
Okay, then why wasn't I some crazy murder baby?
Eh, I think the worst of that stuff got worked out by evolution or something.
So what you really need to be askin' yerself is...
...what cut yer shadow loose?

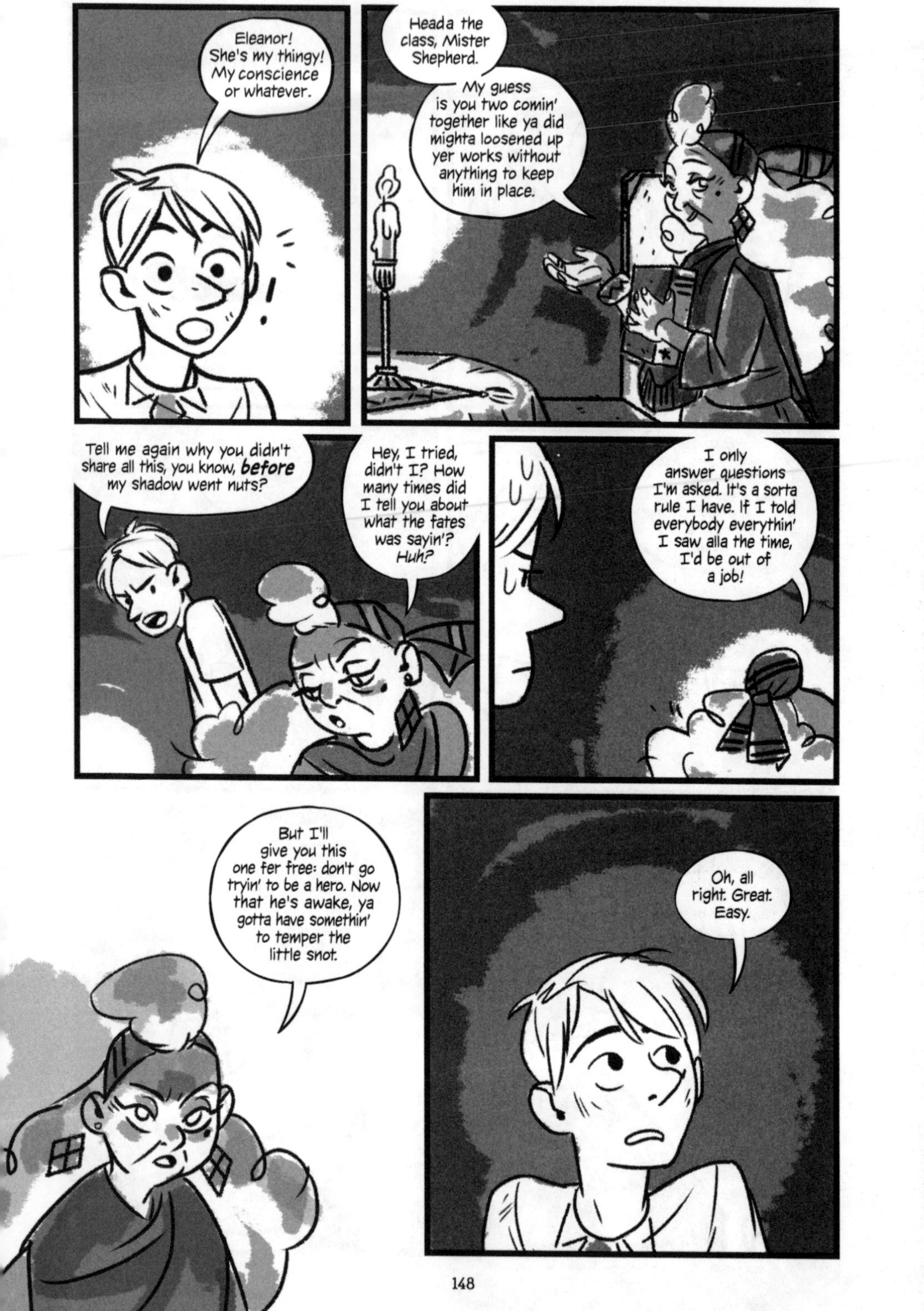

Eleanor! She's my thingy! My conscience or whatever.
Heada the class, Mister Shepherd.
My guess is you two comin' together like ya did mighta loosened up yer works without anything to keep him in place.
Tell me again why you didn't share all this, you know, **before** my shadow went nuts?
Hey, I tried, didn't I? How many times did I tell you about what the fates was sayin'? *Huh?*
I only answer questions I'm asked. It's a sorta rule I have. If I told everybody everythin' I saw alla the time, I'd be out of a job!
But I'll give you this one fer free: don't go tryin' to be a hero. Now that he's awake, ya gotta have somethin' to temper the little snot.
Oh, all right. Great. Easy.

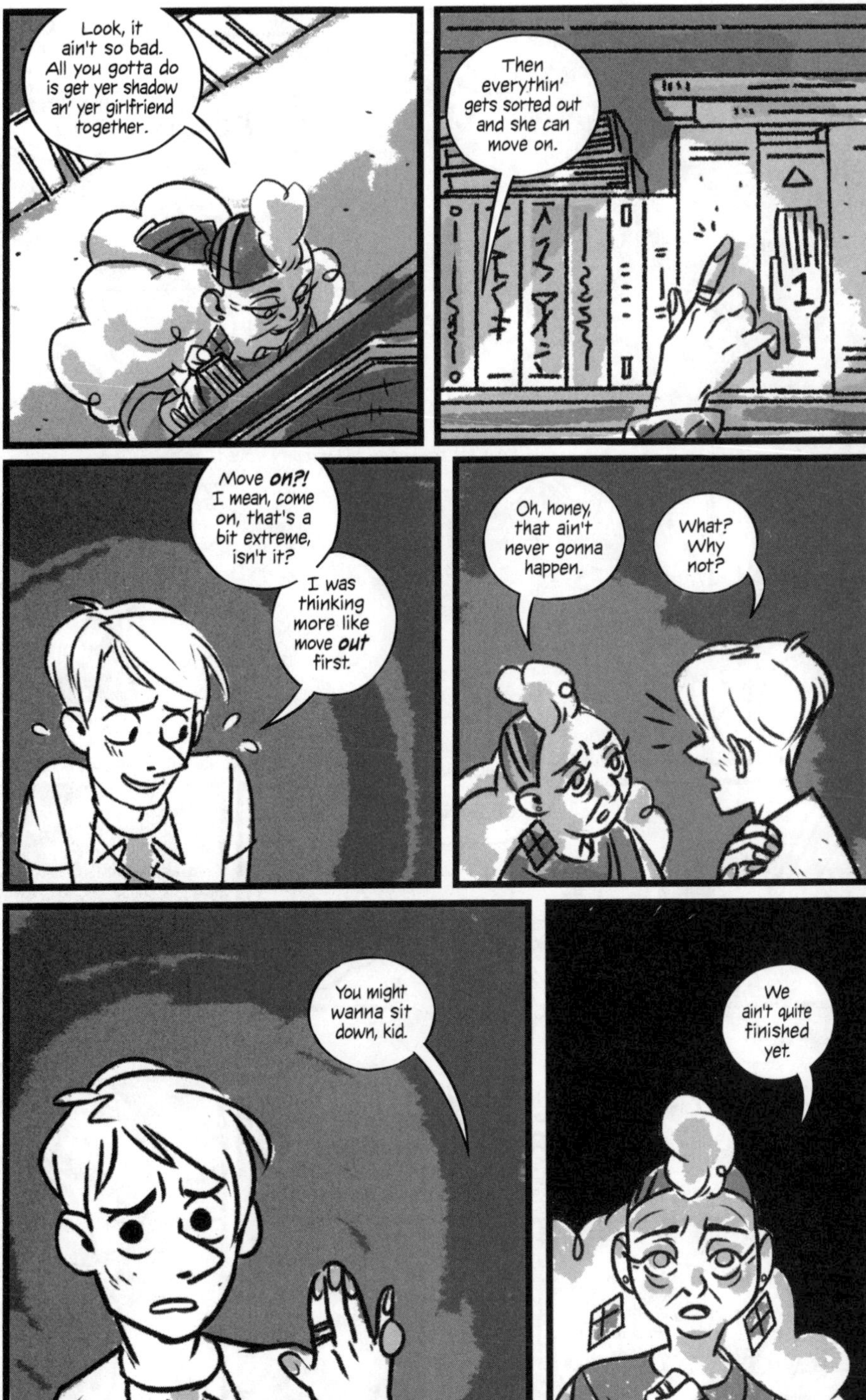
Look, it ain't so bad. All you gotta do is get yer shadow an' yer girlfriend together.
Then everythin' gets sorted out and she can move on.
Move on?! I mean, come on, that's a bit extreme, isn't it?
I was thinking more like move out first.
Oh, honey, that ain't never gonna happen.
What? Why not?
You might wanna sit down, kid.
We ain't quite finished yet.

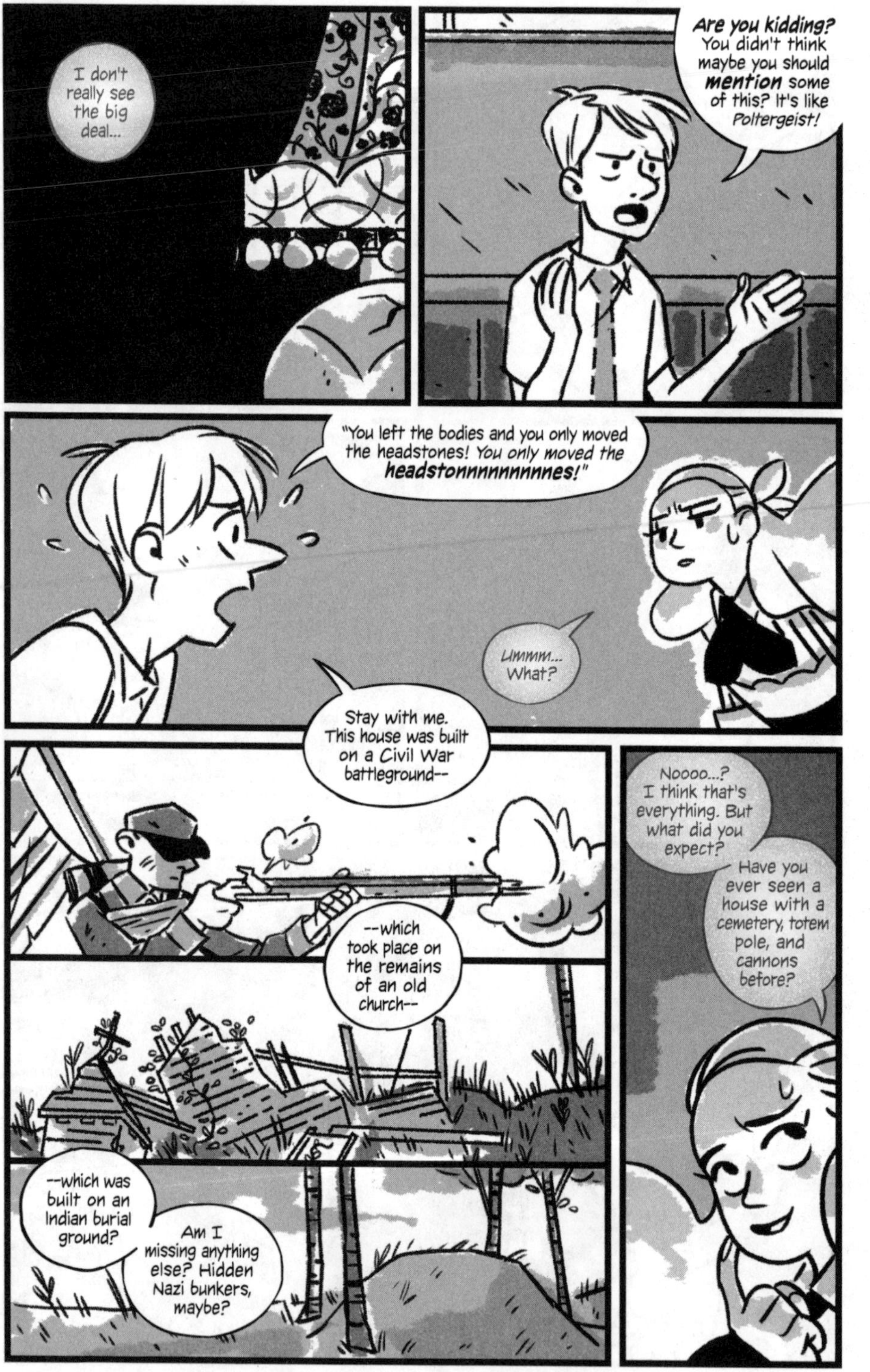
I don't really see the big deal...
Are you kidding? You didn't think maybe you should mention some of this? It's like Poltergeist!
"You left the bodies and you only moved the headstones! You only moved the headstonnnnnnnnnes!"
Ummm... What?
Stay with me. This house was built on a Civil War battleground--
--which took place on the remains of an old church--
--which was built on an Indian burial ground?
Am I missing anything else? Hidden Nazi bunkers, maybe?
Noooo...? I think that's everything. But what did you expect?
Have you ever seen a house with a cemetery, totem pole, and cannons before?

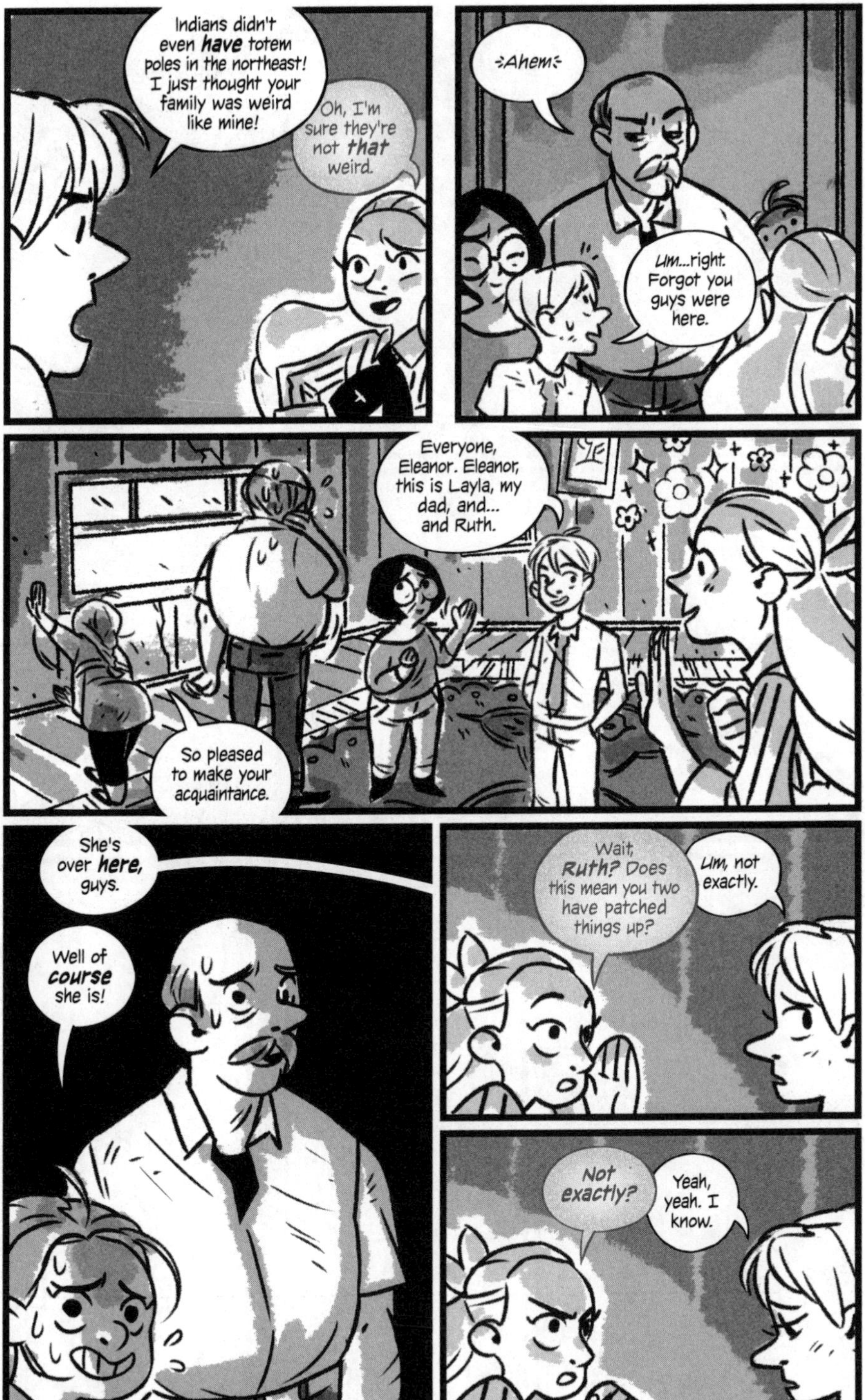

Indians didn't even **have** totem poles in the northeast! I just thought your family was weird like mine!
Oh, I'm sure they're not **that** weird.
Ahem
Um...right. Forgot you guys were here.
Everyone, Eleanor. Eleanor, this is Layla, my dad, and... and Ruth.
So pleased to make your acquaintance.
She's over **here,** guys.
Well of **course** she is!
Wait, **Ruth?** Does this mean you two have patched things up?
Um, not exactly.
Not exactly?
Yeah, yeah. I know.

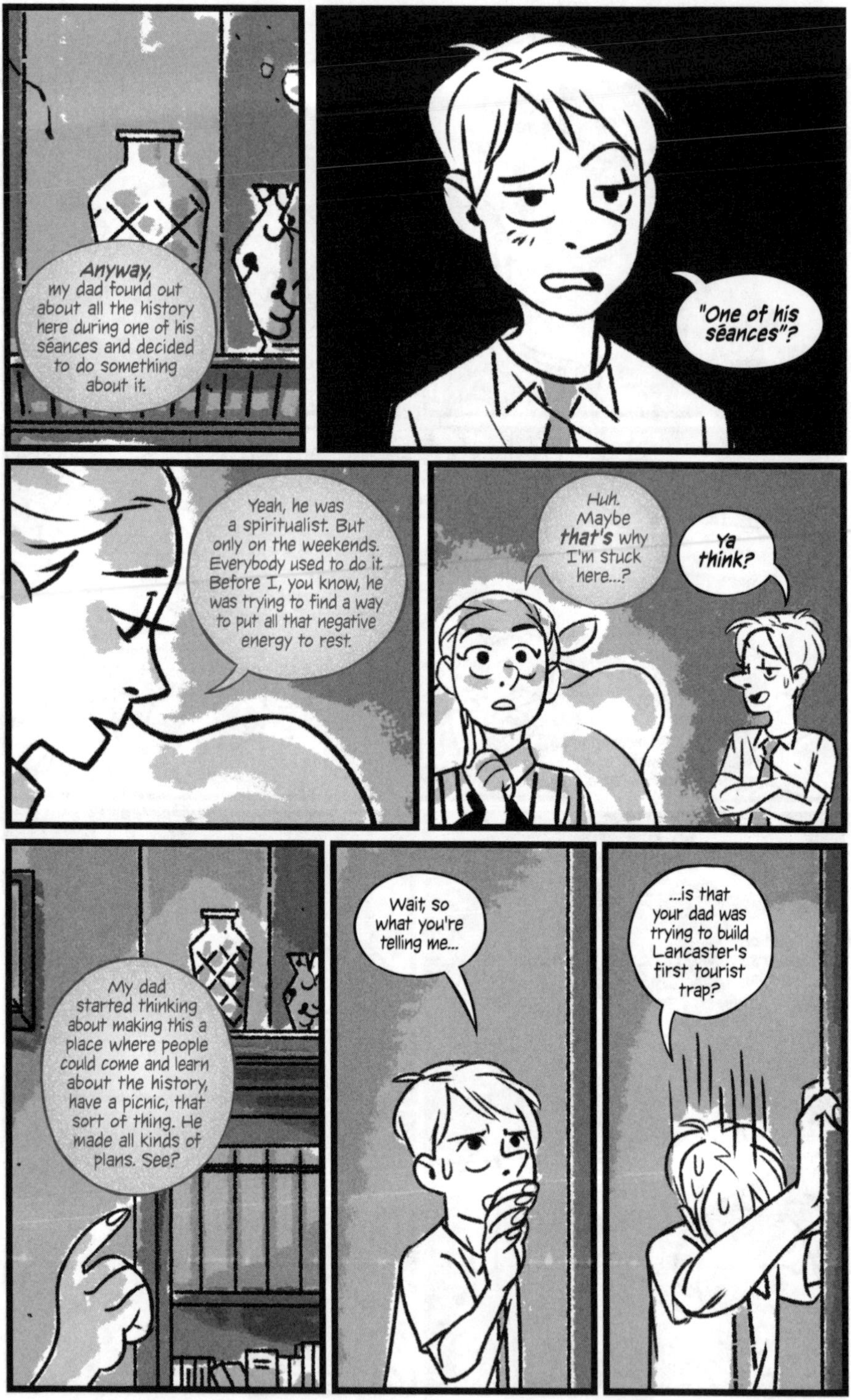

Anyway, my dad found out about all the history here during one of his séances and decided to do something about it.
"One of his séances"?
Yeah, he was a spiritualist. But only on the weekends. Everybody used to do it. Before I, you know, he was trying to find a way to put all that negative energy to rest.
Huh. Maybe that's why I'm stuck here...?
Ya think?
My dad started thinking about making this a place where people could come and learn about the history, have a picnic, that sort of thing. He made all kinds of plans. See?
Wait, so what you're telling me...
...is that your dad was trying to build Lancaster's first tourist trap?

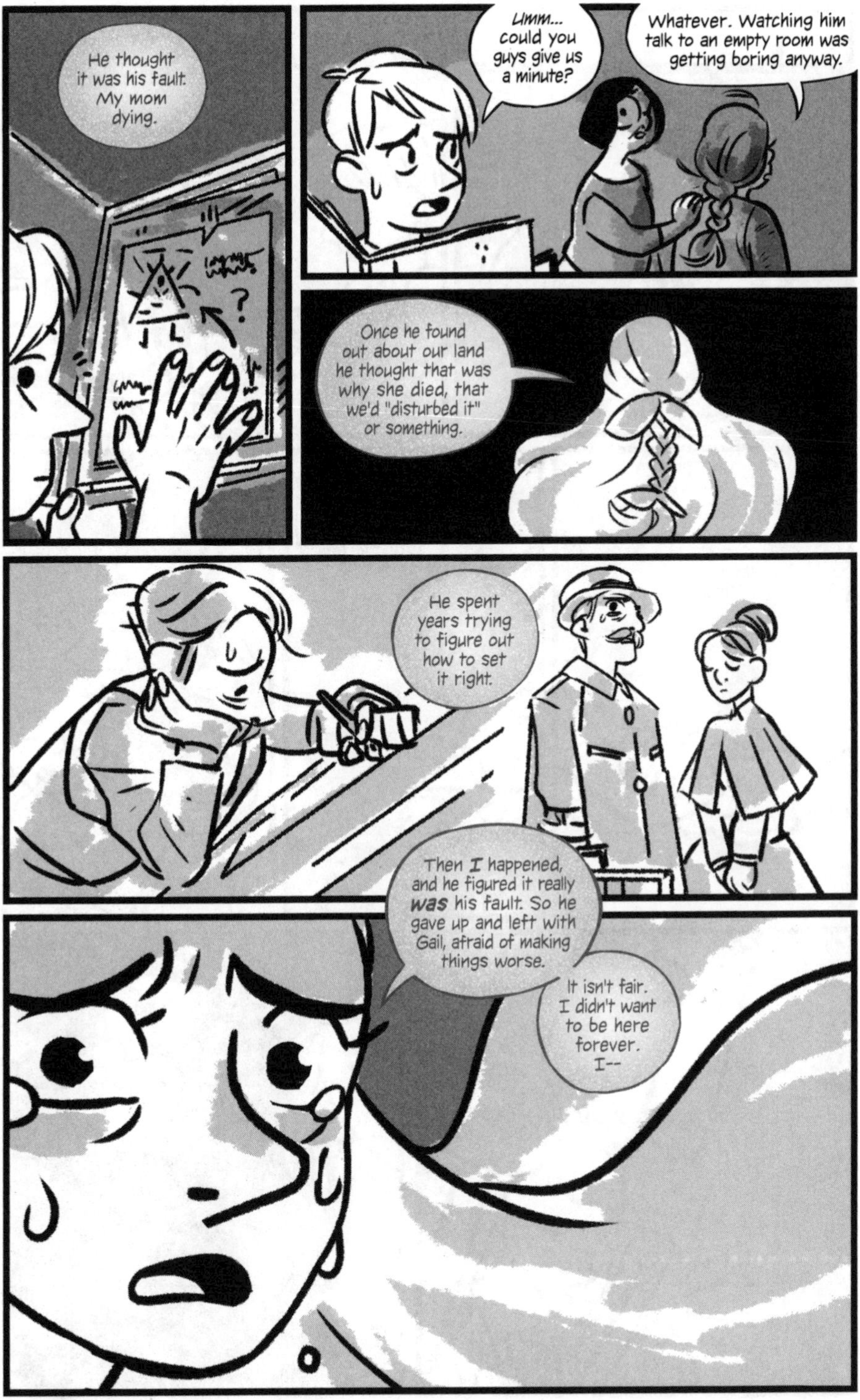
He thought it was his fault. My mom dying.
Umm... could you guys give us a minute?
Whatever. Watching him talk to an empty room was getting boring anyway.
Once he found out about our land he thought that was why she died, that we'd "disturbed it" or something.
He spent years trying to figure out how to set it right.
Then I happened, and he figured it really was his fault. So he gave up and left with Gail, afraid of making things worse.
It isn't fair. I didn't want to be here forever. I--

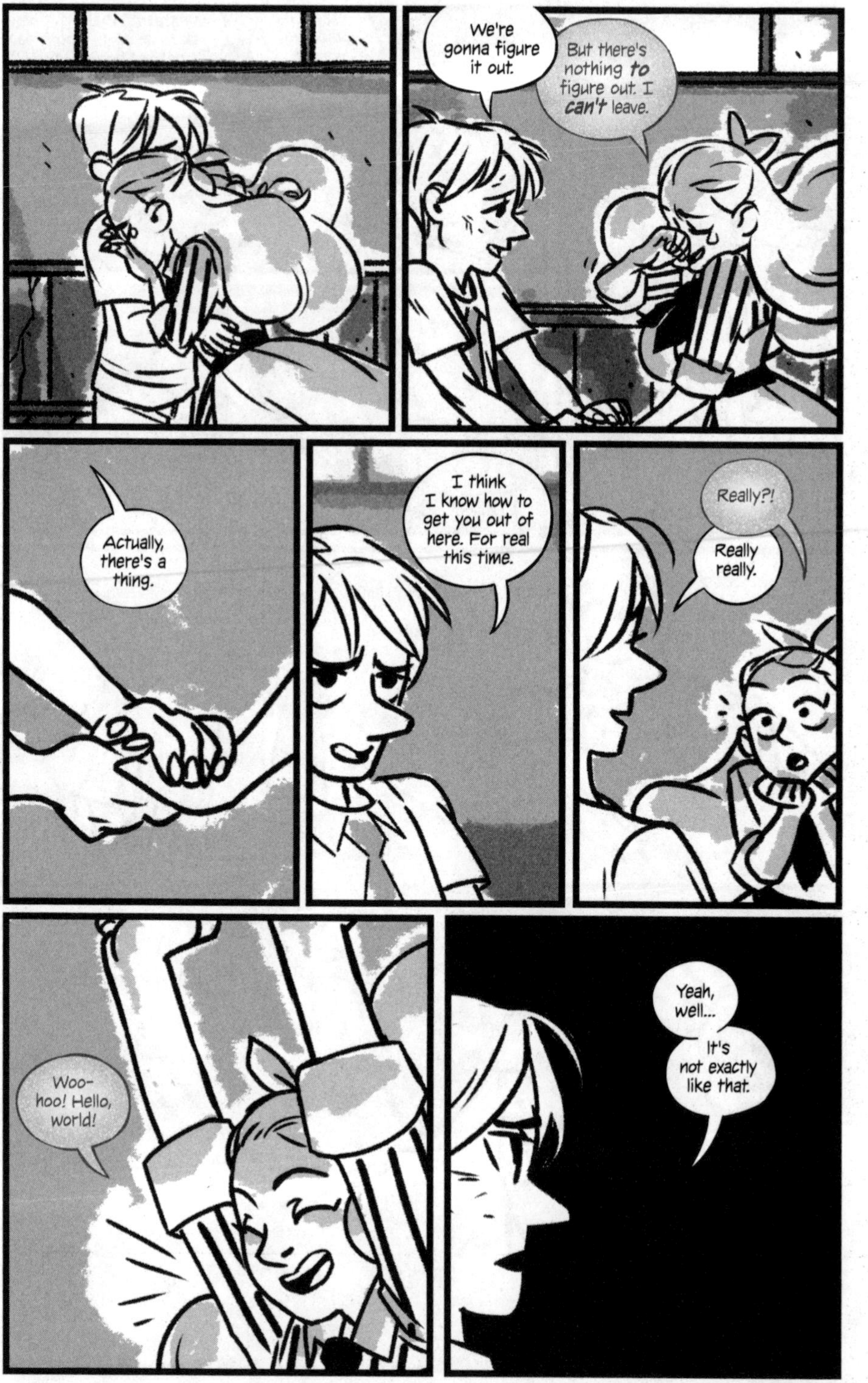
We're gonna figure it out.
But there's nothing *to* figure out. I *can't* leave.
Actually, there's a thing.
I think I know how to get you out of here. For real this time.
Really?!
Really really.
Woo-hoo! Hello, world!
Yeah, well...
It's not exactly like that.

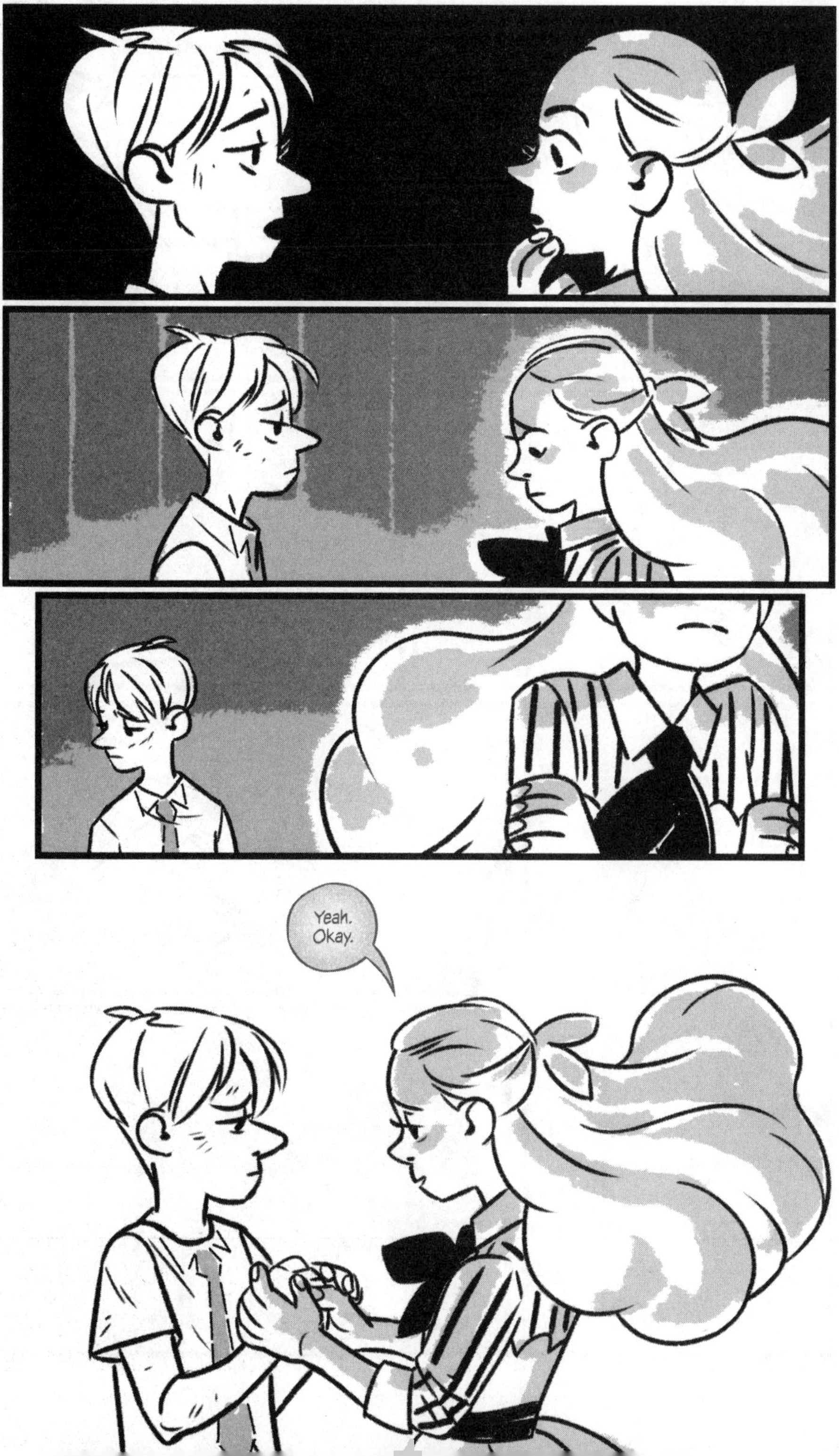
Yeah. Okay.

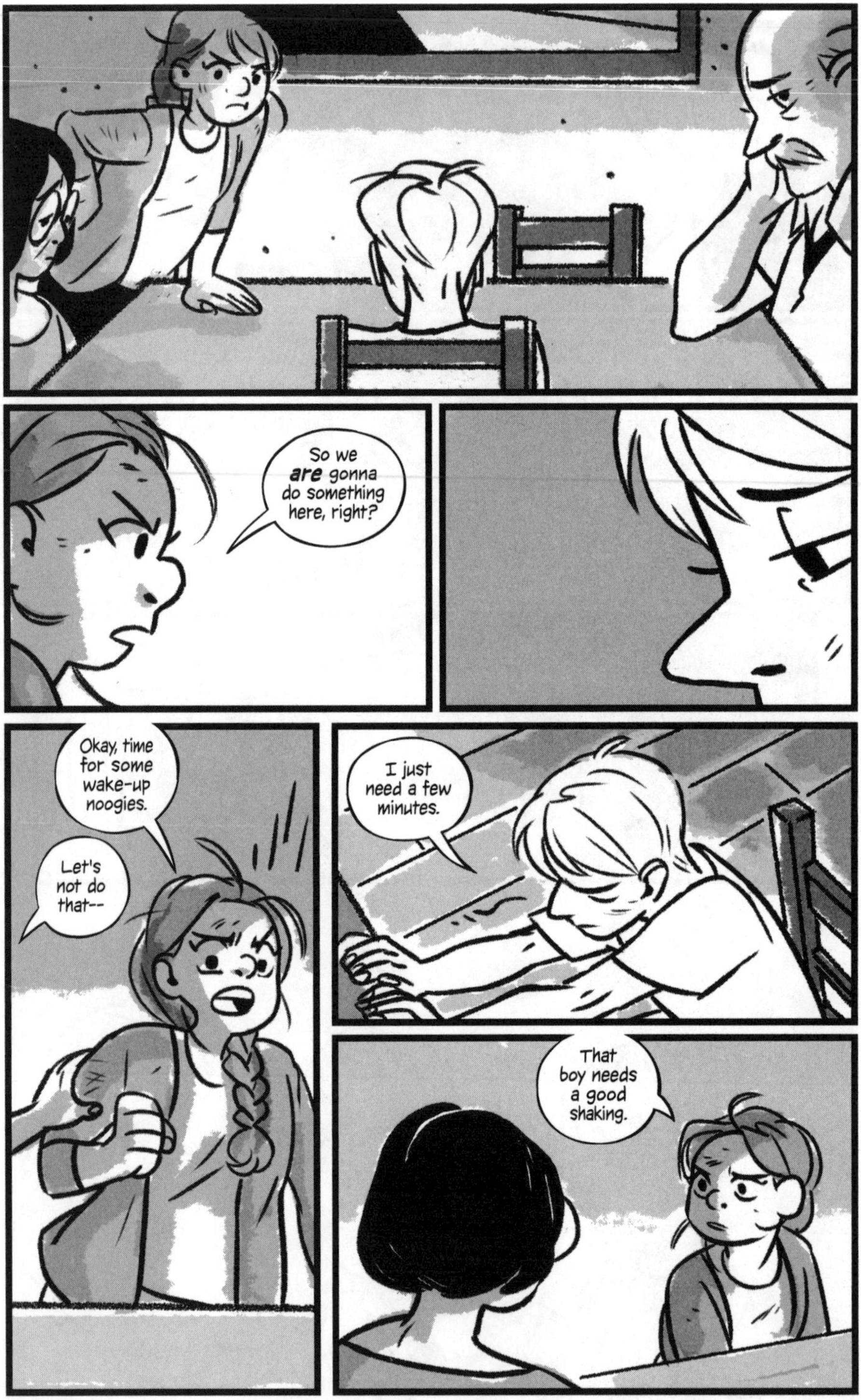
So we **are** gonna do something here, right?
Okay, time for some wake-up noogies.
Let's not do that--
I just need a few minutes.
That boy needs a good shaking.

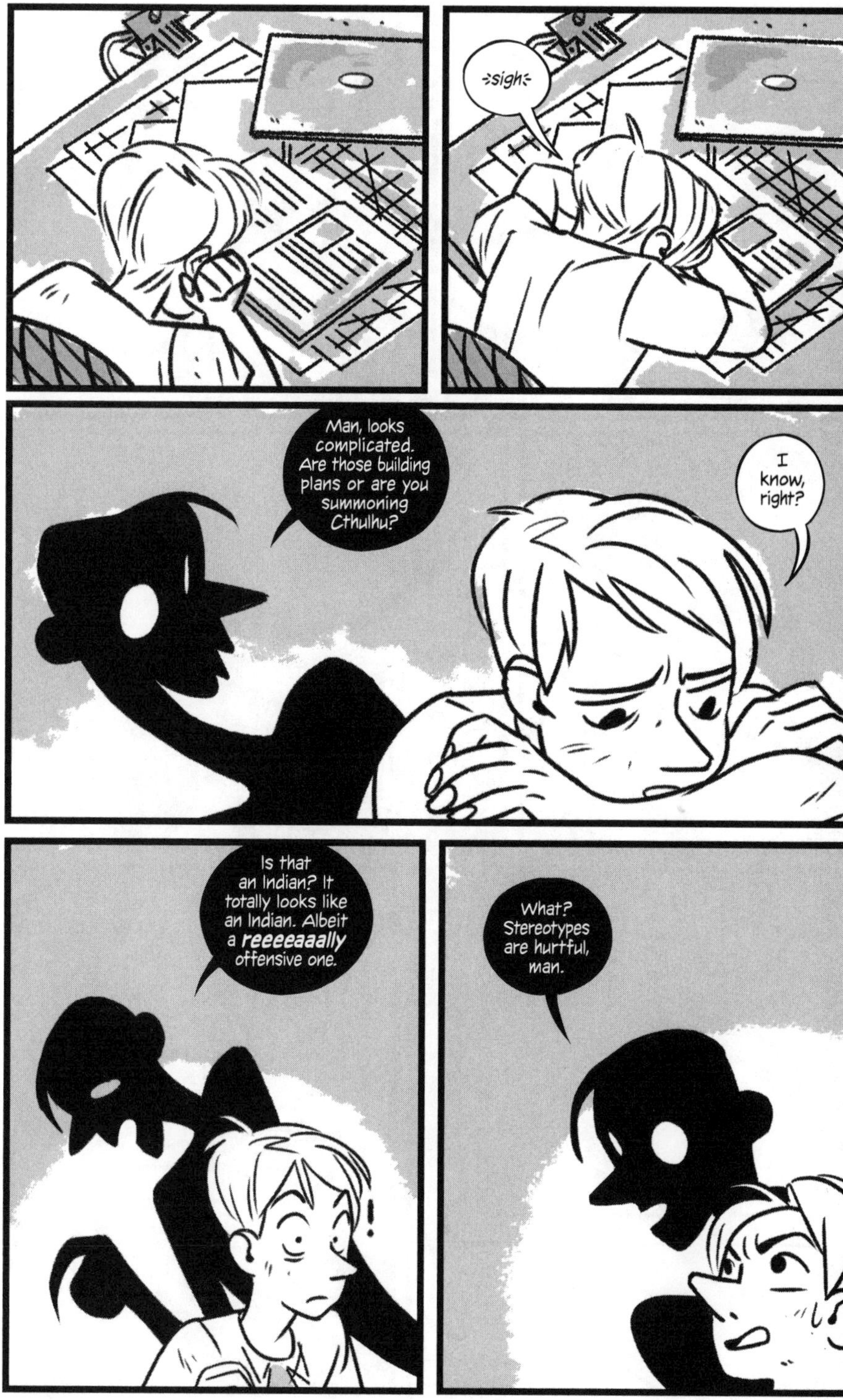

sigh
Man, looks complicated. Are those building plans or are you summoning Cthulhu?
I know, right?
Is that an Indian? It totally looks like an Indian. Albeit a **reeeeaaally** offensive one.
!
What? Stereotypes are hurtful, man.

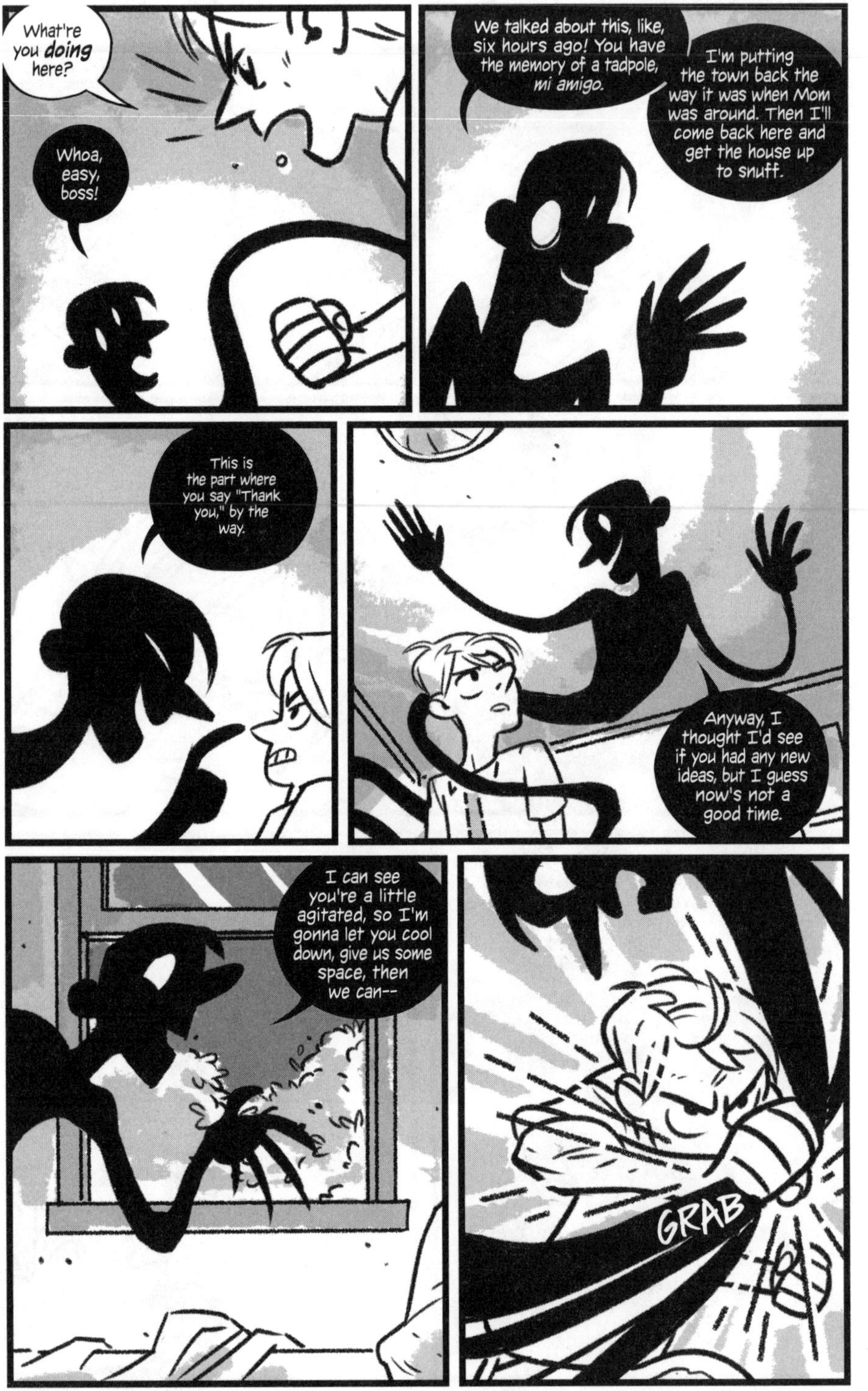

What're you *doing* here?
Whoa, easy, boss!
We talked about this, like, six hours ago! You have the memory of a tadpole, *mi amigo.*
I'm putting the town back the way it was when Mom was around. Then I'll come back here and get the house up to snuff.
This is the part where you say "Thank you," by the way.
Anyway, I thought I'd see if you had any new ideas, but I guess now's not a good time.
I can see you're a little agitated, so I'm gonna let you cool down, give us some space, then we can--
GRAB

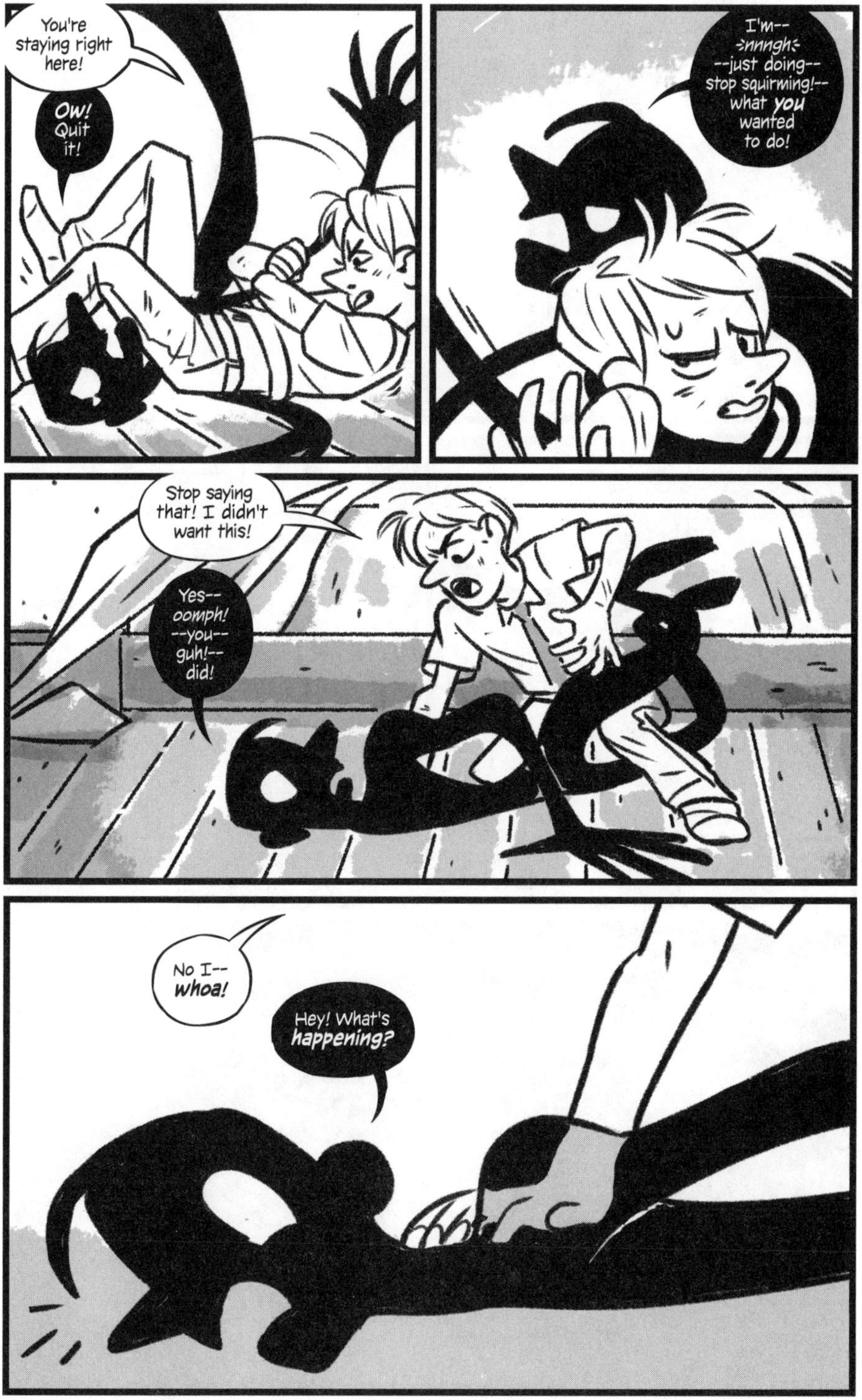
You're staying right here!
Ow! Quit it!
I'm-- nnngh --just doing-- stop squirming!-- what you wanted to do!
Stop saying that! I didn't want this!
Yes-- oomph! --you-- guh!-- did!
No I-- whoa!
Hey! What's happening?

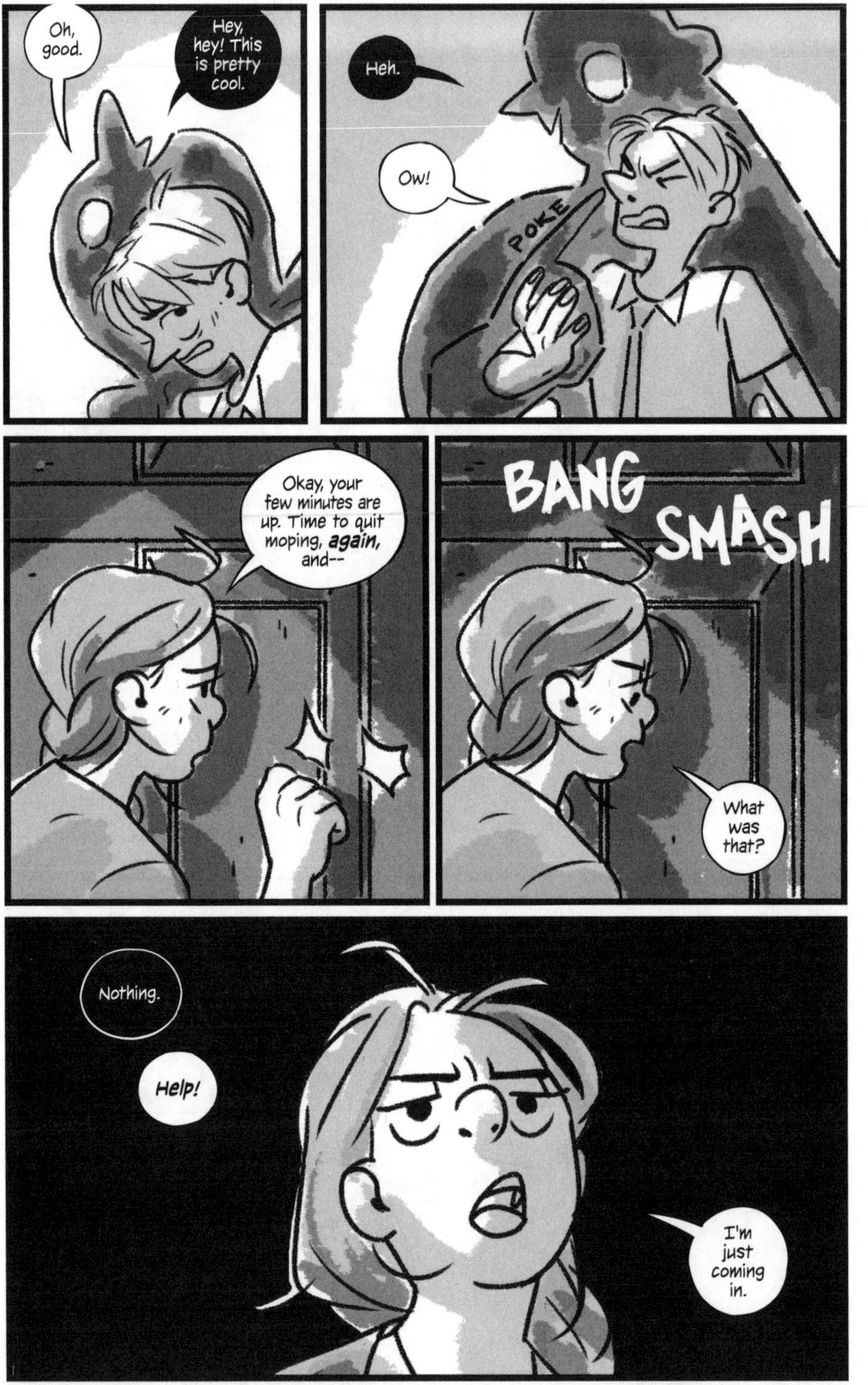

Oh, good.
Hey, hey! This is pretty cool.
Heh.
Ow!
POKE
Okay, your few minutes are up. Time to quit moping, **again,** and--
BANG
SMASH
What was that?
Nothing.
Help!
I'm just coming in.

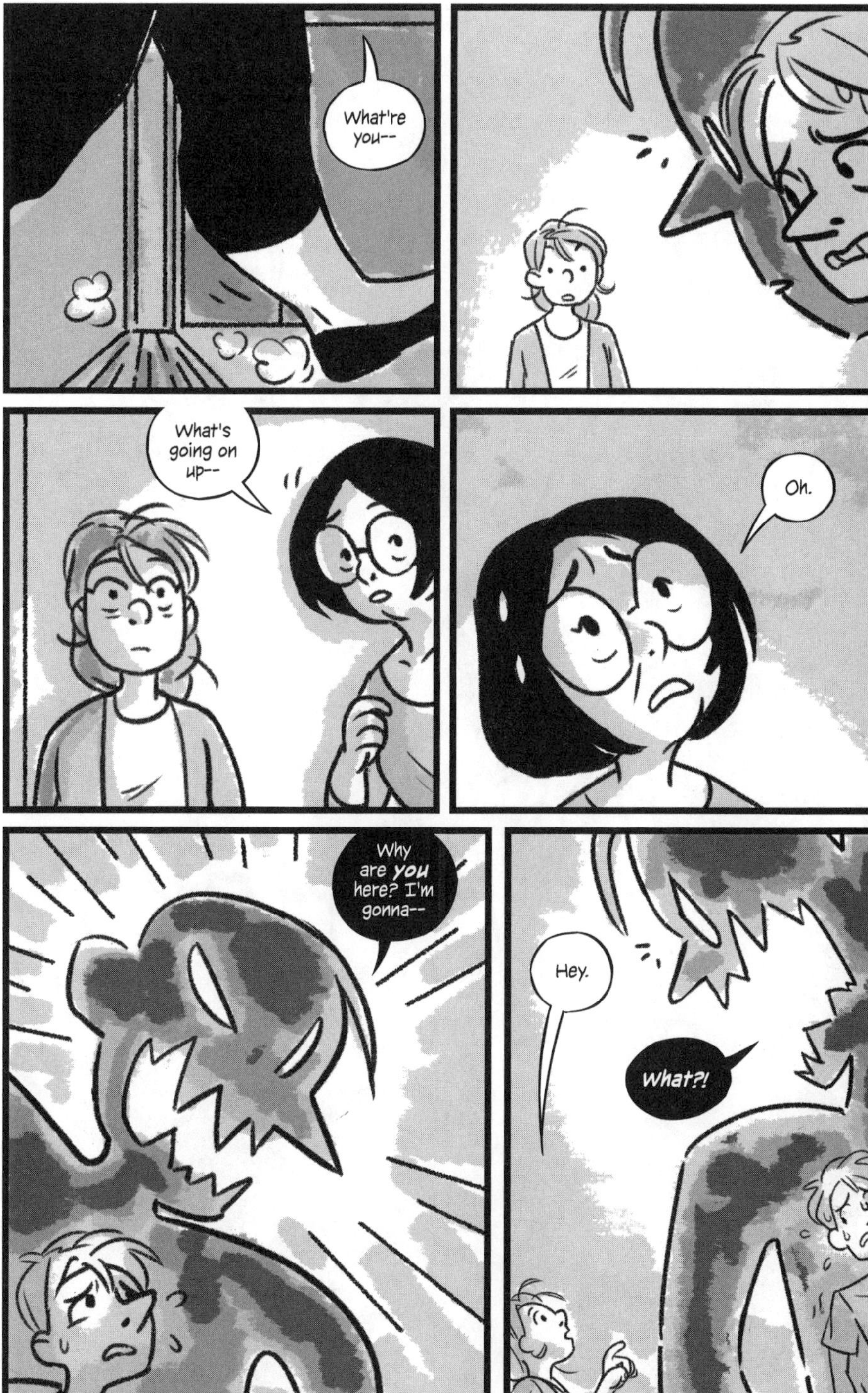
What're you--
What's going on up--
Oh.
Why are *you* here? I'm gonna--
Hey.
What?!

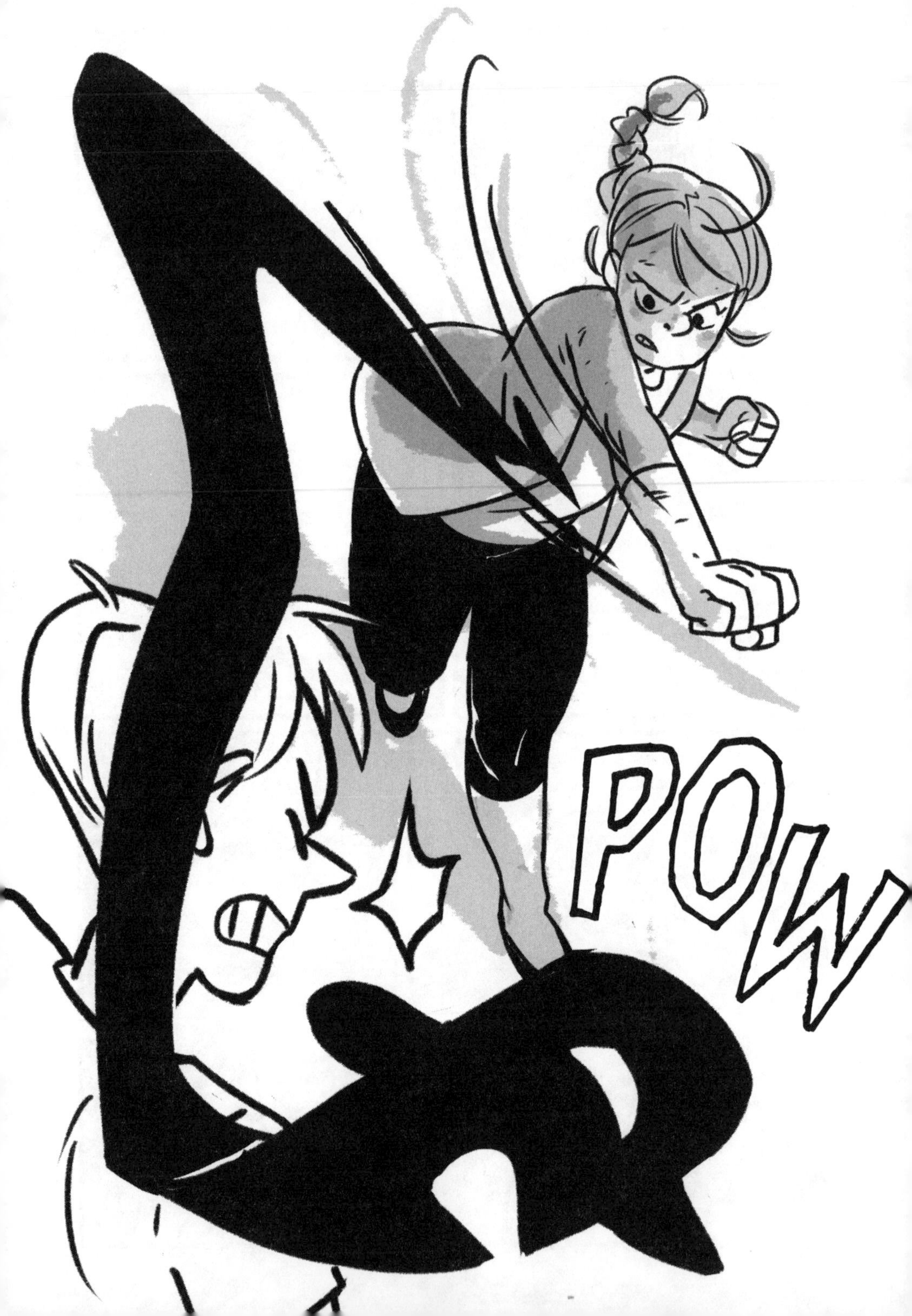
POW

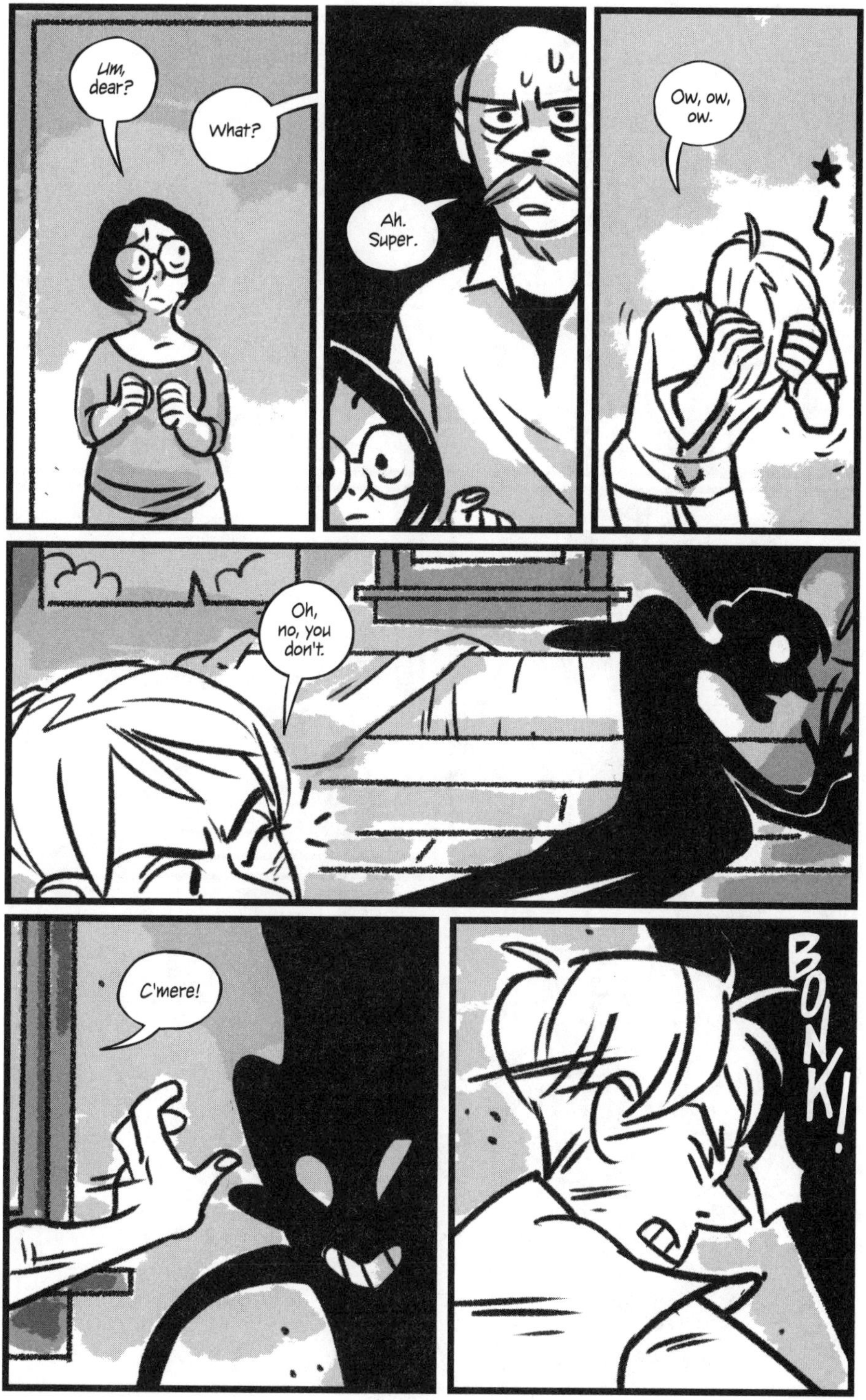
Um, dear?
What?
Ah. Super.
Ow, ow, ow.
Oh, no, you don't.
C'mere!
BONK!

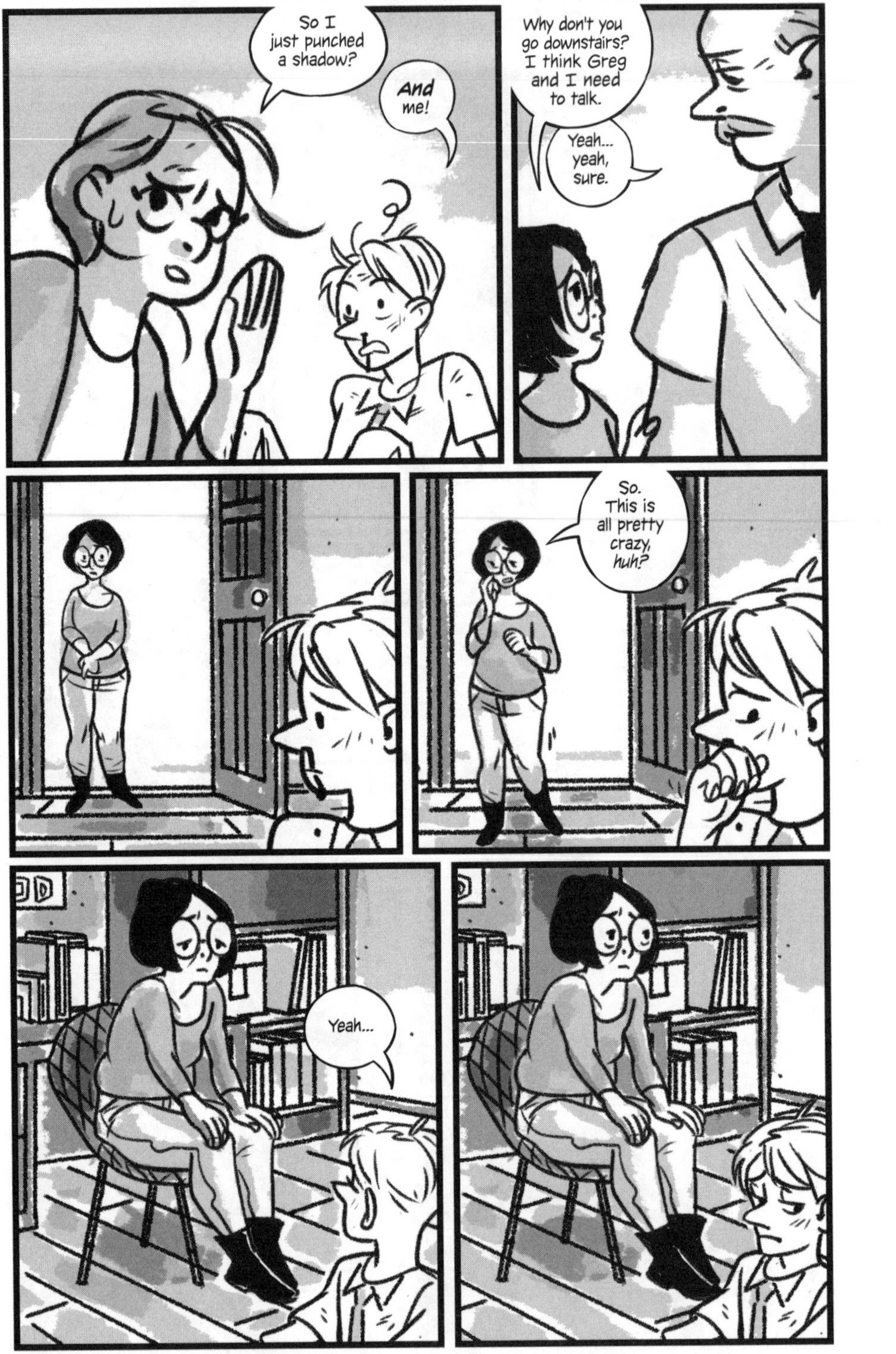
So I just punched a shadow?
And me!
Why don't you go downstairs? I think Greg and I need to talk.
Yeah... yeah, sure.
So. This is all pretty crazy, *huh?*
Yeah...

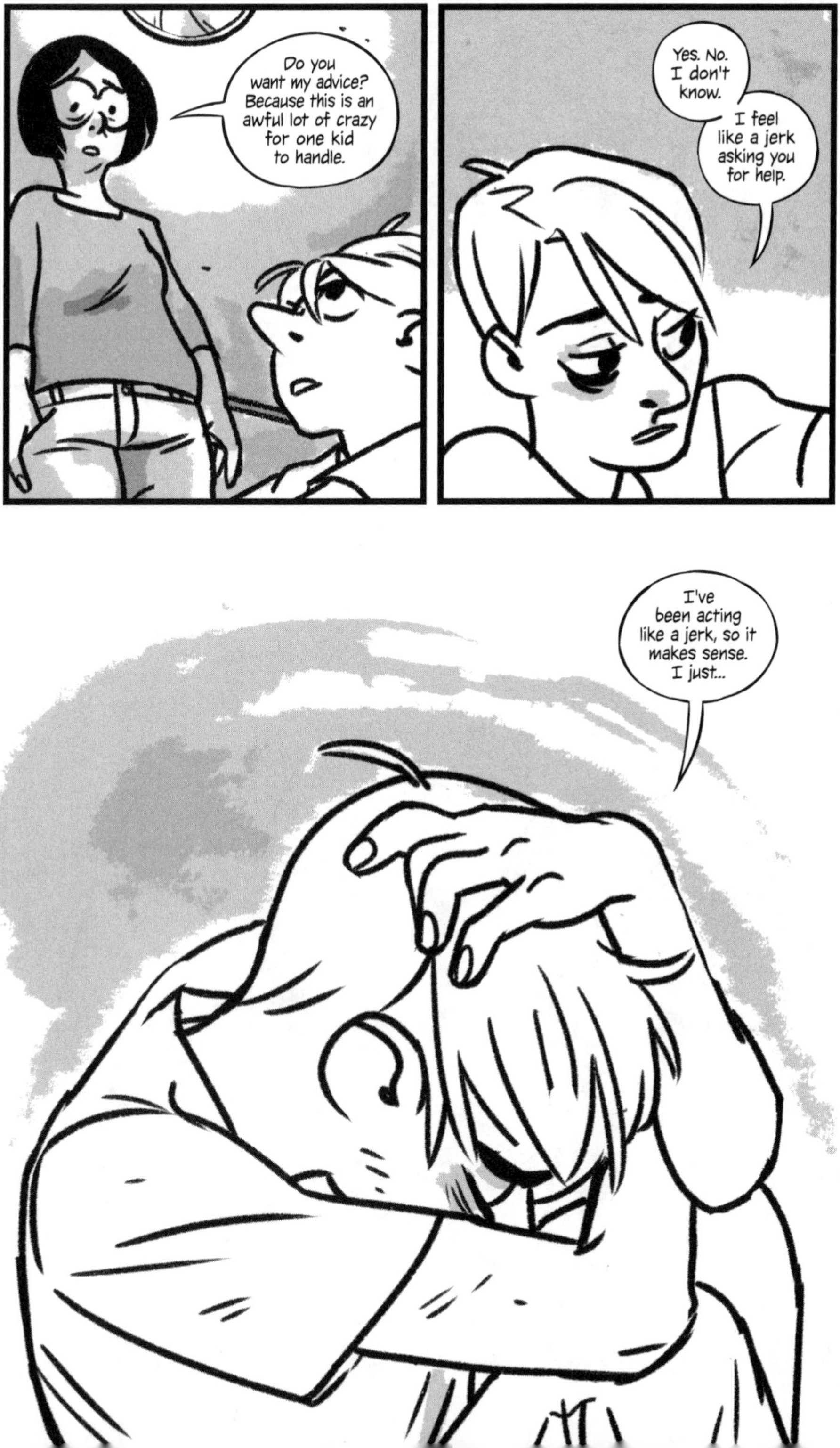
Do you want my advice? Because this is an awful lot of crazy for one kid to handle.
Yes. No. I don't know.
I feel like a jerk asking you for help.
I've been acting like a jerk, so it makes sense. I just...

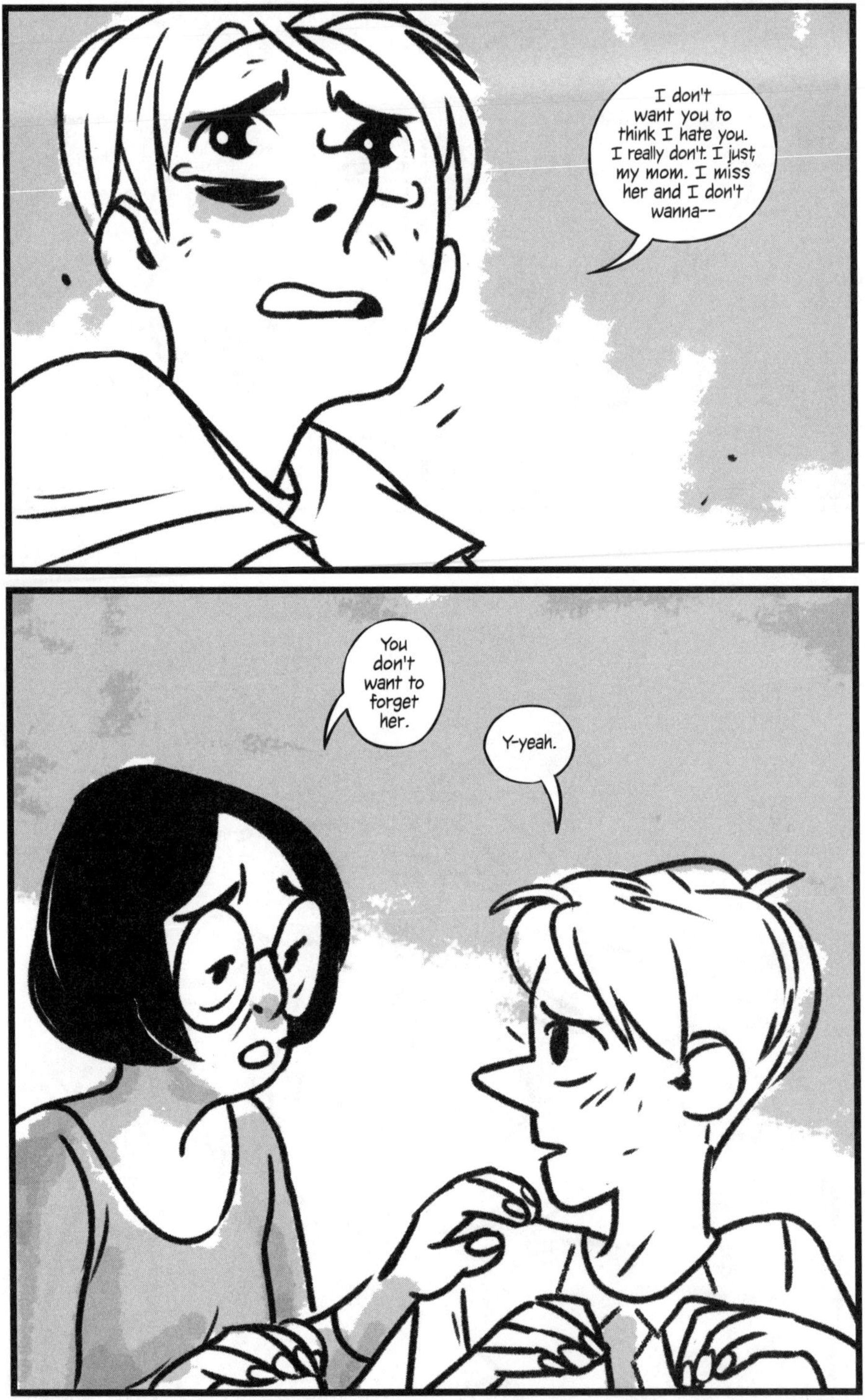
I don't want you to think I hate you. I really don't. I just, my mom. I miss her and I don't wanna--
You don't want to forget her.
Y-yeah.

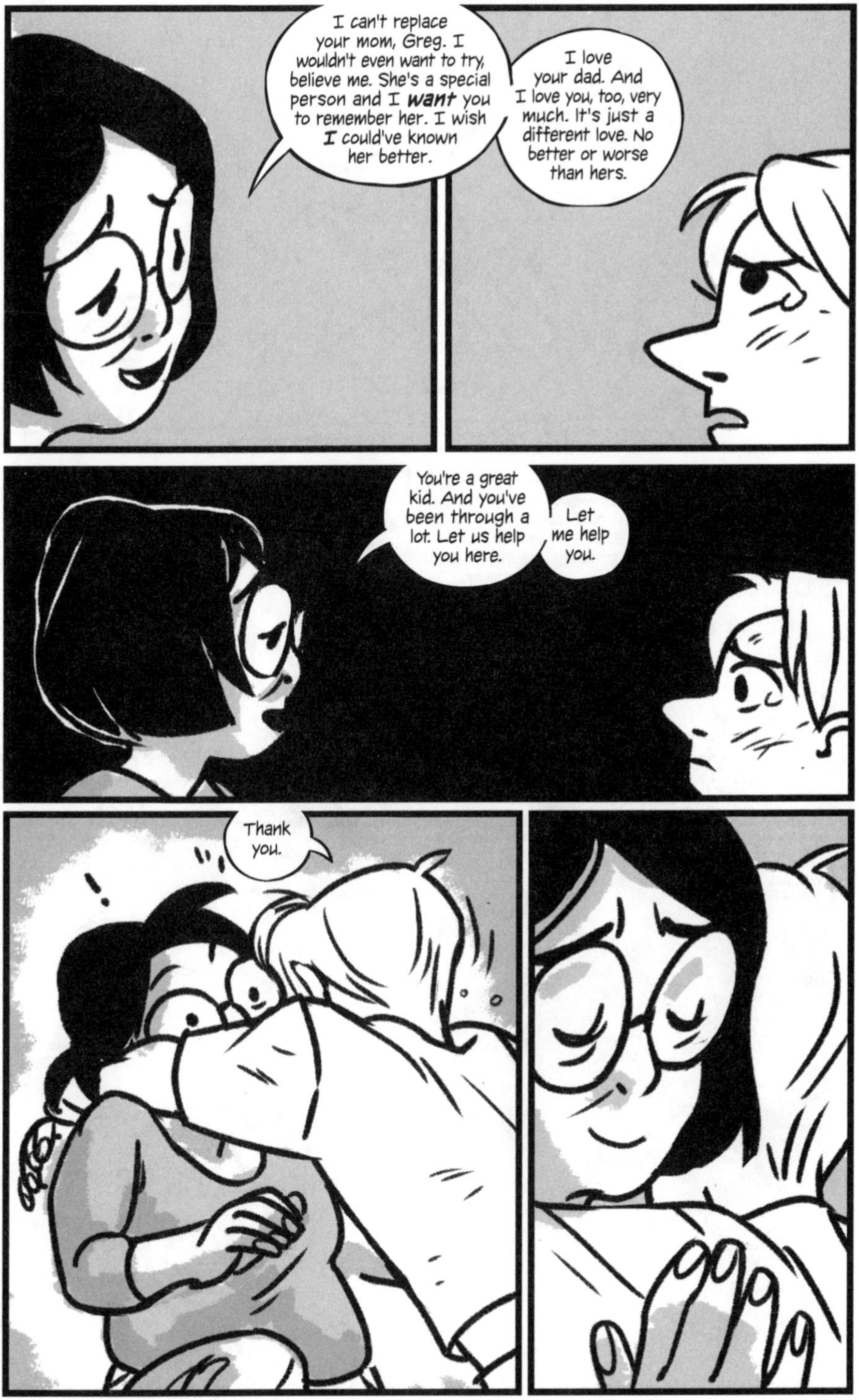
I can't replace your mom, Greg. I wouldn't even want to try, believe me. She's a special person and I *want* you to remember her. I wish *I* could've known her better.
I love your dad. And I love you, too, very much. It's just a different love. No better or worse than hers.
You're a great kid. And you've been through a lot. Let us help you here.
Let me help you.
Thank you.

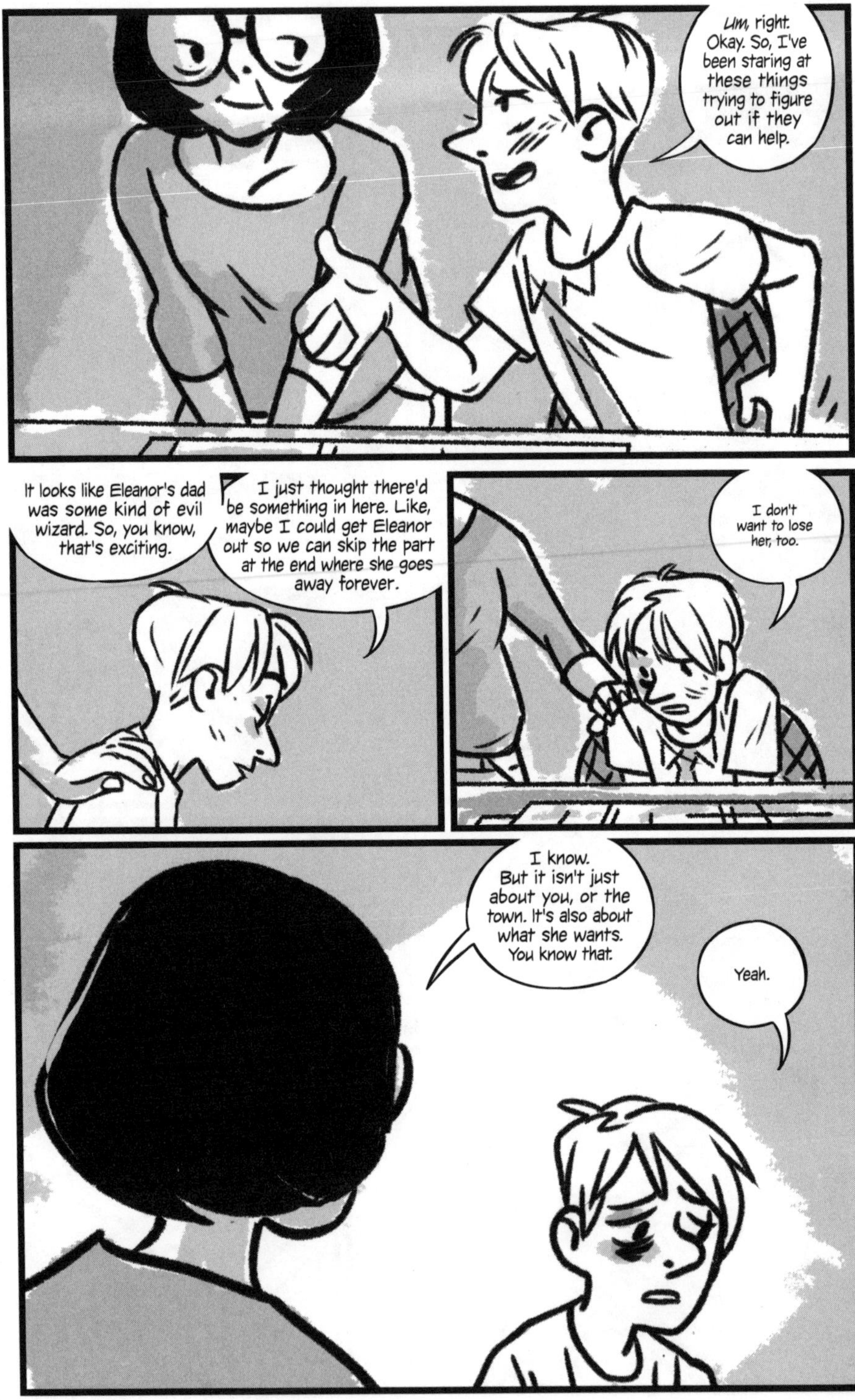
Um, right. Okay. So, I've been staring at these things trying to figure out if they can help.
It looks like Eleanor's dad was some kind of evil wizard. So, you know, that's exciting.
I just thought there'd be something in here. Like, maybe I could get Eleanor out so we can skip the part at the end where she goes away forever.
I don't want to lose her, too.
I know. But it isn't just about you, or the town. It's also about what she wants. You know that.
Yeah.

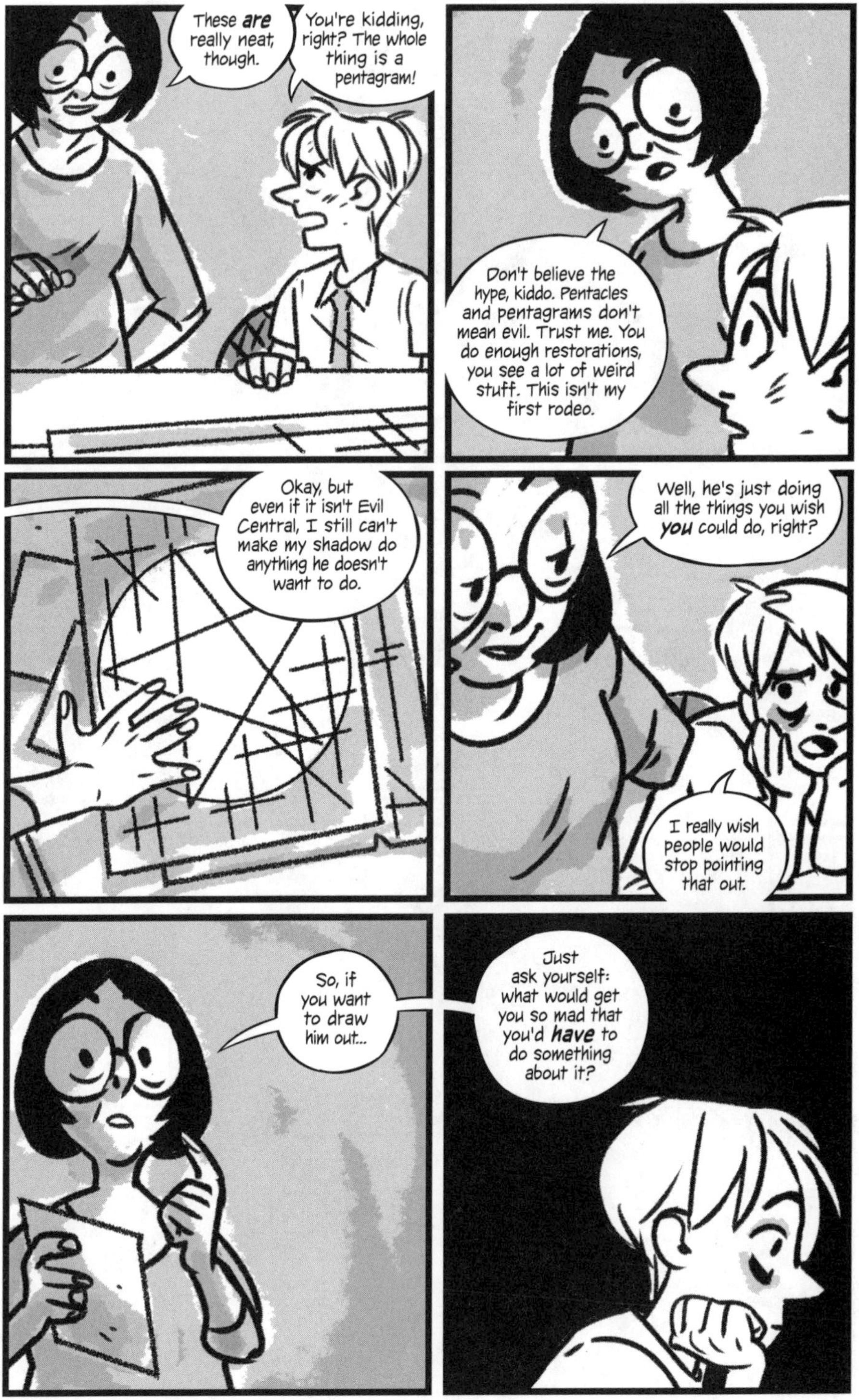
These are really neat, though.
You're kidding, right? The whole thing is a pentagram!
Don't believe the hype, kiddo. Pentacles and pentagrams don't mean evil. Trust me. You do enough restorations, you see a lot of weird stuff. This isn't my first rodeo.
Okay, but even if it isn't Evil Central, I still can't make my shadow do anything he doesn't want to do.
Well, he's just doing all the things you wish you could do, right?
I really wish people would stop pointing that out.
So, if you want to draw him out...
Just ask yourself: what would get you so mad that you'd have to do something about it?

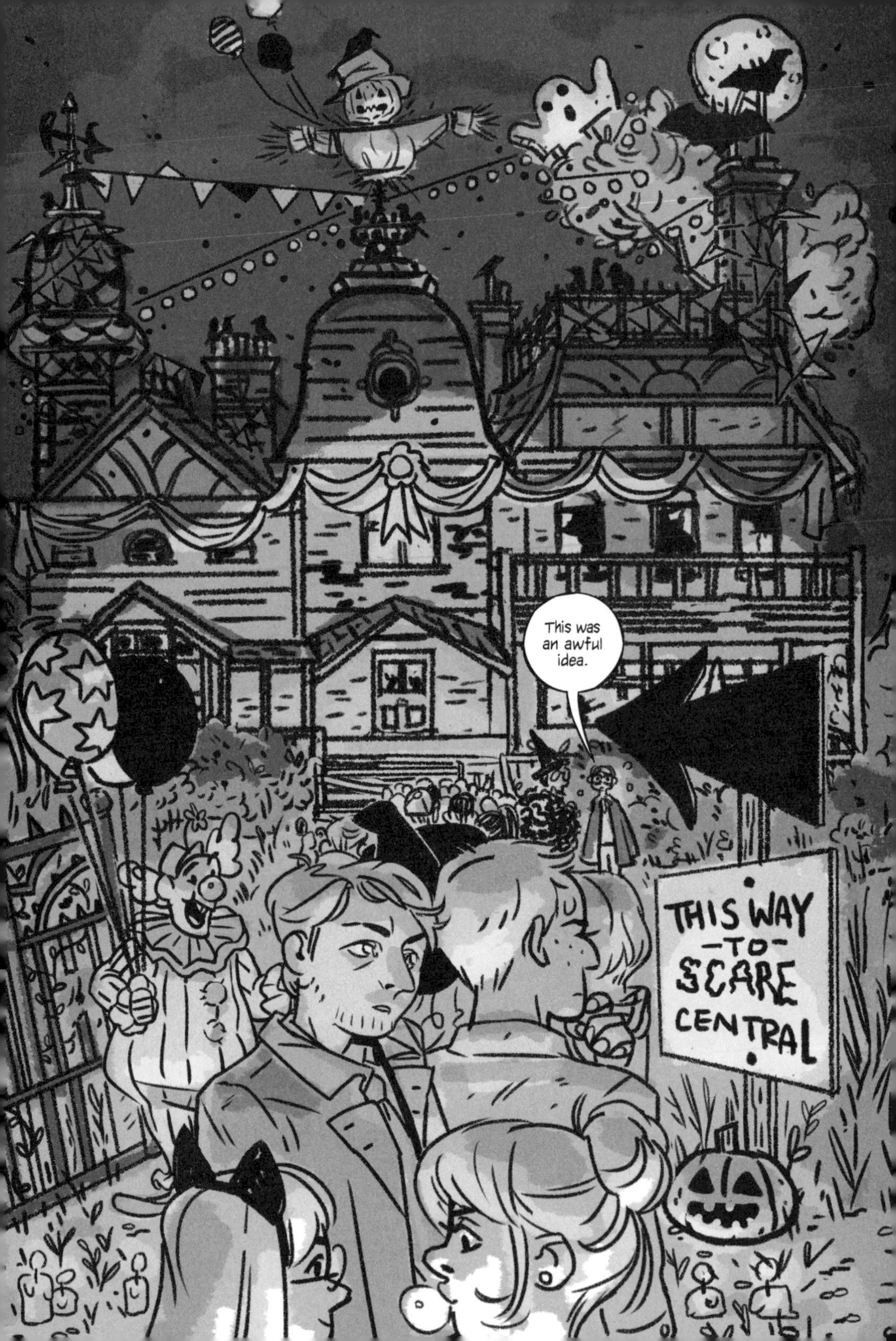
This was an awful idea.
THIS WAY -TO- SCARE CENTRAL

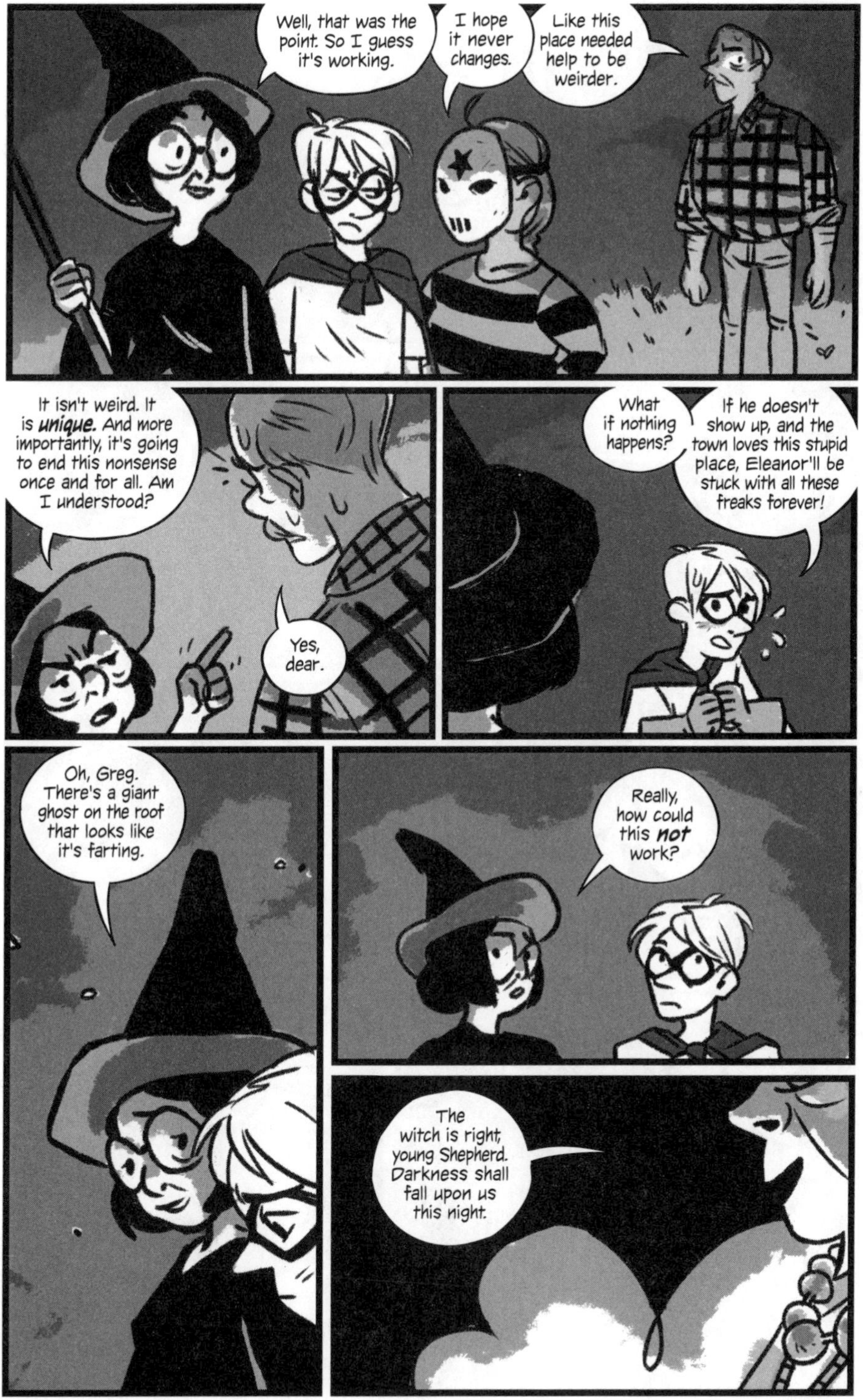

Well, that was the point. So I guess it's working.
I hope it never changes.
Like this place needed help to be weirder.
It isn't weird. It is **unique.** And more importantly, it's going to end this nonsense once and for all. Am I understood?
Yes, dear.
What if nothing happens?
If he doesn't show up, and the town loves this stupid place, Eleanor'll be stuck with all these freaks forever!
Oh, Greg. There's a giant ghost on the roof that looks like it's farting.
Really, how could this **not** work?
The witch is right, young Shepherd. Darkness shall fall upon us this night.

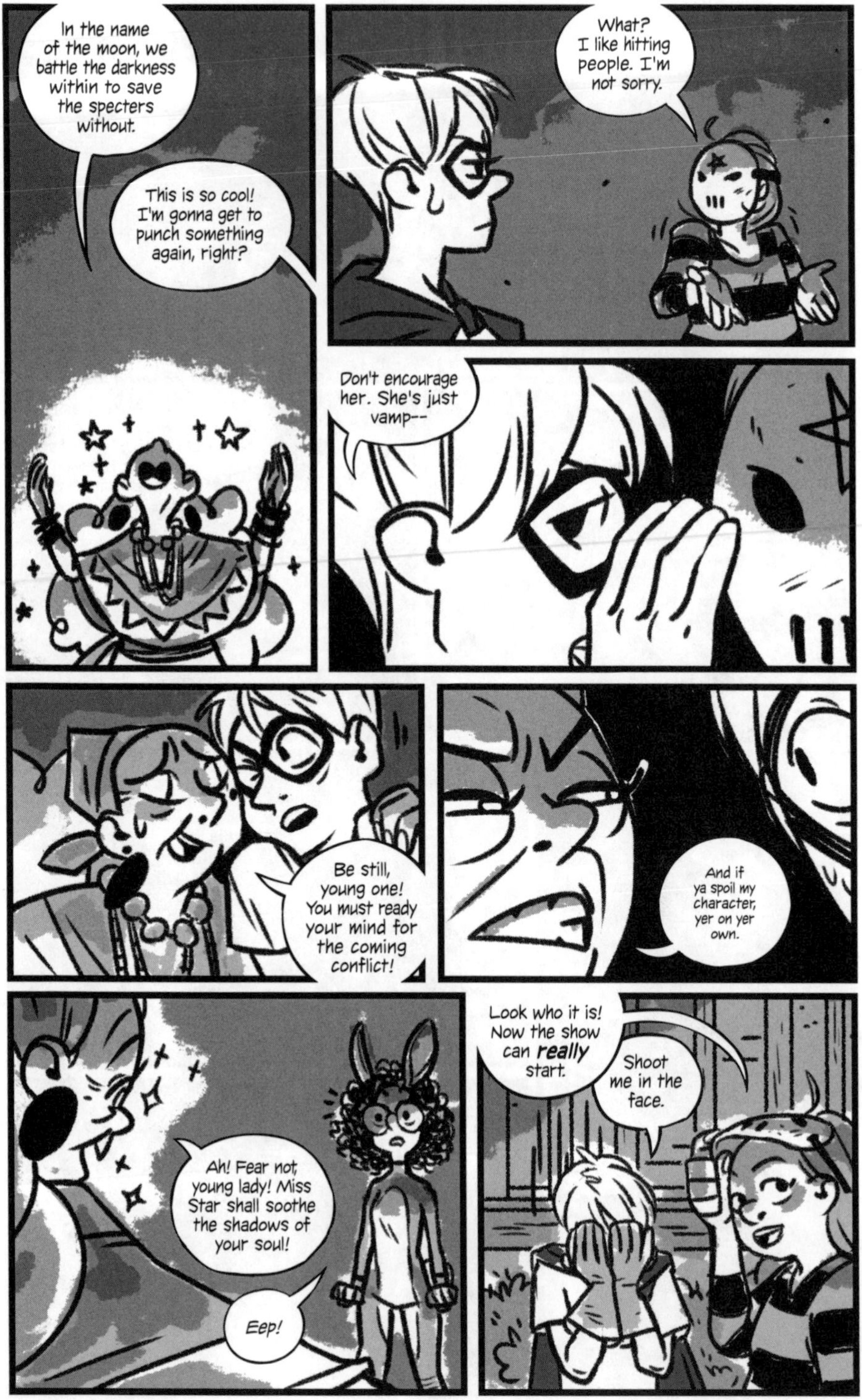
In the name of the moon, we battle the darkness within to save the specters without.
This is so cool! I'm gonna get to punch something again, right?
What? I like hitting people. I'm not sorry.
Don't encourage her. She's just vamp--
Be still, young one! You must ready your mind for the coming conflict!
And if ya spoil my character, yer on yer own.
Ah! Fear not, young lady! Miss Star shall soothe the shadows of your soul!
Eep!
Look who it is! Now the show can *really* start.
Shoot me in the face.

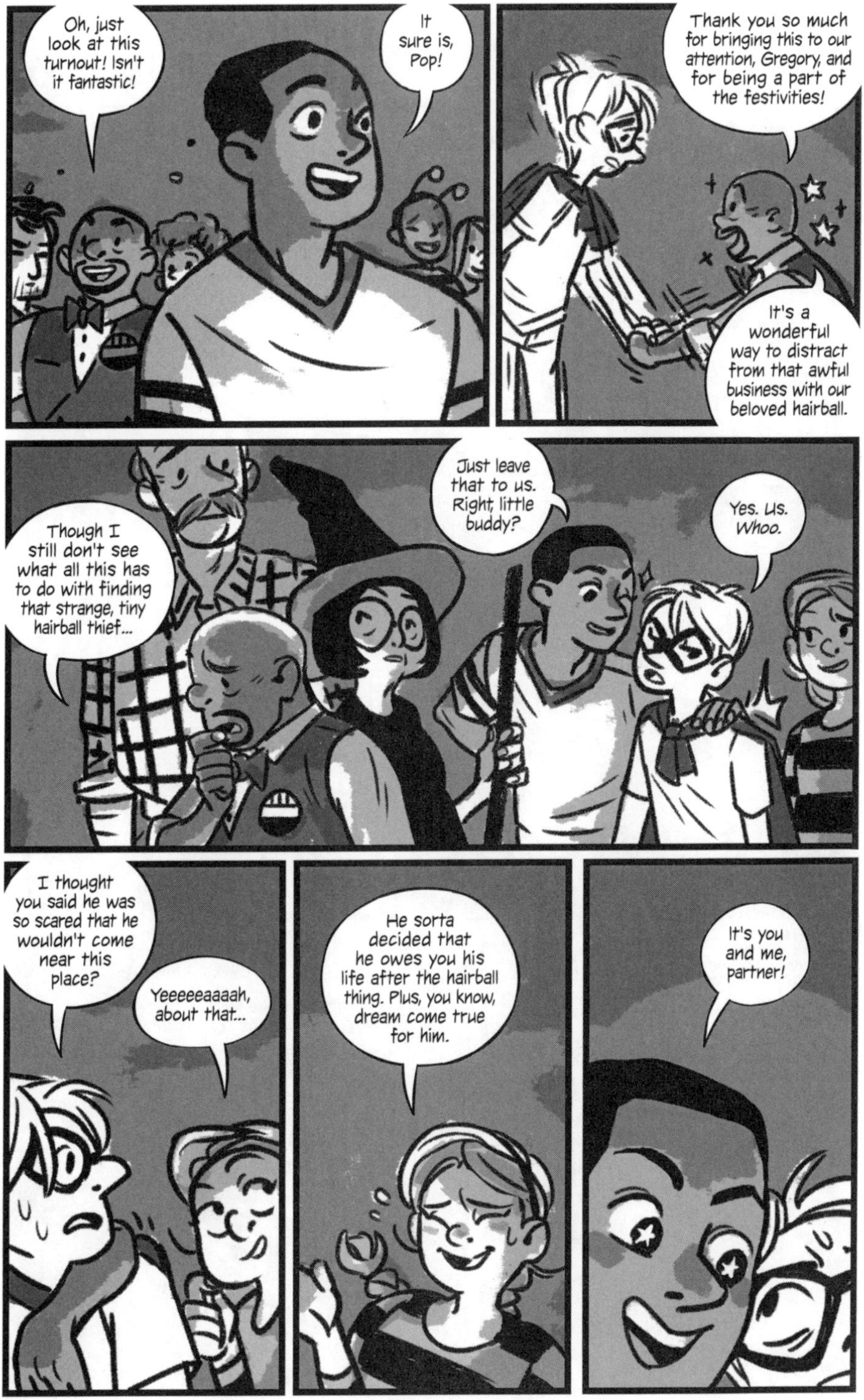
Oh, just look at this turnout! Isn't it fantastic!
It sure is, Pop!
Thank you so much for bringing this to our attention, Gregory, and for being a part of the festivities!
It's a wonderful way to distract from that awful business with our beloved hairball.
Though I still don't see what all this has to do with finding that strange, tiny hairball thief...
Just leave that to us. Right, little buddy?
Yes. Us. Whoo.
I thought you said he was so scared that he wouldn't come near this place?
Yeeeeeaaaah, about that...
He sorta decided that he owes you his life after the hairball thing. Plus, you know, dream come true for him.
It's you and me, partner!

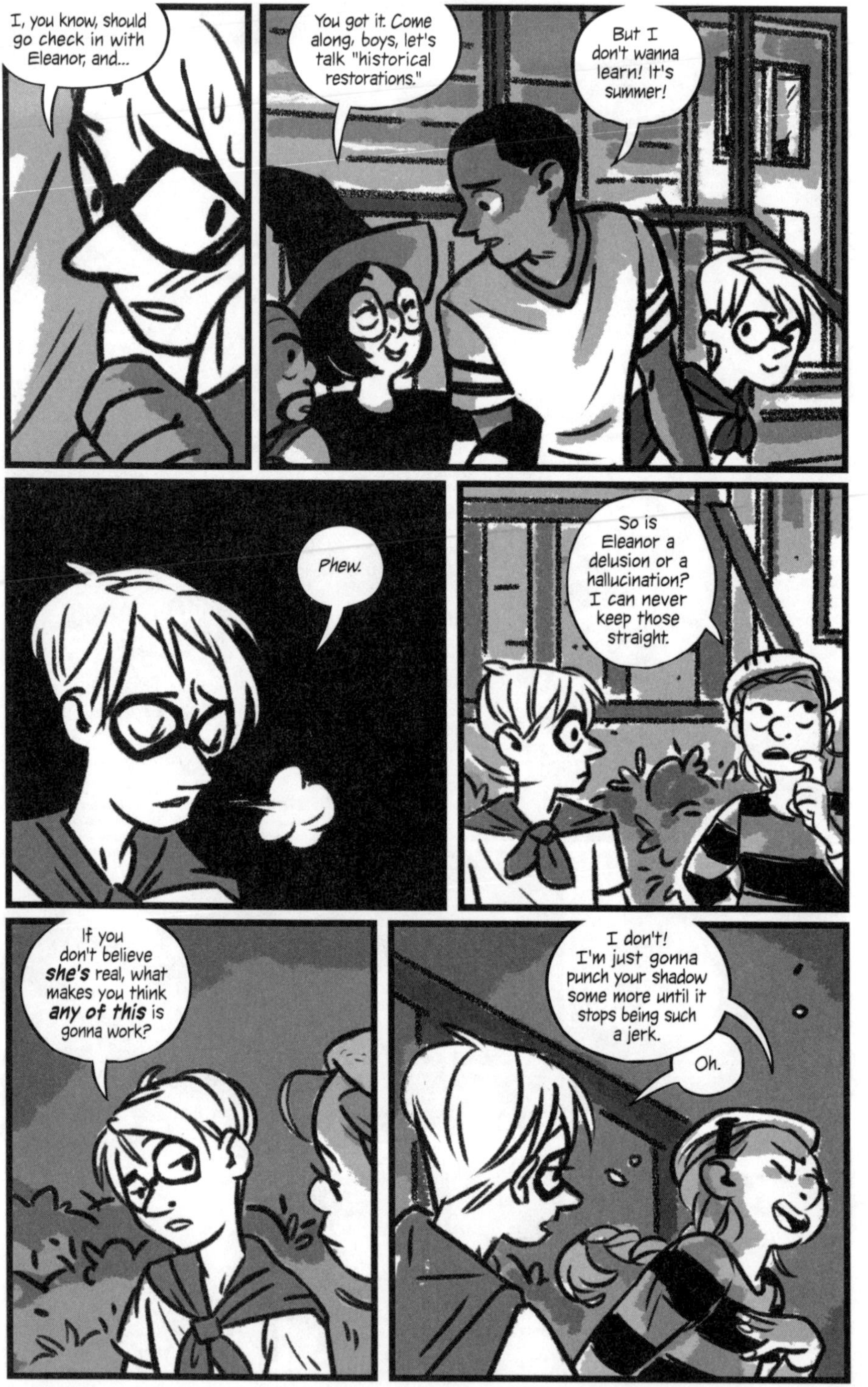

I, you know, should go check in with Eleanor, and...
You got it. Come along, boys, let's talk "historical restorations."
But I don't wanna learn! It's summer!
Phew.
So is Eleanor a delusion or a hallucination? I can never keep those straight.
If you don't believe **she's** real, what makes you think ***any of this*** is gonna work?
I don't! I'm just gonna punch your shadow some more until it stops being such a jerk.
Oh.

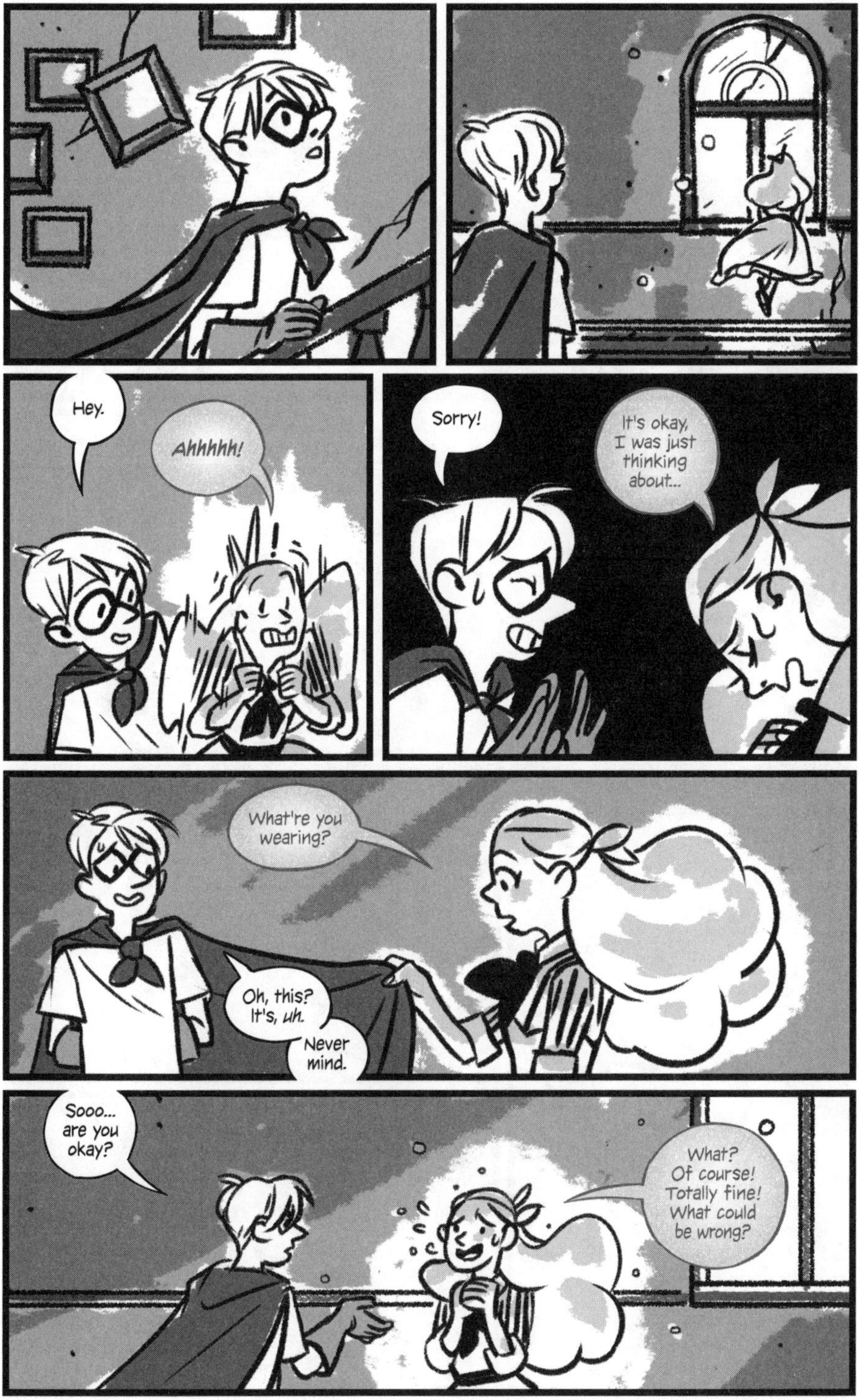
Hey.
Ahhhhh!
Sorry!
It's okay, I was just thinking about...
What're you wearing?
Oh, this? It's, uh.
Never mind.
Sooo... are you okay?
What? Of course! Totally fine! What could be wrong?

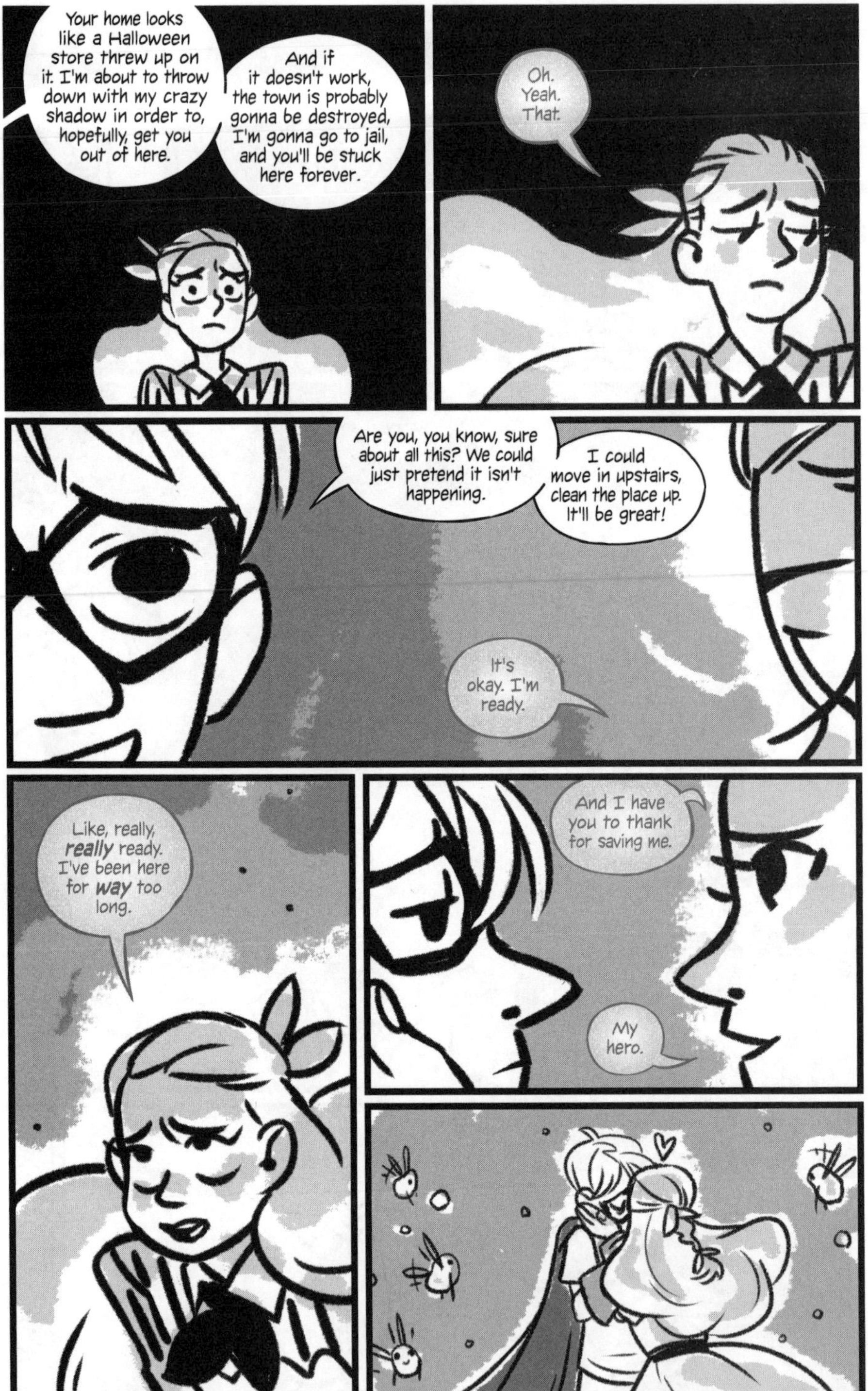
Your home looks like a Halloween store threw up on it. I'm about to throw down with my crazy shadow in order to, hopefully, get you out of here.
And if it doesn't work, the town is probably gonna be destroyed, I'm gonna go to jail, and you'll be stuck here forever.
Oh. Yeah. That.
Are you, you know, sure about all this? We could just pretend it isn't happening.
I could move in upstairs, clean the place up. It'll be great!
It's okay. I'm ready.
Like, really, ***really*** ready. I've been here for ***way*** too long.
And I have you to thank for saving me.
My hero.

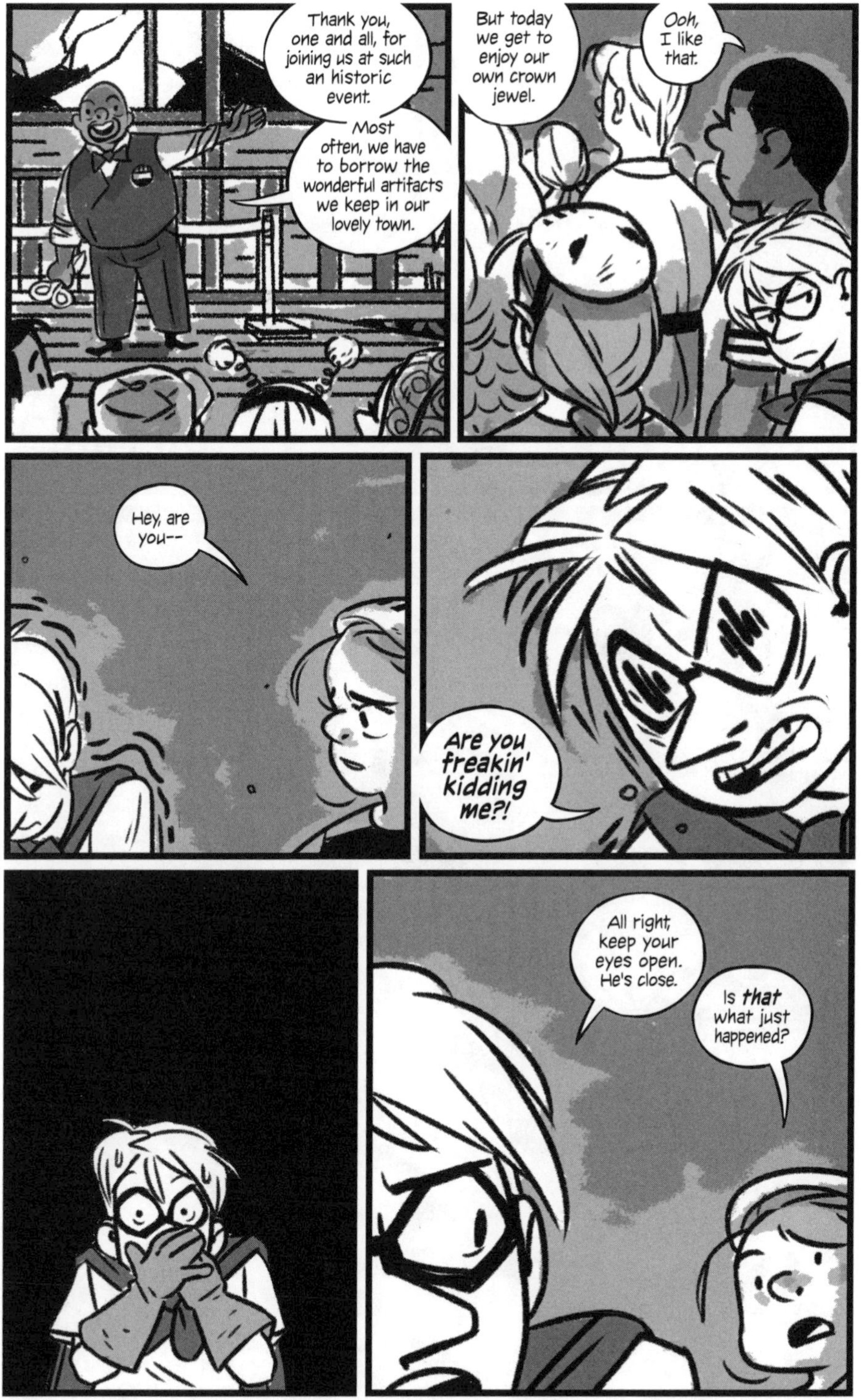
Thank you, one and all, for joining us at such an historic event.
Most often, we have to borrow the wonderful artifacts we keep in our lovely town.
But today we get to enjoy our own crown jewel.
Ooh, I like that.
Hey, are you--
Are you freakin' kidding me?!
All right, keep your eyes open. He's close.
Is *that* what just happened?

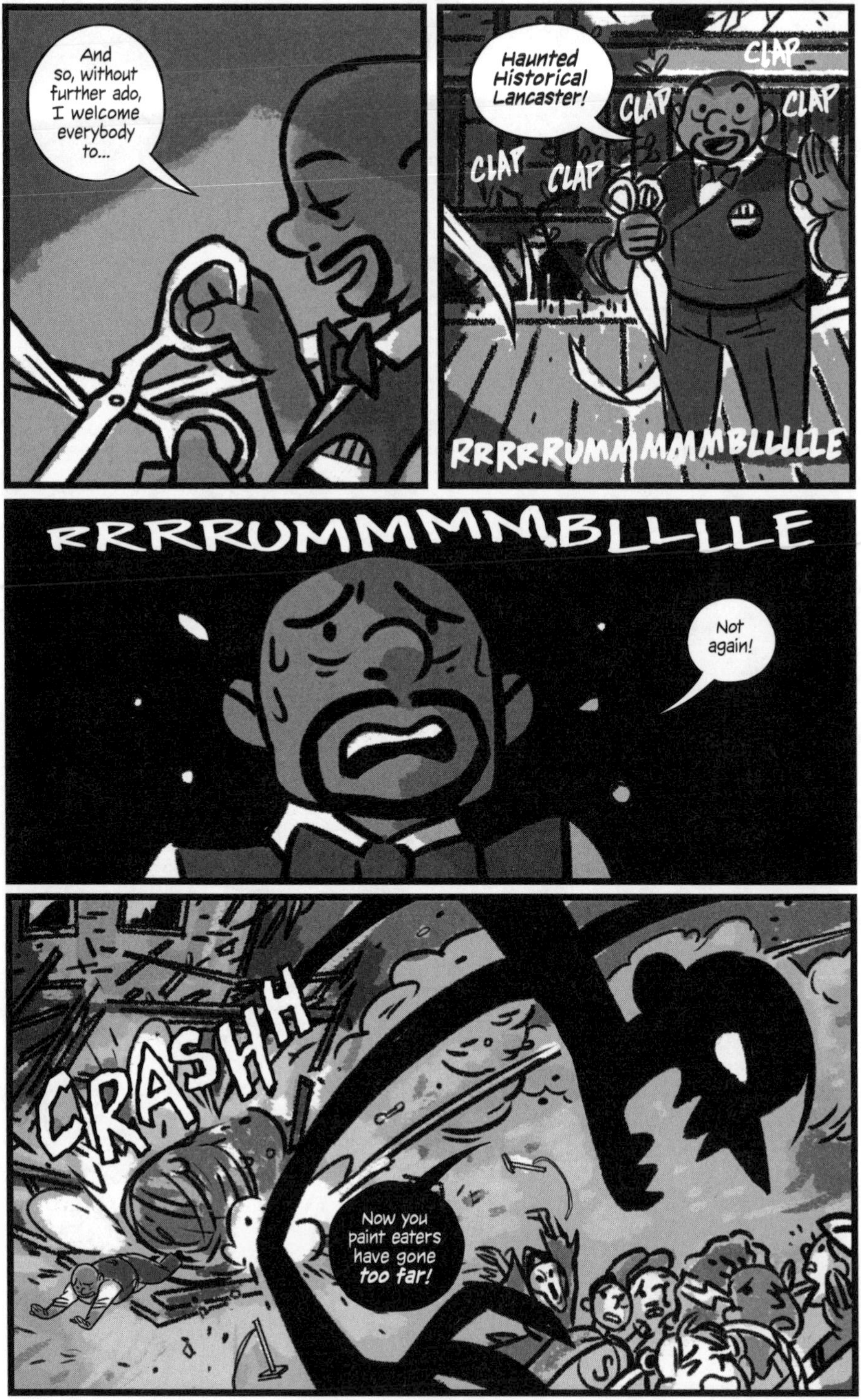
And so, without further ado, I welcome everybody to...
Haunted Historical Lancaster!
CLAP
CLAP
CLAP
CLAP
CLAP
RRRRRUMMMMMBLLLLLE
RRRRUMMMMMBLLLLE
Not again!
CRASHH
Now you paint eaters have gone *too far!*

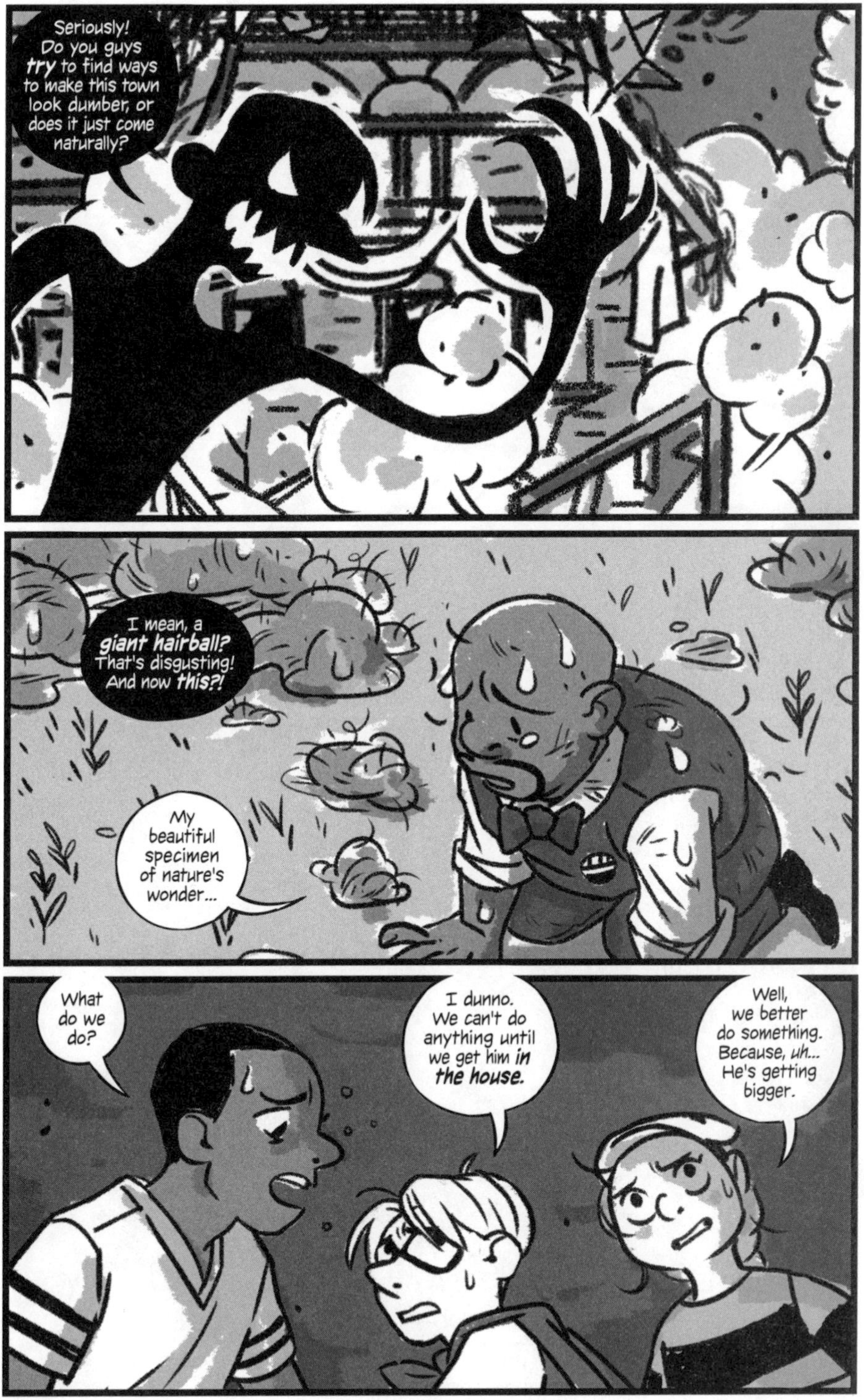
Seriously! Do you guys **try** to find ways to make this town look dumber, or does it just come naturally?
I mean, a **giant hairball?** That's disgusting! And now **this?!**
My beautiful specimen of nature's wonder...
What do we do?
I dunno. We can't do anything until we get him **in the house.**
Well, we better do something. Because, uh... He's getting bigger.

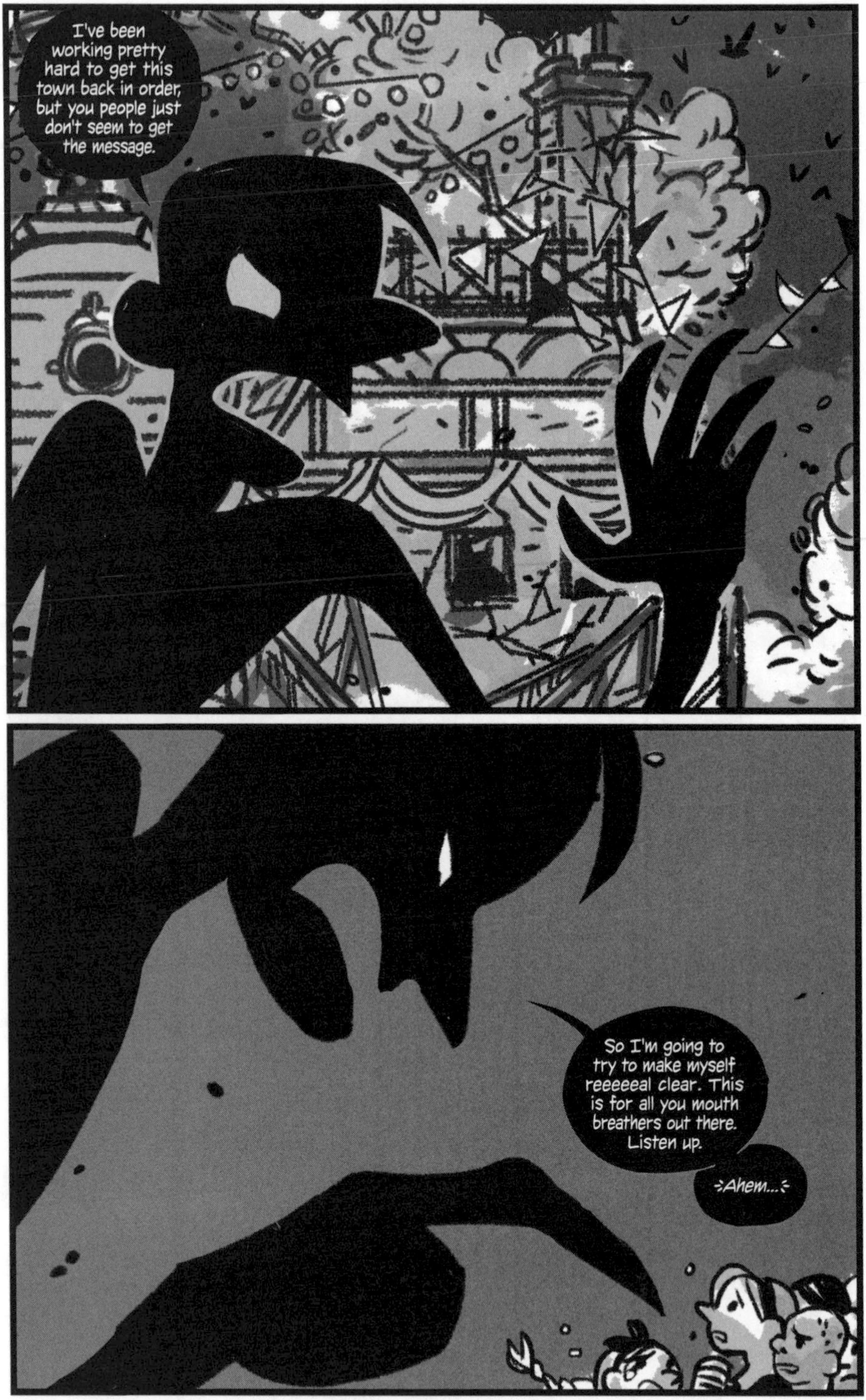
I've been working pretty hard to get this town back in order, but you people just don't seem to get the message.
So I'm going to try to make myself reeeeeal clear. This is for all you mouth breathers out there. Listen up.
Ahem...

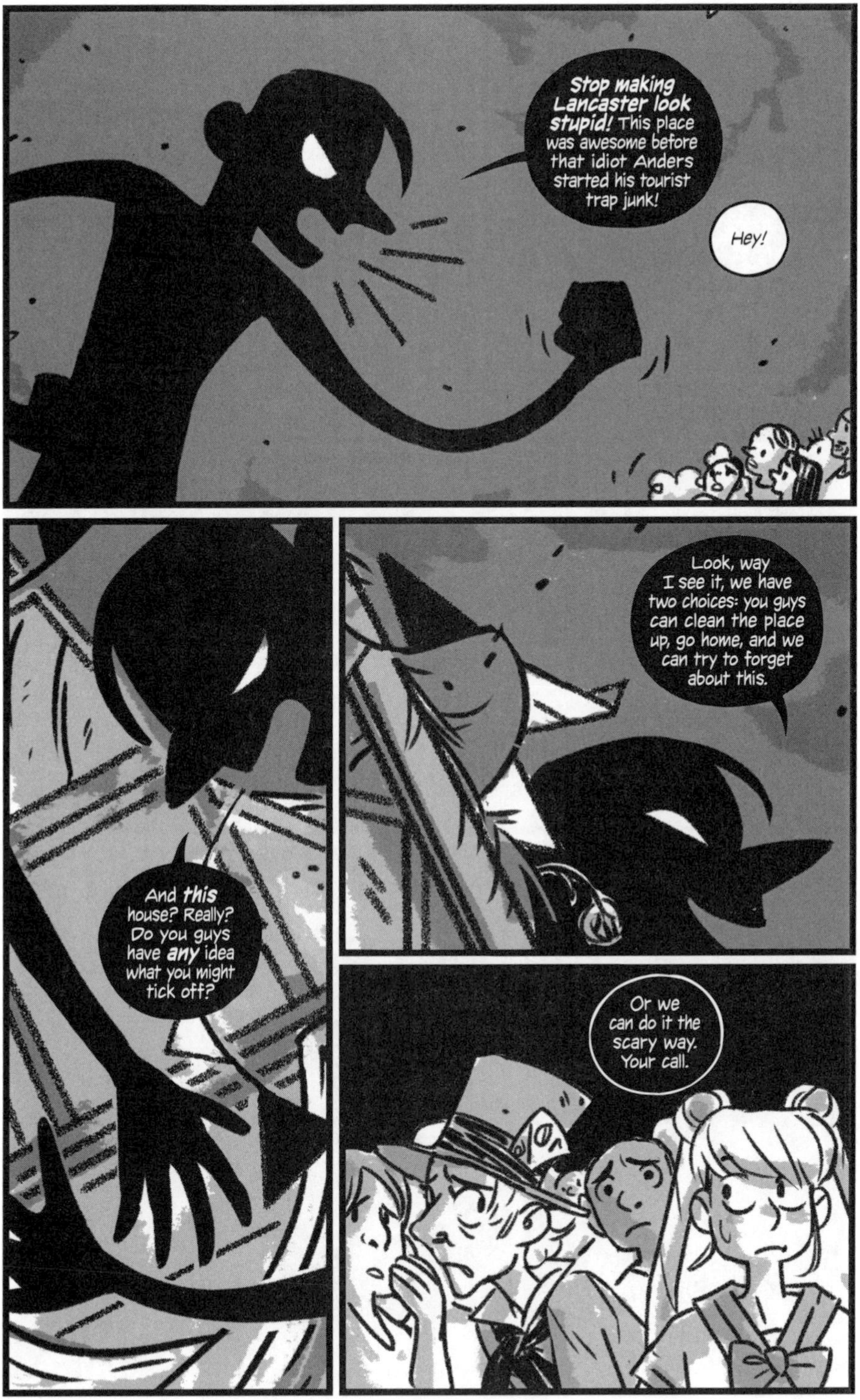
Stop making Lancaster look stupid! This place was awesome before that idiot Anders started his tourist trap junk!
Hey!
And this house? Really? Do you guys have any idea what you might tick off?
Look, way I see it, we have two choices: you guys can clean the place up, go home, and we can try to forget about this.
Or we can do it the scary way. Your call.

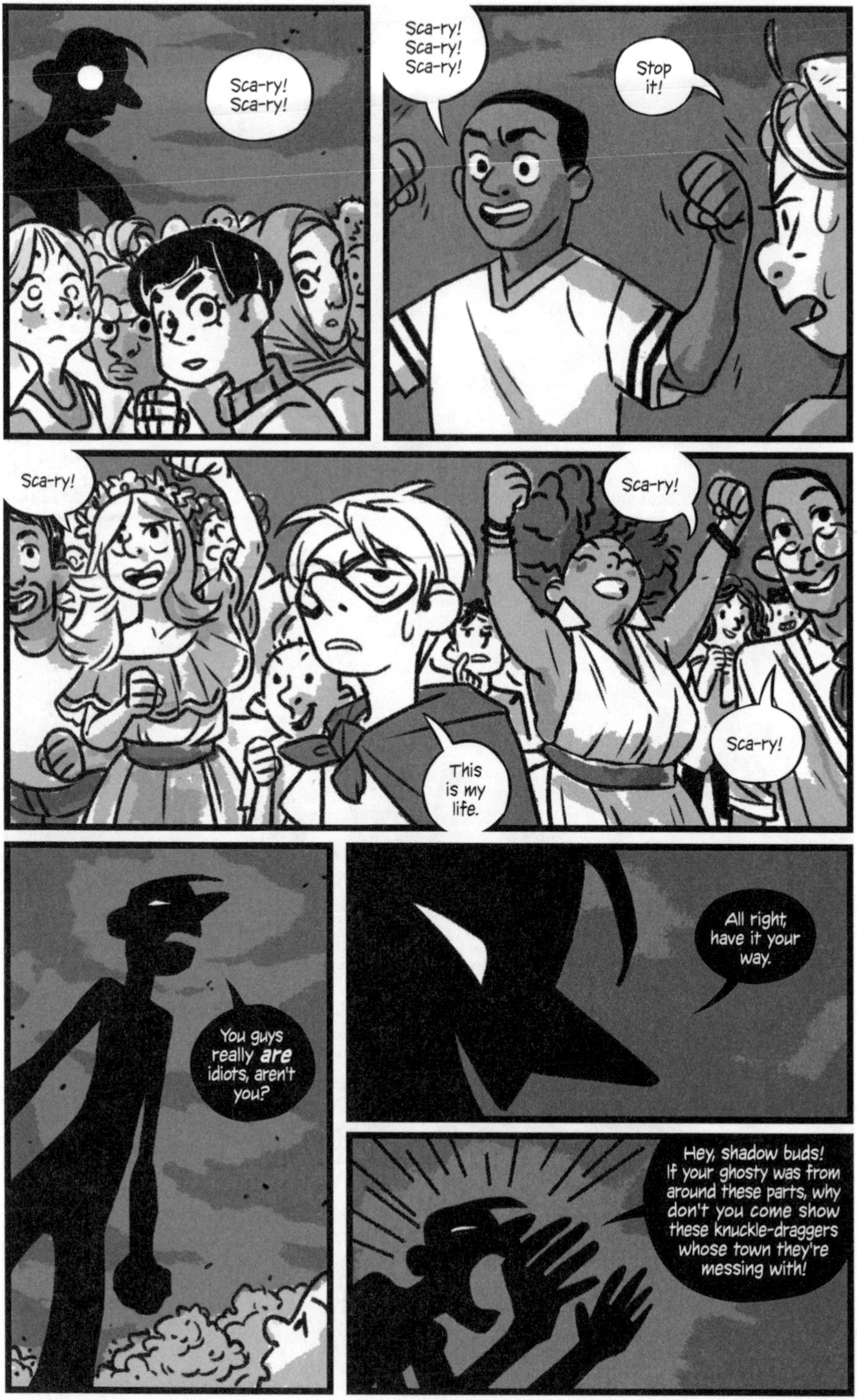
Sca-ry!
Sca-ry!
Sca-ry!
Sca-ry!
Sca-ry!
Stop it!
Sca-ry!
Sca-ry!
This is my life.
Sca-ry!
You guys really **are** idiots, aren't you?
All right, have it your way.
Hey, shadow buds! If your ghosty was from around these parts, why don't you come show these knuckle-draggers whose town they're messing with!

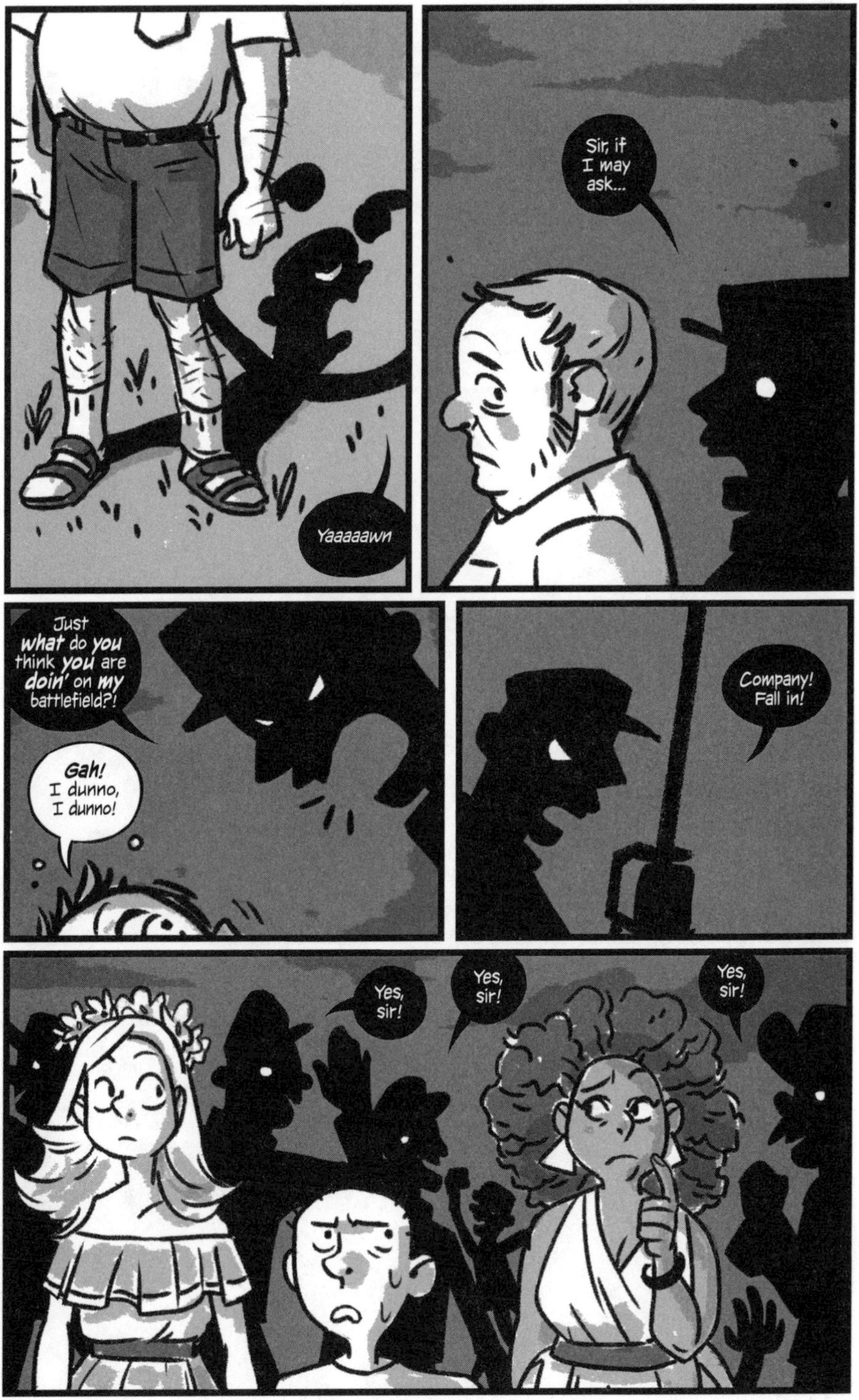
Yaaaaawn
Sir, if I may ask...
Just *what* do *you* think *you* are *doin'* on *my* battlefield?!
Gah! I dunno, I dunno!
Company! Fall in!
Yes, sir!
Yes, sir!
Yes, sir!

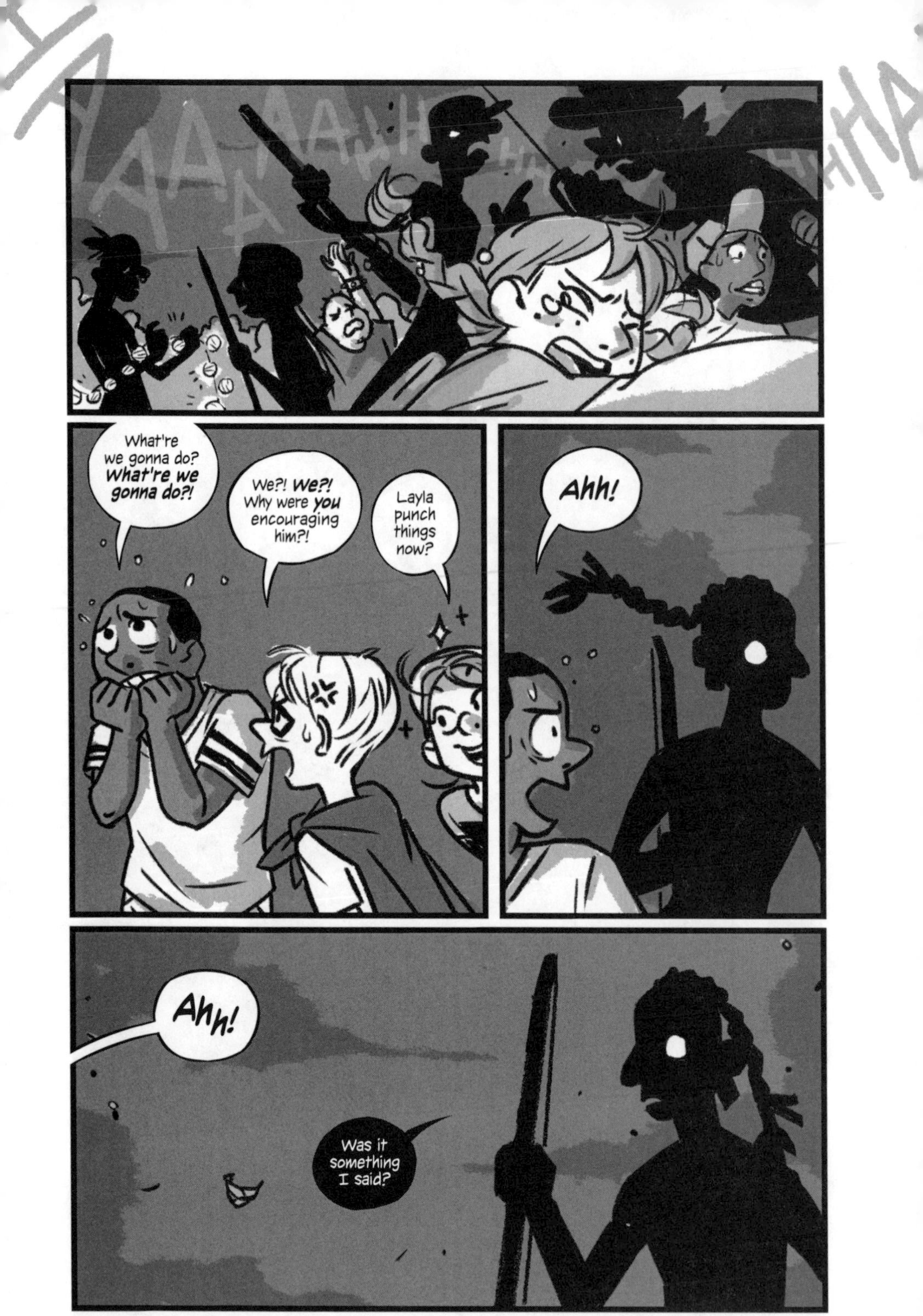

What're we gonna do? What're we gonna do?!
We?! We?! Why were you encouraging him?!
Layla punch things now?
Ahh!
Ahh!
Was it something I said?

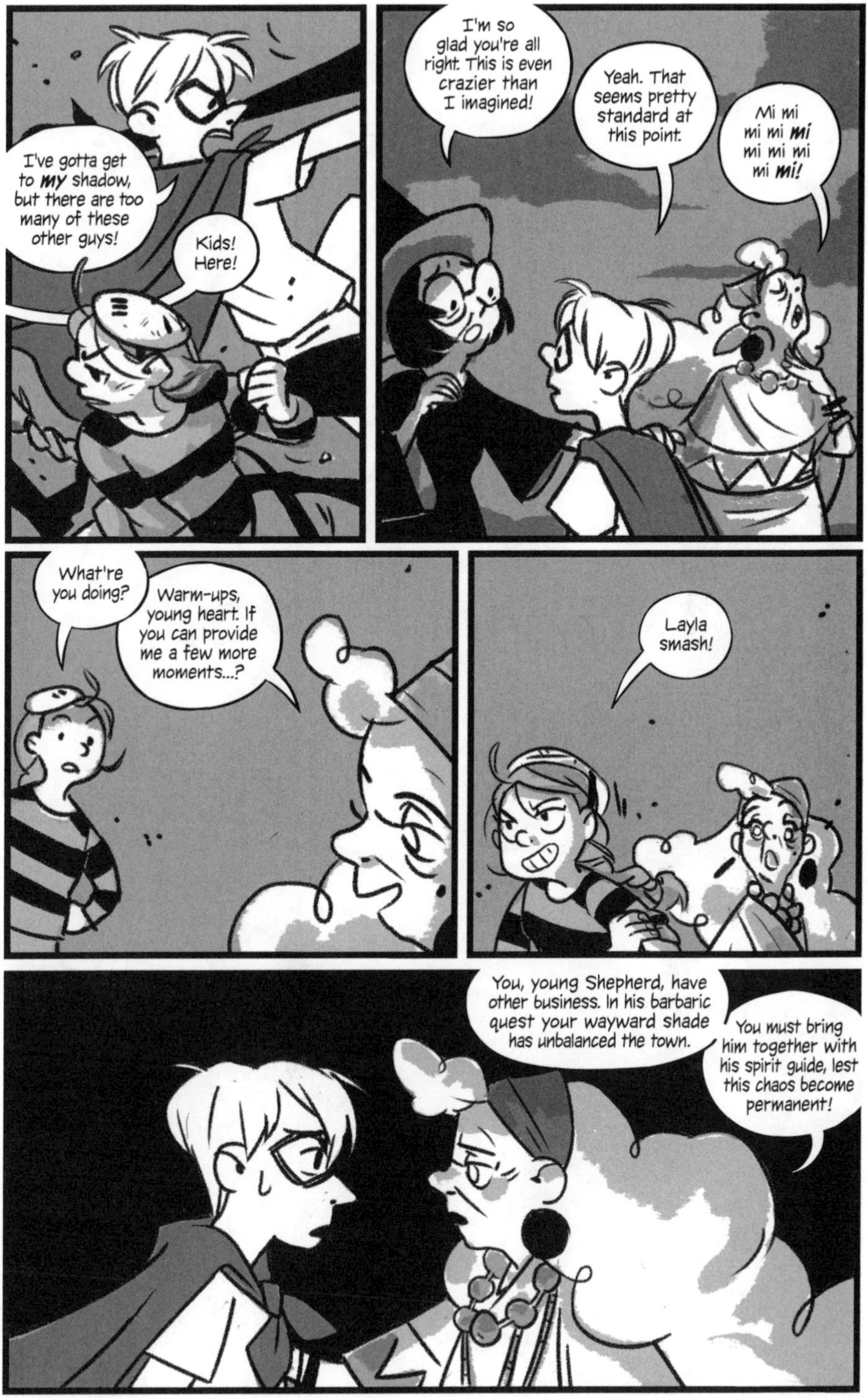
I've gotta get to *MY* shadow, but there are too many of these other guys!
Kids! Here!
I'm so glad you're all right. This is even crazier than I imagined!
Yeah. That seems pretty standard at this point.
Mi mi mi mi *mi* mi mi mi mi *mi!*
What're you doing?
Warm-ups, young heart. If you can provide me a few more moments...?
Layla smash!
You, young Shepherd, have other business. In his barbaric quest your wayward shade has unbalanced the town.
You must bring him together with his spirit guide, lest this chaos become permanent!

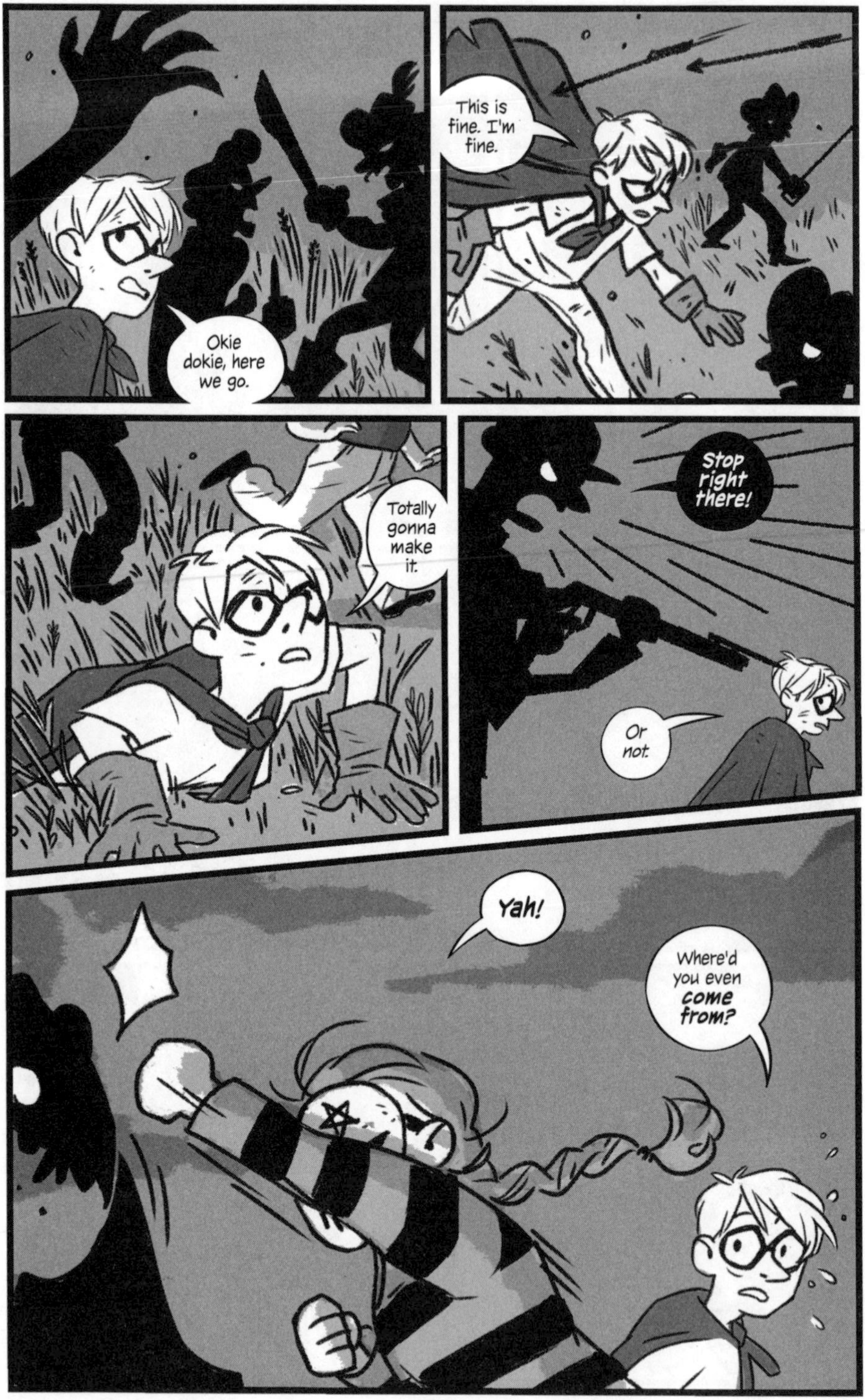
Okie dokie, here we go.
This is fine. I'm fine.
Totally gonna make it.
Stop right there!
Or not.
Yah!
Where'd you even come from?

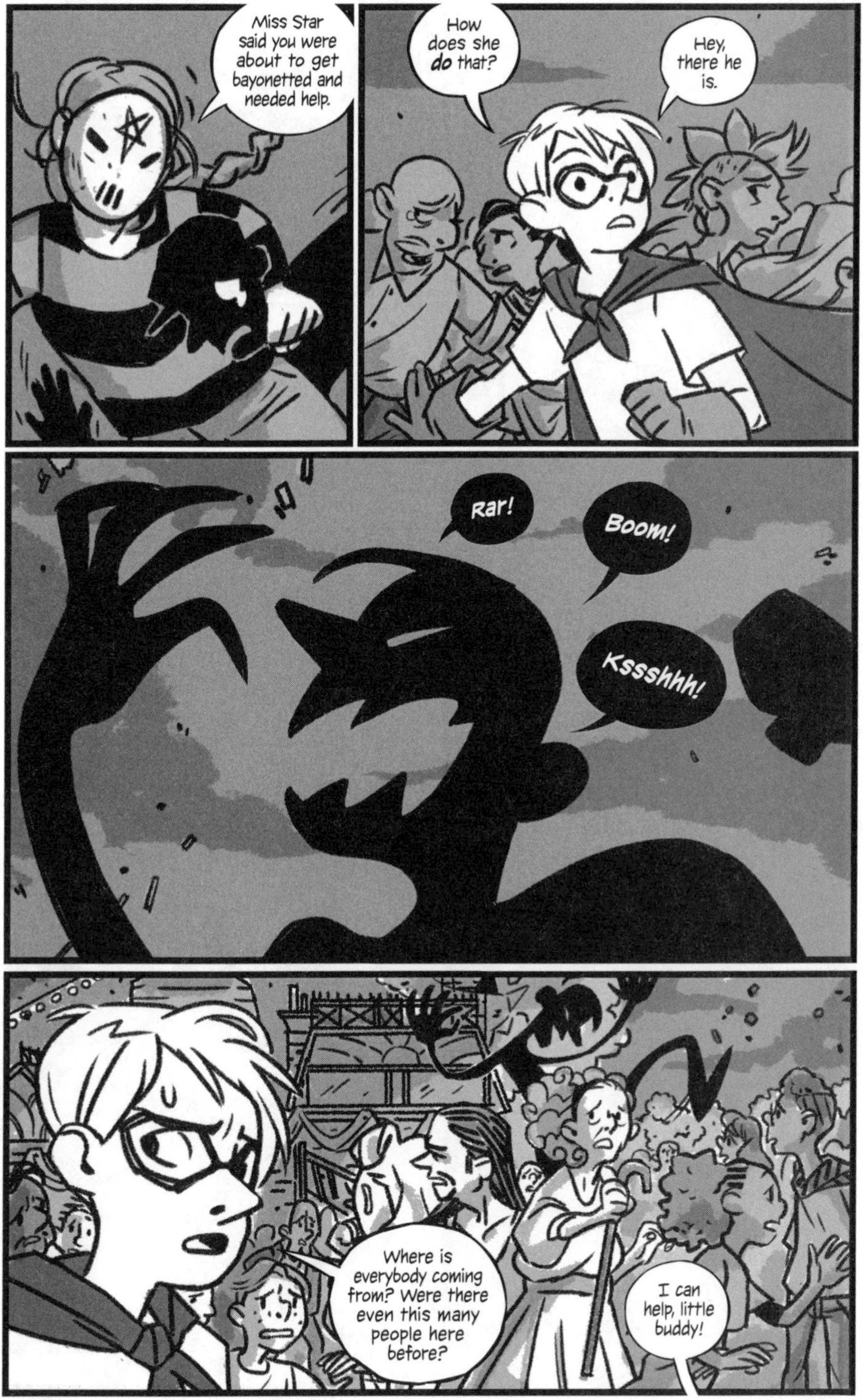
Miss Star said you were about to get bayonetted and needed help.
How does she do that?
Hey, there he is.
Rar!
Boom!
Kssshhh!
Where is everybody coming from? Were there even this many people here before?
I can help, little buddy!

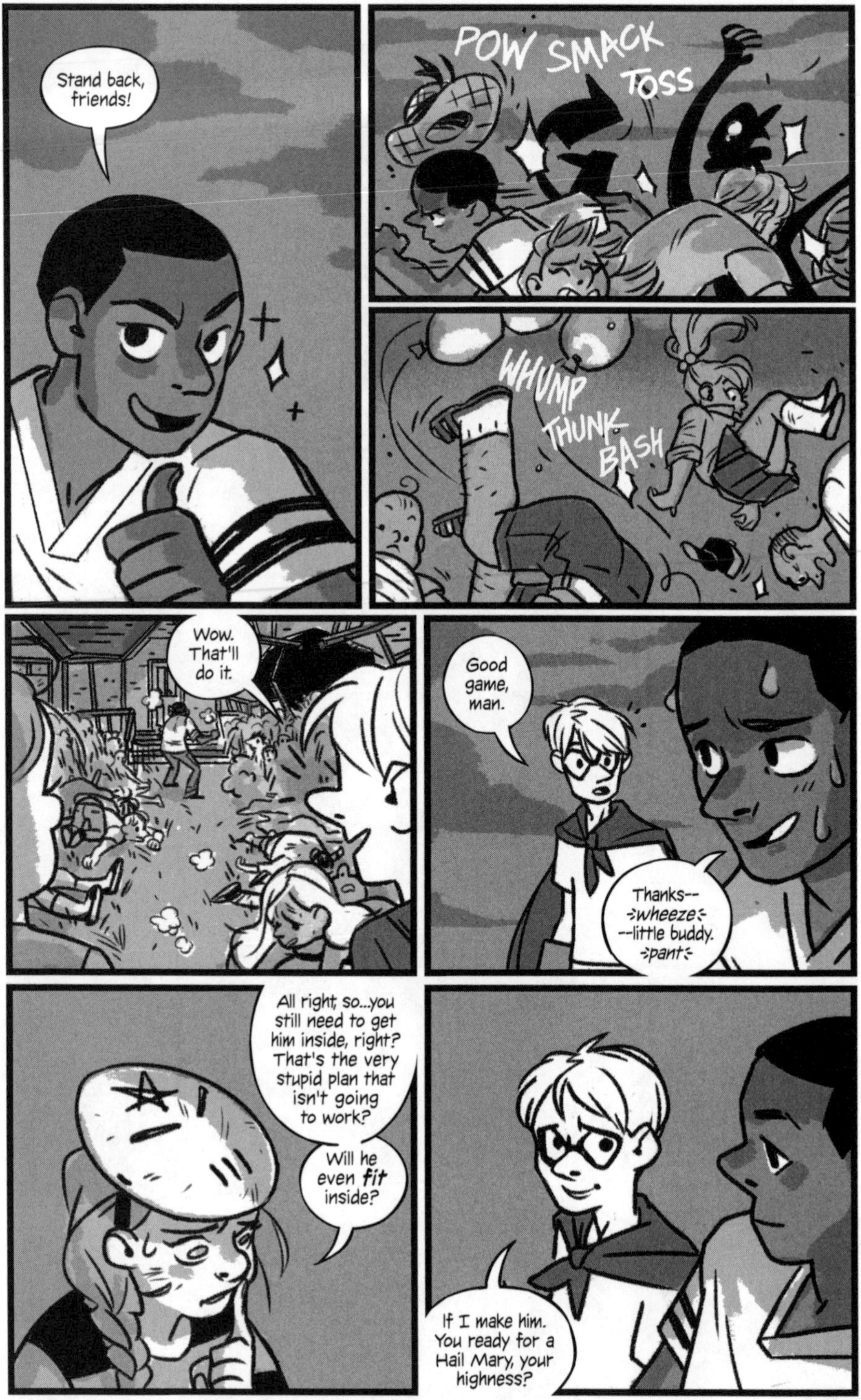

Stand back, friends!
POW SMACK TOSS
WHUMP THUNK BASH
Wow. That'll do it.
Good game, man.
Thanks-- ≈wheeze≈ --little buddy. ≈pant≈
All right, so...you still need to get him inside, right? That's the very stupid plan that isn't going to work?
Will he even *fit* inside?
If I make him. You ready for a Hail Mary, your highness?

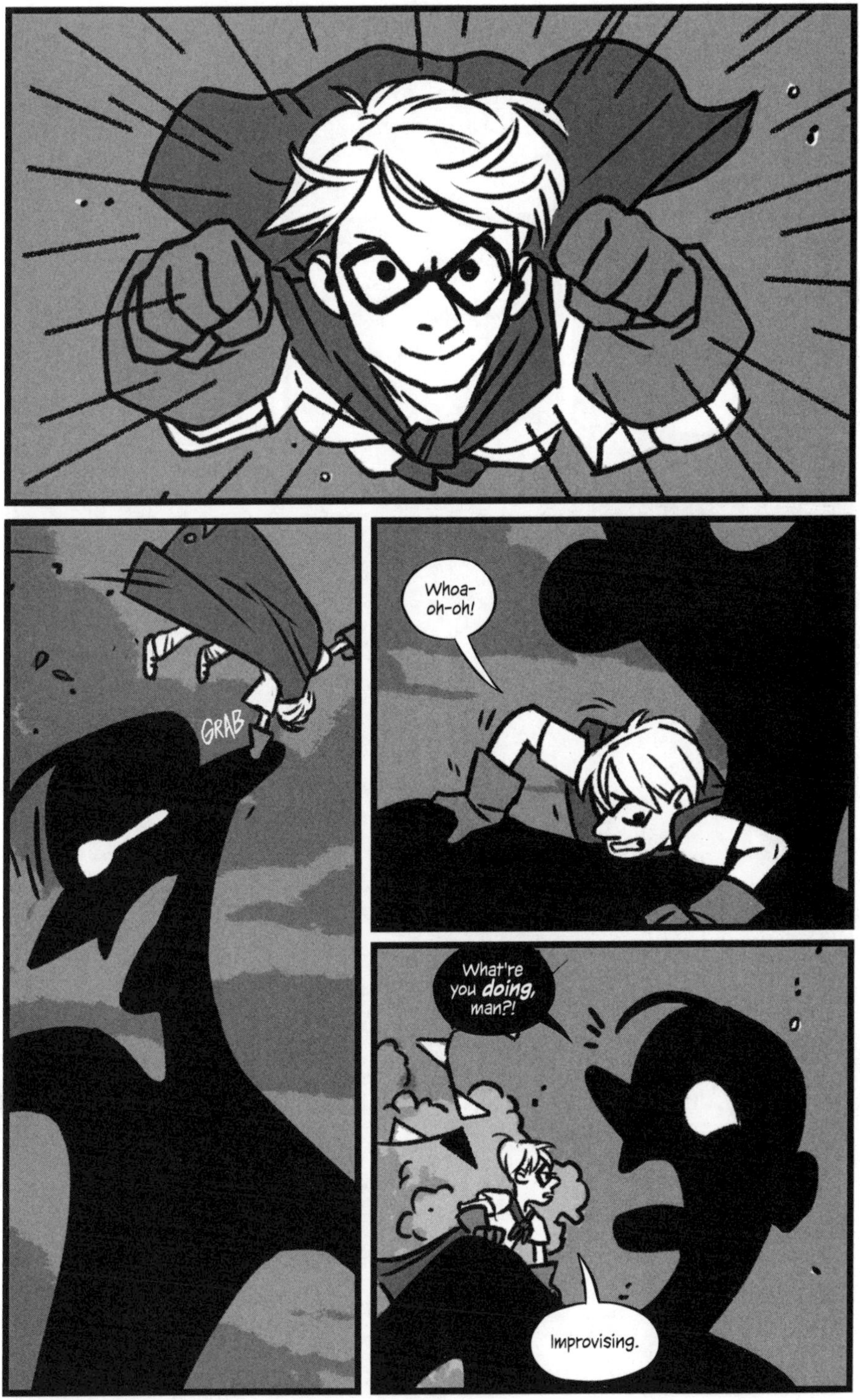
GRAB
Whoa-oh-oh!
What're you doing, man?!
Improvising.

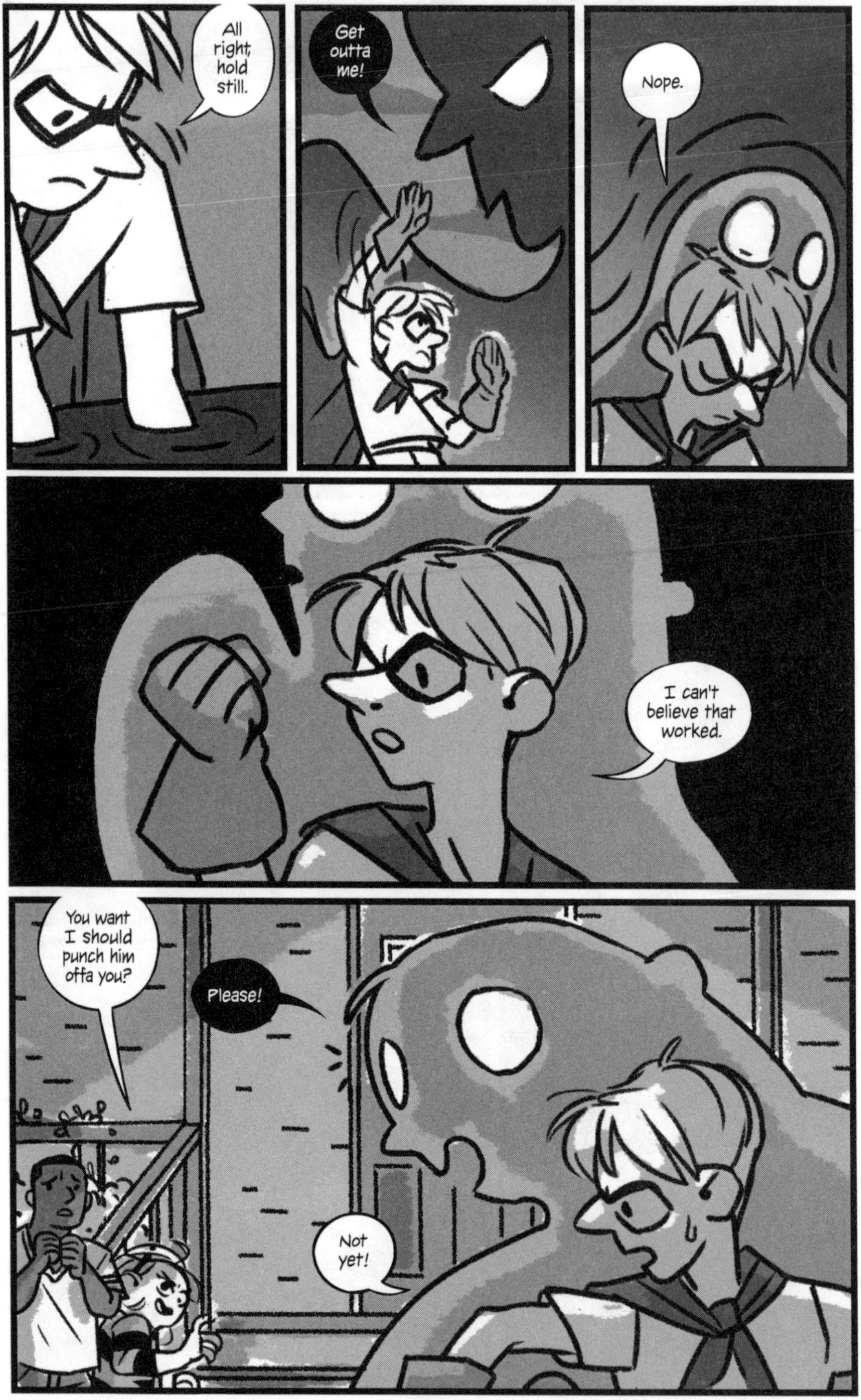
All right, hold still.
Get outta me!
Nope.
I can't believe that worked.
You want I should punch him offa you?
Please!
Not yet!

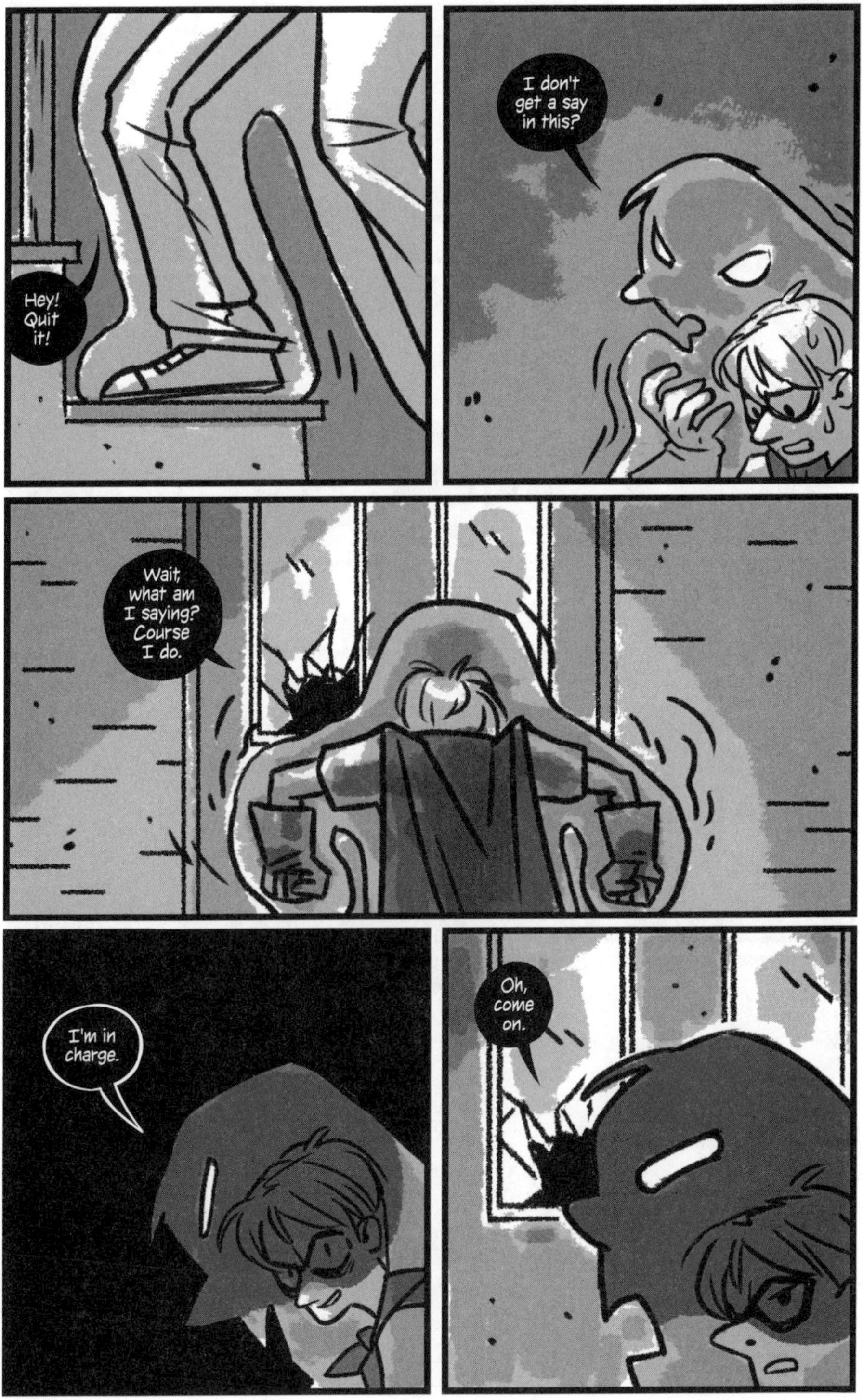
Hey! Quit it!
I don't get a say in this?
Wait, what am I saying? Course I do.
I'm in charge.
Oh, come on.

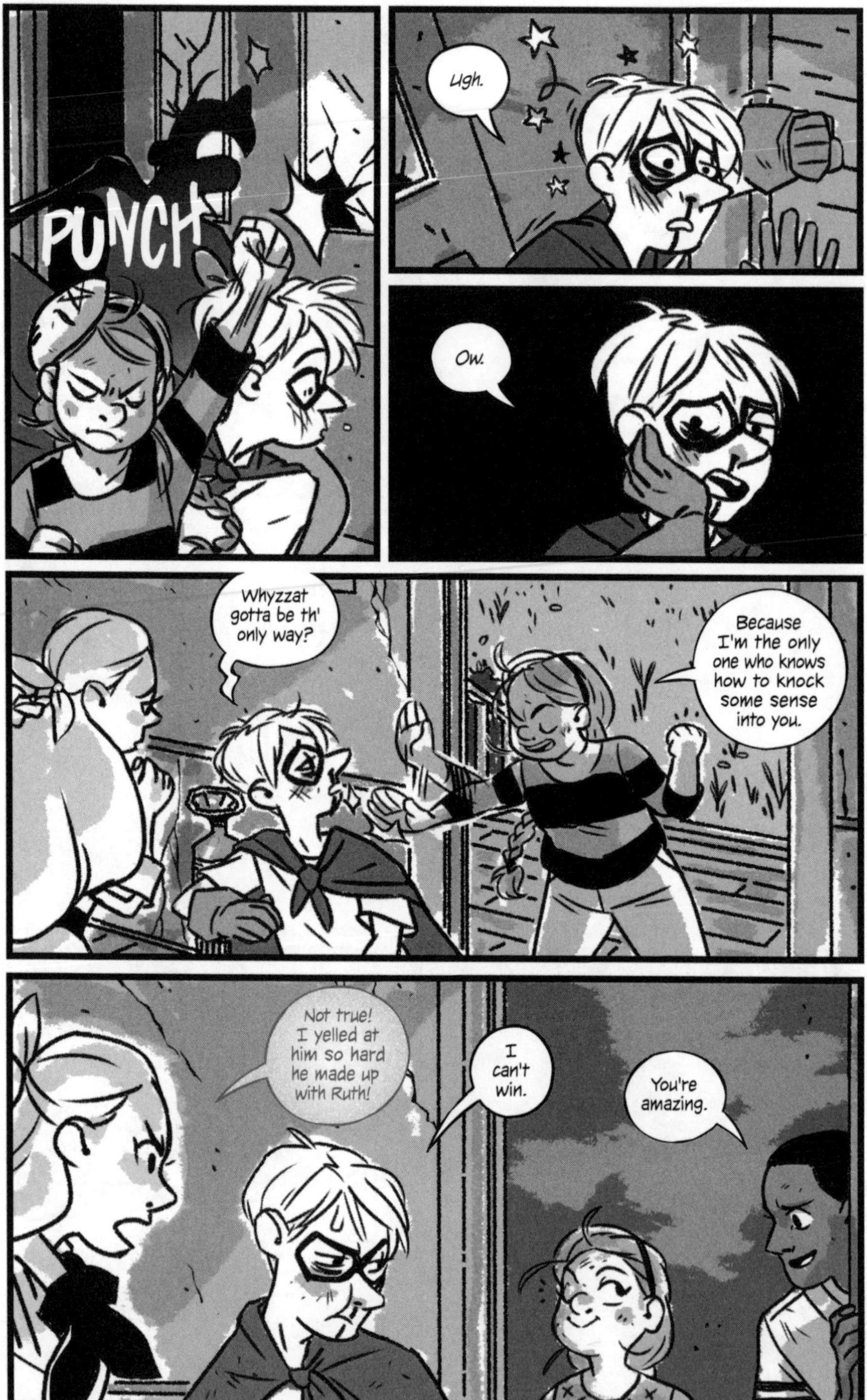
PUNCH
Ugh.
Ow.
Whyzzat gotta be th' only way?
Because I'm the only one who knows how to knock some sense into you.
Not true! I yelled at him so hard he made up with Ruth!
I can't win.
You're amazing.

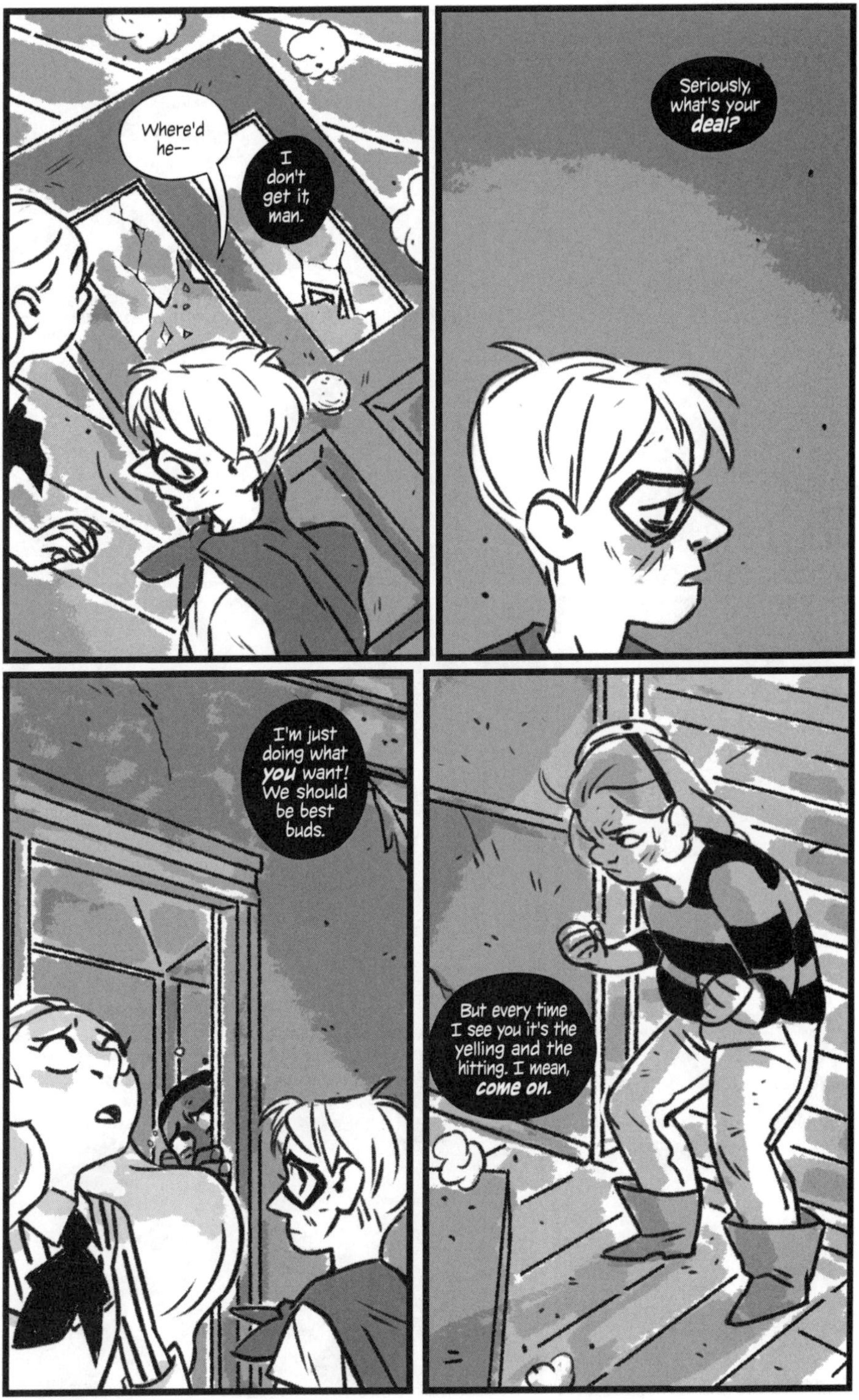
Where'd he--
I don't get it, man.
Seriously, what's your deal?
I'm just doing what you want! We should be best buds.
But every time I see you it's the yelling and the hitting. I mean, come on.

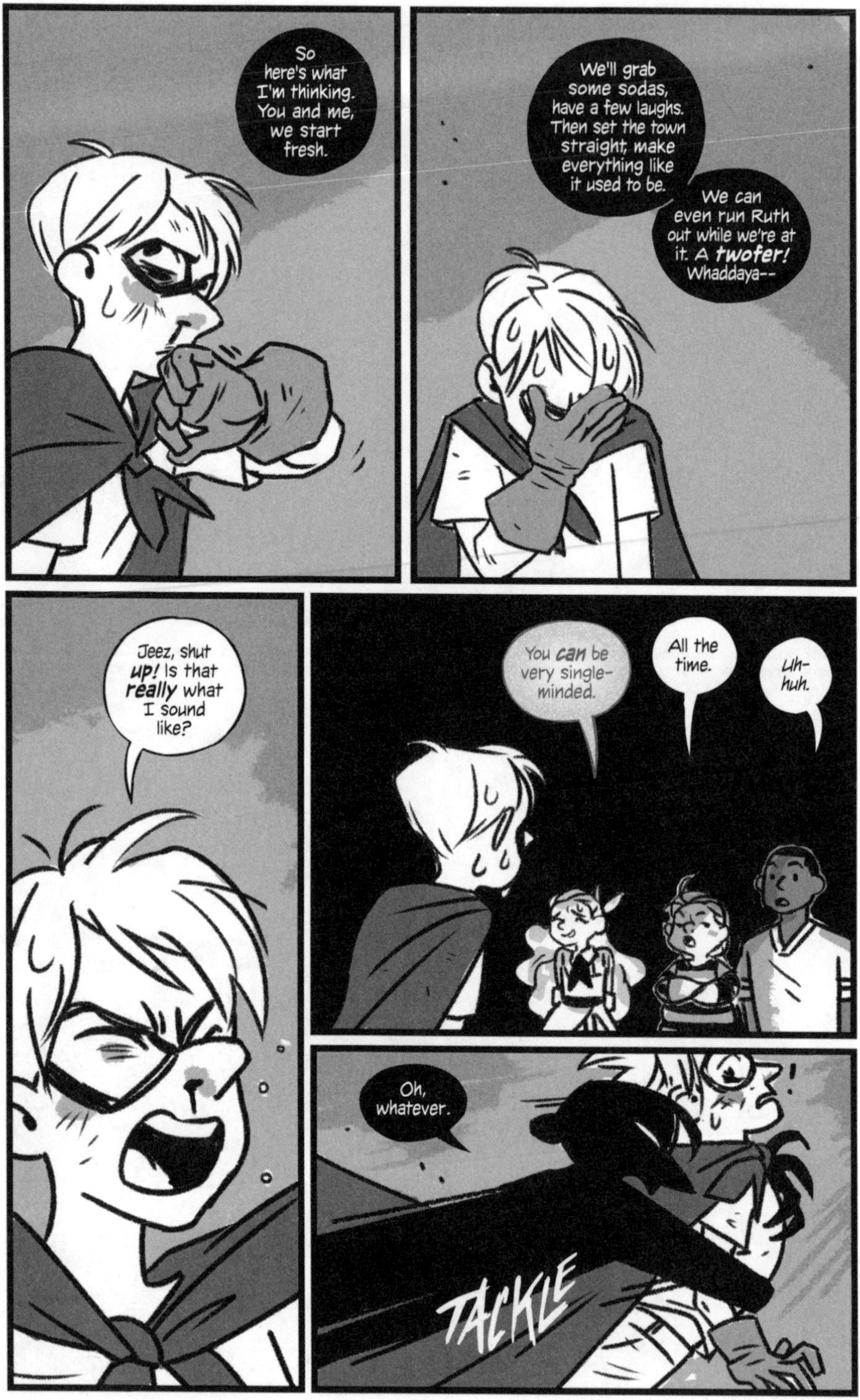

So here's what I'm thinking. You and me, we start fresh.
We'll grab some sodas, have a few laughs. Then set the town straight, make everything like it used to be.
We can even run Ruth out while we're at it. A twofer! Whaddaya--
Jeez, shut up! Is that really what I sound like?
You can be very single-minded.
All the time.
Uh-huh.
Oh, whatever.
TACKLE

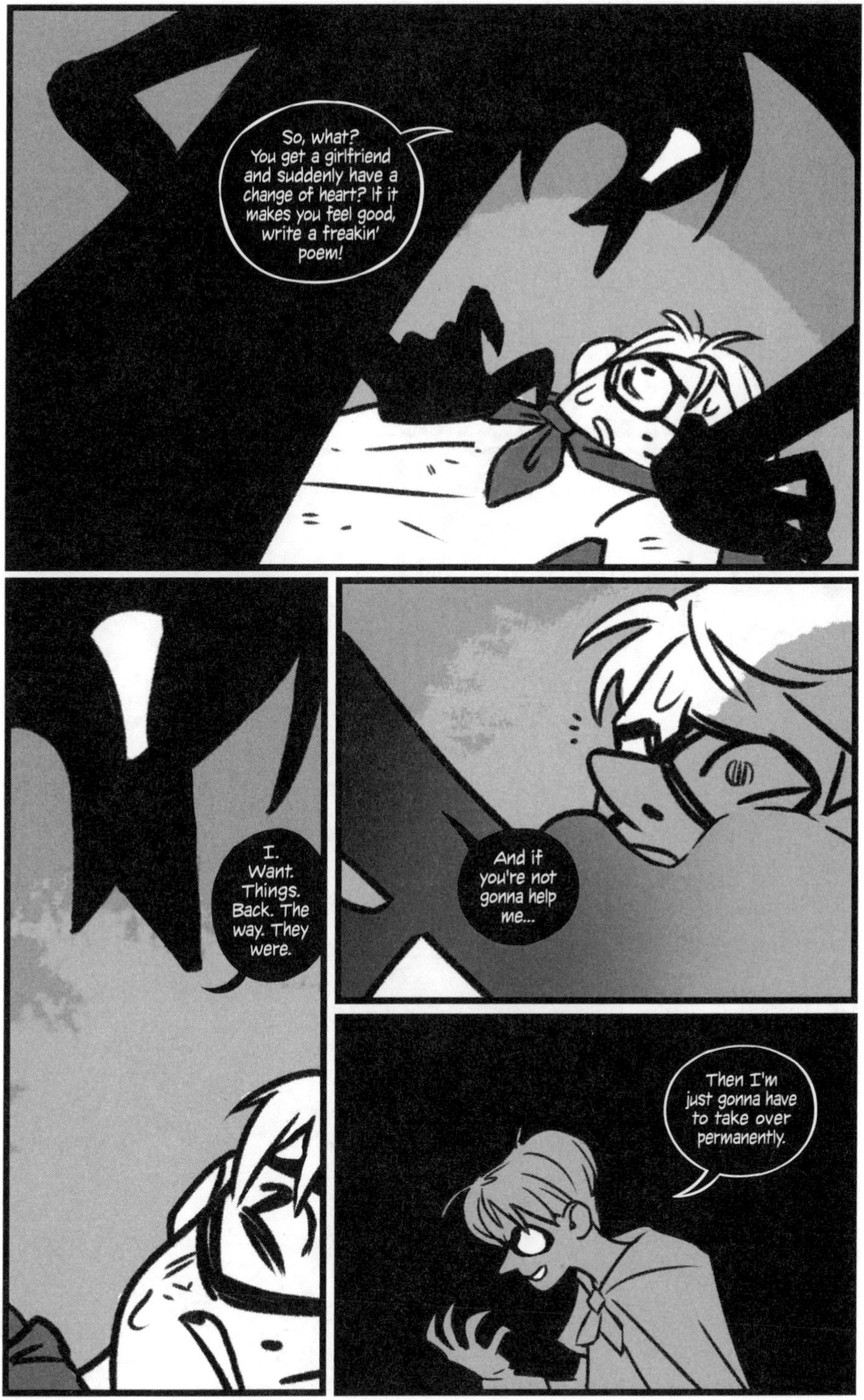
So, what? You get a girlfriend and suddenly have a change of heart? If it makes you feel good, write a freakin' poem!
I. Want. Things. Back. The way. They were.
And if you're not gonna help me...
Then I'm just gonna have to take over permanently.

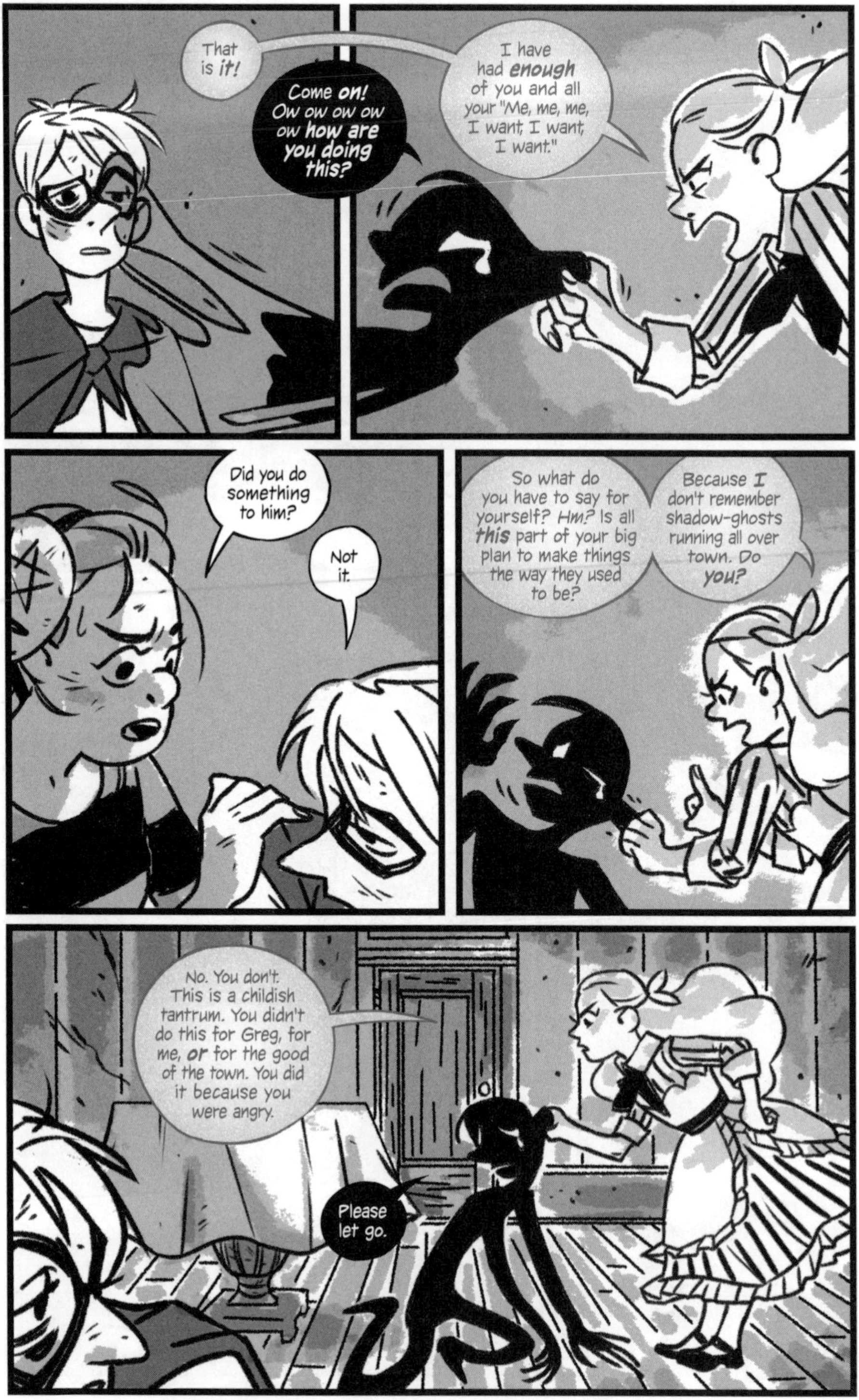
That is *it!*
I have had **enough** of you and all your "Me, me, me, I want, I want, I want."
Come **on!** Ow ow ow ow ow **how are you doing this?**
Did you do something to him?
Not it.
So what do you have to say for yourself? *Hm?* Is all ***this*** part of your big plan to make things the way they used to be?
Because *I* don't remember shadow-ghosts running all over town. Do ***you?***
No. You don't. This is a childish tantrum. You didn't do this for Greg, for me, ***or*** for the good of the town. You did it because you were angry.
Please let go.

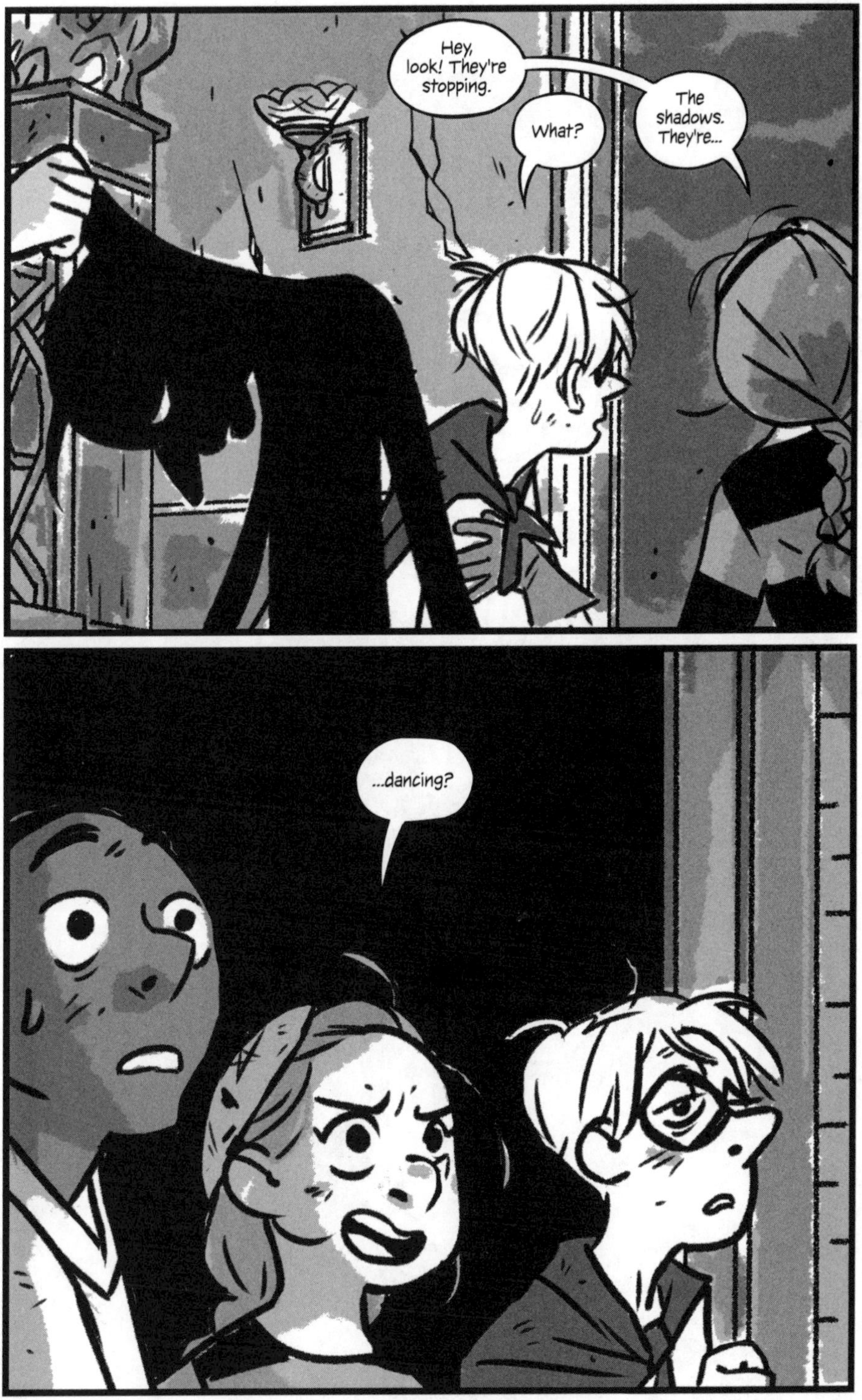
Hey, look! They're stopping.
What?
The shadows. They're...
...dancing?

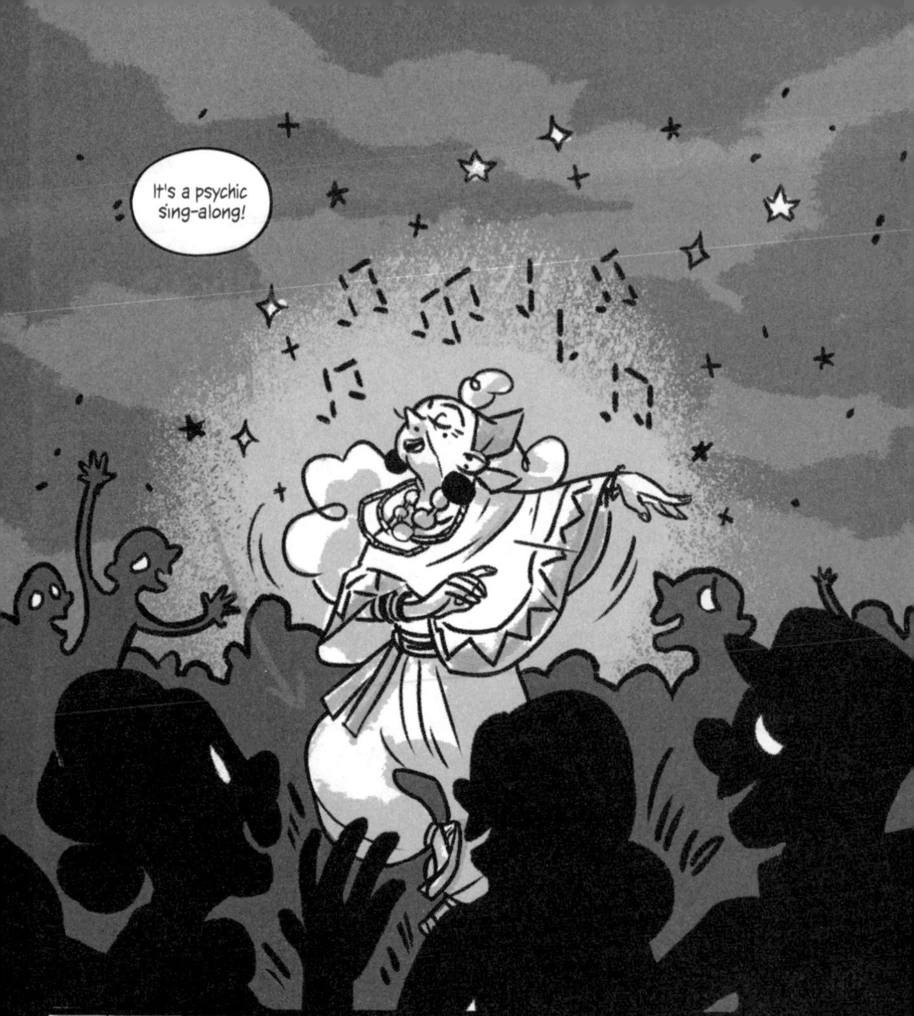
It's a psychic sing-along!

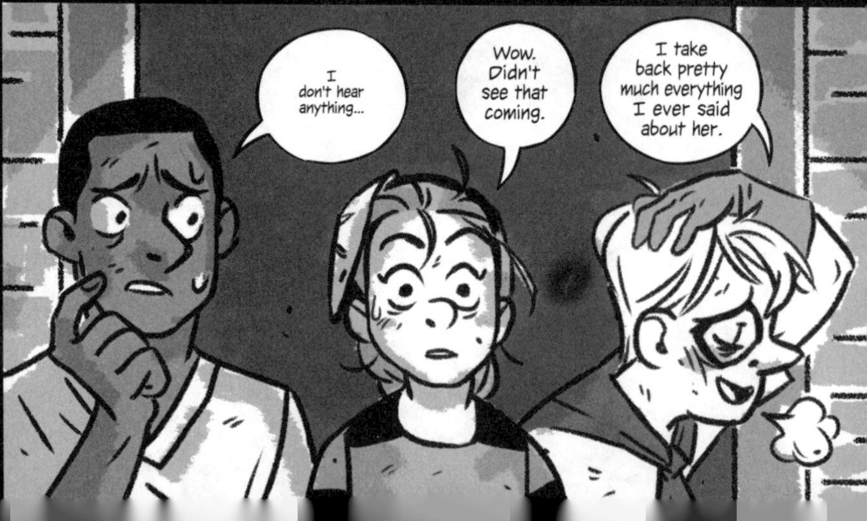
I don't hear anything...
Wow. Didn't see that coming.
I take back pretty much everything I ever said about her.

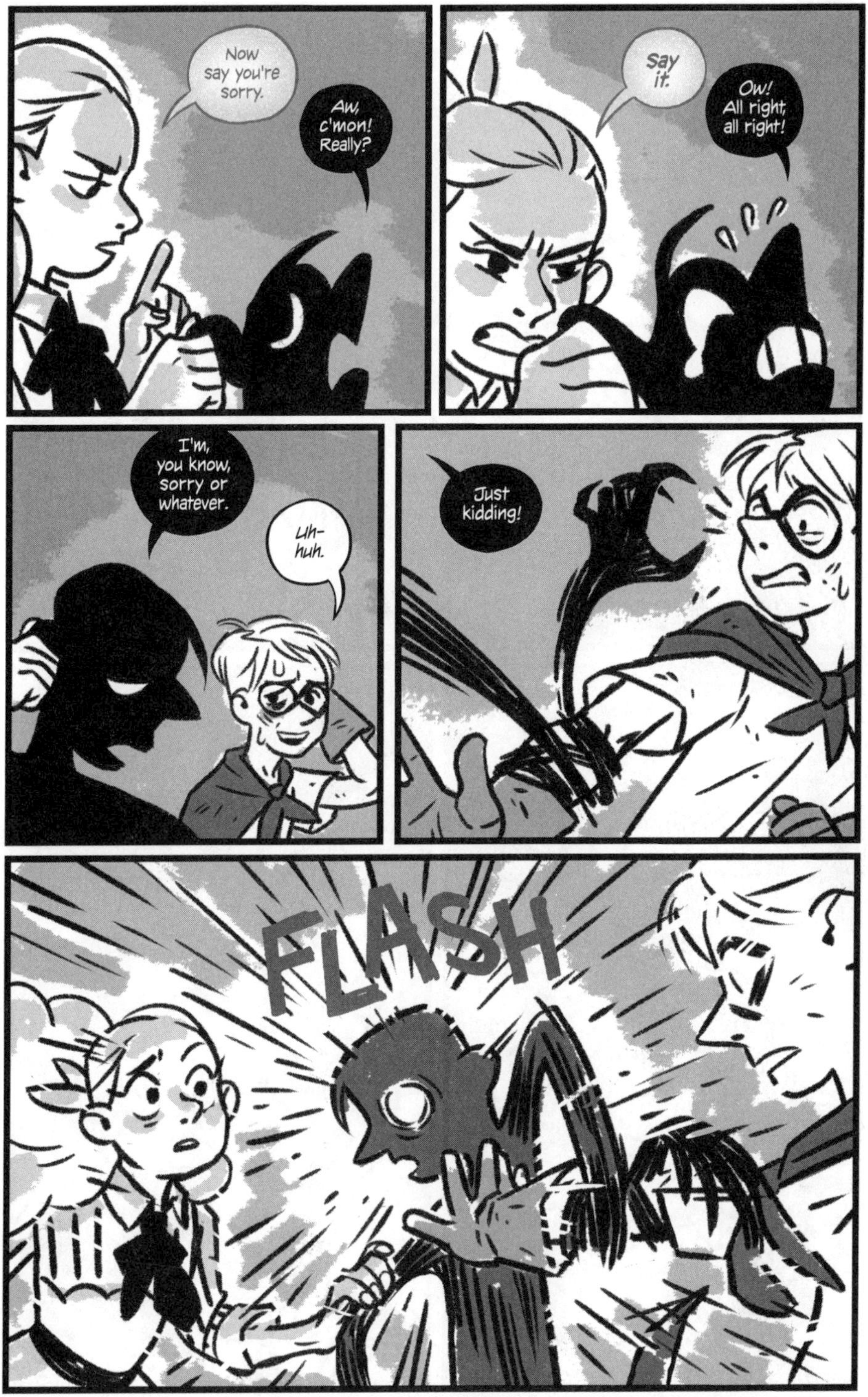
Now say you're sorry.
Aw, c'mon! Really?
Say it.
Ow! All right, all right!
I'm, you know, sorry or whatever.
Uh-huh.
Just kidding!
FLASH

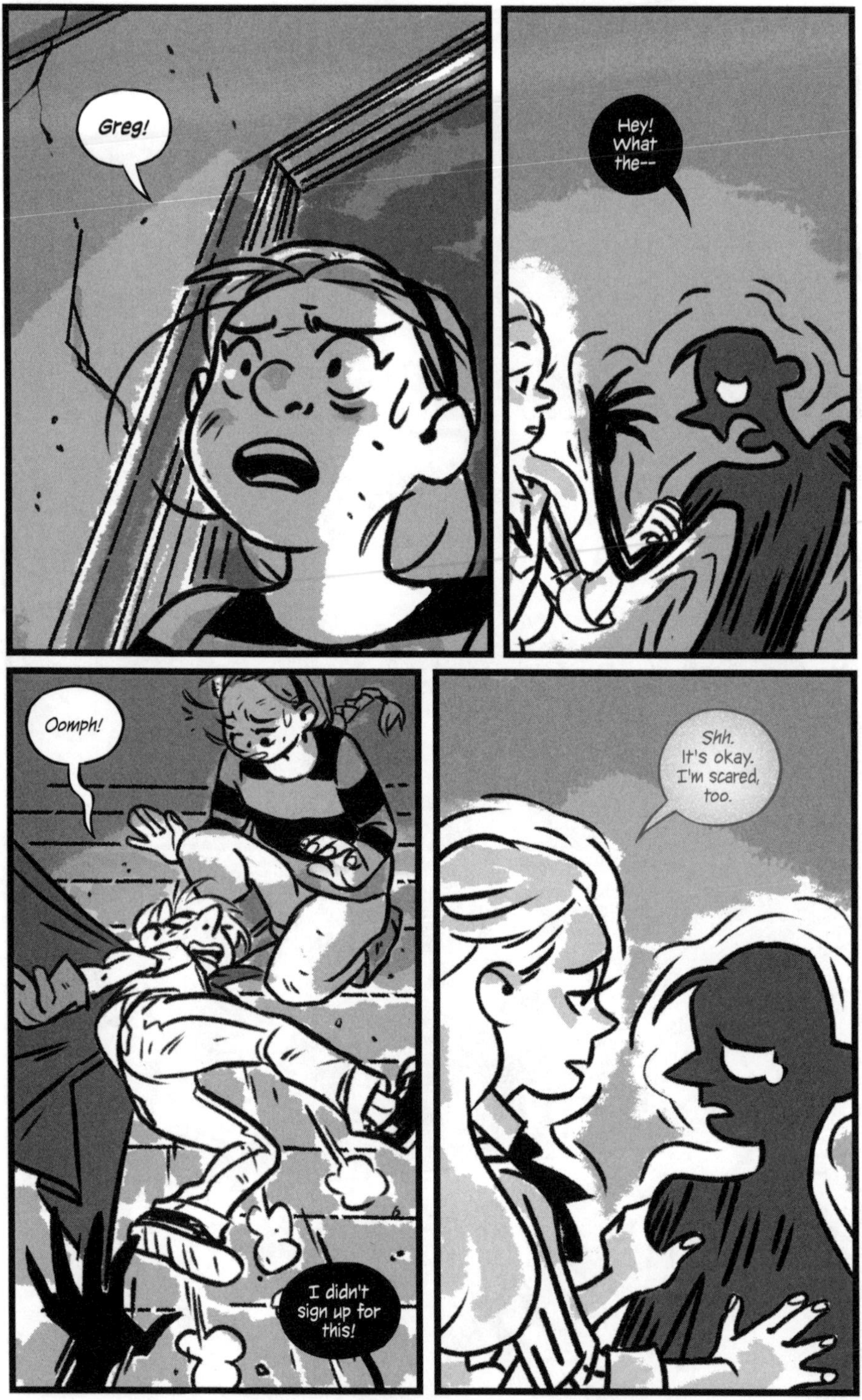
Greg!
Hey! What the--
Oomph!
I didn't sign up for this!
Shh. It's okay. I'm scared, too.

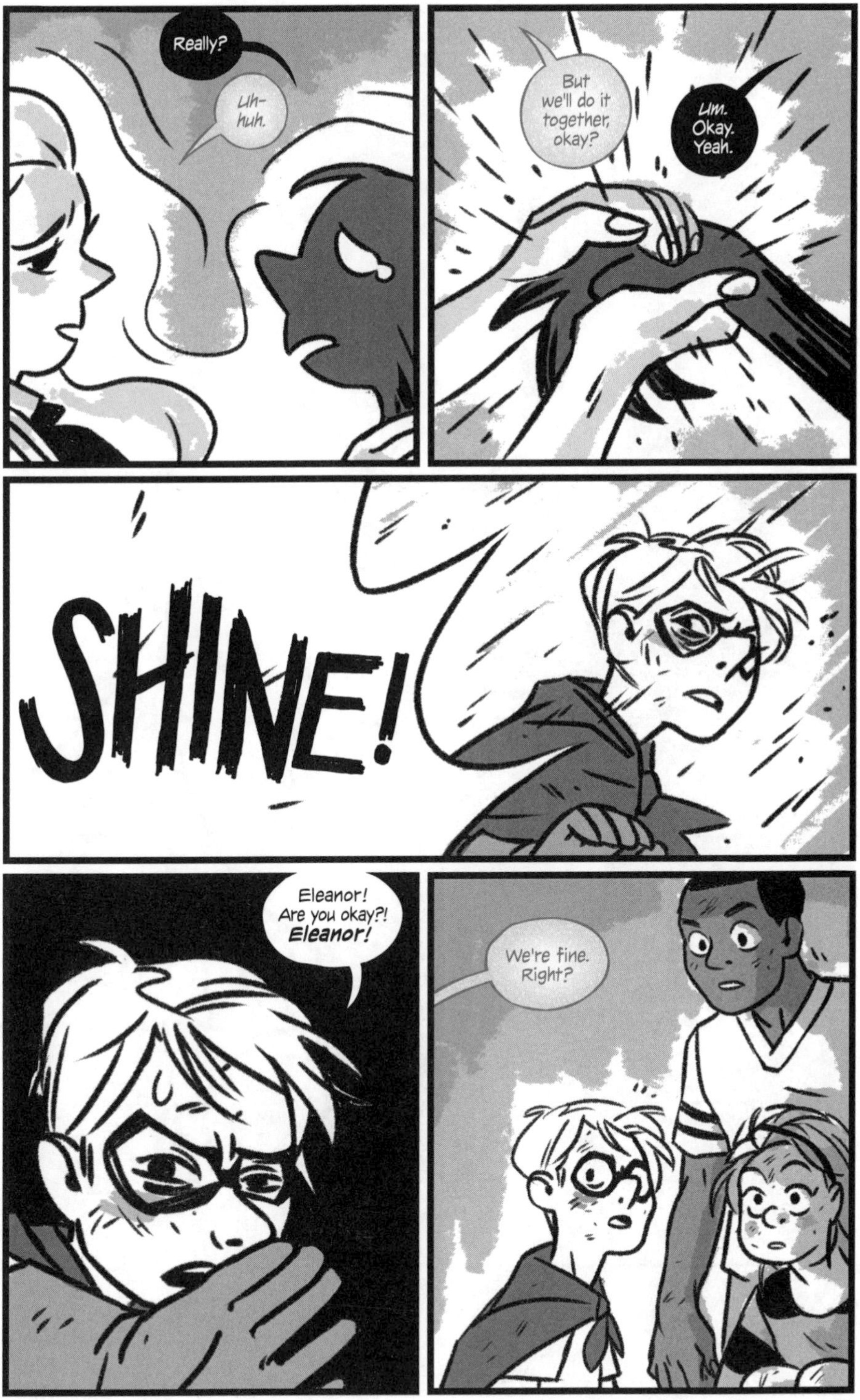

Really?
Uh-huh.
But we'll do it together, okay?
Um. Okay. Yeah.
SHINE!
Eleanor! Are you okay?! **Eleanor!**
We're fine. Right?

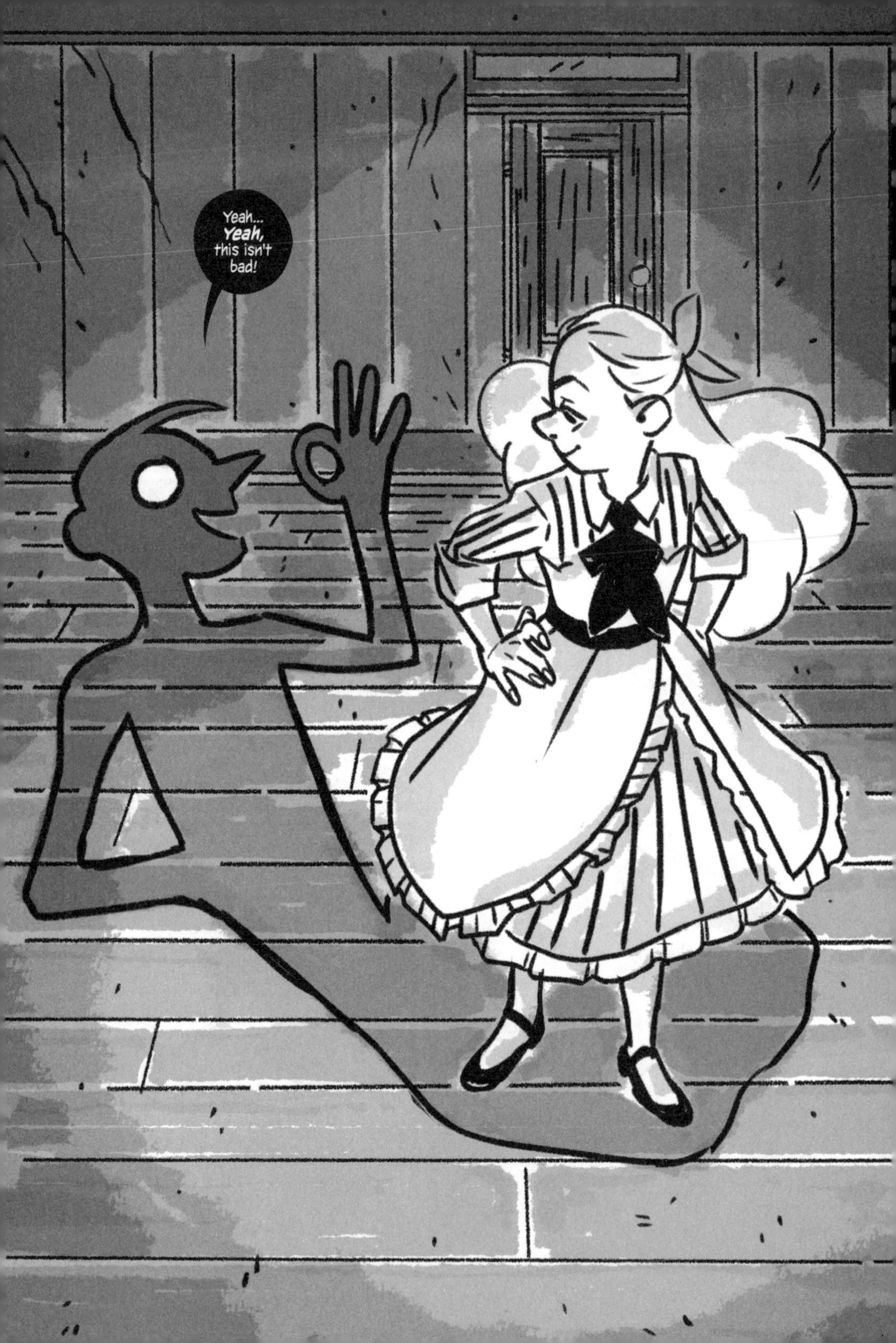
Yeah... **Yeah,** this isn't bad!

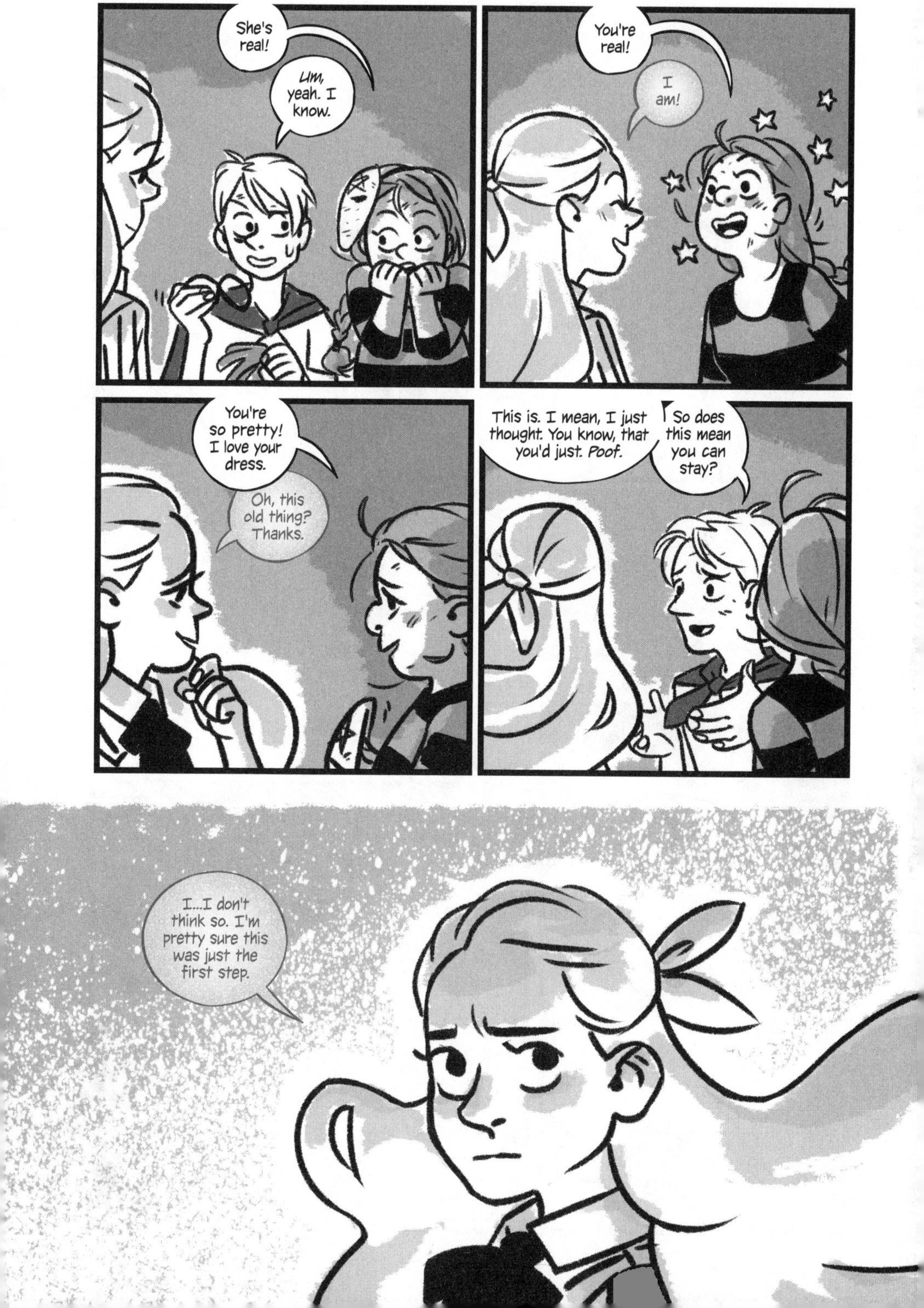
She's real!
Um, yeah. I know.
You're real!
I am!
You're so pretty! I love your dress.
Oh, this old thing? Thanks.
This is. I mean, I just thought. You know, that you'd just. Poof.
So does this mean you can stay?
I...I don't think so. I'm pretty sure this was just the first step.

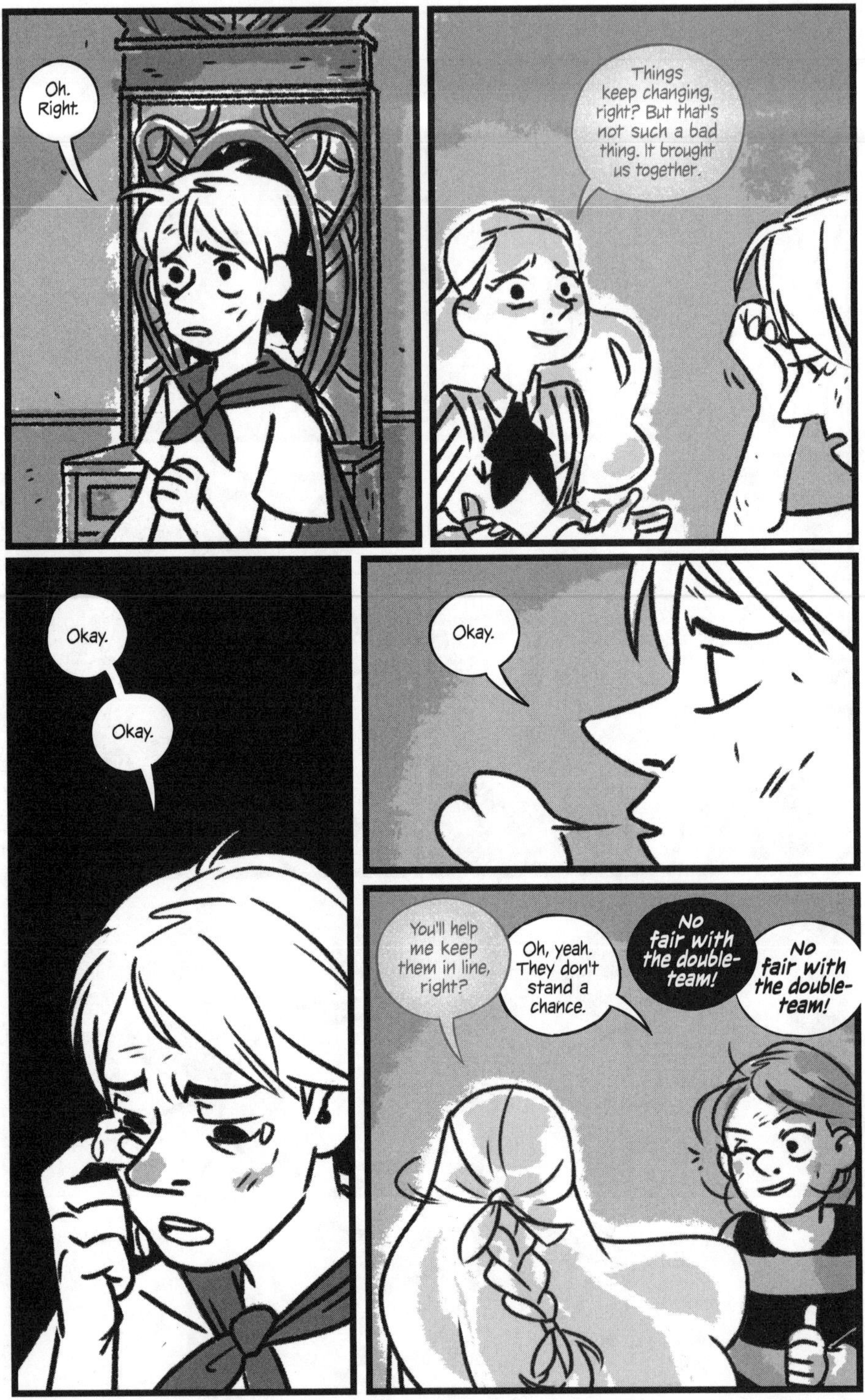
Oh. Right.
Things keep changing, right? But that's not such a bad thing. It brought us together.
Okay.
Okay.
Okay.
You'll help me keep them in line, right?
Oh, yeah. They don't stand a chance.
No fair with the double-team!
No fair with the double-team!

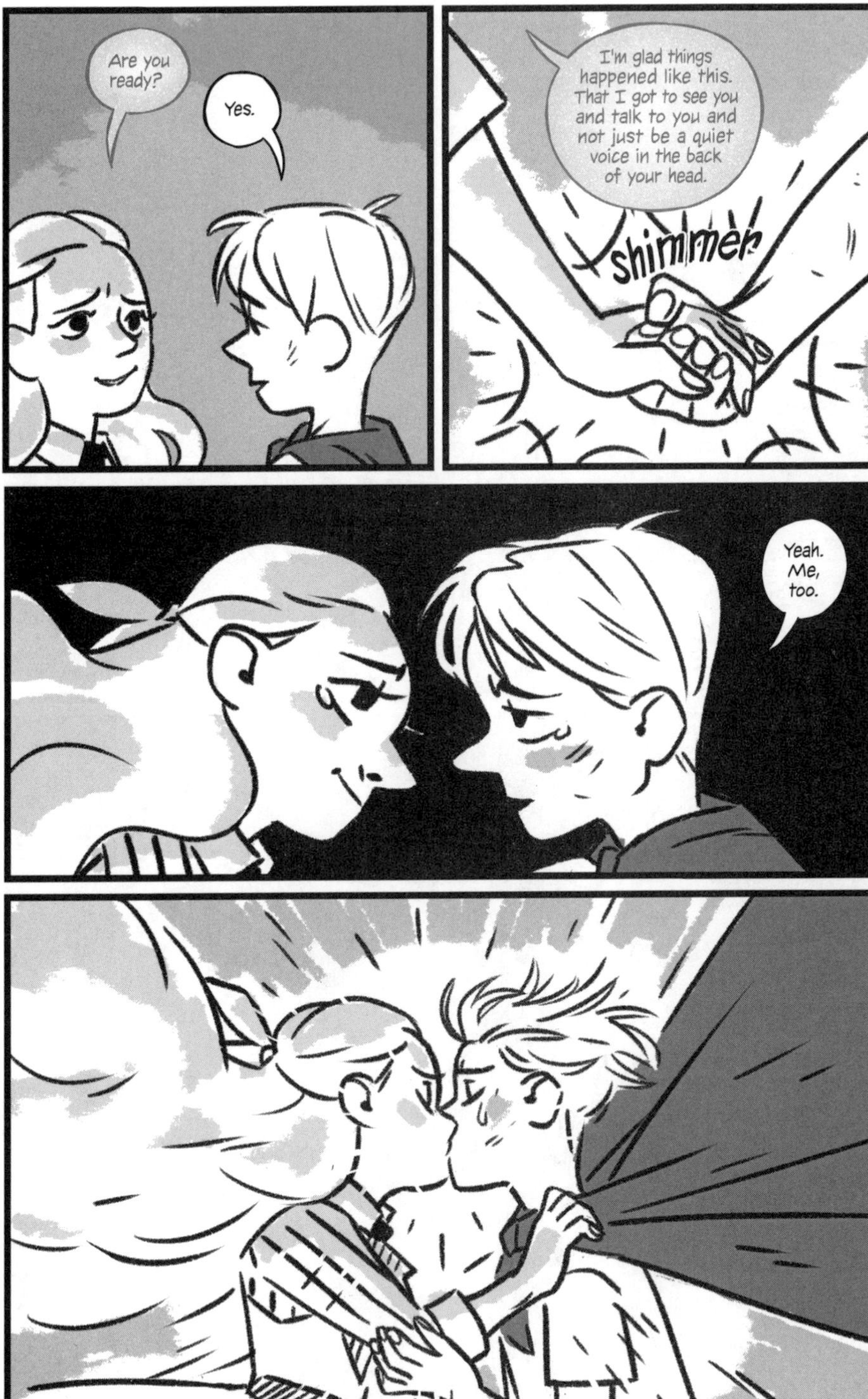
Are you ready?
Yes.
I'm glad things happened like this. That I got to see you and talk to you and not just be a quiet voice in the back of your head.
shimmer
Yeah. Me, too.

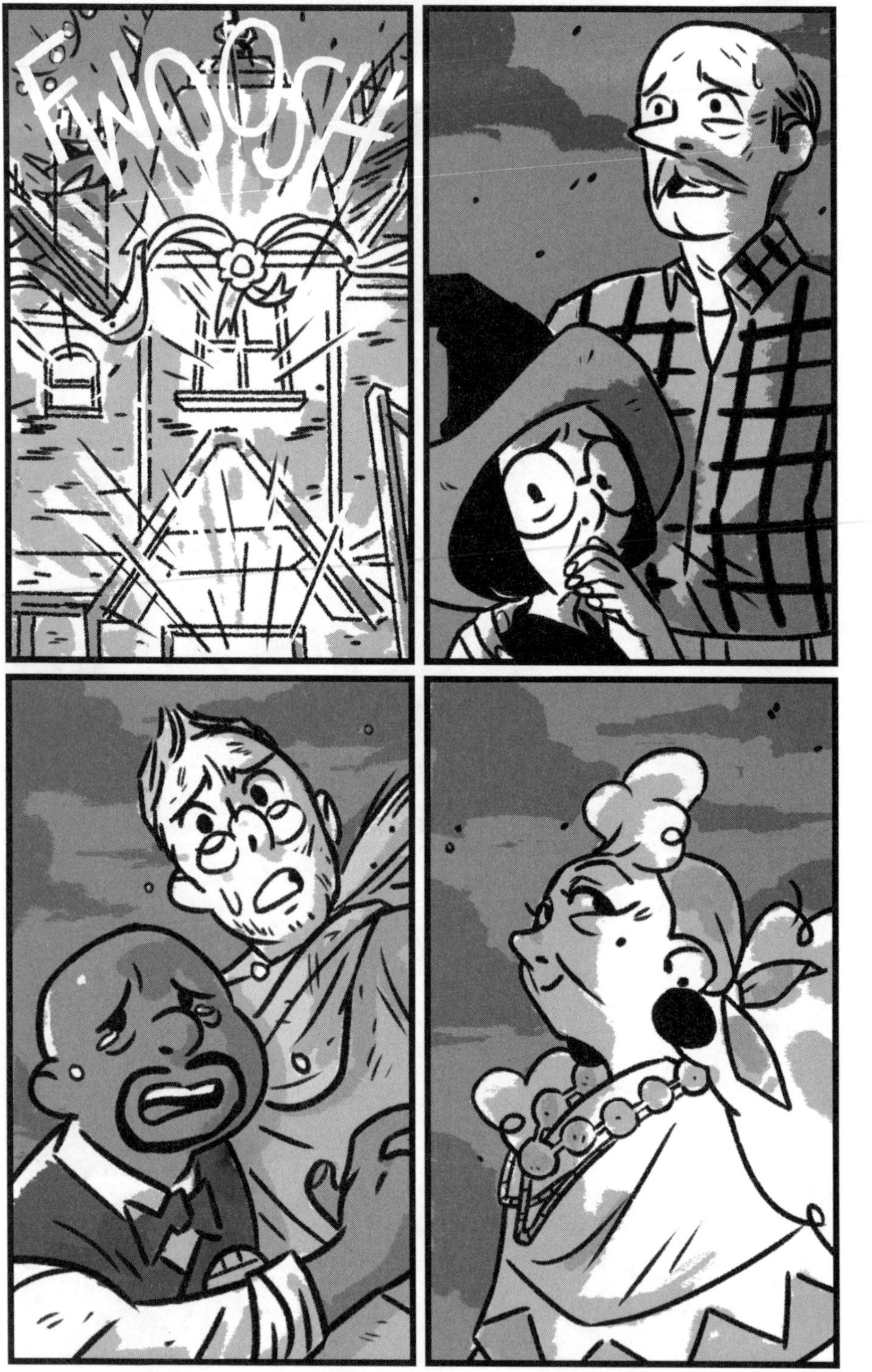
FWOOSH

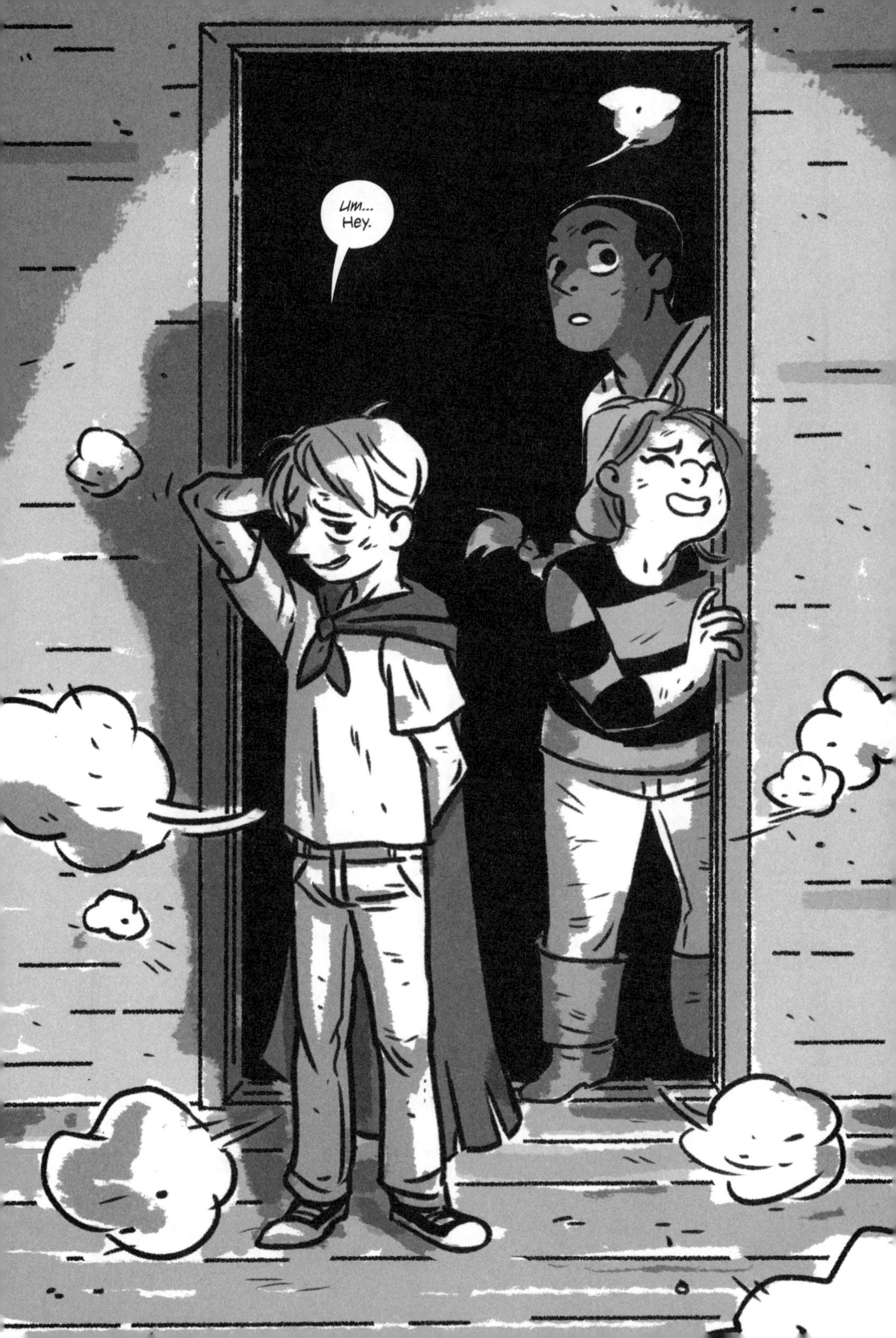
Um... Hey.

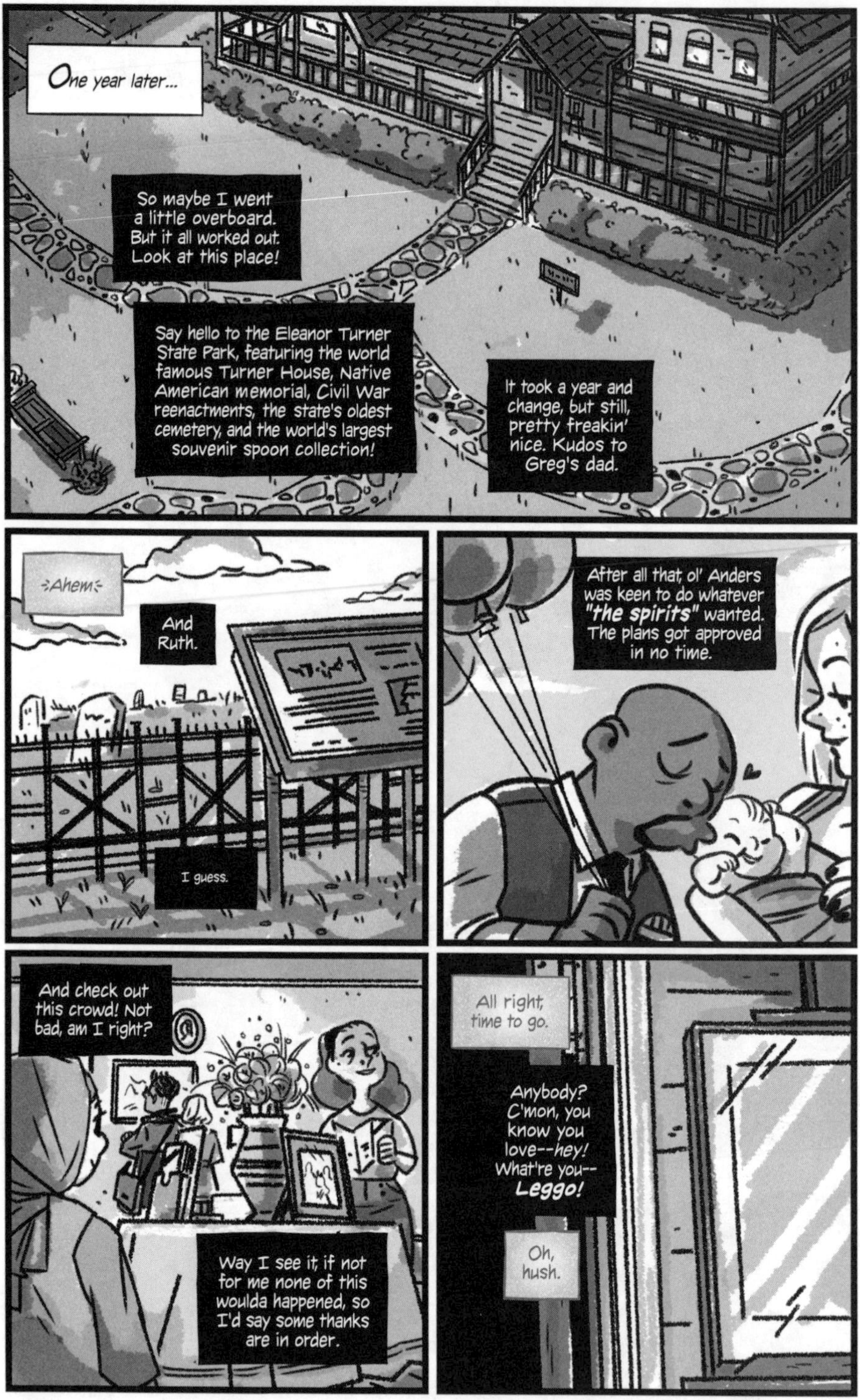
One year later...
So maybe I went a little overboard. But it all worked out. Look at this place!
Say hello to the Eleanor Turner State Park, featuring the world famous Turner House, Native American memorial, Civil War reenactments, the state's oldest cemetery, and the world's largest souvenir spoon collection!
It took a year and change, but still, pretty freakin' nice. Kudos to Greg's dad.
Ahem
And Ruth.
I guess.
After all that, ol' Anders was keen to do whatever "the spirits" wanted. The plans got approved in no time.
And check out this crowd! Not bad, am I right?
Way I see it, if not for me none of this woulda happened, so I'd say some thanks are in order.
All right, time to go.
Anybody? C'mon, you know you love--hey! What're you-- Leggo!
Oh, hush.

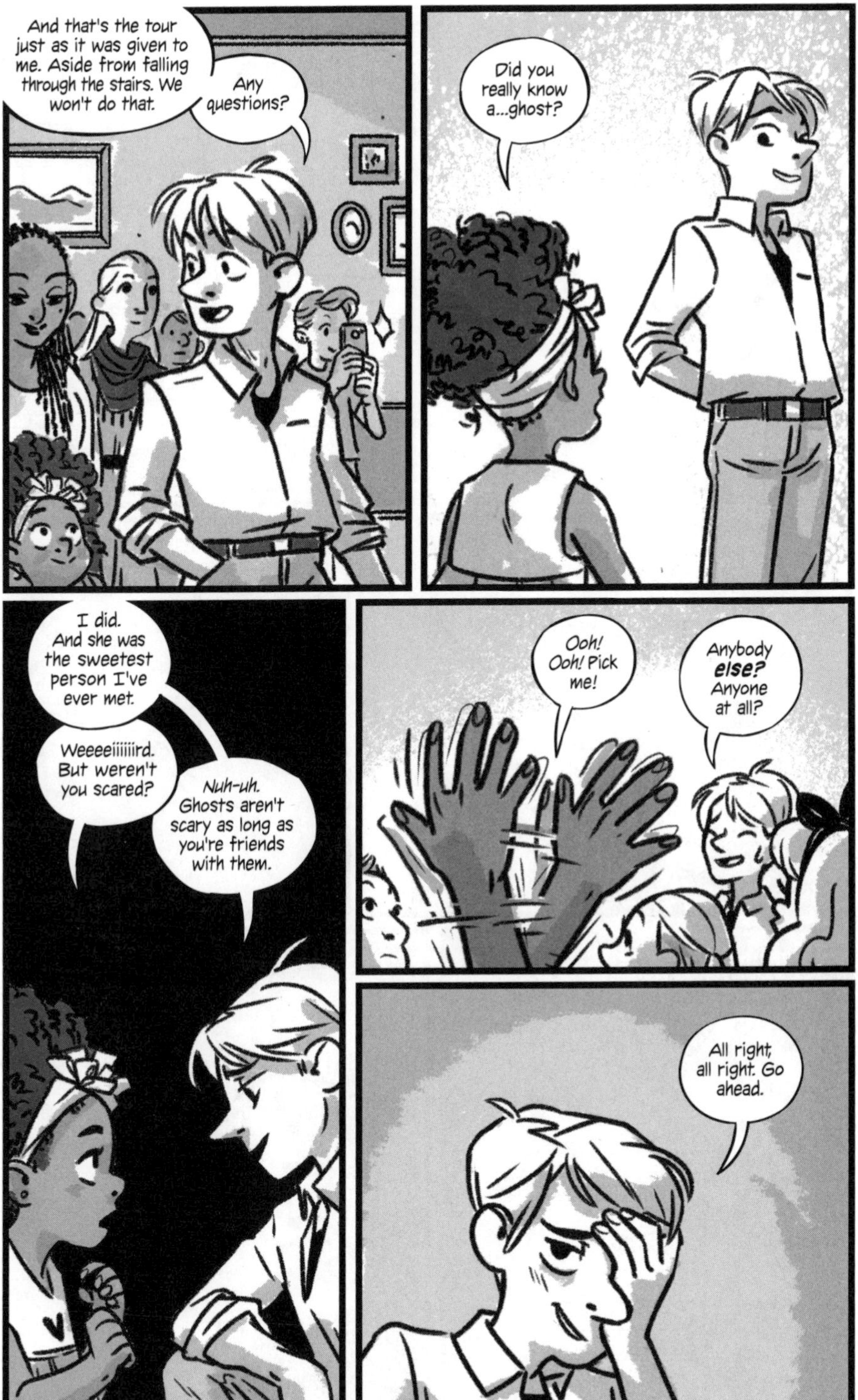
And that's the tour just as it was given to me. Aside from falling through the stairs. We won't do that.
Any questions?
Did you really know a...ghost?
I did. And she was the sweetest person I've ever met.
Weeeeiiiiiiird. But weren't you scared?
Nuh-uh. Ghosts aren't scary as long as you're friends with them.
Ooh! Ooh! Pick me!
Anybody **else?** Anyone at all?
All right, all right. Go ahead.

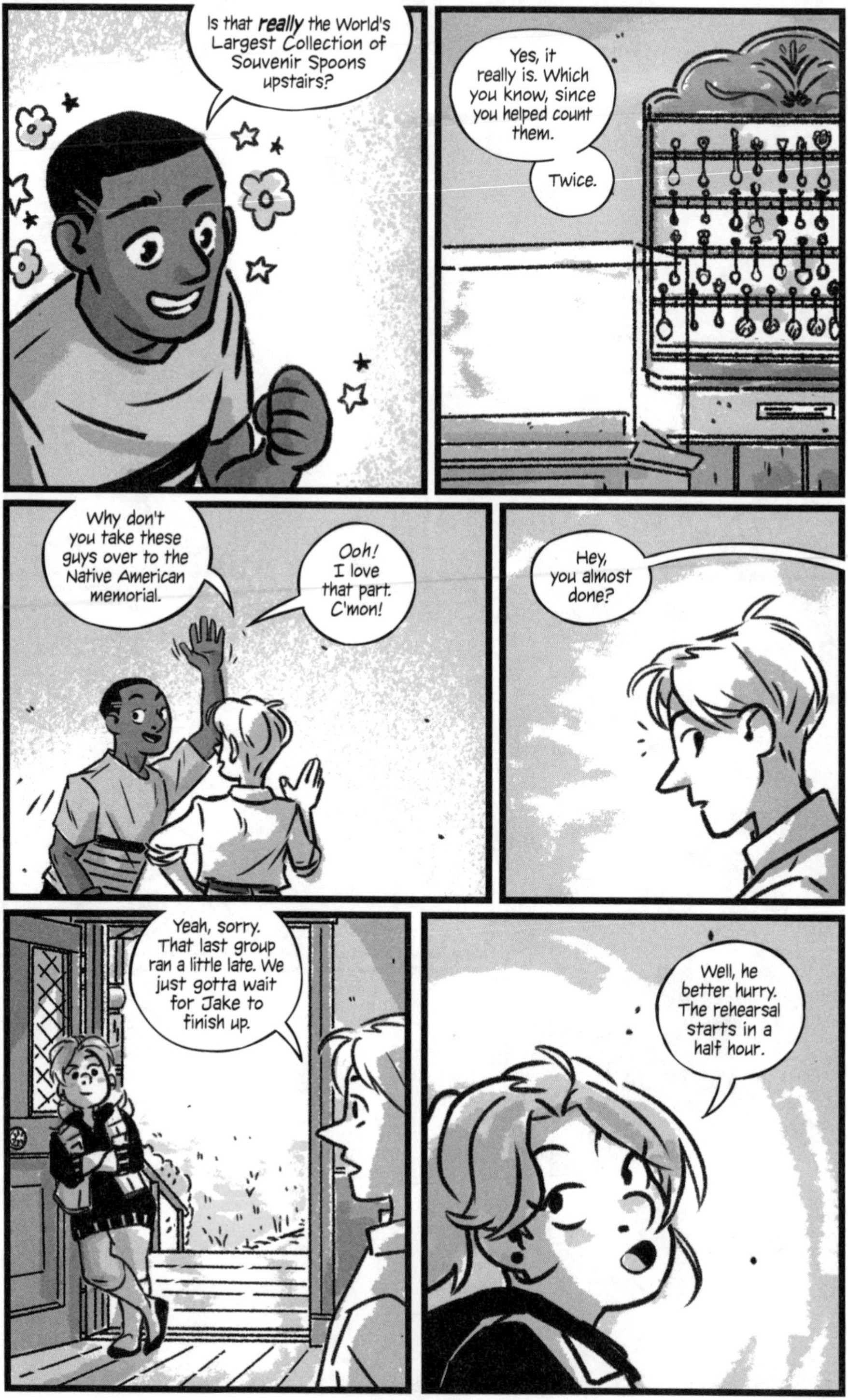
Is that **really** the World's Largest Collection of Souvenir Spoons upstairs?
Yes, it really is. Which you know, since you helped count them.
Twice.
Why don't you take these guys over to the Native American memorial.
Ooh! I love that part. *C'mon!*
Hey, you almost done?
Yeah, sorry. That last group ran a little late. We just gotta wait for Jake to finish up.
Well, he better hurry. The rehearsal starts in a half hour.

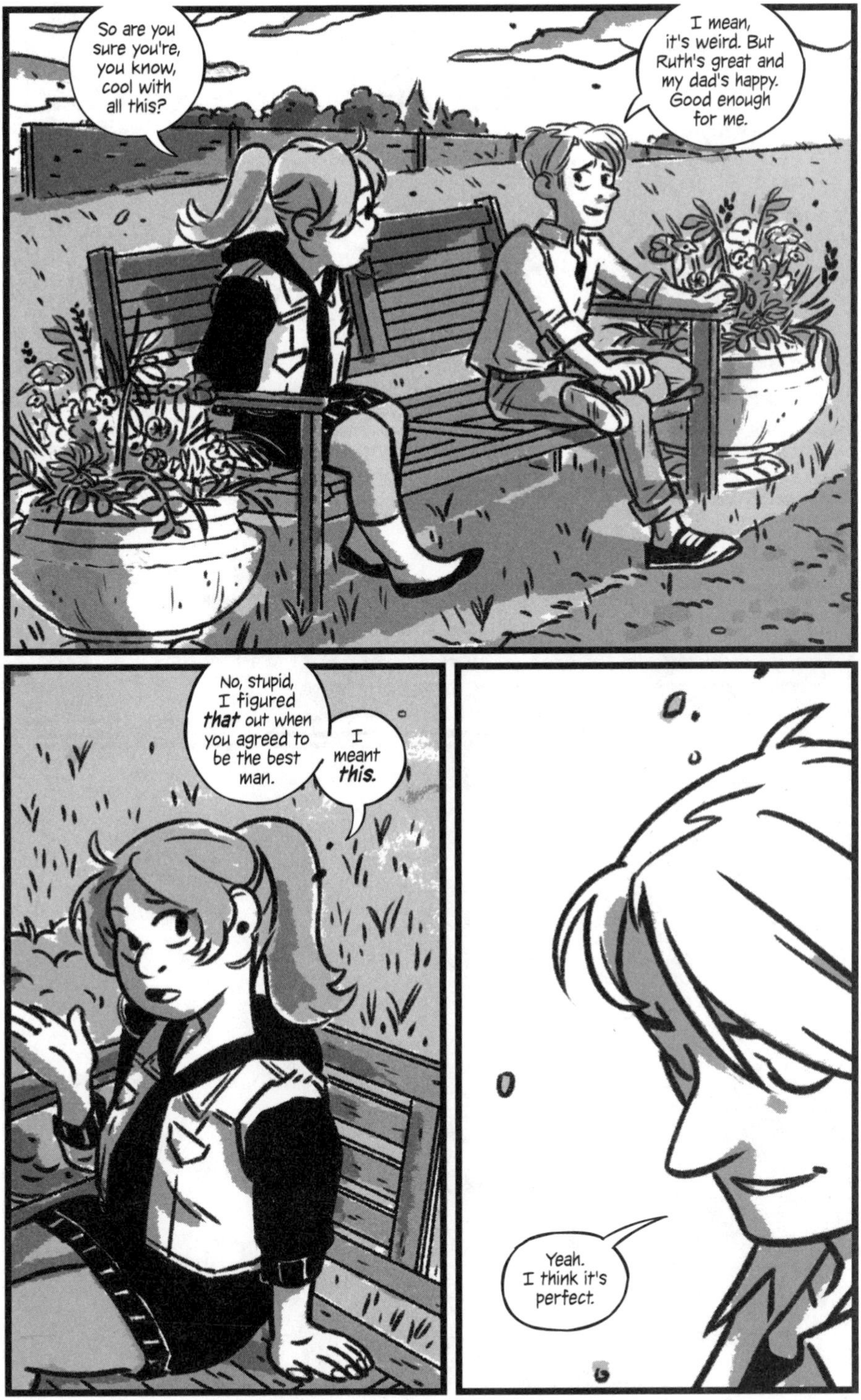
So are you sure you're, you know, cool with all this?
I mean, it's weird. But Ruth's great and my dad's happy. Good enough for me.
No, stupid, I figured *that* out when you agreed to be the best man.
I meant *this*.
Yeah. I think it's perfect.

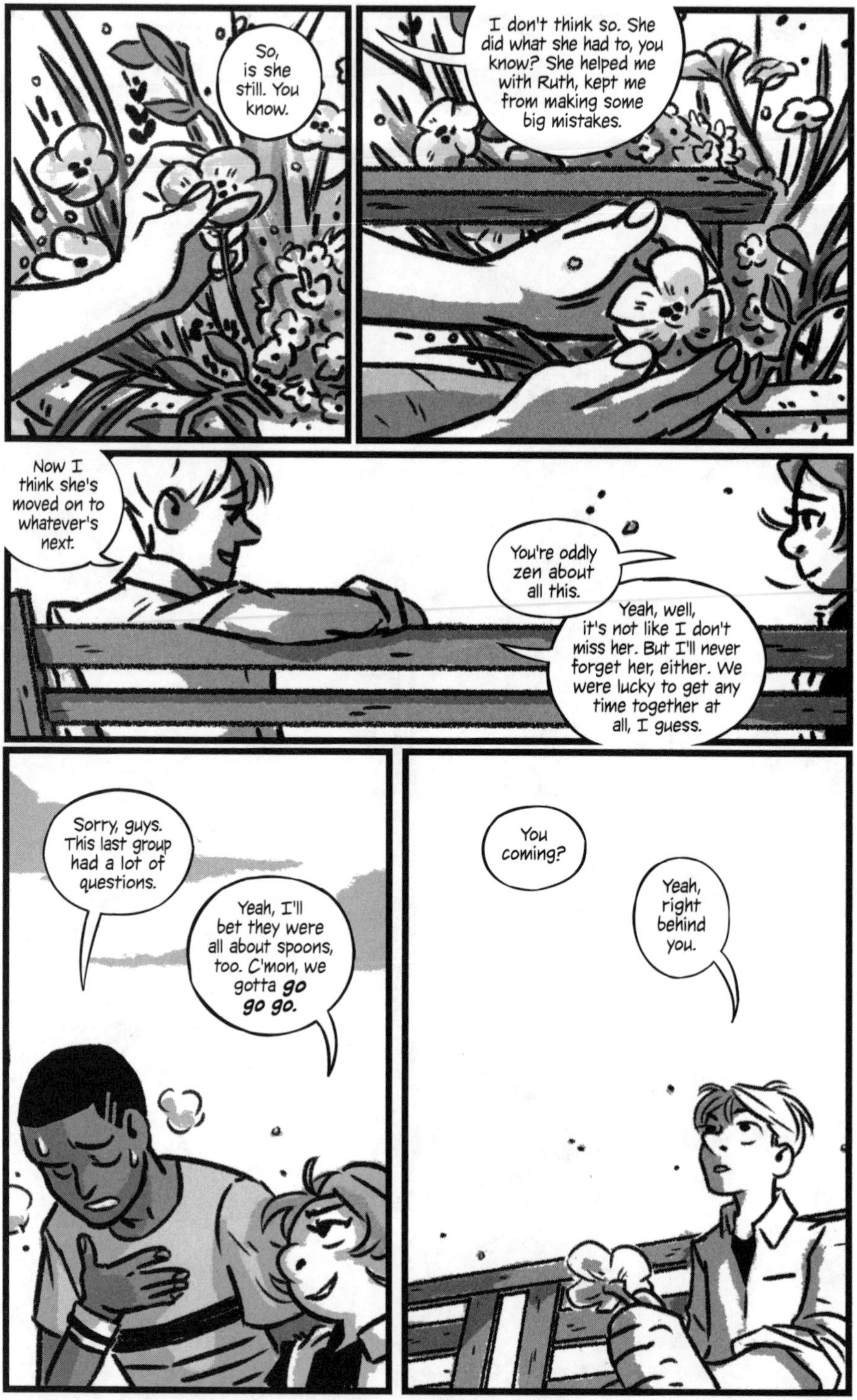
So, is she still. You know.
I don't think so. She did what she had to, you know? She helped me with Ruth, kept me from making some big mistakes.
Now I think she's moved on to whatever's next.
You're oddly zen about all this.
Yeah, well, it's not like I don't miss her. But I'll never forget her, either. We were lucky to get any time together at all, I guess.
Sorry, guys. This last group had a lot of questions.
Yeah, I'll bet they were all about spoons, too. C'mon, we gotta go go go.
You coming?
Yeah, right behind you.

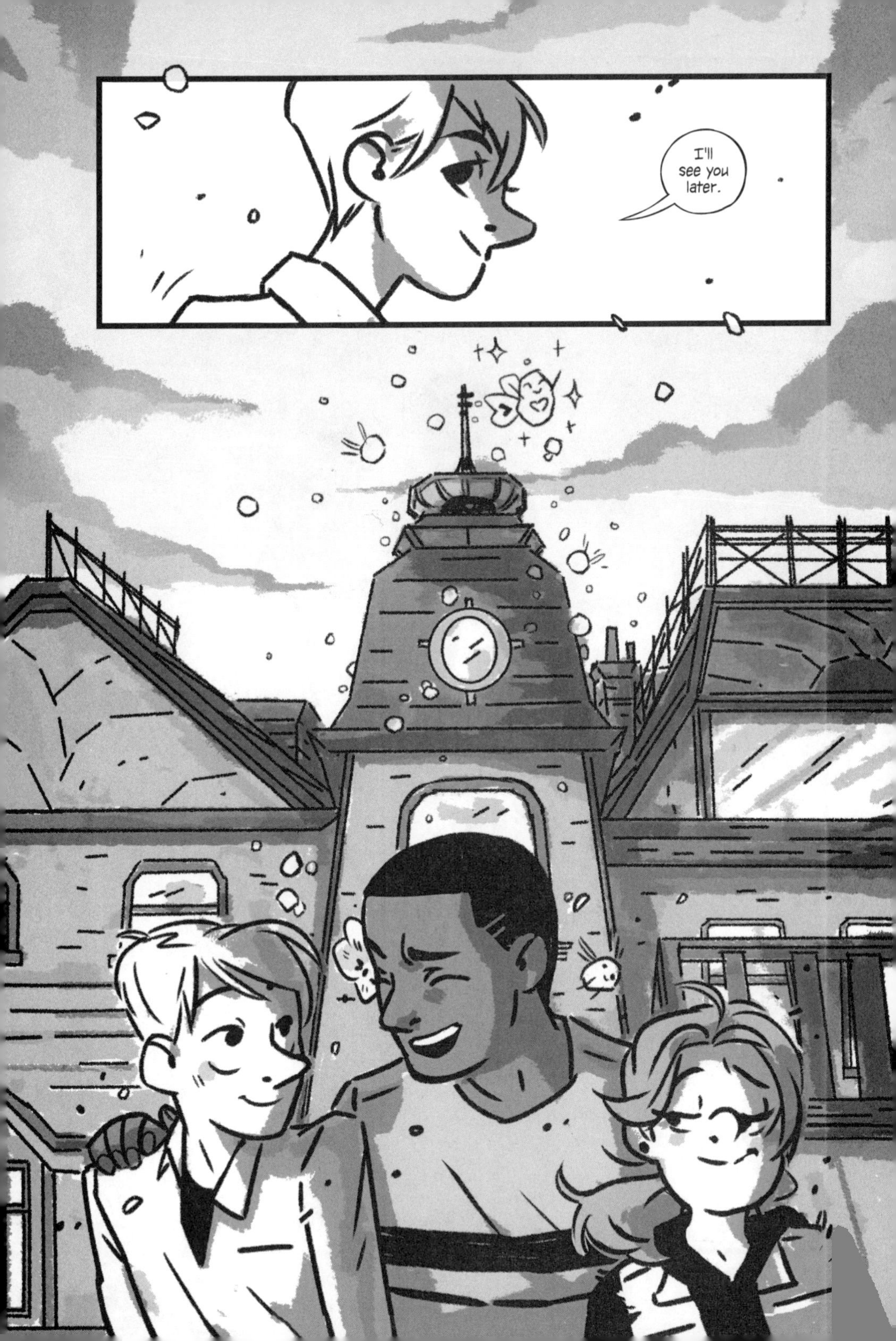
I'll see you later.

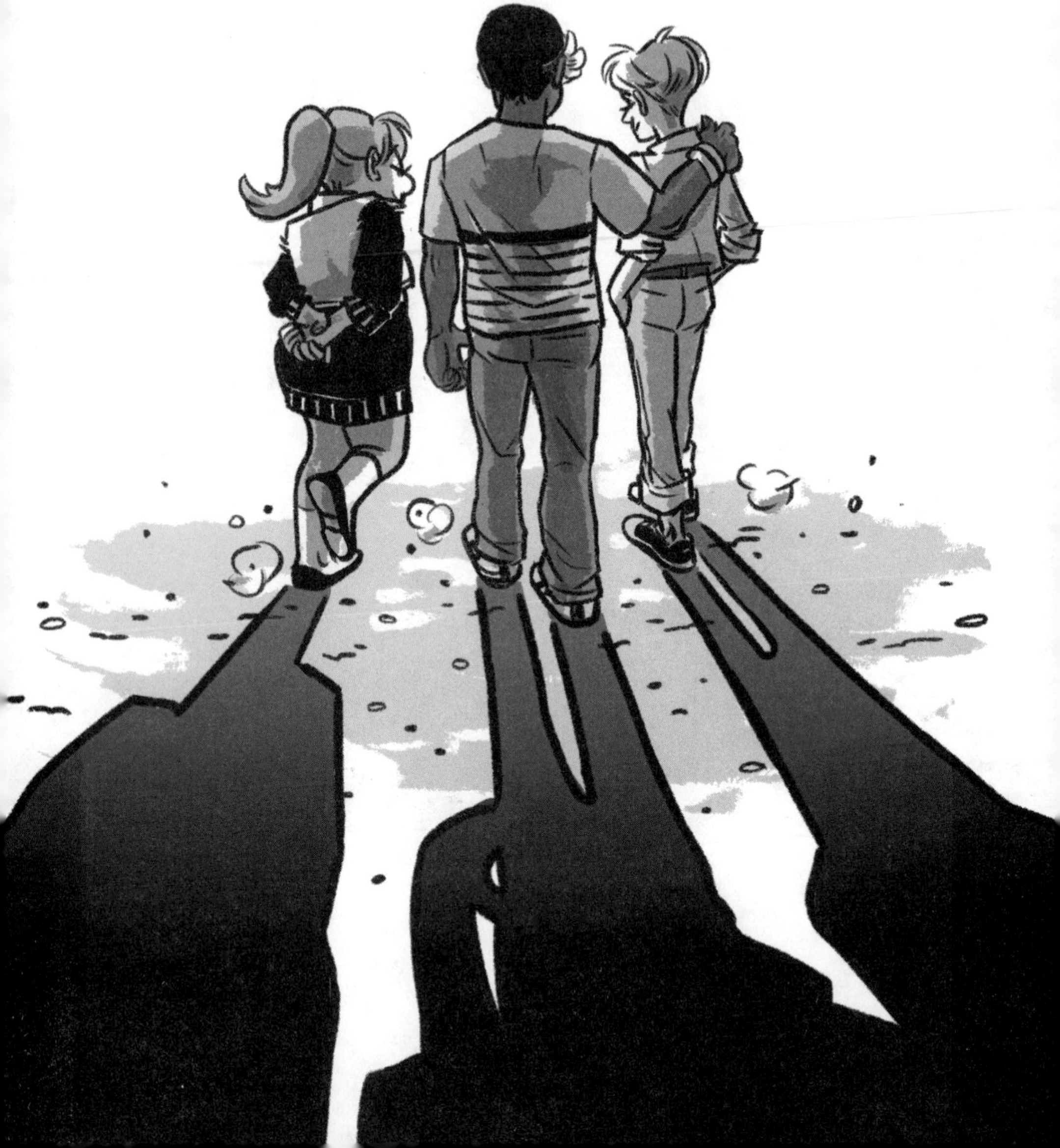

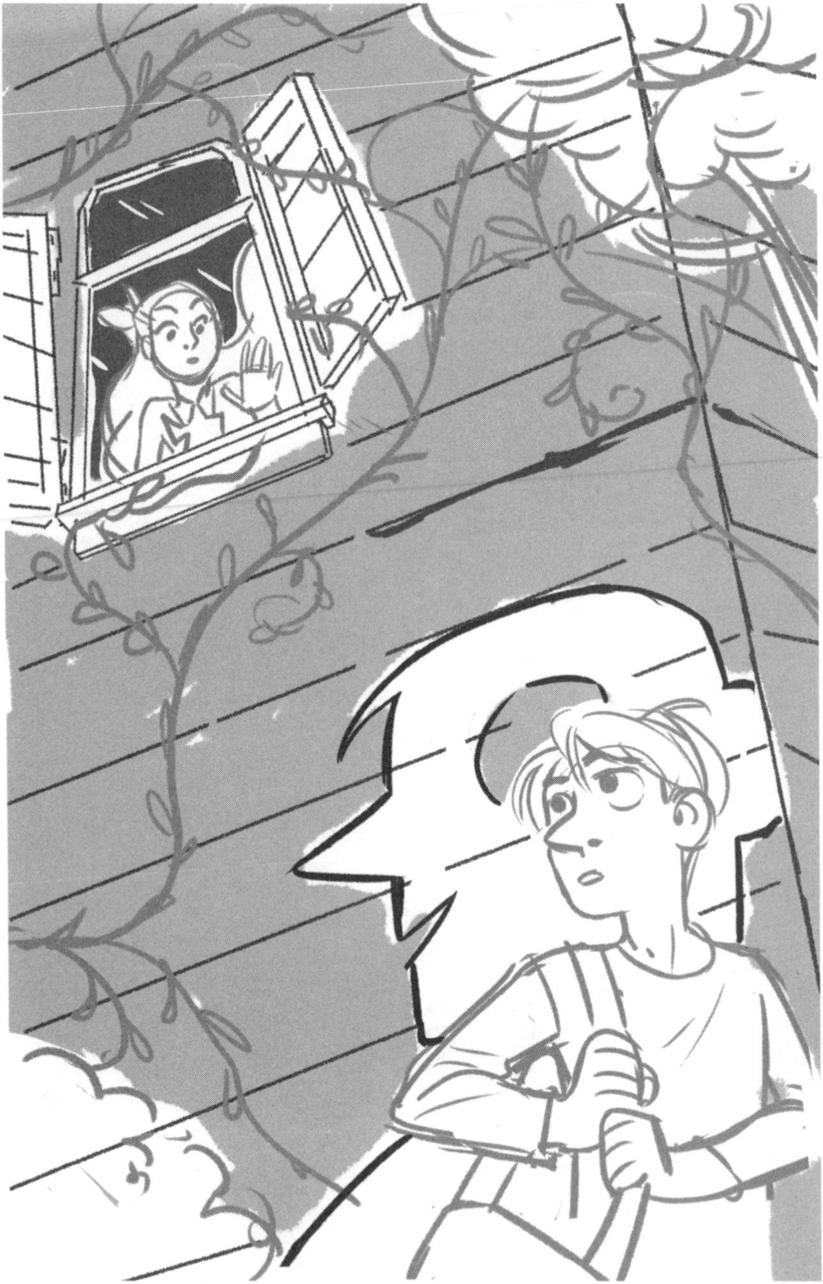

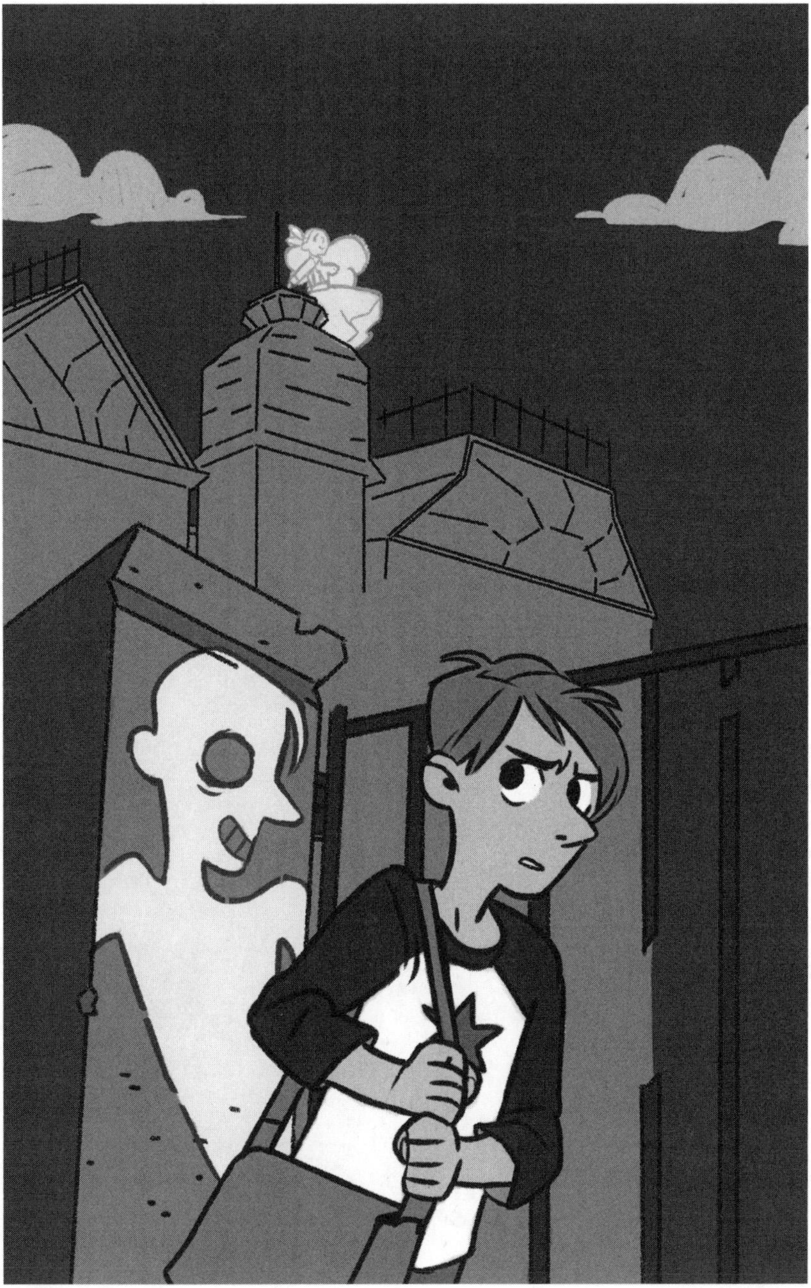

PRELIMINARY CHARACTER DESIGNS

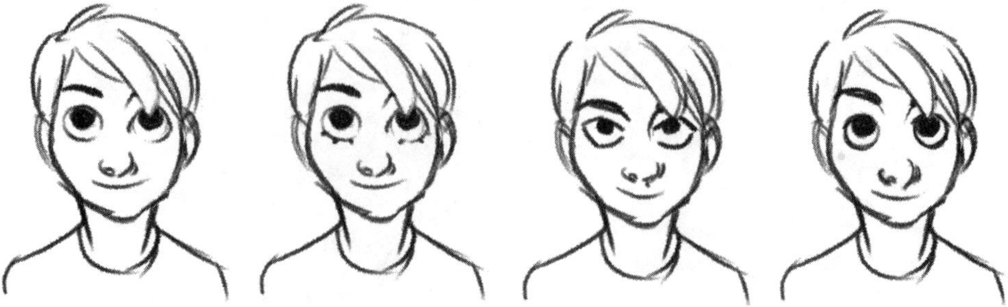

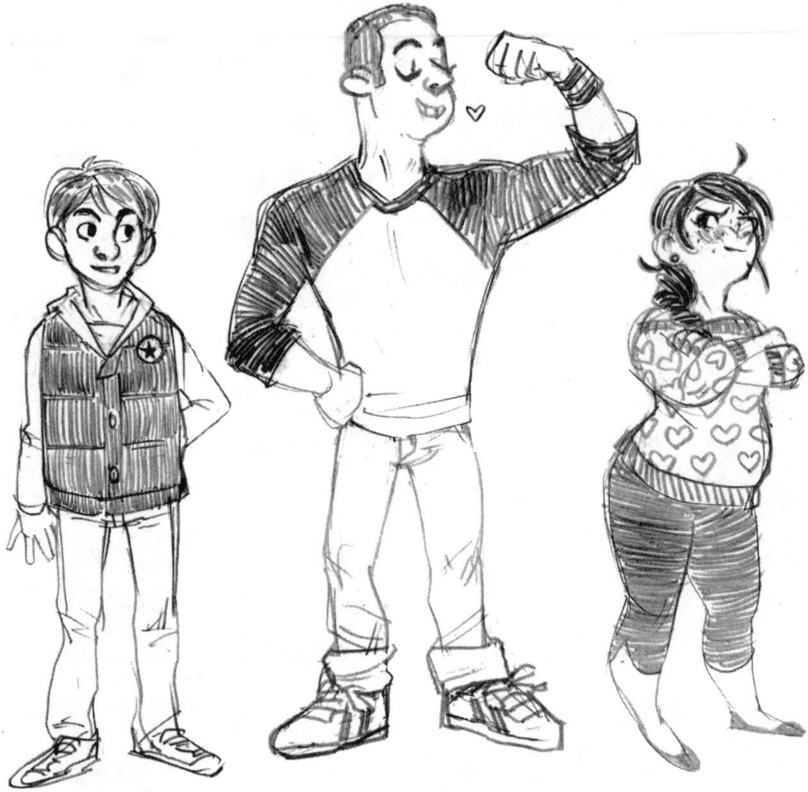

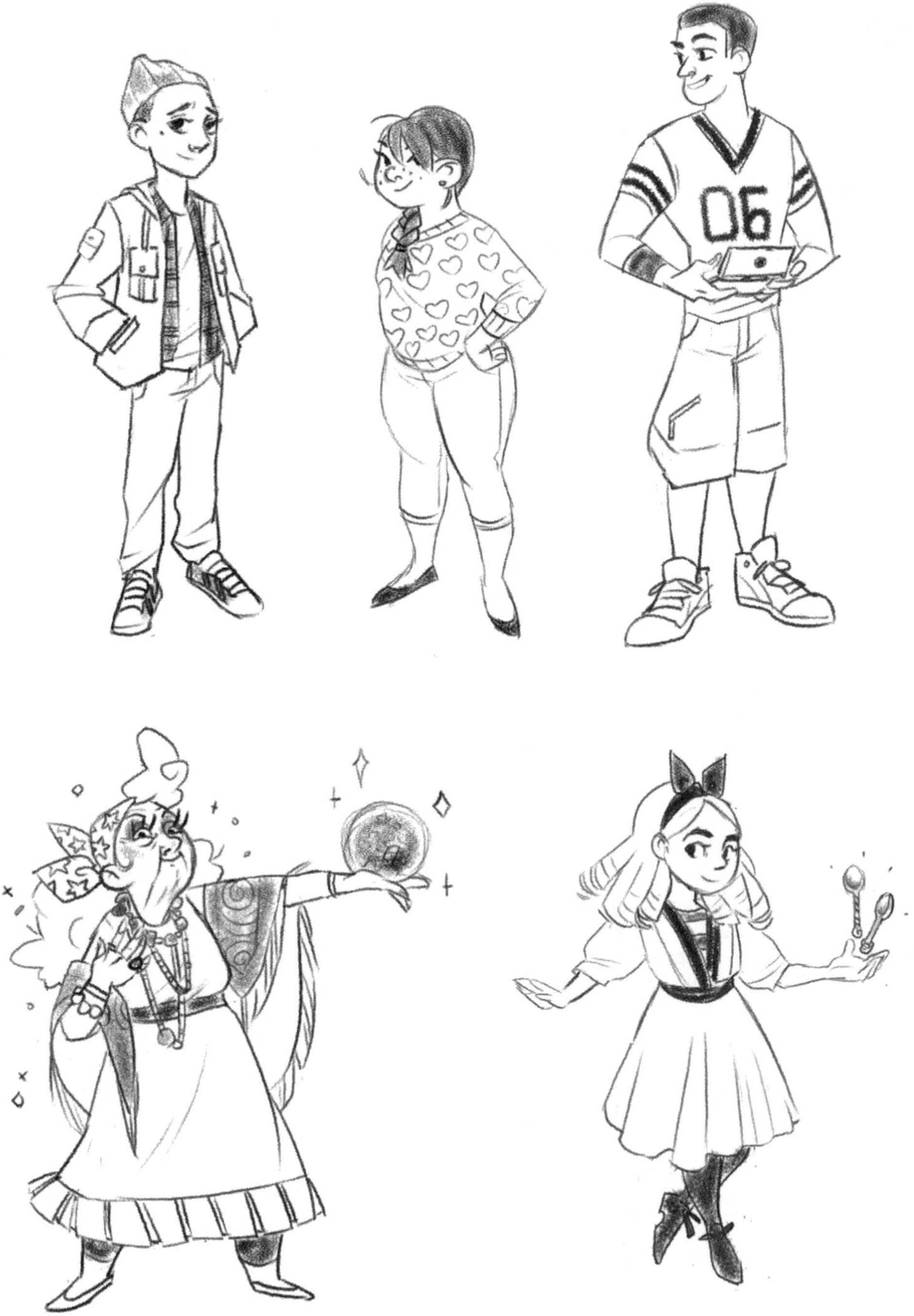
06

Many, many thanks to go around, starting with Mark, for shepherding this script from its earliest days as a short story, and Robyn, for pulling the whole package together with the First Second crew. To Alex and Thomas, two great friends to make comics with, for joining our team in the eleventh hour. To Zack, Kate, and everyone else who read each obsessively revised draft and shared their excellent insight. And of course to Jackie, without whom I'd be missing so much of my heart.
—N. T.

Thank you to all those who have loved and inspired me, especially my father, because he believed in me.
—A. E.

Published by First Second
First Second is an imprint of Roaring Brook Press, a division of Holtzbrinck Publishing Holdings Limited Partnership
175 Fifth Avenue, New York, NY 10010
All rights reserved.

Library of Congress Control Number: 2016945548

ISBN: 978-1-59643-877-4

Our books may be purchased in bulk for promotional, educational, or business use. Please contact your local bookseller or the Macmillan Corporate and Premium Sales Department at (800) 221-7945 ext. 5442 or by e-mail at MacmillanSpecialMarkets@macmillan.com.

First edition 2017

Graytone flats by Alex Eckman-Lawn
Lettering and book design by Thomas Mauer

Printed in the United States of America

Pencilled on paper, scanned, and then inked with Manga Studio.
Toned in Photoshop with the Heavy Smear Wax Crayon brush.

10 9 8 7 6 5 4 3 2 1